Praise for *New York Times* bestselling author Jennifer Weiner

IN HER SHOES

"Weiner's vivid characterizations and her light touch with heavy topics make this follow-up to [her] bestselling debut *Good in Bed* an entertaining romp through family battles and toxic relationships. . . . The book is like spending time with an understanding friend who has a knack for always being great company, brightening the best of times and knowing just how to convince you that not only will you get through the worst, you'll manage to squeeze a laugh or two out of the experience. Bottom line: Wonderful fit."

—People

"Another winner. Known for her very funny approach to serious matters, Weiner is a gifted storyteller. . . ."

—The Hartford Courant

"Irresistible. . . . [Weiner] has a fine eye for detail and a knack for making supporting characters come convincingly to life."

—Washington Post Book World

"A novel as delightful as the author's *Good in Bed*."

—Glamour

"Jennifer Weiner . . . has done it again: another feel-good fractured fairy-tale sure to strike a nerve with modern women. . . . Weiner's easy, intimate, conversational style lets readers bond instantly with her characters."

—The Philadelphia City Paper

"Weiner balances romantic formula with fresh humour, deft characterizations, and literary sensibility."

—Elaine Showalter, *The Guardian* (UK)

"A wonderful contemporary fairy tale. . . . Weiner embroiders serious matters with threads of humor to produce memorable characters and situations. . . . Here's a novel that satisfies on many levels."

—Library Journal

"Heartbreaking and humorous."

—Portland Oregonian

"Satisfying. . . . snappy dialogue and well-crafted characters."

—*Buffalo News*

"[A] winning work. . . . Is this book destined to be another bestseller? You bibbity-bobbity bet."

—*Boston Herald*

"A poignant tale of two damaged girls who need to find themselves so that they can find each other."

—*Kirkus Reviews*

"*In Her Shoes*, Jennifer Weiner's highly anticipated follow-up to *Good in Bed*, speaks to women who have endured the hardships of sibling rivalry or dreamed of trying on someone else's life. It is also an honest look at one woman's struggle with weight. . . . Weiner is at her best. . . . *In Her Shoes* will make readers laugh and perhaps cry."

—*USA Today*

"Weiner laces the stories with her trademark wit, sarcasm, and real world insight. . . . Like other great storytellers, Weiner writes what she knows."

—*Bookreporter*

"Jennifer Weiner, a former newspaper reporter, tells a story with wit and verve. . . . Her second novel, *In Her Shoes*, doubles the dosage."

—*The Dallas Morning News*

"An engaging tale of two very different sisters and the grandmother they've been estranged from since their mother's death. . . . Weiner's second novel is every bit as enjoyable and moving as her first."

—*Booklist*

"Weiner's heroines are cool. They stay plump and still get to sell screenplays, figure out their problems with their parents, have nice apartments and marry doctors and lawyers. Ladies—and gents—everywhere, alert: You can read *Good in Bed* and *In Her Shoes*, munch on chocolate-chip cookies the whole time and not feel like you need to go run a marathon afterward if you want that happy ending for yourself. Without exaggeration, this is revolutionary. It shouldn't be, but it is."

—*The Forward*

GOOD IN BED

"When it comes to pampering, this season's beach-book Queen for a Day is Cannie Shapiro."

—Janet Maslin, *The New York Times*

"*Good in Bed* is a delight, a contemporary Cinderella tale told with intelligence, wit, and style."

—Susan Isaacs, author of *Any Place I Hang My Hat*
and *Almost Paradise*

"A breezy, sweetly oddball urban fairy tale. . . . Jennifer Weiner endows Cannie's story with a lot of brassy heart."

—*The Miami Herald*

"A crackling debut . . . Cannie emerges as one of the most engaging, realistic female characters in years."

—*Entertainment Weekly* (Grade: A)

LITTLE EARTHQUAKES

"Hilarious, heartbreaking, and insightful. Weiner shows that she can write with exquisite tenderness as well as humor."

—*The Miami Herald*

"Immensely readable. . . . Weiner's gift lies in her ability to create characters who both amuse us and make us care."

—*The Washington Post*

"Weiner, a wonderful natural writer and storyteller, renders her characters and their messy, sometimes wrenching lives in details that resonate as the real deal . . . smart, loveable, and mordantly funny."

—*Publishers Weekly* (starred review)

"Lively, witty, and often touching . . . Weiner's snappy dialogue and captivating characters make *Little Earthquakes* endlessly appealing."

—*People*

Also by Jennifer Weiner

Good in Bed
Little Earthquakes
Goodnight Nobody

Jennifer Weiner

In Her SHOES

W

WASHINGTON SQUARE PRESS

NEW YORK   LONDON   TORONTO   SYDNEY

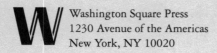
Washington Square Press
1230 Avenue of the Americas
New York, NY 10020

"One Art" from *The Complete Poems, 1927–1979* by Elizabeth Bishop. Copyright
© 1979, 1983 by Alice Methfessel. Reprinted by permission of Farrar, Straus and
Giroux, LLC.

"i carry your heart with me(i carry it in" from *Complete Poems: 1904–1962* by
E. E. Cummings, edited by George J. Firmage. Copyright 1952, © 1980, 1991
by the Trustees for the E. E. Cummings Trust. Used by permission of Liveright
Publishing Corporation.

For Molly Beth

PART ONE

In Her Shoes

ONE

"Baby," groaned the guy—Ted? Tad?—something like that—and crushed his lips against the side of her neck, shoving her face against the wall of the toilet stall.

This is ridiculous, Maggie thought, as she felt him bunching her dress up around her hips. But she'd had five vodka-and-tonics over the course of the last hour and a half, and at this point was not in much of a position to call anything ridiculous. She wasn't even sure she could pronounce the word.

"You're so hot!" Ted or Tad exclaimed, discovering the thong that Maggie had purchased for the occasion.

"I want the thong. In red," she'd said.

"Flame," the salesgirl at Victoria's Secret had replied.

"Whatever," said Maggie. "Small," she added, "extra small if you have it." She gave the girl a quick scornful look to let her know that while she might not know red from flame, she, Maggie Feller, was not worried. She might not have finished college. She might not have a great job—or, okay, after last Thursday, any job at all. The sum total of her big-screen experience might be the three seconds that a sliver of her left hip was visible in Will Smith's second-to-last video. And she might be just barely bumping along while some people, like namely her sister, Rose, went whizzing through

Ivy League colleges and straight into law schools, then into law firms and luxury apartments on Rittenhouse Square like they'd been shot down the water slide of life, but still, she, Maggie, had something of worth, something rare and precious, possessed by few, coveted by many—a terrific body. One hundred and six pounds stretched over five feet and six inches, all of it tanning-bed basted, toned, plucked, waxed, moisturized, deodorized, perfumed, *perfect.*

She had a tattoo of a daisy on the small of her back, the words "BORN TO BE BAD" tattooed around her left ankle, and a plump, pierced red heart reading "MOTHER" on her right bicep. (She'd thought about adding the date of her mother's death, but for some reason that tattoo had hurt more than the other two put together.) Maggie also had D-cup tits. Said tits had been a gift from a married boyfriend and were made of saline and plastic, but this didn't matter. "They're an investment in my future," Maggie had said, even as her father looked hurt and bewildered, and Sydelle the Stepmonster flared her nostrils, and her big sister, Rose, had asked, "Precisely what kind of future are you planning?" in that snotty voice of hers that made her sound like she was seventy. Maggie didn't listen. Maggie didn't care. She was twenty-eight years old now, at her tenth high school reunion, and she was the best-looking girl in the room.

All eyes had been on her as she strolled into the Cherry Hill Hilton in her clinging black spaghetti-strap cocktail dress and the Christian Louboutin stilettos she'd swiped from her sister's closet the weekend before. Rose might have let herself turn into a fat load—a big sister in more ways than one—but at least their feet were still the same size. Maggie could feel the heat of the gazes as she smiled, sashaying over to the bar, hips swaying like music, bangles chiming on her wrists, letting her former classmates get a good look at what they'd missed—the girl they'd ignored, or mocked and called retarded, the one who'd shuffled down the high school hallways swimming in her father's oversized army jacket, cringing against the lockers. Well, Maggie had blossomed. Let them see, let them drool. Marissa Nussbaum and Kim Pratt and especially that bitch Samantha Bailey with her dishwater-blond hair and the fifteen pounds she'd packed on her hips since high school. All the cheerleaders, the ones who'd scorned her or looked right past her. Looked right through her. Let them just feast their eyes on her now . . . or, better yet, let their wimpy, receding-hairlined husbands do the feasting.

"Oh, God!" moaned Ted the Tadpole, unbuckling his pants.

In the next stall, a toilet flushed.

Maggie wobbled on her heels as Ted-slash-Tad aimed and missed and aimed again, jabbing at her thighs and backside. It was like being bludgeoned with a blind snake, she thought, and snorted to herself, a noise that Ted evidently mistook for a groan of passion. "Oh, yeah, baby! You like that, huh?" he demanded, and started poking her even harder. Maggie stifled a yawn and looked down at herself, noting with pleasure that her thighs—firmed from hours on the treadmill, smooth as plastic from a recent waxing—did not so much as quiver, no matter how violent Ted's thrusts got. And her pedicure was perfect. She hadn't been sure about this particular shade of red—not quite dark enough, she'd worried—but it was the right choice, she thought, as she looked down at her toes, gleaming back up at her.

"Jesus CHRIST!" yelled Ted. His tone was one of commingled ecstasy and frustration, like a man who's seen a holy vision and isn't quite sure what it means. Maggie had met him at the bar, maybe half an hour after she'd arrived, and he was just what she had in mind—tall, blond, built, not fat and balding like all the guys who'd been football gods and prom kings in high school. Smooth, too. He'd tipped the bartender five dollars for each round, even though it was an open bar, even though he didn't have to, and he'd told her what she wanted to hear.

"What do you do?" he'd asked, and she'd smiled at him. "I am a performer," she said. Which was true. For the past six months, she'd been a backup singer for a band called Whiskered Biscuit that did thrash-metal covers of 1970s disco classics. So far, they'd booked precisely one gig, as the market for thrash-metal renditions of "MacArthur Park" was not overwhelming, and Maggie knew that she was in the band only because the lead singer was hoping she'd sleep with him. But it was something—a tiny toehold on her dream of being famous, of being a star.

"You weren't in any of my classes," he'd said, tracing his forefinger around and around her wrist. "I would have remembered you for sure." Maggie looked down, toying with one of her auburn ringlets, debating whether she should slide her sandal along his calf, or unpin her hair, letting her curls cascade down her back. No, she hadn't been in his classes. She'd been in the "special" classes, the "remedial" classes, the classes with the scrubs and the burnouts and the big-print textbooks that were a different shape—slightly longer and thinner—than any of the books the other kids carried. You could tuck those books under brown paper covers and shove them in your backpack, but the other kids always knew. Well, fuck them. Fuck all of them. Fuck all the pretty cheerleaders and the guys who'd been happy to fool around with her in the passenger seat of their parents' cars but wouldn't even say "Hi" to her in the halls the next Monday.

"Christ!" yelled Ted again. Maggie opened her mouth to tell him to keep it down, and threw up all over the floor—a clear spill of vodka and tonic, she noted as if from a great distance, plus a few decomposing noodles. She'd had pasta—when? Last night? She was trying to remember her last meal when he grabbed her hips and swung her around roughly so that she was facing the front of the stall, banging her hip against the toilet-paper dispenser in the process. "AGHH!" Ted announced, and came all over her back.

Maggie whirled to face him, moving as quickly as she could through the sloshing vodka/noodle mess on the floor. "Not the dress!" she said. And Ted stood there, blinking, his pants puddled around his knees, his hand still on his dick. He grinned foolishly at her. "That was great!" he said, and squinted at her face. "What was your name again?"

• • •

Fifteen miles away, Rose Feller had a secret—a secret currently splayed flat on his back and snoring, a secret who had somehow managed to dislodge her fitted sheet and kick three pillows to the floor.

Rose propped herself up on her elbow and considered her lover by the glow of the streetlights that filtered through her blinds, smiling a sweet, secret smile, a smile none of her colleagues at the law firm of Lewis, Dommel, and Fenick would have recognized. This was what she had always wanted, what she'd spent her whole life secretly dreaming of—a man who looked at her like she was the only woman in the room, in the world, the only woman who'd ever existed. And he was so handsome, even better looking without his clothes than in them. She wondered if she could take a picture. But the noise would wake him up. And who could she show it to?

Instead, Rose let her eyes take a tour of his body—his strong legs, his broad shoulders, his mouth, half-open, the better to snore with. Rose turned on her side, away from him, drew up the blanket tight under her chin, and smiled, remembering.

They'd been working late on the Veeder matter, which was so boring that Rose could have wept, except the partner on the case was Jim Danvers, and she was so in love with him that she would have spent a week reviewing documents if it meant she'd be close enough to him to smell the good wool of his suit, the scent of his cologne. It got to be eight o'clock, and then it got to be nine, and finally they sealed the last of the pages into the messenger's pouch and he looked at her with his movie-star smile and said, "Do you want to get a bite to eat?"

They went to the bar in the basement of Le Bec-Fin, where a glass of wine turned into a bottle, where the crowd dwindled and the candles burned down until it was midnight and they were alone and the conversation stuttered to a stop. While Rose was trying to figure out what to say next—something about sports maybe?—Jim reached for her hand and murmured, "Do you have any idea how beautiful you are?" Rose shook her head because, really, she had no idea. Nobody had ever told her she was beautiful, except her father, once, and that didn't really count. When she looked in the mirror, she saw nothing but an ordinary girl, a plain Jane, a grown-up bookworm with a decent wardrobe—size fourteen, brown hair and brown eyes, thick, straight eyebrows, and a chin that jutted forward slightly as if to say, *You and what army?*

Except she'd always harbored the secret hope that someday, somebody would tell her that she was beautiful, a man who'd slide her hair out of its ponytail, slip her glasses off her face, and look at her like she was Helen of Troy. It was one of the main reasons she'd never gotten contacts. And so she'd leaned forward, every fiber of her being quivering, staring at Jim, waiting for more of the words she'd always wanted to hear. But Jim Danvers just grabbed her hand, paid the bill, and whisked her out the door, up to her apartment, where he'd pulled off her shoes, shucked her skirt, kissed his way from her neck down her belly, and spent forty-five minutes doing things to her that she'd only dreamed of (and seen once on *Sex and the City*).

She shivered deliciously, pulling the comforter up to her chin, reminding herself that this could be trouble. Sleeping with a colleague went against her personal code of ethics (an easy code to maintain, she admitted, because she'd never had a colleague who'd wanted to sleep with her). More problematic, though—relationships between partners and associates were explicitly forbidden by firm rules. Both of them could be disciplined if anyone found out. He'd get in trouble. She'd probably be asked to leave. And she'd have to find another job, start all over again—another round of interviews, boring half-days spent reciting the same answers to the same questions: *Have you always wanted to be a lawyer? What areas of the law appeal to you the most? What kind of practice do you see yourself developing? How would you fit in with this firm?*

Jim hadn't been like that. He interviewed her when she came to Lewis, Dommel, and Fenick. It was a beautiful September afternoon three months ago when she walked into the conference room, in her navy blue interview suit, with the folder full of firm PR clutched to her chest. After five years at Dillert McKeen she'd been looking for a change—a slightly smaller firm that would give her more responsibilities. This was her third interview of the week, and her feet, in navy Ferragamo pumps, were killing her, but one look at Jim Danvers had banished all thoughts of aching feet and other firms. She'd been expecting a standard-issue partner—fortyish, balding, bespectacled, carefully avuncular with potential female colleagues. And there was Jim, standing at the window, and when he turned to greet her, the late-afternoon light turned his blond hair into a golden crown. Not standard issue at all, and not fortyish, either— maybe thirty-five, Rose thought, a baby partner, five years older than she was, and so handsome. That jaw! Those eyes! The tantalizing whiff of aftershave he left in his wake! He was the kind of guy who'd always been strictly off-limits to Rose as she'd toiled through high school, college, and law school, keeping her nose to the grindstone and her grades in the stratosphere. But when he'd smiled, she'd caught a glint of silver against his teeth. A retainer, she saw, her heart lifting, blossoming inside of her chest. So maybe he wasn't perfect. Maybe there was hope.

"Ms. Feller?" he asked, and she nodded, not trusting her voice. He smiled at her, crossed the room in three long steps, and took her hand in his.

It had started, for her, at that moment—the sun behind him, his hand wrapped around hers, sending bolts of electricity shooting straight between her legs. She'd felt something she'd only read about, something she wasn't even sure that she believed in—passion. Passion as hot and steamy as anything from her Harlequin romances, passion that stole the breath right out of her throat. She looked at the smooth skin of Jim Danvers's neck and wanted to lick it, right there in the conference room.

"I'm Jim Danvers," he said.

She cleared her throat. Her voice was breathy, husky, a wanton rasp. "I'm Rose." Shit. What was her last name again? "Feller. Rose Feller. Hi."

It had started so slowly between them—the glance held a beat too long while waiting for the elevator, a hand that would linger at the small of her back, the way his eyes would seek her out in a crowd whenever the associates and partners wound up in a meeting together. Meanwhile, she gleaned whatever gossip she could. "Single," said her secretary. "Extremely single," said a paralegal. "Serial heartbreaker," whispered a first-year associate as she reapplied her lipstick in the ladies' room mirror. "And I hear he's good." Rose had blushed, washed her hands, and fled. She didn't want Jim to have a reputation. She didn't want him discussed in bathrooms. She wanted him to be hers alone. She wanted him to tell her she was beautiful, again and again.

In the apartment upstairs, a toilet flushed. Jim grunted in his sleep. When he rolled over, she felt his foot brush against her shin. Oh, dear. Rose ran an experimental toe up the length of her calf. The news was not good. She'd been meaning to shave her legs, had been meaning to shave them for some time, kept promising she'd shave them before she went to her aerobic class, but she'd last attended class three weeks ago, and she'd been wearing tights to work every day, and . . .

Jim rolled over again, pushing Rose to the absolute edge of the mattress. She stared unhappily at her living room, which might as well have borne a sign: Single Girl, Lonely, Late '90s. A trail of his-and-hers clothing lay on the floor beside five-pound bright yellow dumbbells propped up next to a Tae Bo tape that was still in its original plastic shrink-wrap. The treadmill she'd bought to fulfill a get-in-shape New Year's Resolution three New Years ago was draped with her dry cleaning. There was a half-empty Passionberry Punch wine cooler on the coffee table, four shoe boxes from Saks piled by the closet, and a half-dozen romance novels beside her bed. Disaster, Rose thought, wondering what she could do before dawn to give her apartment the appearance of being inhabited by someone with an interesting life. Was there an all-night emporium that sold throw pillows and bookcases? And was it too late to do something about her legs?

As quietly as she could, she reached for the portable phone and crept into the bathroom. Amy answered on the first ring. "Wassup?" she asked. In the background, Rose could hear Whitney Houston wailing, which meant that her best friend was watching *Waiting to Exhale* for the hundredth time. Amy wasn't black, but that didn't stop her from trying.

"You won't believe it," Rose whispered.

"Did you get laid?"

"Amy!"

"Well, did you? I mean, why else would you be ringing me now?"

"Actually," said Rose, flicking on the light and studying her glowing face in the mirror, "actually, I did. And it was . . ." She paused, and gave a little hop in the air. "It was so good!"

Amy whooped. "Way to go, girlfriend! So who's the lucky guy?"

"Jim," Rose breathed. Amy whooped even louder.

"And it was unbelievable!" said Rose. "It was . . . I mean, he's so . . ."

Her call waiting beeped. Rose stared at the phone unbelievingly.

"Ooh, popular girl," Amy said. "Call me back!"

Rose clicked over, glancing at her watch. Who'd be calling her at almost one in the morning? "Hello?" She could hear loud music, voices—a bar, a party. She slumped against the bathroom door. Maggie. Big surprise.

The voice on the other end was young, male, and unfamiliar. "Is this Rose Feller?"

"Yes. Who's this, please?"

"Um . . . well, my name's Todd."

"Todd," Rose repeated.

"Yeah. And, um . . . well, I'm here with your sister, I guess. Maggie, right?"

In the background, Rose could hear her sister's drunken shout.

"Little sister!" Rose scowled, grabbing a bottle of shampoo—"specially formulated for thin, limp, lifeless hair"—and tossed it under the sink, reasoning that if Jim stayed for a shower, he didn't need to be confronted with evidence of her problem locks.

"She's . . . um. Sick, I think. She had a lot to drink," Todd continued, "and she was . . . well . . . I don't know what else she was doing, really, but I found her in the bathroom and we were kind of hanging out for a while, and then she kind of passed out, and now she's, um, getting kind of loud. She told me to call you first, though," he added. "Before she passed out."

Rose could hear her sister shouting, "I'm King of the World!" "How nice of her," she said, throwing her prescription zit cream and a box of pantyliners in after the shampoo. "Why don't you just take her home?"

"I don't want to really get involved. . . ."

"Tell me, Todd," Rose began pleasantly, in the voice she'd practiced in law school, the one she imagined using to sucker witnesses into telling her what she needed to know. "When you and my sister were hanging out in the bathroom, what exactly was going on?"

There was silence on the other end.

"Now, I don't need to know specifics," said Rose, "but I'm inferring that you and my sister are already, to use your word, 'involved.' So why don't you be a stand-up guy about it and take her home?"

"Look, I think she needs help, and I've really got to go. . . . I borrowed my brother's car, I've got to get it back . . ."

"Todd . . ."

"Well, is there someone else I should call?" he asked. "Your parents? Your mother or something?"

Rose felt her heart stop. She closed her eyes. "Where are you?"

"The Cherry Hill Hilton. The high school reunion." Click. Todd was no more.

Rose leaned against the bathroom door. Here it was—her real

life, the truth of who she was, barreling down on her like a bus with bad brakes. Here was the truth—she wasn't the kind of person Jim could fall in love with. She wasn't what she'd made herself out to be—a cheerful, uncomplicated girl, a normal girl with a happy, orderly life, a girl who wore pretty shoes and had nothing more pressing on her mind than whether *ER* was a rerun this week. The truth was in the exercise tape she didn't have time to unwrap, let alone exercise to; the truth was her hairy legs and ugly underwear. Most of all, the truth was her sister, her gorgeous, messed-up, fantastically unhappy and astonishingly irresponsible sister. Only why tonight? Why couldn't Maggie have let her enjoy this one night?

"Fuck," she groaned softly. "Fuck, fuck, fuck." And then Rose padded back into her bedroom, groping for her glasses, sweatpants, boots, and car keys. She scribbled a quick note for Jim ("Family emergency, be back soon") and hurried to the elevator, steeling herself to drive off into the night and pull her sister's chestnuts out of the fire yet again.

The hotel had a "Welcome! Class of '89" banner still drooping from the front door. Rose stomped through the lobby—all faux marble and crimson carpet—and into the deserted lounge, which smelled of cigarette smoke and beer. There were tables covered in cheap red-and-white paper tablecloths with plastic pom-poms as centerpieces. In the corner, a guy and a girl were making out, leaning drunkenly against the wall. Rose squinted toward them. Not Maggie. She walked to the bar, where a man in a stained white shirt was putting away glasses and where her sister, in a tiny dress that was inappropriate for November—or, really, for any appearance in public—was slumped on a barstool.

Rose paused for a minute, considering her strategy. From a distance, Maggie looked just fine. You didn't notice the smeared makeup, the reek of booze and barf that surrounded her like a thick cloud, until you got up close.

The bartender gave Rose a sympathetic look. "She's been here for half an hour," he said. "I've been watching out for her. She's just had water to drink."

Terrific, Rose thought. *Where were you when she was probably getting gang-banged in the bathroom?*

"Thanks," she said instead, and shook her sister's shoulder. Not gently. "Maggie?"

Maggie opened one eye and scowled. "Leame lone," she said.

Rose gathered the straps of her sister's black dress and lifted. Maggie's butt rose six inches off the seat. "Party's over."

Maggie tottered to her feet and kicked Rose sharply in the shin with one silver sandal. Make that one Christian Louboutin silver stiletto sandal, Rose noticed as she looked down, one silver sandal coveted for three months, purchased just two weeks ago, and, she'd thought, still snug in its shoe box. One silver sandal now stained and splotched with the sticky residue of she didn't want to know what.

"Hey, those are mine!" Rose said, shaking her sister by her dress. *Maggie,* she thought, feeling the familiar fury coursing through her veins. Maggie takes *everything.*

"Fuck youuuu!" Maggie brayed, and twisted her body from side to side, trying to free herself from Rose's grasp.

"I can't believe you!" Rose hissed, hanging on to the straps as Maggie thrashed, and the toes of Maggie's shoes—*her* shoes— kicked at her shins. *Insult to injury,* she thought, imagining the bruises she'd find in the morning. "I haven't even worn them yet!"

"Easy there," the bartender called, clearly hoping that this was going to turn into a sister-on-sister catfight.

Rose ignored him and half dragged, half carried her sister out of the bar and deposited Maggie in her passenger seat.

"If you're going to throw up," Rose advised, yanking the seat belt around her sister, "give me a little advance warning."

"I'll send a telegram," Maggie muttered, reaching into her purse for her lighter.

"Oh, no," said Rose, "don't even think about smoking in here." She flicked on the lights, wrenched the steering wheel to the right, and started driving out of the deserted parking lot and onto the highway, heading toward the Ben Franklin Bridge and Bella Vista, where Maggie had the most recent in her extended series of apartments.

"Not this way," said Maggie.

"Okay," said Rose. Her hands tightened on the wheel in frustration. "So where are we going?"

"Take me to Sydelle's," Maggie mumbled.

"Why?"

"Just take me, okay? Jesus. I don't need to play twenty questions."

"Of course not," Rose said tightly. "I'm just your personal taxi driver. No need to give me an explanation. Just call my number and I'll show up."

"Bitch," Maggie said thickly. Her head lolled against the back of the seat, rolling back and forth each time Rose yanked on the wheel.

"You know," Rose said, in her most reasonable tone, "it is possible to attend one's high school reunion and not wind up drinking so much vodka that you don't even notice that you've passed out in the ladies' room."

"Whaddare you, a DARE officer?" asked Maggie.

"It's possible," Rose continued, "to simply attend, to reacquaint yourself with old friends, to dance, to dine, to drink responsibly, to wear clothes that you've bought for yourself instead of the ones you've taken from my closet . . ."

Maggie opened her eyes and stared at her sister, noting the large white plastic hair clip. "Hey, 1994 called," she said. "It wants its hairstyle back."

"What?"

"Don't you know that nobody wears those anymore?"

"So why don't you tell me what the really fashionable girls are wearing when they have to go pick up their drunk sisters in the middle of the night," said Rose. "I'd love to know. Have Nicky and Paris Hilton launched a line for us yet?"

"Whatever," Maggie mumbled, staring out the window.

"Are you happy this way?" Rose continued. "Drinking every night, running around with God knows who . . ."

Maggie rolled down the window and ignored her.

"You could go back to school," said Rose. "You could get a better job."

"And be just like you," Maggie said. "Wouldn't that be fun? No sex in, what's it been, Rose, three years? Four? When was the last time a guy looked at you?"

"I could have plenty of guys looking at me if I wore your clothes," Rose said.

"Like they'd fit," said Maggie. "Your *leg* wouldn't fit into this dress."

"Oh, right," said Rose. "I forgot that being a size zero is the most important thing in the world. Because it's obviously made you so successful and happy." She honked the horn longer than was necessary to get the car in front of her to move. "You've got problems," Rose said. "You need help."

Maggie threw back her head, cackling. "And you're just perfect, right?"

Rose shook her head, thinking of what she could say to shut her sister up, but by the time she'd formulated her line of attack, Maggie's head was resting on the window, her eyes shut tight.

Chanel, the golden retriever—Sydelle the Stepmonster's dog—turned in wild circles up and down the length of the yard as Rose drove up the driveway. A light went on in an upstairs bedroom, and another light appeared in the downstairs hall as Rose grabbed Maggie by her straps and hauled her onto her feet.

"Get up," she ordered.

Maggie stumbled in her sister's grasp, weaving up the driveway until she arrived at the front door of the oddly shaped modern house that their father and stepmother called home. The hedges were pruned into tortured curlicues, per Sydelle's instructions, and the doormat read, "Welcome Friends!" Rose had always figured the mat had come with the house, as their stepmother was neither particularly welcoming nor especially friendly. Maggie staggered up the path and bent over. Rose thought she was throwing up until she saw Maggie flip over one of the flagstones and fish out a key.

"You can go now," said Maggie, leaning against the door and fumbling with the lock. She waved good-bye without turning around. "Thanks for the ride; now, get lost."

The front door flew open as Sydelle Levine Feller stepped out into the night, lips pursed, bathrobe belted tightly around her five foot figure, face gleaming with skin cream. In spite of hours of exercise and thousands of dollars' worth of Botox shots and the recent addition of tattooed eyeliner, Sydelle Levine Feller was not a pretty woman. For one thing, she had tiny, dull brown eyes. For another, she had enormous, flaring nostrils—the kind of thing Rose always figured that the surgeons couldn't correct, because surely Sydelle had to have noticed that she could easily fit a Hebrew National salami up each one.

"She's drunk," Sydelle said, her nostrils flaring. "What a surprise." As always, she addressed her most hurtful remarks to the air three inches to the left of the recipient's face, as if she were directing her observation to some invisible onlooker who would undoubtedly see her side of things. Rose could remember dozens—no, hundreds—of those catty observations zinging past her own left ear . . . and Maggie's. *Maggie, you need to apply yourself to your schoolwork. Rose, I don't think you need a second helping.*

"Can't get anything by you, can I, Sydelle?" asked Maggie. Rose snorted in spite of herself, and for a moment, the two of them were a team again, united against a common, formidable enemy.

"Sydelle, I need to talk to my father," said Rose.

"And I," Maggie announced, "need to use the facilities."

Rose looked up and saw the glint of her father's glasses through the bedroom window. His tall, thin, slightly stooped frame was floating in pajama bottoms and an old T-shirt, and his fine gray hair drifted up around his bald spot. *When did he get so old?* Rose thought. He looked like a ghost. In the years since they'd been married, Sydelle had gotten more vivid—her lipstick increasingly brighter, her highlights ever more golden—and her father had faded, like a photograph left in the sun. "Hey, Dad!" she called. Her father turned toward her voice and started to open the window.

"Darling, I'll take care of this," Sydelle called up toward the bedroom window. Her words were sweet. Her tone was icy. Michael Feller paused with his hands at the bottom of the window, and Rose could imagine his face crumpling into its familiar expression of sadness and defeat. An instant later, the light flicked off, and her father vanished from view. "Shit," Rose muttered, although she wasn't surprised. "Dad!" she yelled again, helplessly.

Sydelle shook her head. "No," she said. "No, no, no."

"This episode brought to you by the word *No,*" said Maggie, and Rose laughed, then returned her attention to her stepmother. She remembered the first day Sydelle had showed up at their apartment. Their father had been dating her for two months and had gotten dressed up for this occasion. Rose recalled him tugging at the sleeves of his sport jacket, readjusting the knot of his tie. "She's very excited about meeting both of you," he told Rose, who was then twelve, and Maggie, who was ten. Rose remembered thinking that Sydelle was the most glamorous woman she'd ever seen. She'd worn gold bracelets and gold earrings and shiny gold sandals. Her hair was streaked with ash and copper, her eyebrows were plucked to thin golden parentheses. Even her lipstick had a golden tinge. Rose was dazzled. It wasn't until later that she noticed Sydelle's less-lovely features—the way that her mouth fell naturally into a frown, how her eyes were the color of a muddy puddle, the nostrils that loomed like twin Lincoln Tunnels in the center of her face.

At dinner, Sydelle slid the bread basket out of her reach. "None for us!" she'd simpered, with what Rose thought was supposed to be a conspiratorial wink. "We girls need to watch our figures!" She pulled the same trick with the butter. When Rose made the mistake of reaching for a second helping of potatoes, Sydelle pursed her lips. "It takes the stomach twenty minutes to send a message to the brain that it is full," she lectured. "Why don't you wait a while and see if you really want those?" Her father and Maggie got ice cream for dessert. Rose got a dish of grapes. Sydelle had nothing. "I don't care for sweets," she said. The whole performance made Rose feel like throwing up . . . throwing up, and then sneaking back to the refrigerator for a belated bowl of ice cream. Which, if she remembered correctly, was exactly what she'd done.

Now she stared at Sydelle, imploring, wanting desperately to be done with this task, to drop Maggie off and hurry back to Jim . . . if he was even still there.

"I'm very sorry," Sydelle said, in a tone indicating that she was really anything but sorry. "If she's been drinking, she can't come in."

"Well, I haven't been drinking. Let me talk to my father."

Sydelle shook her head again. "Maggie is not your responsibility," she recited, parroting the speech she'd no doubt memorized from a Tough Love book. Or, more likely, a Tough Love pamphlet. Sydelle wasn't much of a reader.

"Let me talk to him," Rose said again, knowing it was hopeless.

Sydelle turned her body so that she was blocking the doorway, as if Rose and Maggie might try to sneak in past her. And Maggie wasn't improving the situation.

"Hey, Sydelle!" she cawed, shoving her sister aside. "You look great!" She squinted at her stepmother's face. "You did something new, right? Chin lift? Cheek implant? Li'l Botox? What's your secret?"

"Maggie," Rose whispered, grabbing her sister's shoulders and telepathically begging her to shut up. Which Maggie didn't do.

"Way to spend our inheritance!" she howled.

Sydelle finally looked right at them, instead of at the space between the two girls. Rose could practically hear what she was thinking, which was that her daughter, the much-vaunted Marcia, would never behave in such a fashion. Marcia—or My Marcia, as she was commonly called—was eighteen and a freshman at Syracuse by the time Sydelle and her father had wed. My Marcia, as Sydelle never tired of reminding Rose and Maggie, wore a perfect size six. My Marcia had been a member of the National Honor Society and the homecoming court. My Marcia had joined the best sorority at Syracuse, had graduated with honors, had worked for three years as an assistant to one of the top interior decorators in New York City before marrying a dot-com gazillionaire and gracefully retreating into motherhood and a seven-bedroom showplace in Short Hills.

"You both need to leave," said Sydelle, and closed the door, leaving Maggie and Rose out in the cold.

Maggie stared up at the bedroom window, perhaps hoping that their father would toss his wallet down. Finally, she turned and headed to the driveway, pausing only to yank one of Sydelle's curlicued hedges out of the ground and throw it at the doorstep, where it landed in a rattling shower of dirt. As Rose watched, Maggie pulled off the purloined high heels and hurled them at her sister on the lawn. "Here you go," she said.

Rose's hands curled into fists. She should have been in her apartment, in bed with Jim. Instead, here she was, in the middle of the night, in the middle of a frozen lawn in New Jersey, trying to help her sister, who didn't even want to be helped.

Maggie crossed the lawn on her bare feet and began limping down the road. "Where do you think you're going?" Rose called.

"Somewhere. Anywhere." Maggie said. "Don't worry about me, I'll be okay." She'd made it almost to the corner before Rose caught up.

"Let's go," Rose said roughly. "You can stay with me." Even as the words were exiting her lips, her internal alarms were sounding shrieking whoops of warning. Inviting Maggie to stay was like offering to host a hurricane, which she'd learned the hard way five years ago when Maggie had moved in with her for three horrible weeks. Maggie in your house meant that money would go missing along with your best lipstick, favorite pair of earrings, and costliest shoes.

Your car would vanish for days at a time and reappear with an empty gas tank and brimming ashtrays. Your house keys would disappear, and your clothes would waltz off their hangers, never to be seen again. Maggie in residence meant mess and confusion, dramatic scenes, tears and fights and hurt feelings. It meant the end of any peace and quiet she might have been foolish enough to hope for. Quite possibly, she thought with a shudder, it meant the end of Jim.

"Come on," Rose said again.

Maggie shook her head back and forth, a child's exaggerated no.

Rose sighed. "It'll only be for the night," she said. But at the touch of Rose's hand on her shoulder, Maggie whirled around. "No it won't," she said.

"What?"

"Because I got evicted again, all right?"

"What happened?" asked Rose, and restrained herself from adding, "this time."

"I got mixed up," Maggie muttered.

Mixed up, Rose had long ago learned, was Maggie's shorthand for the ways the world confounded her, the ways that her learning disabilities had her hamstrung and crippled. Numbers tripped her up, fractions and directions and balancing a checkbook were absolute impossibilities. Tell her to double a recipe and she couldn't. Ask her to find her way from Point A to Point B and Maggie would usually wind up at Point K, where she'd unfailingly locate a bar and have a few guys clustered around her by the time Rose showed up to retrieve her.

"Fine," said Rose. "We'll figure it out in the morning."

Maggie wrapped her arms around herself, and stood, skinny and shivering. She really should have been an actress, Rose thought. It was a shame all of this dramatic ability never got put to better use than extracting cash, shoes, and temporary housing from her family.

"I'll be fine," said Maggie. "I'll just stay here until it gets light, and then . . ." She sniffled. Goose bumps dotted her arms and shoulders. "I'll find somewhere to go."

"Come on," said Rose.

"You don't want me," Maggie repeated sadly. "Nobody does."

"Just get in the car." Rose turned and started walking toward the driveway, and she wasn't a bit surprised when, after a moment, Maggie followed. There were some things in life you could always count on, and Maggie needing help, Maggie needing money, Maggie just plain *needing* was one of them.

Maggie was quiet during the twenty-minute ride to Philadelphia, while Rose tried to decide how she was going to keep her sister from noticing that there was a pantsless partner in her bed. "You take the couch," she whispered once they were in her apartment, hurrying to snatch Jim's suit off the floor. Maggie didn't miss a thing.

"My, my," she drawled. "What have we here?" Her hand darted into the bundle of clothing in Rose's arms and emerged, seconds later, triumphantly clutching Jim's wallet. Rose grabbed for it, but Maggie jerked it away. *So it begins,* thought Rose.

"Give that back," she whispered. Maggie flipped the wallet open.

"James R. Danvers," she recited loudly. "Society Hill Towers, Philadelphia, Pee-Aye. Very nice."

"Shh!" Rose whispered, casting an alarmed glance at the wall behind which James R. Danvers presumably slumbered.

"Nineteen sixty-four," Maggie read in a stentorian voice. Rose could practically hear the gears turning as Maggie struggled to do the math. "He's thirty-five?" she finally asked. Rose grabbed the wallet from Maggie's hand.

"Go to sleep," she hissed.

Maggie selected a T-shirt from the clothes draped over Rose's treadmill and pulled her dress over her head. "Don't say it," she warned.

"You're too thin," Rose blurted, shocked by the sight of the prominent sweep of Maggie's collarbone and the individual bumps of her vertebra, made all the more pathetic by her ridiculous store-bought breasts.

"And you haven't been using the Ab Master I bought you," Maggie retorted, yanking the shirt over her head and snuggling into the couch.

Rose opened her mouth, then shut it. *Just get her to sleep,* she told herself.

"Your boyfriend looks cute, though," Maggie said, and yawned. "Could you bring me a glass of water and two Advils, please?"

Rose ground her teeth, but fetched the medication and the water, and watched Maggie gulp the pills, chug the water, and close her eyes without so much as a "thank you." In her bedroom, Jim still lay on his side, snoring softly. She rested one hand lightly on his arm.

"Jim?" she whispered. He didn't move. Rose contemplated crawling into bed with him, dragging the blankets up over her head and handling the morning in the morning. She glanced back at the door, looked down at Jim, and realized that she couldn't. She couldn't sleep with a naked man with her sister in the next room. Her job was, and had always been, to set an example for Maggie. Shacking up with a man who was sort of her boss didn't qualify. And what if he wanted sex again? Maggie would overhear, or worse, walk in, and stare. And laugh.

Instead, Rose pulled an extra blanket from the foot of the bed, grabbed a pillow from the floor, tiptoed back into the living room, and arranged herself on the armchair, thinking that in the annals of romantic history, this was probably the worst way a night like hers could end. She shut her eyes and listened for Maggie's breathing, the way she always had through all the years they'd shared a bedroom. Then she rolled over, trying to stretch out as much as she could. Why didn't she at least get the couch? Why had she invited Maggie over at all? Just then, Maggie started talking.

"Remember Honey Bun?"

Rose closed her eyes in the darkness. "Yes," she said. "I remember."

Honey Bun had come to them in the spring, when Rose was eight and Maggie was six. Their mother, Caroline, had woken them up early on a Thursday morning. "Shh, don't tell!" she'd whispered, hurrying them both into their best party dresses, then having them put on sweaters and coats on top. "It's a special surprise!" They'd called good-bye to their father, still lingering over coffee and the business section, hustled past the kitchen where the countertops were crammed with boxes of chocolate and the sink was filled with dirty dishes, and climbed into the station wagon. Instead of turning into the school entrance, the way she did most mornings, Caroline steered right past it, and kept going.

"Mom, you missed the turn!" called Rose.

"No school today, honey," their mother singsonged over her shoulder. "Today's a special day!"

"Yay!" said Maggie, who'd gotten the coveted front seat.

"Why?" asked Rose, who'd been looking forward to the day at school because it was Library Day and she'd get to pick out more books.

"Because something very exciting has happened," their mother said. Rose could remember exactly how her mother looked that day, the way her brown eyes glowed, and the gauzy turquoise scarf she'd wrapped around her neck. Caroline started talking very quickly, her words tumbling over each other, looking over her shoulder to tell Rose the big news. "It's candy," she said. "Fudge, really. Well, different than fudge. Better than fudge. Like divinity. Have you girls ever had that?"

Rose and Maggie shook their heads.

"I was reading in *Newsweek* about this woman who made cheesecakes," Caroline rambled, speeding around a curve and lurching to a stop at a traffic light. "And all of her friends raved about the cheesecakes, and first she got one supermarket in her neighborhood to carry them, and then she got a distributor, and now her cheesecakes are carried in eleven states. Eleven!"

A chorus of honks came from behind them. "Mom," said Rose. "Green light."

"Oh, right, right," said Caroline, stepping on the gas. "So last night I was thinking, well, I can't make cheesecake, but I can make fudge. My mother made the best fudge in the world, with walnuts and marshmallows, so I called her for the recipe and I was up all night, making batches and batches, had to go to the supermarket twice for ingredients, but here!" And she jerked the wheel sideways, pulling into a gas station. Rose noticed that her mother's fingernails were broken and sooty brown, as if she'd been digging through dirt. "Here! Try!" She reached into her purse and came up with two wax-paper-wrapped squares. "R and M Fudge," they read, in what looked to Rose like eyeliner.

"I had to improvise, of course, the packaging will change, but taste it and tell me whether that's not the best fudge you've ever had in your life!"

Rose and Maggie unwrapped the fudge. "Delicious!" said Maggie, with her mouth full.

"Ooh, yum," said Rose, struggling to swallow the lump of fudge, which was sticking in her throat.

"R and M for Rose and Maggie!" said their mother, starting to drive again.

"Why can't it be M and R?" asked Maggie.

"Where are we going?" asked Rose.

"To Lord and Taylor," their mother said gaily. "I thought about supermarkets, of course, but what I decided is that this is really a gourmet product, not a grocery item, and it should be sold in boutiques and department stores."

"Does Dad know about this?" asked Rose.

"We're going to surprise him," said Caroline. "Take off those sweaters and make sure your faces are clean. We're making a sales call, girls!"

Rose turned on her side, remembering the rest of the day—the manager's polite smile when her mother had upended her handbag on the costume jewelry counter and dumped out two dozen squares of wax-paper-wrapped R and M fudge (and two squares reading "M and R," which Maggie had changed in the car). How their mother had whisked them up to the girls' department and bought them matching rabbit-fur muffs. How they'd had lunch in the Lord and Taylor tearoom, cream-cheese-and-olive sandwiches with the crusts cut off, tiny pickles barely longer than Rose's baby finger, slices of angel food cake with strawberries and whipped cream. How beautiful their mother looked, her cheeks flaring pink, her eyes sparkling, her hands fluttering like birds, ignoring her own lunch as she described her sales ideas, her marketing plans, how R and M Fudge would be as popular as Keebler or Nabisco. "We're starting small, girls, but everyone has to start somewhere," she'd said. Maggie nodded and told Caroline how good the fudge was and asked for seconds on sandwiches and cake, and Rose sat there, trying to force down a few bites of her lunch and wondering whether she'd been the only one to notice the manager's raised eyebrows and overly polite smile when all that candy came cascading onto the countertop.

After lunch they went walking through the mall. "Each of you can get one present," their mother said. "Anything you want. Anything at all!" Rose asked for a Nancy Drew book. Maggie wanted a puppy. Their mother didn't hesitate.

"Of course a puppy!" she'd said, her voice rising. Rose noticed other shoppers staring at the three of them—two little girls in party dresses, one woman in a skirt printed with red poppies and a turquoise scarf, tall and beautiful, carrying six shopping bags and talking way too loud. "We should have gotten a puppy a long time ago!"

"Dad's allergic," Rose said. Her mother either didn't hear, or decided to ignore her. She grabbed her daughters by their hands and hurried them over to the pet shop, where Maggie picked out a small tan cocker spaniel puppy and named it Honey Bun.

"Mom was nuts, but she was fun, wasn't she?" Maggie asked in her underwater voice.

"Yeah, she was," said Rose, remembering how they'd come home, laden with shopping bags and Honey Bun's cardboard carrying case, to their father sitting on the couch, still in his suit and tie from work, waiting.

"Girls, go to your room," he'd said, taking Caroline by the hand and leading her to the kitchen. Rose and Maggie, carrying Honey Bun in her box, walked quietly upstairs, but even through the closed bedroom door, they could hear their mother's voice rising to a shriek. *Michael, it was a good idea, it was a legitimate business idea, there's no reason it won't work, and I just bought the girls a few treats, I'm their mother, I can do what I want, I can take them out of school once in a while, it doesn't matter, we had a nice day, Michael, a special day, a day they'll always remember, and I'm sorry I forgot to call the school, but you shouldn't have worried, they were with me and I'M THEIR MOTHER I'M THEIR MOTHER I AM THEIR MOTHER. . . .*

"Oh, no," Maggie whispered, as the puppy started to whine. "Are they fighting? Is it our fault?"

"Shh," said Rose. She gathered the puppy into her arms. Maggie's thumb crept into her mouth as she leaned against her sister, and they listened to their mother's screams, now punctuated with the sound of things being thrown and things breaking, and their father's murmur, which seemed to consist of a single word: *Please.*

"How long did we have Honey Bun?" asked Maggie. Rose twisted in the armchair and struggled to remember.

"A day, I think," she said. It was coming back to her now. The next morning, she'd gotten up early to walk the dog. The hallway was dark; their parents' bedroom door was closed. Their father was sitting at the kitchen table alone.

"Your mother's resting," he said. "Can you take care of the dog? Can you get breakfast for yourself and Maggie?"

"Sure," said Rose. She gave her father a long look. "Is Mom . . . is she okay?"

Her father sighed, and restacked the newspaper. "She's just tired, Rose. She's resting. Try to keep quiet, and let her rest. Take care of your sister."

"I will," Rose promised. When she came home from school that afternoon, the dog was gone. Her parents' bedroom door was still closed. And here she was, twenty-two years later, still keeping that promise, still taking care of her sister.

"It was really good fudge, wasn't it?" asked Maggie. In the dark, she sounded like her six-year-old self—happy and hopeful, a merry little girl who wanted to believe everything her mother told her.

"It was delicious," said Rose. "Good night, Maggie," she said, in a tone she hoped would make it clear that she wasn't interested in any more discussion.

When Jim Danvers opened his eyes the next morning, he was alone in the bed. He stretched, scratched himself, then got to his feet, wrapped a towel around his waist, and went in search of Rose.

The bathroom door was locked, and he could hear water running behind it. He knocked gently, sweetly, seductively, even, imagining Rose in the shower, Rose's skin flushed and steamy, Rose's bare chest beaded with water . . .

The door swung open, and a girl who was not Rose stalked out.

"Hlgho," said Jim, struggling for some combination of "hello" and "who are you?"

The strange girl was slender, with long reddish-brown hair piled on top of her head, a delicate heart-shaped face, and full pink lips. She had painted toenails, tanned legs that stretched toward her chin, and hard nipples (he couldn't help but notice) poking against the threadbare front of her T-shirt. She scowled at him sleepily. "Was that even English?" she asked. Her eyes were wide and brown and rimmed with layers of liner and sleep-smeared mascara—hard, watchful eyes, the color of Rose's eyes, but somehow very different.

Jim tried it again. "Hello," he said. "Is, um, Rose around?"

The strange girl cocked her thumb toward the kitchen. "In there," she said. She leaned against the wall. Jim became aware that a towel was all he was wearing. The girl cocked one leg behind her, resting her foot flat against the wall, and eyed him slowly, up and down.

"You're Rose's roommate?" he guessed, unable to remember whether Rose had mentioned a roommate.

The girl shook her head, just as Rose rounded the corner, fully clothed, shoes and lipstick on, with two cups of coffee in her hands.

"Oh!" she said, and stopped so quickly that coffee sloshed backward, splashing her wrists and the front of her blouse. "Oh. You guys have met?"

Mutely, Jim shook his head. The girl said nothing . . . just kept staring at him with a small, sphinxlike grin.

"Maggie, this is Jim," Rose said. "Jim, this is Maggie Feller. My sister."

"Hello," said Jim, and bobbed his head, clutching his towel tightly.

Maggie gave a short nod. They stood there for an instant, the three of them, Jim feeling ridiculous in his towel, Rose, with coffee dripping from her sleeves, and Maggie staring back and forth between them.

"She came last night," said Rose. "She was at her high-school reunion, and . . ."

"I don't think he needs details," said Maggie. "He can wait for the *E! True Hollywood Story* like everyone else."

"Sorry," said Rose.

Maggie sniffed, turned on her heel, and stalked back to the living room. Rose sighed. "Sorry," she said again. "It's always a production with her."

Jim nodded. "Hey," he said quietly, "I want to hear all about it. Just give me a minute . . ." he said, nodding toward the bathroom.

"Oh!" said Rose, "oh, I'm sorry."

"Don't worry," he said, whispering, nuzzling her cheek and the soft flesh of her neck with his stubble. She trembled, and the remaining coffee quivered in the cups.

When Jim and Rose left a half-hour later, Maggie had returned to the couch. One bare foot and smooth, naked calf poked out from the blankets. Rose was sure she wasn't sleeping. She was certain that this—the tanned curve of her sister's leg, the scarlet toenails—was a calculated display. She hustled Jim out the door, thinking that this had been what she'd wanted—to perform the classic kittenish Hollywood wake-up, all smudgy and glamorous and gorgeous, with the slow fluttering of eyelashes, the contented smile. And now Maggie got to be the smudgy, sexy, glamorous one, while she was bustling around like Betty Crocker, offering people coffee.

"Are you working today?" he asked. She nodded.

"Work on the weekends," he mused. "I'd forgotten what being an associate was like." He kissed her good-bye at her front door—a brisk, businesslike peck—and looked in his wallet for his parking stub. "Huh," he said, frowning, "I could've sworn there was a hundred bucks in here."

Maggie, Rose thought to herself, even as she reached into her wallet for a twenty. Maggie, Maggie, Maggie, who always makes me pay.

TWO

Morning. Ella Hirsch lay alone in the center of her bed and assessed her various aches, pains, and maladies. She began with her cranky left ankle, progressed to her throbbing right hip, paused at her intestines, which felt both empty and knotted at the same time, and moved steadily upward, past the breasts that were shrinking each year, up over her eyes (the cataract surgery last month had been a success), and on to the hair that she wore unfashionably long and dyed a warm auburn—her one vanity.

Not bad, not bad, thought Ella, as she swung first her left leg, then her right one, out of the bed, resting her feet lightly on the cool tiled floor. Ira, her husband, had never wanted tiles—"Too hard!" he'd said, "Too cold!" And so they'd had wall-to-wall carpeting. Beige. The day shiva was over, Ella had been on the phone, and two weeks later, the carpet was gone and she had her tile—a creamy white marble that felt smooth under her feet.

Ella put her hands on top of her thighs, rocked back and then forth, once and then twice, and struggled, groaning slightly, out of the queen-sized bed—her second apres-Ira purchase. It was the Monday after Thanksgiving, and Golden Acres, "a retirement community for active seniors," was unusually quiet, because most of those active seniors had spent the holiday with their children and grandchildren. Ella, too, had celebrated, in her own little way. She'd had a turkey sandwich for dinner.

She smoothed out her quilt and considered the day—breakfast, and the poem she had to finish, then she'd take the trolley to the bus stop and take the bus to her weekly volunteer session at the pet shelter. Then she'd come home for lunch and a nap, and maybe she'd read for an hour or two—she was halfway through taping a book of Margaret Atwood short stories for the vision impaired. Dinner was early—"Four o'clock's the late seating here," she'd heard somebody joking, and it was funny because it was true—and then the Clubhouse had Movie Night. Another empty day, stuffed as full as she could manage.

She'd made a mistake, moving here. Florida had been Ira's idea. "A new start," he'd said, fanning the brochures out over the kitchen table, with the lights glinting off his bald spot, his gold watch and wedding ring. Ella had barely glanced at the glossy photographs of sandy beaches, surf and palm trees, white buildings with elevators and wheelchair ramps and showers with built-in stainless steel grab bars. She'd thought only that Golden Acres, or any of the dozen communities just like it, would be a good place to hide. No more former friends and neighbors to stop her at the post office or the grocery store, to place well-meaning hands on her forearm and say, *How are you two holding up? How long has it been now?* She'd been almost happy, almost hopeful, packing up their house in Michigan.

She hadn't known, couldn't have guessed, could never have figured that the whole point of a retirement community was children. They hadn't showed that in the brochures, she thought bitterly—how every living room she'd visit would have every available surface crammed with pictures of children, grandchildren, great-grandchildren. How every conversation would eventually make its way back to that most precious commodity. *My daughter loved that movie. My son bought a car just like that. My granddaughter's applying to college. My grandson said that senator's a crook.*

Ella kept herself apart from the other women. She stayed busy. Pet shelter, hospital, Meals on Wheels, shelving books at the library, pricing goods at the thrift store, the column she wrote for the Acres's weekly newspaper.

On that morning, she sat at her kitchen table, a cup of hot tea in front of her, with sunshine gleaming on her tiled floor, and took out her notebook and pen. She was going to finish the poem she'd started last week. Not that she was much of a poet, but Lewis Feldman, the editor of the *Golden Acres Gazette,* had come to her in desperation after the regular poet had broken her hip. The deadline was Wednesday, and she wanted to have Tuesday free for revisions.

"Just Because I'm Old," was the title she'd come up with. "Just because I'm old," the poem began, "because my step's a little slow, because my hair has gotten gray, because I nap most ev'ry day . . ."

And that was as far as she'd gotten. She sipped her tea, considering. Just because she was old . . . well, what?

"I AM NOT INVISIBLE," she wrote, in big bold capital letters. Then she crossed it out. It wasn't true. She did feel she'd turned sixty and been erased, somehow, and had been invisible for the last eighteen years. Real people—young people—looked right through her. But "invisible" would be a very hard word to rhyme.

She decided to come back to 'invisible' and wrote, beneath it, "I matter." *Matter* should be easier . . . but then, what could she rhyme that with? "I can make a good cake batter?" "I can hear the trolley's clatter?" "Even though I've gotten fatter?"

Yes! *Fatter* was good. People at Golden Acres would identify. Especially, she thought with a smile, her almost-friend Dora, who volunteered at the thrift shop with her. Dora wore elastic-waist everything, and always ordered whipped cream with dessert. "I spent seventy years watching what I ate," she'd say, spooning a mouthful of hot fudge or cheesecake. "My Mortie's gone now, so why should I worry?"

"I matter. Even thought I've gotten fatter, I'm still here," Ella wrote. "I have ears to hear the sounds of life around me . . ."

Which was true, she mused. Except the sounds of life at Golden Acres were, if she was perfectly honest, the constant drone of traffic, the occasional wail of the ambulance siren, and people picking fights with each other because they'd left their clothes in the communal dryer at the end of the hall, or put plastic bottles into the "glass only" recycling bin. Not exactly the stuff of poetry.

"The ocean's gentle thunder," she wrote instead. "The sound of children laughing. The music of sun and smiles."

There. That was good. The ocean part was even possible— Golden Acres was a mile away from the shore. The trolley went there. And "the music of sun and smiles." Lewis would like that. In his life before Golden Acres, Lewis had run a chain of hardware stores in Utica, New York. He liked editing—"newspapering," he called it—a lot better. Every time she saw him, he had a red grease pencil tucked behind his ear, as if he might be called upon at any minute to dash off a headline, or edit some copy.

Ella closed her notebook and took a sip of her tea. Eight-thirty, and it was already getting hot. She rose from her seat thinking only of the full day she had before her, the full week after that. Only, as she walked, she could hear the very thing she'd written about—the sound of children's laughter. Boys, from the sound of it. She could hear their shouts, and their sandals slapping as they ran back and forth along the corridor outside of her door, chasing the tiny, darting chameleons who sunned themselves on the ledge, most likely. They were Mavis Gold's grandsons, she thought. Mavis had mentioned she was getting ready for a visit.

"I got one! I got one!" called one of the boys, his voice full of excitement. Ella closed her eyes. She should go outside and tell them not to be afraid, that the chameleons had more to fear from their clumsy, sweaty boy-palms and boy-fingers than the boys had to fear from the chameleons. She should go and tell them to stop shouting before Mr. Boehr in 6-B came out and started yelling about his insomnia.

Instead, she turned her face from the window before she let herself open the blinds and look at the boys. Children hurt . . . even though it had been more than fifty years since her daughter had been a child, and more than twenty years since she'd last seen her granddaughters.

Ella set her lips in a tight line and walked resolutely toward the bathroom. She wouldn't go down that road today. She wouldn't think about the daughter-who-was-gone, or the grandchildren she would never get to know, about the life that was snatched away from her, excised as cleanly and completely as a tumor, leaving not even a scar for her to cherish, to remember it by.

THREE

More and more, Rose Feller was starting to think that her boss had lost his mind.

Sure, she knew that everyone thought his or her boss was crazy. All of her friends—well, Amy—had the usual spate of complaints: the unreasonable demands, the inconsiderate treatment, the drunken ass-patting at the company picnic.

But now, filing into the conference room for the pep rally that Don Dommel had instituted as a Friday afternoon ritual, Rose was once again faced with the possibility that one of her firm's founding partners wasn't just eccentric or odd, or any of those polite adjectives reserved for powerful men, but he was actually honest-to-God nuts.

"People!" the man of the hour bellowed, thwacking a PowerPoint chart of the firm's billable hours with his fist. "We have GOT to do BETTER than THIS! THIS," he continued, "is GOOD, but not GREAT. And with the talent we've got, even GREAT is NOT GOOD ENOUGH! We have to GRIND DOWN the handrail of mediocrity and OLLIE OVER to excellence!"

"Huh?" muttered the associate on Rose's right. He had frizzy gingery hair and his skin, pale as skim milk, was a badge of honor in this place, the sure sign that he was making his minimum billable hours and, hence, not getting out much. Simon Something, Rose thought.

Rose shrugged at him, and slumped in her seat. How many law firms had pep rallies, anyhow? she thought. How many associates had received custom-made skateboards with the words "DOMMEL LAW" painted on the top, instead of the customary cash, for their holiday bonuses last year? How many managing partners delivered weekly speeches couched almost exclusively in sports metaphors, followed by an overamplified rendition of "I Believe I Can Fly"? How many law firms had theme music at all? Not many, Rose thought sourly.

"Is an Ollie a person or a thing?" Simon Something persisted. Rose gave another shrug, hoping, as she did each week, that Dommel's Xtreme gaze wouldn't fall on her. Don Dommel had always been a jock, Rose knew. He'd jogged through the seventies, felt the burn during the eighties, even finished a few triathalons before plunging headlong into the brave new world of extreme sports and taking his law firm along with him. At some point past his fiftieth birthday he'd decided that conventional exercise, no matter how strenuous, just wasn't enough. Don Dommel didn't just want to be fit, he wanted to be edgy and hip, radical and cool. Don Dommel wanted to be a fifty-three-year-old lawyer on a skateboard. Don Dommel, apparently, saw no contradiction between those two things.

He bought two specially-made skateboards and found a semi-homeless kid who seemed to live in Love Park to coach him (technically, the kid worked in the mail room, but nobody'd ever seen so much as the tip of his dreadlocks down there). He constructed a wooden ramp inside of the law firm's parking garage, spent every lunch hour on it, even after he'd broken his wrist, bruised his tailbone, and developed a limp that had him lurching through the firm's halls like an imperfectly rehearsed drag queen.

And it wasn't enough that he himself wanted to become an urban warrior. Don Dommel had to extend his vision to the entirety of the firm. One Friday, Rose had come into work and found a nylon jersey shoved into her mail slot, with her last name on the back above the words *I Can Fly!* "Please," Rose had said to her secretary. "I can barely walk before I've had my coffee." But the jerseys weren't optional. A firm-wide e-mail said that all associates should wear them every Friday. The week after that, once she'd reluctantly tugged the jersey over her shoulders, Rose had put her mug under the coffee dispenser only to find that it, plus all of the firm's water-coolers and soda machines, were dispensing only Gatorade. Which, the last time Rose had checked, wasn't caffeinated. Which meant it was going to do her no good at all.

So now she sat miserably in a seat in the center of the third row with her fly jersey pulled over her suit jacket, sipping warm sports beverage and wishing desperately that she had coffee. "This is getting ridiculous," she murmured to herself, as Dommel once again dispensed with the afternoon's advertised topic ("Effective Depositions," Rose remembered) in favor of a video of Tony Hawk highlights.

"Psst," said Simon, out of the corner of his mouth, as Dommel tore into a cringing first-year. ("YOU! DO YOU BELIEVE YOU CAN SOAR?")

Rose glanced at him. "Psst? Did you actually just say 'psst'? Are we in a detective novel?"

Simon raised his eyebrows in an exaggerated sneaky manner and opened a brown paper bag. Rose's nose twitched at the scent of coffee. Her mouth watered. "Want some?" he whispered.

She hesitated, looked around, considered the breaches of etiquette involved in sipping someone else's coffee, then decided that if she didn't get some caffeine, she'd be a jittery, worthless mess for the rest of the day. She ducked her head and gulped.

"Thanks," she whispered. He nodded, just as Don Dommel's white-hot gaze fell upon him.

"YOU!" roared Dommel. "WHAT'S YOUR DREAM?"

"To be six foot ten," Simon answered without hesitation. A ripple of laughter started in the back of the room. "And to play for the

Sixers." The laughter swelled. Don Dommel stood on the stage looking bewildered, as if his audience of loyal associates had suddenly turned into donkeys. "Maybe not as a center. I'd be happy to play guard," Simon continued. "But if that's not going to happen . . ." He paused, and looked up at Don Dommel. "I'd settle for being a good lawyer."

Rose giggled. Don Dommel opened his mouth, then shut it, then lurched across the stage. "THAT!" he finally announced, "THAT is the SPIRIT I'm looking for. I want EACH and EVERY ONE OF YOU to go BACK and THINK about that kind of WINNING ATTITUDE!" Dommel concluded. Rose had pulled her jersey off over her suit jacket and wadded it into her purse before his mouth was shut.

"Here," Simon said, offering her his cup of coffee. "I've got more in my office, if you want this one."

"Oh, thanks," Rose said, taking the cup, still scanning the sea of departing bodies for Jim's. She caught up with him by the receptionist's desk.

"What in God's name was that about?" she asked.

"Why don't you come into my office, and we can discuss it," he said, for the benefit of anyone within earshot, smiling a wicked smile, for her benefit alone. He closed the door and whirled her into his arms.

"Umm, do I detect dark roast?" he asked, kissing her.

"Don't rat me out," said Rose, kissing him back.

"Never," he growled, lifting her hips *(Oh, God,* thought Rose, *don't let him hurt himself!)* and settling her on his desk. "Your secrets," he said, kissing her neck, "are safe," and now his lips were sliding down her cleavage and his hands were busy with her buttons, "with me."

FOUR

At eleven o'clock the following Monday morning, Maggie Feller opened her eyes and stretched her arms over her head. Rose was gone. Maggie walked to the bathroom, where she drank thirty-two ounces of water and continued with her in-depth examination of her habitat, starting with the medicine cabinet, where the shelves were so well-stocked it seemed as if her sister expected a dire medical emergency to befall Philadelphia, and that she alone would be called upon to play Florence Nightingale to the city's entire population.

There were bottles of painkillers, boxes of antacids, a jumbo-sized jug of Pepto-Bismol, a family-sized box of Band-Aid bandages, and a Red Cross–approved first-aid kit. There was Midol and Advil and Nuprin, NyQuil and DayQuil, cough syrup and cold tablets and tampons. Here was a girl who made good use of the coupons at CVS, Maggie thought, as she sorted through Ace bandages and multivitamins, calcium tablets and dental floss, rubbing alcohol and hydrogen peroxide, prescription-strength benzoyl peroxide and four unopened toothbrushes. Where was the eyeliner? Where were the blush and the concealer that her sister so desperately needed? Maggie hadn't found anything cosmetic except for a single half-used lipstick. There was makeup remover—a tub of

Pond's cold cream—but no makeup. What did Rose think? That somebody was going to sneak into her apartment in the dead of night, tie her up, put makeup on her face, and then leave?

Plus, there wasn't so much as a single condom or tube of spermicide, although there was an unopened package of Monistat—so just in case her celibate sister somehow managed to get a yeast infection from a toilet seat or something, she'd be ready. It was probably on sale, Maggie snorted, helping herself to a bottle of Midol.

The bathroom was also minus a scale. Which wasn't a surprise, given Rose's history with bathroom scales. When they were teenagers, Sydelle had taped a laminated chart on the girls' bathroom wall. Each Saturday morning, Rose would stand on the scale, her eyes shut and her face impassive, as Sydelle recorded the number and then sat on the toilet seat, quizzing Rose about what she'd eaten during the week. Even now, Maggie could hear her stepmother's too-sweet voice. *You had a salad? Well, what kind of dressing was on it? Was it fat free? Are you sure? Rose, I'm only doing this to help you. I've got your best interests at heart.*

Yeah, right, Maggie thought. As if Sydelle was ever interested in anyone but herself, and her own daughter. In the bedroom, Maggie pulled on a pair of her sister's sweatpants and continued her inventory, gathering what she called Information.

"You're a very smart girl," her old teacher Mrs. Fried used to tell her, back in elementary school. Mrs. Fried, with her gray curls and impressive shelf of a bosom, with her beaded eyeglass chain and knitted sweater vests, had taught Maggie what was euphemistically called "enrichment" (and what was known to the students as "special ed") from second grade through sixth. She was a kind, grandmotherly woman who'd become Maggie's ally, especially during her first months in a new school, in a new state. "Part of what makes you so smart is that you can always think of another way to get the job done. So if you don't know what a word means, what do you do?"

"Guess?" guessed Maggie.

Mrs. Fried smiled. "Figure it out through context, is how I'd

put it. It's all about finding solutions. Solutions that work for you."
Maggie had nodded, feeling pleased and flattered, which were not
normally ways she felt during class. "So imagine you are on your
way to the Vet, for a concert, but there's a big traffic jam. Would
you go home? Skip the concert? No," Mrs. Fried had said, before
Maggie'd had a chance to ask her who was playing at this theoretical concert so she could figure out how much effort it was worth.
"You'd just find another way to get there. And you're smart enough
to do it really well." In addition to figuring out a word's meaning
from context, Mrs. Fried's alternative strategies taught Maggie to
add numbers if she couldn't multiply them, to chart out a paragraph's meaning, circling the subject, underlining the verbs. In the
years since school, Maggie had come up with a few new strategies of
her own, like Information, which could be defined as knowing
things about people that they didn't want or expect you to know.
Information was always useful, and it was usually easy to come by.
Through the years Maggie secretly perused credit-card bills and
diaries, bank statements and old photographs. In high school, she'd
located a battered copy of *Forever* between Rose's mattress and box
spring. Rose had turned over her allowance for almost an entire
school year before deciding that she didn't care if Maggie told her
father how she'd dog-eared the pages with sex scenes.

Maggie snooped over to her sister's desk. There were gas bill,
electric bill, phone bill, and cable bill, all neatly paper-clipped
together, the return envelopes already bearing stamps and address
labels. Here was a receipt from Tower Records, which told her that
Rose had purchased (and worse, paid full price for) a copy of George
Michael's greatest hits. Maggie pocketed it, sure that it would be
useful, even if she wasn't sure how. A receipt from Saks for a pair of
shoes. Three hundred and twelve dollars. Very nice. A schedule of
classes at the gym, six months out of date. No surprise there.
Maggie closed the drawer and moved on to what was sure to be the
depressing terrain of Rose's closet.

She flipped through the hangers, shaking her head at the

clothes that ranged in shade from black to brown, with the occasional gray sweater thrown in for fun. Drab, drab, drab. Boring suits all in a row, and dowdy sweater sets, a half-dozen skirts designed to hit Rose in the dead center of her calves, as if she'd picked them out to give her legs the illusion of maximum thickness. Maggie could have helped her. But Rose didn't want help. Rose thought her life was fine. Rose thought it was everyone else who had the problems.

There was a time, when they were little girls, that people thought they were twins, with their matching pigtails and identical brown eyes and the defiant way their jaws poked forward. Well, not anymore. Rose was maybe an inch or two taller, and at least fifty pounds heavier, maybe more—Maggie could make out a faint slackening under her jawline, the beginning of the dread double chin. She had shirts in her closet from Lane Bryant, which Maggie didn't even want to touch, although she knew that fat wasn't contagious. And Rose just didn't care. Her hair, shoulder-length, was usually shoved into an untidy bun or ponytail or, worse, done up in one of those plastic clips that everyone else in the world had tacitly agreed to stop wearing five years ago. Maggie wasn't even sure where Rose was still finding them—dollar stores, probably—but somehow she had an endless supply, even though Maggie made it a point to toss a few in the trash whenever she visited.

Maggie took a deep breath, pushing the last jacket aside, and began with the thing she'd been saving for dessert—her sister's shoes. As always, what she saw dazzled her and made her feel sick, like a little kid who'd gorged on too much Halloween candy. Rose, fat, lazy, unfashionable Rose, Rose who couldn't be bothered to exfoliate or moisturize or polish her fingernails, had somehow managed to acquire dozens of pairs of the absolutely most perfect shoes in the world. There were flats and stilettos and high-heeled Mary Janes, suede loafers so buttery soft you wanted to rub them against your cheek, a pair of Chanel sandals that were little more than a slim leather sole and wisps of gold wire and ribbon. There were knee-high Gucci boots in glossy black, ankle-high Stephane Kelian boots in cinnamon, a pair of crimson cowgirl boots with hand-stitched jalapeño peppers winding up the sides. There were lace-up Hush Puppies in raspberry and lime; there were Sigerson Morrison flats and Manolo Blahnik mules. There were Steve Madden loafers and, still in their Saks box, a pair of Prada kitten heels, white, with white-and-yellow daisies appliquéd over the toes. Maggie held her breath and eased them on. As always—as all of Rose's shoes did—they fit her perfectly.

It wasn't fair, she thought, stalking into the kitchen in the Pradas. Where was Rose going to wear a pair of shoes like these, anyhow? What was the point? She scowled and opened a cabinet. Whole Wheat Total. All-Bran. Golden raisins and brown rice. Jesus Christ, she thought, wrinkling her nose. Was it National Healthy Colon week? And there were no Fritos, no Cheetos, no Doritos . . . nothing at all from the all-important Ito food group. She rummaged through the freezer, past the veggie burgers and pints of whole fruit all-natural sorbet sitting in a row until she hit pay dirt—a pint of Ben and Jerry's New York Superfudge Chunk, still in its brown paper bag. Ice cream had always been her sister's go-to comfort food, Maggie thought, grabbing a spoon and proceeding back to the couch, where a section of newspaper sat at the center of the coffee table, with a red pen laid beside it. Maggie picked it up. Today's classified ads, thoughtfully provided by big sister Rose. Of course.

Well, she thought, this was a pretty pass. That was one of the things Mrs. Fried used to say. Whenever something would go wrong in the classroom—a spilled can of paint, a lost book—Mrs. Fried would clasp her hands across her chest and shake her head until her eyeglass chain rattled and say, "Well, this is a pretty pass!"

But even Mrs. Fried couldn't have predicted this, thought Maggie, eating ice cream with one hand and circling classified ads with the other. Not even Mrs. Fried could have seen Maggie Feller's downfall coming as swiftly as it had, so that Maggie still felt as if somewhere between the ages of fourteen and sixteen she'd walked off the edge of a cliff and had been falling ever since.

Elementary school and junior high had been fine, she remembered, spooning the cool creaminess even faster past her lips (and not noticing when she accidentally dropped a chocolate-covered walnut on the shoe). She'd had to go to "enrichment" during recess three days a week, but not even that had mattered much, because she was still the prettiest, most fun girl in her class, the girl with the cutest outfits, the best Halloween costumes that she'd make herself, the most interesting ideas of what to do during recess. And after her mother died and they'd moved to New Jersey, when her father would be at work in the afternoons and Sydelle would be off at some volunteer committee thing and Rose, of course, would be busy with the chess club or debate team, she'd been the girl with access to an empty house and an unlocked liquor cabinet. She'd been popular. It was Rose who'd been the nerd, the geek, the loser, Rose who'd skulked around with her thick glasses hiding half her face and dandruff silting her shoulders, Rose who'd been the one the girls had laughed at.

She could close her eyes and still remember one afternoon at recess. She'd been in fourth grade and Rose was in sixth. Maggie was heading to play hopscotch with Marissa Nussbaum and Kim Pratt when Rose had strolled right through a game of dodgeball, oblivious, holding a book up to her eyes.

"Hey, move it!" one of the older boys, a sixth-grader, shouted, and Rose raised her head and looked puzzled. *Move, Rose,* Maggie thought as hard as she could, as Kim and Marissa tittered. Rose kept walking, not picking up the pace, when another one of the big boys picked up the ball and threw it at her, as hard as he could, grunting with the effort. He'd been aiming for her body, but his aim wasn't good, and he hit Rose in the back of her head. Rose's glasses went flying. Her books flew out of her arms as she staggered forward, got her feet tangled, and fell flat on her face.

Maggie's heart stopped beating. She stood as if she'd been

frozen, stood as still as the circle of sixth-grade boys, who'd looked at each other uneasily, as if they were trying to decide whether this was still funny, or whether they'd really hurt this girl and could get in trouble. And then one of them—Sean Perigini, most likely, the tallest boy in sixth grade—started laughing. And then they were all laughing, all the sixth-grade boys, and then all the kids who'd been watching, as Rose, of course, started to cry, and then wiped the snot off her face with a palm that was bleeding from her fall and started groping around for her glasses.

Maggie had stood there, part of her knowing she shouldn't let them do that, and part of her thinking, cruelly, *Let Rose figure it out. She's the one who's such a loser. She brought this on herself.* Plus, Maggie wasn't the one who fixed things. Rose was. So she'd stood, watching, for what felt like an unbearably long time, until Rose found her glasses. One of the lenses was cracked, Maggie saw, as Rose lurched to her feet, gathering her books, and . . . oh, no. Her sister's pants had split right down the back and Maggie and everyone else could see her underwear, her Holly Hobbie underwear, which raised the pointing and laughing to a hysterical pitch. *Oh, God,* thought Maggie, feeling sick, *why did Rose have to wear those today?*

"You're going to have to pay!" Rose was shouting at Sean Perigini, holding her broken glasses and probably with no idea that everyone could see her underwear. The laughter built. Rose's eyes swept the playground, past the kickball game, past the kids on the swing sets and jungle gym, through the big kids, the fifth and sixth graders shrieking and clutching each other as they laughed at her, until finally she caught sight of Maggie, standing between Kim and Marissa on the little section of grass beside the flower bed that was, by unspoken consent, reserved for the most popular girls. Rose squinted at Maggie, and Maggie could read the hatred and misery in her sister's eyes as clearly as if Rose had walked over and shouted in her face.

I should help, a voice inside of her whispered again. But Maggie just stood there, watching, listening to the other kids laugh, thinking that this was somehow some dark part of the bargain that had made her the pretty one.

She was safe, Maggie thought fiercely, as Rose wiped her face, gathered her books, and, ignoring the taunts and laughter and the singsonged catcalls of "Hol-ly! Hob-bie!" that a few of the fifth-grade girls had already taken up, walked slowly back into the school. Maggie'd never make the mistake of wandering through a dodgeball game and she'd certainly never wear cartoon-character underwear. She was safe, she thought, as Rose pushed through the double glass doors and headed inside—to the principal's office, no doubt. "Do you think she's okay?" Kim had asked, and Maggie had tossed her head scornfully. "I think she's adopted," she'd said, and Kim and Marissa had giggled, and Maggie had laughed, too, even though the laughter felt like gravel in her chest.

And then, as fast as a dodgeball flying through the air to whack her unsuspecting head, everything changed. When, exactly? Her fourteenth year, at the tail end of eighth grade, in the gap between junior high, where she'd ruled, and high school, where everything had fallen apart.

It had started with the standardized assessment test. "Nothing to worry about!" Mrs. Fried's junior-high replacement had said in a falsely cheerful voice. The new "enrichment" teacher was ugly, with caked-on makeup and a wart next to her nose. She'd told Maggie that she could take an untimed version of the test. "You'll do fine!" But Maggie stared at the page of blank bubbles that she was supposed to fill in with her number two pencil, feeling her heart sink, knowing that it wasn't going to be fine. *You're a smart girl,* Mrs. Fried had told her a dozen times. But Mrs. Fried was gone, back in the elementary school. High school was going to be different. And that test—"just for our records! Results kept confidential!"—had somehow tripped her up and ruined everything. She wasn't supposed to have seen her scores, but her teacher had left a copy on the desk, and Maggie had peeked, first trying to read the words upside down and then just grabbing the thing and flipping it around so that she could read it. The words hit her like a hammer. "Dyslexic," it said. "Learning disabled." It might as well have read, "You're dead," Maggie thought, because that was what those words really meant.

"Now, Maggie, let's not get hysterical," Sydelle had said that night, after the teacher had called to share the "confidential" results. "We'll get you a tutor!"

"I don't need a tutor," Maggie had said furiously, feeling tears scalding her throat.

Rose, sitting in the corner of Sydelle's white-on-white living room, had looked up from *Watership Down.* "It might help, you know."

"Shut up!" Maggie had said, the forbidden words flying out of her mouth. "I'm not stupid, Rose, so just shut up!"

"Maggie," their father had said, "nobody's saying you're stupid. . . ."

"That test said I was stupid," said Maggie. "And you know what? I don't even care. And why'd you have to tell her?" she demanded, pointing her finger at Sydelle. "And her?" Maggie continued, pointing at Rose. "It's none of her business!"

"We all want to help," Michael Feller had said, and Maggie had ranted that she didn't need help, she didn't care what the dumb test said, she was smart just like Mrs. Fried had always said. No, she didn't need a tutor, no she didn't want to go to private school, she had friends, unlike some people she could name, she had friends and she wasn't stupid no matter what the test said, and plus even if she was stupid, she'd rather be stupid than ugly like four-eyes in the corner, even if she was stupid, that was okay, it was no biggie, she'd be fine.

But she wasn't fine. When she started high school, her friends were placed in the honors-level courses, and Maggie had been sent to the remedial classes, with no friendly Mrs. Fried to tell her that she wasn't a dummy or a retard, that her brain just worked a little differently, and that they'd figure out tricks to get her through. She got stuck with the indifferent teachers—the burned-out older ones who just wanted to be left alone, like Mrs. Cavetti, who wore cock-eyed wigs and too much perfume, or Mrs. Learey, who'd give them in-class reading assignments and then spend the entire period fill-ing photo albums with endless pictures of her grandchildren.

Maggie figured it out fast—the worst teachers got the worst kids as punishment, for being bad teachers. The worst kids got the worst teachers as punishment for being poor—or dumb. Which in this fancy town were often interpreted as the same thing. Well, Maggie figured, if she was someone's punishment, she'd act like punishment. She stopped bringing her books to class and started toting a toolbox-sized makeup kit instead. She'd take polish off her nails during the lectures, reapply a different shade during the pop quiz, after she'd answered all of the questions with the same let-ter—A for one class, B for the next. Multiple-choice quizzes were all these teachers ever came up with. "Maggie, please come to the blackboard," one of the crappy teachers would drone. Maggie would shake her head without lifting her eyes from her makeup mirror. "Sorry, can't help," she'd call, fluttering her fingertips. "I'm drying."

She should have flunked everything, should have been left back in every grade. But the teachers kept passing her—probably because they didn't want to see her again the next year. And her friends moved farther and farther away from her with each new school year. She tried for a while, and Kim and Marissa tried, too, but eventually the gap got too wide. They were playing field hockey, they were joining student council, they were taking SAT prep courses and visiting colleges, and she'd been left behind.

By sophomore year, Maggie decided that if the girls were going to ignore her, the guys certainly wouldn't. She started wearing her hair piled high and her cleavage leveraged higher by lace underwire bras that peeked through her shirts. She'd arrived for the first day of school in low-slung jeans that barely clung to the ridge of her hips, high-heeled black leather boots, and a consignment-store lace bustier beneath the army jacket she'd swiped from her father.

Lipstick, nail polish, enough eye shadow to paint a small wall with, an armful of black rubber bracelets, and big, floppy fabric bows in her hair. She took her cues from Madonna, whom she idolized, Madonna, who was just starting to have her videos played on MTV. Maggie devoured every scrap of information about the singer she could find—every magazine interview, every newspaper profile— and marveled at the similarities. They both had dead mothers. They were both beautiful, both talented dancers who'd studied tap and jazz since they were little girls. They were both street-smart, with sex appeal to spare. Boys buzzed around Maggie like flies, buying her packs of cigarettes, inviting her to parties where no parents were present, keeping her cup filled, holding her hand, walking her into an unused bedroom or the backseat of a car when it got late.

It took a while for Maggie to notice that they weren't calling, or asking her to dances, or even saying hello to her in the halls. She'd cried about it—late at night, when Rose was asleep, when nobody could hear her—and then she'd decided not to cry. None of them were worth her tears. And they'd all be sorry, ten years down the road, when she was famous and they were nothings, stranded in this shitty little town, fat and ugly and unfamous, not special at all.

So that was high school. Cringing around the edges of the pop- ular crowd like some kicked dog still holding on to the memories of the days when they'd petted and praised her. Parties on weekends at the house of whoever's parents were away. Beer and wine, joints or pills, and they'd be drunk and, eventually, she figured it was easier if she was drunk, too, if things were a little blurry around the edges and she could imagine seeing what she wanted in their eyes.

And Rose . . . well, Rose hadn't gone through the kind of John Hughes metamorphosis where she shed her glasses, got a good hair- cut, and the football captain fell in love with her at the prom. But she did change in smaller ways. She stopped having dandruff, for one thing, thanks to Maggie's not-so-subtle trick of leaving large bottles of Head and Shoulders in the shower. She still wore glasses, still dressed like a geek, but somewhere along the line she'd acquired a friend—Amy, who was, in Maggie's opinion, just as weird as Rose was—and didn't seem bothered by the fact that the pretty girls still laughed at her, or ignored her, and still occasionally referred to her as Holly Hobbie. Rose was in the honors classes, Rose got straight A's. Maggie would have dismissed all of those things as further signs of her sister's social hopelessness except that those accomplishments had started to matter.

"Princeton!" Sydelle had said, over and over, when Rose was a senior and her acceptance letter had come in the mail. "Well, Rose, this is quite an achievement!" She'd actually cooked Rose's favorite foods for dinner—fried chicken and biscuits and honey—and she hadn't said a word when Rose reached for seconds. "Maggie, you must be very proud of your sister!" she'd said. Maggie had just rolled her eyes in an unspoken "whatever." Like Princeton was such a big deal. Like Rose was the only person who'd ever succeeded in spite of a dead mother. Well, Maggie had a dead mother, too, but did she get extra points for that? No, she did not. She just got questions. From neighbors. From teachers. From everyone who knew her sister. "Can we expect great things from you?" Well, obviously, they couldn't, Maggie thought, inking an emphatic red circle around an ad for waitresses at a "busy, successful Center City restaurant." She'd got the body, Rose had gotten the brains, and now it was looking like brains might count for more.

So Rose graduated from Princeton while Maggie put in a few half-hearted semesters at the local community college. Rose had gone to law school, and Maggie had waitressed at a pizza parlor, done baby-sitting and housecleaning, dropped out of bartending school when the instructor tried to stick his tongue in her ear after the lesson on martinis. Rose was plain, and fat, and frumpy, and up until this morning Maggie had never known her to have a boyfriend except for, like, ten minutes in law school. Yet somehow she was the one with the great apartment (well, the apartment that could have been great if Maggie had decorated it), and with money and friends, the one people looked at with respect. And this guy,

Jim Whatever, was cute in a semi-nerdy way, and Maggie just bet that he was rich, too.

It wasn't fair, thought Maggie, stalking back to the kitchen. It wasn't fair their mother had died. It wasn't fair that she'd somehow used up her handful of good years by junior high and was now living in her sister's shadow, doomed to watch Rose get everything she wanted, while she got nothing at all. She crumpled up the empty container of ice cream, gathered the newspaper, and was getting ready to toss them both when something in the paper caught her eye. It was the magic word: *auditions*. Maggie dropped the ice-cream carton and turned her full attention to the newspaper. "MTV Announces Auditions for VJs," she read. Excitement rose within her like a balloon, along with panic—what if she'd missed it? She scanned the story as rapidly as she could. *December 1. Open call. In New York.* She could be there! She'd tell Rose she had a job interview, which was technically sort of the truth, and she'd get Rose to lend her money for a bus ticket, and clothes. She'd need an outfit. She'd have to buy something new; she could see that instantly; nothing she had was even remotely right. Maggie folded the newspaper carefully and hurried to her sister's closet to see which shoes she'd wear to the Big Apple.

FIVE

Lewis Feldman ushered Mrs. Sobel into his office—a converted closet with the words *Golden Acres Gazette* stenciled on the glass—and closed the door behind them.

"Thank you for coming," he said, pulling the red grease copyediting pencil from behind his ear and setting it on his desk. Mrs. Sobel perched on a chair, crossed her ankles, and clasped her hands in her lap. She was a tiny woman with blue hair and a blue wool cardigan sweater and blue veins pulsing in her hands. He gave her what he hoped was a reassuring smile. She gave him a tentative nod.

"Let me just begin by saying how grateful I am for your help," he said. "We were really in a pinch." Which was true—ever since the *Gazette*'s previous food critic, the Noshing Gourmet, had suffered a heart attack that had landed him facedown in a western omelet, Lewis had been stuck recycling old reviews, and the natives had been getting restless, not to mention tired of reading about the Rascal House yet again.

"This was a very fine first effort," he said, spreading the tear sheet on his desk, so Mrs. Sobel could see what her review looked like, laid out on the page. "Italian Restaurant Tempts Tastebuds," read the headline, beneath a drawing of a winking little bird—the Early Bird, of course—with a cartoon worm clutched in its beak. "I had just a few suggestions," said Lewis, as Mrs. Sobel gave another trembly little nod. He braced himself—running hardware stores hadn't been nearly as tough as taking the fragile egos of retired women in his hands on a biweekly basis—and began to read.

" 'Mangiamo's Italian Restaurant is located in the shopping mall on Powerline Road, next to where the Marshall's used to be, and across from the frozen yogurt shop. It looks like it should be easy to get to, but my husband, Irving, had a very difficult time making the left-hand turn.' "

Mrs. Sobel gave another nod, this one slightly more assertive. Lewis kept reading.

" 'The restaurant has red carpet, white tablecloths with small candles on them. The air conditioner is turned up very high, so you should bring a sweater if you go to Mangiamo's. The minestrone soup was not the way I make it. It had kidney beans, which neither I nor Irving enjoy. The Caesar salad was good, but it is made with anchovies, so if you are allergic to fish, you should get the house salad instead.' " And now Mrs. Sobel was leaning forward eagerly, nodding along, repeating the words in a low, breathless whisper.

" 'For entrees, Irving wanted the chicken parmesan, even though cheese does not agree with him. I had the spaghetti and meatballs, because I thought Irving would eat that. Sure enough, the chicken was hard for him to chew, so he had my meatballs, which were soft.' " Lewis looked at Mrs. Sobel, who was leaning forward, eyes bright.

"See, here's the thing," he said, wondering whether Ben Bradlee and William Shawn had ever had problems like this. "What we're trying to do is be objective."

"Objective," Mrs. Sobel repeated.

"We're trying to give a snapshot of what it's like to eat at Mangiamo's."

She nodded again, confusion replacing the eagerness in her eyes.

"So when you talk about the left-hand turn, and how it was difficult to make, or how the way they make their soup isn't the way you make yours . . ." *Be careful,* Lewis, he told himself, picking up his pencil and tucking it securely behind his ear again. "Well, those are interesting things, and very nicely written, but they might not be exactly helpful to other people who are going to be reading this and using it to decide whether they want to go there."

Now Mrs. Sobel drew herself up straight, a trembling reed of indignation. "But those things are true!" she said.

"Of course they're true," Lewis soothed her. "I'm just wondering whether they're useful. Like, the air-conditioning, and telling people to bring a sweater. That's a very, very useful detail. But the section on the soup . . . not every reader needs to see the restaurant's soup placed in the context of your soup." And then he smiled, and hoped the smile would work. He thought it probably would. His wife, Sharla—Sharla of blessed memory, dead for two years—had always told him he could get away with anything because of his smile. He wasn't a handsome man, he knew. He had a mirror, and while his eyes weren't so great anymore, he could still tell that he was much more Walter Matthau than Paul Newman. Even his earlobes had wrinkles. But the smile was still working. "I'm sure that any soup would suffer, being compared to your soup."

Mrs. Sobel sniffed. But she was looking decidedly less offended.

"Why don't you take this home with you, take another look at it, and try to ask yourself, with everything you're writing, whether it's going to help"—he thought for a minute, then pulled a name out of the air—"Mr. and Mrs. Rabinowitz decide whether to go there for dinner."

"Oh, the Rabinowitzes would never go there," said Mrs. Sobel. "He's very cheap." And then, when Lewis was still sitting behind his desk, utterly nonplussed, she gathered her purse and cardigan and the copy of her story and marched grandly out the door, past Ella Hirsch, who was on her way in.

Ella, Lewis noticed with great relief, neither trembled or nodded. She wasn't nearly as ancient, or fragile, as Mrs. Sobel. She had clear brown eyes and reddish hair that she wore pulled back in a twist, and he'd never once seen her in polyester pants, which were preferred by most of the Acres's female residents.

"How are you?" she asked.

Lewis shook his head. "Honestly, I'm not quite sure," he told her.

"That doesn't sound good," she said, handing him her neatly typed poem. Would he have had a little bit of a crush on Ella even if she wasn't the best writer at the *Golden Acres Gazette?* Probably, Lewis decided. Except he didn't think she was interested. The times he'd invited her for coffee to talk about story ideas, she'd seemed happy to come along, and just as happy when the coffee was gone and she could tell him good-bye.

"Thanks," he said, setting her papers in his in box. "So what are you up to this weekend?" he asked, trying to sound casual.

"I'm at the soup kitchen tomorrow night, and then I've got two books for the blind to read," she said. It was polite, Lewis thought, but it was still a refusal. Had she read that book that all the women were passing around the pool a couple years ago, the one that talked about playing hard to get and had caused eighty-six-year-old Mrs. Asher to hang up on him, mid-edit, after declaring that she was a creature unlike any other and that, as such, it was incumbent upon her to end all phone calls with men?

"Well, thanks for the poem. You're the only one who made your deadline. As usual," Lewis said. Ella gave him a faint smile and headed for the door. Maybe it was his looks, he thought glumly. Sharla had bought him a bulldog calendar for one of the anniversaries they'd celebrated together in Florida, and he'd accused her of trying to tell him something. She'd given him a resounding kiss on his cheek and told him that while his modeling career was probably dead in the water, she loved him anyhow.

Lewis shook his head, hoping to clear away the memories, and picked up Ella's poem. "Just Because I'm Old," he read, and smiled at the line that read "I AM NOT INVISIBLE," and decided that Ella was worth yet another try.

SIX

Rose Feller leaned across the table. "The usual stipulations, counselor?" she asked. The opposing counsel—a whey-faced man in an unfortunate greenish gray suit—nodded, even though Rose would have bet that he didn't know what "the usual stipulations" actually were any more than she did. But every deposition she'd ever attended had started out with the lawyer in charge saying "the usual stipulations," and so she said it, too.

"Okay, if everyone's ready, we'll begin," she said, with a confidence that was more feigned than felt, as if she'd done hundreds of depositions by herself, instead of just two. "My name is Rose Feller, and I am an attorney at Lewis, Dommel, and Fenick. Today I'm representing the Veeder Trucking Company and Stanley Willet, the comptroller of Veeder, who's present and sitting to my left. This is the deposition of Wayne LeGros—" She paused and glanced across the table at the witness, hoping for confirmation that she was pronouncing his last name correctly. Wayne LeGros refused to meet her eyes. "Wayne LeGros," she continued, deciding that if she was saying it wrong he'd speak up, "the president of Majestic Construction. Mr. LeGros, could you begin by giving us your name and address?"

Wayne LeGros, who was short, fiftyish, with iron-gray hair in a buzz cut and a heavy class ring on one thick finger, swallowed hard.

"Wayne LeGros," he said loudly. "I live at five-thirteen Tasker Street. In Philadelphia."

"Thank you," Rose said. In truth, she sort of felt sorry for the guy. She'd never been deposed, except in law school, in mock trial, but she was sure it wasn't fun. "Can you tell us your job title?"

"President. Majestic," said loquacious Mr. LeGros.

"Thank you," Rose said again. "Now, as I'm sure your counsel has explained, we're here today to gather information. My client is contending that you owe them . . ." she glanced down fast at her notes. "Eight thousand dollars, for the lease of equipment."

"Dump trucks," LeGros offered.

"That's right," said Rose. "Can you tell us how many trucks were leased?"

LeGros shut his eyes. "Three."

Rose slid a piece of paper across the table. "This is a copy of the lease agreement you signed with Veeder. I've already had the court reporter mark it as Plaintiff's Exhibit fifteen-A." The court reporter nodded. "Could I ask you to read the parts I've highlighted?"

LeGros took a deep breath and squinted at the page. "It says Majestic agrees to pay Veeder two thousand dollars a week for three dump trucks."

"Is that your signature?"

LeGros took a minute to study the photocopy. "Yep," he finally said. "It's mine." A note of petulance had crept into his voice, and he'd pulled the class ring off his finger and was spinning it on the conference table.

"Thank you," said Rose. "Now, was this project in Ryland completed?"

"The school? Yeah."

"And was Majestic Construction paid for its work?"

LeGros nodded. His attorney raised his eyebrows at him. "Yeah," LeGros said.

Rose slid another sheet of paper across the table. "This is

Plaintiff's sixteen-A—a copy of your invoice to the Ryland School Board, marked 'paid in full.' Was that account paid?"

"Yeah."

"So you were paid for the work you did on the project?"

Another nod. Another dirty look from his attorney. Another "yeah." For the next half-hour, Rose painstakingly led LeGros through a stack of stamped invoices and notices from a collection agency. It wasn't the stuff of Grisham thrillers, she thought as she slogged onward, but if she was lucky it would get the job done.

"So the job in Ryland was completed, and you paid your subcontractors?" Rose summarized.

"Yeah."

"Except not Veeder."

"They got theirs," he mumbled. "They got paid for other things."

"Pardon me?" Rose asked politely.

"Other things," LeGros repeated. He ducked his head. Spun his ring. "Things they owed other companies. Things they owed my dispatcher," he said, biting off each syllable. "Why don't you ask him about my dispatcher?"

"I certainly will," Rose promised. "But right now, it's your deposition. It's your turn to tell your story."

LeGros stared down again, at the ring, at his hands.

"Tell me your dispatcher's name," she prodded gently.

"Lori Kimmel," LeGros muttered.

"And where does she live?"

He stared down sullenly. "Same place I do. Fifth and Tasker."

Rose felt her pulse spike. "She's your . . ."

"My lady friend," said LeGros, with a look on his face that said, *Want to make something of it?* "Ask him," he said, sticking a thumb toward Stanley Willet. "Ask him," he repeated. "He knows all about her."

LeGros's lawyer laid a hand on his forearm, but LeGros would not be stopped.

"Ask him about the overtime she worked! Ask him about how

she never got paid! Ask him about how when she left the company, he said he'd pay her vacation and sick days, and never did!"

"Could we take a break?" LeGros's attorney. Rose nodded. The court reporter raised her eyebrows. "Sure," said Rose. "Fifteen minutes." She ushered Willet into her office as LeGros and his attorney huddled in the hall.

"What's this about?"

Willet shrugged. "The name sounds familiar. I could make a few calls . . ."

Rose nodded toward her telephone. "Hit nine," she said. "I'll be back in a minute." She hurried to the bathroom. Depositions made her nervous, and being nervous made her have to pee, and . . .

"Ms. Feller?" It was LeGros's attorney. "Can I speak to you for a minute?" He pulled her into the conference room. "Look," he said. "We'd like to settle."

"What happened?"

The lawyer shook his head. "You can probably fill in the blanks. His girlfriend used to work for your guy. As best I can tell, she left without giving notice and figured she was entitled to all of her vacation and sick pay. Veeder told her to forget about it, and I think that my guy figured he could just bill Veeder for what she said she was owed."

"You didn't know that?"

The lawyer shrugged. "I just got this case two weeks ago."

"So he'll . . ." Rose let her voice trail off suggestively.

"Pay it back. All of it."

"Plus interest. This has gone on for three years," said Rose.

LeGros's lawyer winced. "One year's interest," he said. "We'll write you a check right now."

"Let me run it by my client," said Rose. "I'll recommend that he accept." Her heart was racing, her blood pounding in her veins. Victory! She felt like doing a dance. Instead she returned to Stan Willet, who was staring at her diplomas.

"They want to settle," she said.

"Good," he said, without turning toward her. Rose swallowed her disappointment. Of course he wasn't going to be as excited as she was. To him eight thousand dollars was pocket change. But still! She couldn't wait to tell Jim how well she'd done! She ran through the terms. "They're willing to write us a check today, which means you won't waste time chasing after the money. My recommendation is that we accept."

"Fine," he said, his eyes still on the glass frames and Latin writing of her diplomas. "Write it up, send it over." Finally, he turned toward her. "Good stuff in there." He cracked a thin smile. "Bury them in paper, right?"

"Right," Rose agreed, feeling her heart sink. She'd been brilliant! Well, maybe not brilliant in a flashy way, but competent. Extremely competent. Goddamnit, she'd hunted down every last little memo, every single bill, every solitary scrap of paper that proved her client's case! She walked Stan Willet to the elevator, hurried back to her office, and dialed Jim's extension.

"They settled," she said happily. "Eight thousand plus a year's interest."

"Nice job," he said, sounding pleased. Pleased, and distracted. She could hear the click of his mouse in the background. "Can you write me up a memo?"

Rose felt as though he'd dumped ice water on her head. "Sure," she said. "I'll have it done this afternoon."

Jim's voice softened. "Congratulations," he said. "I'm sure you were great."

"I buried them in paper," said Rose. She could hear Jim breathing, and the sound of other voices in the background.

"What was that?"

"Nothing." She set down the phone without saying good-bye. Instantly, a message popped up on her screen. From Jim. She clicked it open.

"Sorry I couldn't talk more," it read, then—her heart lifted as she read the words—"can I stop by tonight?"

She typed her response. "YES!" And then she sat back in her chair, beaming, feeling pleased, thinking that everything was finally right in her world. She was a professional success. It was Friday night, and she wouldn't be alone. She had a man who loved her. True, she also had her little sister camping out on her couch, but that wouldn't last forever, she thought, and started typing up the memo.

Euphoria lasted until four in the afternoon; happiness until six; and by the time nine o'clock rolled around and Jim still hadn't put in an appearance, Rose's mood was dipping toward miserable. She headed to the bathroom, where her ever-helpful little sister had left an article from *Allure* taped to the mirror. "This Season's Best Brows!" read the headline. And there were tweezers on the sink.

"Okay," Rose said to herself. "I can take a hint." At least this way, if—when—Jim came, he'd find her waiting with perfectly plucked brows. Rose peered at herself in the mirror and decided that her life would be easier if she'd just been born a different kind of girl. Not really different, but a better, prettier, more polished, slightly thinner version of the person she already was. The thing was, of course, she had no idea, really, of how to be anything other than what she was. And it wasn't for lack of trying.

When she was thirteen years old, Rose and Maggie Feller moved into Sydelle's house. "It just makes sense!" Sydelle said sweetly. "I've got plenty of room." The house was a four-bedroom modern monstrosity painted a flat, brilliant white, and looked out of place on a street full of Colonials, like a spaceship that had crash-landed in the cul-de-sac. Sydelle's house—and Rose never thought of it any other way—had huge windows and odd angles and strangely-shaped rooms (a dining room that was almost a rectangle, a bedroom that was not quite a square). The rooms were full of glass tables, glass-and-metal furniture with pointed edges, and mirrors everywhere, including a mirrored wall in the kitchen that showed every stray fingerprint, every deep breath—and every bite or nibble that everyone in the kitchen ever took. Plus, there were digital scales in every bathroom, including the downstairs powder room, and a variety of magnets with diet-related slogans on the refrigerator. The one Rose remembered best had a picture of a cow contentedly munching grass beneath the legend "Holy Cow! Are you eating again?" Every glittering, reflective surface, every magnet and every scale seemed to conspire with Sydelle to send the message that Rose was inadequate, unfeminine, not pretty enough, and way too big.

The week they'd moved in, Rose had asked her father for money.

"Is there something special you need?" he asked, staring at her with concern. Rose never asked him for money above the five dollars in allowance she got each week. Maggie was the one who regularly hit him up—she wanted Barbie dolls, a new lunch box, scented Magic Markers and glittery stickers, and a poster of Rick Springfield for her wall.

"School supplies," Rose said. He gave her a ten-dollar bill. She walked to the drugstore and purchased a small notebook with a purple cover. For the rest of the school year she'd used it to write down her careful notations of what women did. It was her secret project. Sydelle, she knew, would be happy to tell her what women did and did not do, say, wear, and, most important, eat, but Rose wanted to figure it out for herself. Looking back, she figured she must have had some dim idea that she was supposed to have magically absorbed the pertinent information at some point in her girlhood . . . and the fact that she hadn't, and that Sydelle felt she had room to issue proclamations on skin care and calorie counting, was an indictment of her dead mother. Which, of course, made Rose all the more determined to puzzle it out on her own.

"Nails curved, not straight!" she would write . . . or "no dumb jokes!" She convinced her father to buy her a yearlong subscription to *Seventeen* and *Young Miss* magazines, and she'd saved up her allowance to buy herself a copy of a paperback called *How to Be Popular!* that she'd seen advertised in the back of both magazines. She had studied those pages as carefully as any Talmudic scholar had ever pored over the sacred texts. She would watch her teachers, neighbors, her sister, even the hair-netted ladies in the cafeteria, and try to figure out how girls and women were supposed to be. It was like a math problem, she told herself, and once she solved it, once she'd figured out the equation of shoes plus clothes plus hairdo plus the right kind of personality (and, of course, once she'd figured out how to approximate the right kind of personality), she'd get people to like her. She'd be popular, like Maggie.

Of course it had been a disaster, she thought, wiping her breath off the mirror and leaning in close with the tweezers. All of her planning and note taking had been for nothing. Popularity was a code she couldn't crack. No matter how many pages she'd filled, no matter how often she'd imagined sitting with Missy Fox and Gail Wylie in the high-school cafeteria, her purse slung over the back of her chair, her Diet Coke and Baggies of carrots before her, it had never worked out right.

By high school, she'd given up on clothes and makeup, on hair and nails. She quit reading the advice columns and the stories in her magazines that dictated everything from how to talk to a guy to the precise angle of an eyebrow's arch. She abandoned the hope that she'd ever be pretty or popular, and kept what was left of her fashion focus on shoes. Shoes, she reasoned, could not be worn incorrectly. There were no variables with shoes, no collars to turn up or down, no cuffs to roll or leave unrolled, no piece of jewelry or hairdo that would make or break (in Rose's case, mostly break) the outfit. Shoes were shoes were shoes, and even if she wore them with the wrong things, she couldn't wear them the wrong way. Her feet would always look right. She'd look the popular-girl part, from the ankles down, even if from the ankles up she was still a loser.

It was only natural that she'd be thirty years old and clueless about almost anything style-related except for the relative merits of nubuck versus suede or the shape of this season's heels. Rose sighed and squinted at herself. Crooked. "Shit," she said, and raised the tweezers. The doorbell chimed.

"Coming!" Maggie sang.

"Oh, no," said Rose. She hurried out of the bathroom, shoving past her sister, who shoved her right back.

"Jesus, what is your problem!" Maggie demanded, rubbing her shoulder.

"Just move!" said Rose, groping for her wallet, extracting a wad of bills, and shoving them toward Maggie. "Go away! Go see a movie!"

"It's almost ten," Maggie pointed out.

"Find a late show!" said Rose, and flung open the door. And there was Jim, smelling faintly of cologne and more strongly of scotch, with a dozen red roses in his arms. "Hello, ladies," he said.

"Ooh, pretty!" said Maggie, taking the flowers. "Rose, put these in a vase," she said, handing them off to her sister. "May I take your coat?" she asked Jim.

Jesus! Rose gritted her teeth and walked to the kitchen. When she got to the living room, Maggie and Jim were sitting side by side on the couch. Maggie showed no signs of leaving . . . and, Rose noticed, the money she'd given her had magically disappeared. "So Jim!" Maggie said brightly, leaning toward him, her bountiful cleavage on display, "how have you been?"

"Maggie," said Rose, balancing herself on the arm of the couch, which was the only available seating, "don't you have plans?"

Her sister gave her an evil smile. "Not at all, Rose," she said. "I'm in for the night."

SEVEN

On Monday morning, Maggie Feller hopped off the bus, slung her backpack over her shoulder, and wove deftly through Port Authority. It was nine-thirty, and the auditions started at nine, and she would have been earlier, except she hadn't been able to decide between the caramel leather Nine West boots (with boot-cut jeans) or the Stuart Weitzman Mary Janes (with pencil skirt and fishnet stockings).

She turned the corner at Forty-second Street and her heart sank. There had to be a thousand people out in front of the MTV studio windows, jamming every inch of the sidewalk, crowding the little strip of grass in the center of Broadway.

Maggie stopped a girl in a cowboy hat. "Are you here for the auditions?"

The girl made a sour face. "I was. But they took the first three thousand people, and told the rest of us to go home."

Maggie's heart sank even further. This would not do. This would not do at all! She hurried through the crowd as fast as her high heels would carry her, finally locating a harried-looking woman with a walkie-talkie and a jacket with a yellow "MTV" logo on the back. *Confidence,* Maggie told herself, and tapped the woman on her shoulder.

"I'm here for the audition," she announced.

The woman shook her head. "Sorry, hon," she said, without looking up from her clipboard. "Doors are closed."

Maggie reached into her backpack, grabbed her purloined bottle of Midol, and rattled it in the woman's face. "I have a medical condition," she said.

The woman looked up and cocked her eyebrow. Maggie wrapped her fingers around the label, but not fast enough. "Midol?"

"I have debilitating cramps," Maggie announced. "And I'm sure that you're familiar with the Americans with Disabilities Act."

Now the woman was staring at her curiously.

"You can't discriminate against me just because of my troubled uterus," Maggie said.

"Are you serious?" the woman grumbled . . . but Maggie could see that she was more amused than irritated.

"Look, just give me a chance," she pleaded. "I came all the way from Philadelphia!"

"There are people here who came all the way from Idaho."

Maggie rolled her eyes. "Idaho! Do they even have cable there? Look," she continued, "I went through extensive preparations to be here."

The woman raised her eyebrows.

"Would it interest you to know," Maggie continued, "that I've had a very personal portion of my anatomy waxed into the MTV logo?"

For one dizzying instant, Maggie thought the woman was actually going to ask to see. Instead, she laughed, scribbled something on her clipboard, and beckoned to Maggie. "I'm Robin. Follow me," she said. Once she'd turned, Maggie jumped into the air, clicked her heels together, and gave a little shriek of glee. She'd made it! Well, she'd made it part of the way, she thought, hurrying after Robin. Now it was just a question of wowing the judges, and she'd be home free.

• • •

Inside, the corridors were even more jammed than the sidewalks had been. There were guys with cornrows and bandanas and jeans that drooped toward the floor rapping softly to themselves, gorgeous girls in miniskirts and low-cut tops preening into hand-held mirrors. Maggie quickly deduced that most of them were in their early twenties, and subtracted five years from her age on the form Robin gave her to fill out.

"Where are you from?" asked the girl in front of her, a tall, skinny girl who'd done herself up like Ginger Spice.

"Philadelphia," said Maggie, figuring that she had nothing to lose by being gracious. "I'm Maggie."

"I'm Kristy. Are you nervous?" asked the girl.

Maggie signed her form with a flourish. "Not really. I don't even know what they want us to do."

"Talk into the camera for thirty seconds," said Kristy, and sighed. "I wish they'd have us perform or something. I've taken dance classes since I was four. I can do tap and jazz, I can sing, I've got a monologue memorized . . ."

Maggie gulped. She'd taken dance classes, too—twelve years' worth—but no acting, and the only thing she'd memorized for the occasion was Rose's address, so MTV would know where to send flowers after she'd won. Kristy ran her fingers through her hair. "I don't know," she murmured, piling her hair on top of her head, then letting it tumble back down toward her shoulders. "Up or down?"

Maggie studied Kristy. "How about a French twist? Here," she said, digging in her backpack for her hairbrush, hairspray, bobby pins, and elastics. The line inched forward. By the time Maggie made it to the front, three hours had flown by, and she'd done Kristy's hair and redone her makeup, smoothed glittery gold eyeshadow onto an eighteen-year-old named Kara, and lent Latisha, who'd been behind her in the line, Rose's Nine West boots.

"Next!" called the bored-looking guy behind the camera.

She took a deep breath, feeling no nerves at all, feeling nothing but a supreme confidence, a blazing joy as she stepped into the tiny blue-carpeted cubicle beneath the circle of burning-hot light. Behind the cameraman, Robin grinned and gave her a thumbs-up.

"Tell us your name, please," she said.

Maggie smiled. "I'm Maggie May Feller," she said, her voice low and clear. God, she could see herself on the monitor hanging overhead! She sneaked a quick peek, and there she was! On TV! Looking terrific!

"Maggie May?" asked Robin.

"My mother named me after the song," said Maggie. "I think she always knew that I was destined for musical greatness."

Robin scanned Maggie's form. "It says here you used to be a waitress."

"That's right," said Maggie, licking her lips. "And I think that's given me the perfect experience to work with rock stars."

"What do you mean?" Robin asked.

"Well, once you've handled frat boys having waffle fights, you can handle anything," Maggie said. "And when you're a waitress, you see all kinds of people. You've got your girls on diets who have all kinds of weird allergies." She raised her voice to a snotty soprano. " 'Are there peanuts in this?' Which is fine, except they ask it about everything. Including iced tea. You've got picky vegetarians, vegans, the Zone dieters, diabetics, macrobiotics, macrobiotic Zone diabetics with high blood pressure who can't have salt . . ." And now she was off and running, ignoring the lights, ignoring the competition, ignoring even Robin and the guy in the baseball cap. It was just her and the camera, the way it was always meant to be. "And if you've ever had to dump iced coffee in some guy's lap because he was trying to leave his tip in your cleavage, well, you're not going to be afraid of Kid Rock."

"What kind of music do you like?" asked Robin.

"All kinds," said Maggie. She licked her lips and tossed her hair. "Madonna's my idol. Except for the whole yoga thing. I just can't get into that. Of course, I'm a singer, too, in a band called Whiskered Biscuit . . ."

The guy behind the camera started laughing.

"Perhaps you're familiar with our soon-to-be hit single, 'Lick Me Where I'm Pink'?" Maggie asked.

"Could you sing us a little bit?" asked the cameraman.

Maggie beamed. This, finally, was what she'd been waiting for. She pulled her hairbrush out of her backpack and used it as a microphone, tossing her hair and wailing, "Lick me where I'm pink! Pour yourself a drink! Don't wanna hear your problems, what am I, your fucking shrink?" She wondered, fleetingly, whether it was okay to say "fuck" on MTV, and then figured that the damage was done.

"Anything else we should know about you, Maggie?" Robin asked.

"Only that I'm ready for prime time," Maggie said. "And if Carson Daly's ever single again, you've got my number." She blew the camera a kiss, then stuck out her tongue, mockingly, flashing her piercing at the camera.

"Way to go!" Kristy whispered. And Latisha was applauding, and Kara gave her a thumbs-up, and Robin hurried out of the booth into the line, tapped Maggie on her shoulder, grinned, and pulled her down a corridor to where a group of a dozen other people were waiting. "Congratulations," she whispered. "You've made the callbacks."

"You're where?" Rose demanded.

"I'm in New York!" Maggie yelled into her cell phone. "MTV's having auditions for VJs, and guess who got a callback!"

There was silence on the other end of the line. "You told me you had a job interview," Rose finally said.

Maggie's face flushed. "What do you think this is?"

"A wild-goose chase," Rose said.

"God, can't you even be happy for me?" The girl next to her, a six-foot-tall amazon in a leather catsuit, scowled at her. Maggie scowled back and moved to a corner of the waiting room.

"I'd be happy if you got a job."

"I'm going to get a job!"

"Oh, you know for sure that MTV's going to hire you? And what are they paying?"

"A lot," said Maggie sullenly. In truth, she wasn't sure what the job paid . . . but it had to be a lot. It was on television, right? "More than what you're making. You know what I think? I think you're jealous."

Rose sighed. "I'm not jealous. I just want you to give up this whole crazy fame thing and get a job, instead of wasting your money going to New York."

"And be just like you," Maggie said. "No thanks." She slipped the phone into her purse, and stared furiously at the ground. Fucking Rose! Why had she thought that her sister would be happy for her, or impressed with hearing how she'd talked her way into the auditions and wowed everyone? Well, she thought, reaching into her purse for her lipstick, she'd just show Big Sistershit. She'd ace the audition, she'd get the job, and the next time Rose saw her she'd be on TV, larger than life and twice as lovely.

"Maggie Feller?"

Maggie took a deep breath, gave her mouth a final touch of lipstick, and headed back to capture her dream. This time, they led her to a larger room where three blinding-bright lights perched high on stainless-steel scaffolds shone down on her. Robin smiled at Maggie from over her clipboard and pointed toward a television set.

"Have you ever read off a TelePrompTer?" Robin asked.

Maggie shook her head.

"Well, it's easy," she said, demonstrating. She walked over a masking-tape X on the floor and faced the screen. "Coming up next!" she read, her voice loud and enthusiastic. "We've got the hot new debut from the Spice Girls! And don't touch that remote, 'cause you'll see Britney Spears within the hour!"

Maggie stood, staring at the television set. The words rolled down the screen, then reversed themselves and zipped back up so fast that Maggie felt instantly queasy. She could read. She could read just fine. Just not as fast as other people. And not while the words were moving around like this!

She realized that Robin was staring at her. "Okay?"

"Oh, sure!" said Maggie. She walked to the taped X on shaking legs. "Coming up next," she whispered to herself. She shook her hair, licked her lips. The lights shone down on her, as merciless as fire. She felt sweat form at her hairline. "Whenever you're ready," called the cameraman.

"Coming up next," Maggie began with a confidence she didn't feel. The words started to roll down the screen. "We've got . . ." She stared at the screen. The words wiggled some more. "The debutt video from the Spice Girls! And . . ." Oh, shit. "Debut," she whispered. "Debut!" she said, out loud, and wondered for perhaps the millionth time in her life why words weren't spelled the way they were pronounced. The cameraman was laughing, only not in a nice way. She peered at the screen, praying with all of her heart, *please just let me be able to read this okay. A B.* Something with a *B* and a *Y.* What? "Boyz II Men?" she guessed. "Yes, Motown Philly's back again! And . . ."

The cameraman was staring at her curiously. So was Robin. "Are you okay?" she asked. "Can you see the screen all right? Do you want to try again?"

"Coming up next!" Maggie said, much too loudly. *Please, God,* she thought, as hard as she could. *I'll never ask you for anything else again, only just let me be able to do this.* She stared at the screen, trying as hard as she could, as the *b*'s flipped into *d*'s and the *w*'s turned upside down. "We've got a lot of great music, right after this next commercial here . . ." And now the words had dissolved into incomprehensible hieroglyphics, and Robin and the cameraman were both staring at her with expressions she could read just fine. Pity.

"Coming up next, we've got the same crap we played for you yesterday," Maggie snarled as she turned on her heel—make that

Rose's heel—and blundered toward the door, swiping at her eyes. She ran through the waiting room, almost knocking over Ms. Catsuit, and had shoved her way into the hall, but not before she heard Robin's voice for the last time, saying, "Next!" and, "Let's hurry up, people; we've got a lot of you left to get through."

EIGHT

Lewis Feldman stood on the landing, a bouquet of tulips in one hand, a box of chocolates in the other, and a sense of trepidation as heavy as a winter coat hanging on his shoulders. Did this ever get any easier? he wondered, taking a deep breath and staring up at Ella Hirsch's door.

"The worst thing she can say is no," he reminded himself. He shifted the tulips to his left hand and the chocolates to his right, and stared down at his pants, which, in spite of his best efforts in the laundry room, were wrinkled and had a suspicious stain below one of the pockets, as if a pen had exploded—which, Lewis thought glumly, was probably exactly what had happened.

A no wouldn't kill him, he reminded himself. If the small heart attack he'd had three years ago hadn't killed him, certainly Ella Hirsch's rejection wouldn't, either. And there were other fish in the sea, fish who'd flopped right out of the water and into his boat before he'd even thought to bait a hook. But he hadn't been interested in Lois Ziff, who'd dropped by two weeks after Sharla's funeral with a kugel and her blouse undone an extra button's worth, exposing a bonus three inches of wrinkled cleavage. He hadn't been interested in Bonnie Begelman, who'd slipped an envelope through his door last month with two movie tickets and a note saying she'd be happy to join him "when you're ready." In the days after Sharla's death, in the weeks when he endured daily visits from what he'd come to think of as the Casserole Brigade, dozens of women with concerned faces and Tupperware, he hadn't thought he'd ever be ready, even though she'd given him her blessing.

"Find someone," she'd told him. She was in the hospital for the last time, and they both knew it, even though that truth remained unspoken between them. He was holding her hand, the one without the IV needles in it, and he'd leaned forward to brush her thin hair off her forehead.

"Sharla, let's not talk about this," he'd said. She'd shaken her head and stared at him, her blue eyes lit with a familiar spark—a spark he hadn't seen much of since the day he'd come home to find her sitting quietly on the couch. He'd looked at her and known, even before she raised her head, even before he'd she'd told him, *It's back. The cancer came back.*

"I don't want you to be alone," she said. "I don't want you turning into one of those unpleasant widowers. You'll eat too much sodium."

"Is that all you're worried about?" he teased her. "My sodium?"

"Those men get nasty," she said. Her eyes were slipping shut. He held her straw to her lips so she could sip. "Self-righteous and crotchety. I don't want it happening to you." Her voice was fading. "I want you to find someone."

"Do you have anyone in mind?" he asked. "Anyone special you've noticed?"

She didn't answer. He thought she was asleep—eyelids slipped shut, thin chest rising and falling slowly beneath the fresh bandages—but she said something else to him. "I want you to be happy," she said, each word coming in a separate puff of breath. He'd bowed his head, afraid that if he looked at her, his wife, the woman he'd loved and lived with for fifty-three years, he'd start crying and wouldn't be able to stop. So he sat by her bed and held her hand and whispered into her ear how much he loved her. He thought, when she'd died, that he'd never even want to look at another woman again, and the neighbor ladies, with their kugels and their cleavage, didn't appeal. Nobody had until now.

It wasn't that Ella reminded him of Sharla—at least, not physically. Sharla had been small, and with age she'd only gotten smaller. She'd had round blue eyes and bobbed blond hair, a too-big nose and a too-big bottom that she'd despaired of, and she'd loved coral lipstick and costume jewelry: necklaces of painted glass beads, dangly earrings that flashed and glittered when she moved. She'd reminded him of some tiny, exotic bird with iridescent plumage and a high, sweet song. Ella was different. She was taller, with fine features—a sharp nose, a firm jawline—and the long auburn locks she kept twined around her head, even though all of the other ladies at Golden Acres had short hair. Ella reminded him a little bit of Katharine Hepburn—a Jewish Katharine Hepburn, not quite so regal, or terrifying, a Hepburn steeped in some secret melancholy.

"Hepburn," he muttered. He shook his head at his own foolishness and started up the steps. He wished his shirt weren't wrinkled. He wished he had a hat.

"Well, hello!"

Lewis was so startled he actually jumped a little bit, and stared at a woman whose face he didn't recognize.

"Mavis Gold," the woman supplied. "And where are you off to, all dressed up?"

"Oh . . . just . . ."

Mavis Gold clapped her hands, causing her tanned upper arms to jiggle in a celebratory fashion. "Ella!" she whispered—a whisper so loud that cars on the Causeway probably heard it, Lewis thought. She ran one fingertip appreciatively over the top of a tulip. "They're beautiful. You're such a gentleman." Mavis beamed at him, kissed his cheek, and thumbed away the lipstick she'd left. "Good luck!"

He nodded, took a deep breath, repositioned his gifts for the last time, and turned the doorbell's crank. He listened for a radio, a television set, and heard nothing but Ella's feet padding quickly across the floor.

She opened the door and looked at him with a puzzled expression. "Lewis?"

He nodded, suddenly tongue-tied. She was wearing blue jeans, the kind that came only as far as the middle of her calves, and a loose white shirt and no shoes. Her feet were bare, long, and pale, beautifully shaped, with a polish the color of mother-of-pearl on the nails. Her feet made him want to kiss her. Instead, he swallowed hard.

"Hello," he said. There. That was a start.

A furrow appeared between Ella's eyebrows. "Was the poem too long?"

"No, no, the poem was fine. I'm here because . . . well, I was wondering if . . ." *Come on, old man!* he told himself. He'd been in a war; he'd buried a wife; he'd watched his son become a Republican with a Rush Limbaugh bumper sticker on the back of his minivan. He'd survived worse things than this. "Would you like to have dinner with me?"

He could see her getting ready to shake her head even before it happened. "I . . . I don't think so."

"Why not?" It came out louder than he'd intended.

Ella sighed. Lewis took advantage of her momentary silence. "Okay if I come in?" he asked.

She looked reluctant as she opened the door and ushered him inside. Her apartment wasn't cluttered, as so many of the smallish rooms at Golden Acres tended to become, when tenants tried to cram a lifetime's worth of possessions into space that was never meant to hold very much. Ella's apartment had tiled floors, cream-colored walls, the kind of white sofa that, in Lewis's experience, was much better in theory than in practice, especially if you had grandchildren, and the grandchildren liked grape juice.

He sat at one end of the couch. Ella sat at the other, looking flustered as she tucked her bare feet underneath her.

"Lewis," she began.

He got to his feet.

"Please don't leave. Let me explain," she said.

"I'm not leaving, I'm finding a vase," he told her.

"Wait," she said, sounding alarmed at the thought of him going through her things. "I'll do it." She hurried into the kitchen and produced a vase from a cabinet. Lewis filled it with water, put the tulips inside, came back to the living room, and set it in the center of her coffee table.

"There," he said. "Now, if you're going to say no, you'll have to look at those tulips every day and feel guilty," he said.

She looked, for an instant, as if she might be getting ready to smile . . . then the look was gone, as if he'd imagined it.

"The thing of it is," she started.

"Hold on," he said. He opened the box of candy. "You go first," he said.

She waved the box away. "Really, I can't . . ."

He put on his glasses and unfolded the candy map. "The dark chocolate hearts have cherry cordial inside," he reported. "And those roundish ones are nougat."

"Lewis," she said firmly. "You're a wonderful person, and . . ."

"But," he said. "I hear a *but* coming." He got up again, went to her kitchen, put water on to boil. "Where's your good china?" he called.

"Oh," she said, hurrying after him.

"Don't worry," he said. "I'm just making us a cup of tea."

Ella looked at him, then at the kettle. "Okay," she said, and pulled two mugs advertising the Broward County Public Library from a shelf. Lewis dropped tea bags into the mugs, located her sugar bowl (filled with packets of Sweet 'n Low), and set it on the table, alongside a pint of lactose-free milk.

"Are you always this handy?" she asked.

"I wasn't always," he said. He opened the refrigerator, found a lemon in back of her vegetable crisper, and sliced it as he talked.

"Then my wife got sick, and she knew . . . well. She knew. So she gave me lessons."

"Do you miss her?" Ella asked.

"Every day," he said. "I miss her every day." He set her cup on a saucer and carried it over to the table. "How about you?"

"Well, I never met your wife, so I can't say that I miss her . . ."

"A joke!" He applauded, and sat down beside her and studied the table. "I think it still needs something," he said. He opened Ella's freezer. "May I?"

She nodded, looking slightly dazed. He dug around until he found a familiar-shaped object that he instantly recognized as frozen Sara Lee pound cake. It had been a favorite of Sharla's. More than once he'd woken up in the middle of the night to find her in front of the television set, watching infomercials and munching on a hunk of thawed pound cake. Usually those nights signaled the conclusion of one of her twice-yearly grapefruit-and-tuna-fish diets, and she'd come back to bed with a guilty smile and a mouth that tasted like butter. *Kiss me,* she'd whisper, sliding her nightgown over her shoulders. *Let's burn off some of those bad old calories.*

He handed the cake to Ella. "Okay?"

She nodded, and put the cake into the microwave. Lewis sipped his tea and watched her move. Her hips looked original, he thought, and laughed at himself for noticing something like that. Adam, one of his grandsons, had told him during his last visit that he could tell just by looking whether a woman's chest was real or not, and Lewis had decided that he had the same talent for hip joints.

"What are you smiling about?"

He gave a small shrug. "My grandson."

Her face crumpled like a paper bag. She quickly smoothed it back again, so fast he wasn't sure he'd seen what he'd seen, which was despair. He wanted to reach over and hold her hands, hold her hands and ask her to tell him what was wrong, what hurt enough to make her look that way. He actually started to move his hands across the table when he noticed she was staring down as if a roach had just crawled out of the pound cake.

"What?"

She pointed at the cuffs of his shirt. Lewis looked down. One cuff was missing a button, and the other one was badly frayed and slightly browned.

"Did you burn that?" Ella asked.

"I guess I must have," Lewis said. "I'm not so great with the iron."

"Oh," said Ella. "I could . . ." She closed her mouth abruptly and smoothed her hair, looking flustered. Lewis saw his chance, an inflatable raft bobbing in the waves, and grabbed for it with all his might.

"Give me some lessons?" he asked humbly. *Forgive me, Sharla,* he thought, imagining he'd have to hide all the notes she'd left him, the boxes and bottles carefully labeled "for colors" and "for whites."

Ella was wavering. "Well," she said. The microwave chirped. Lewis fetched the cake. He served Ella a slice, then cut one for himself.

"I know it's an imposition," he said, "and I know how busy you are. But since my wife died, I'm kind of at loose ends. Last week I actually tried to figure out whether it would be easier to just buy new clothes every month or so . . ."

"Oh, don't do that!" said Ella. "I'll help you." He could tell that her assent had come at a cost, that there was a battle going on behind her eyes, her sense of obligation and sympathy warring with her fierce desire to be alone. "Just let me get my book."

Her book turned out to be a four-inch-thick marvel of scheduling, a half-illegible maze of scribbles and arrows and phone numbers and Post-it notes. "Let's see," said Ella, scrutinizing each page. "Wednesday I'm at the hospital . . ."

"What's wrong?"

"I rock babies," Ella said. "Thursday's the soup kitchen, then the hospice, Friday is Meals on Wheels . . ."

"Saturday?" Lewis asked. "Not to frighten you, but I'm almost out of underwear."

Ella made a noise in the back of her throat that sounded almost like laughter. "Saturday," she agreed.

"Good," he told her. "Five o'clock? I'll take you to dinner once we're done."

He was out the door before she could think to say anything to him, and as he whistled his way down the hall, he was unsurprised to see Mavis Gold, who claimed that she was on her way to the laundry room, in spite of the visible absence of her laundry.

"How'd it go?" she whispered. He gave her a thumbs-up and smiled as she clapped her hands. Then he hurried home to spill ink on his pants and pull a few buttons off his favorite shirt.

NINE

"Okay," Rose called from her seat in front of her computer. "Name, got that. Address, you can use mine." Her fingers flew over the keyboard. "Objective?"

"To get a job," said Maggie, who was sprawled on the couch with her face buried under half an inch of what she'd informed her sister was a pore-reducing clay mask.

"How about if we say 'a position in retail'?" asked Rose.

"Whatever," said Maggie, flicking on the TV. It was Saturday morning, five days after her ignominious audition, and MTV was introducing the winner of the VJ contest—a pretty, bubbly brunette with a pierced eyebrow. "Coming up next, we'll have the debut of the Spice Girls's latest video!" the girl burbled. Maggie flipped quickly away.

"Listen," said Rose. "I'm trying to help you. Could you please pay attention?"

Maggie made a huffing noise and clicked the TV off.

"Employment history," Rose prompted.

"Huh?"

"You know, your other jobs. Maggie, haven't you ever done a résumé before?"

"Oh, sure," said Maggie. "All the time. You know, just like you go to the gym."

"Other jobs," Rose repeated.

Maggie stared longingly at the cigarettes in her purse, but she knew that lighting up would result in either Rose's lung-cancer lecture or her my-house-my-rules rap. "Okay," she said, and closed her eyes. "T.J.Maxx," she began. "For six weeks. October through right before Thanksgiving." She sighed. She'd actually liked that job. She'd been good at it, too. When she worked the dressing room, she wouldn't just give her customers the plastic tag and point them toward the dressing room. She'd take the clothes, lead them in, open a cubicle, and hang each garment neatly, the way they did it at the fancy department stores and boutiques downtown. And when the women came out to spin and squint in front of the three-way mirror, tightening a belt or untucking a shirt, Maggie would be there, offering suggestions, telling them honestly (but carefully) when an outfit didn't flatter, hurrying back to the racks to find another size or another color, or something else entirely, something totally different, something they'd never even imagined themselves wearing, but something that Maggie could see. "You're a jewel!" she could remember one of her ladies saying, a tall, sleek, black-haired woman who would have looked great in anything, but looked especially great in the outfit Maggie'd put together—a little black dress with the perfect black leather bag and black slingback pumps, plus a belt of gold links that she'd rescued from the clearance bin. "I'm going to tell the manager how much help you've been!"

"What happened?" asked Rose.

Maggie kept her eyes shut. "I quit," she mumbled. In fact, what had happened was what usually happened with her jobs—things would be going fine until she ran up against something. There was always something. In this case, it was the cash register. She'd scanned a coupon for ten percent off, and it hadn't gone through. "Well, can't you just do it manually?" the customer had demanded.

Maggie had scowled at her, and stared at the total. One hundred and forty-two dollars. So ten percent was . . . She bit her lip. "Fourteen dollars!" said the woman. "Come on!" At which point Maggie had straightened up slowly, paged the manager, and turned to the next customer in line with a sweet smile.

"Can I help you?"

"Hey!" the ten-percent woman had said. "You didn't finish me!"

Maggie ignored her as the next customer in line piled her sweaters and jeans onto the belt and Maggie flicked open a plastic bag. She knew what was going to happen. The woman was going to call her stupid. And there was no way Maggie was going to stand for that. She didn't even want to be here. Her talents were wasted on the cash register, her time was better spent in the dressing room, where she could actually help people instead of just work the scanner like a robot.

The supervisor came hurrying over, register keys jingling against her chest. "What's the problem?"

The ten-percent woman pointed a finger at Maggie. "She couldn't ring up my coupon."

"Maggie, what's the problem?"

"It wouldn't go through," Maggie had muttered.

"Well, ten percent," said the supervisor. "Fourteen dollars!"

"Sorry," Maggie muttered, staring at the floor, as the customer had rolled her eyes. At the end of her shift, when the supervisor had started to say something about how there was a calculator available or how she could always ask for help, Maggie had taken off her polyester pinny, dropped her name tag onto the floor, and walked out the door.

"Okay," said Rose. "But if they ask, tell them you didn't find it challenging enough."

"Fine," said Maggie, and stared at the ceiling as if the high-lights of her employment history were inscribed there, a retail-and-fast-food version of the Sistine Chapel. "Before T.J.Maxx, I was at the Gap, and before that I was at Pomodoro Pizza, and before that

was the Starbucks on Walnut Street, and then I was at the
Limited—no, wait, that's wrong. I was at Urban Outfitters first,
and the Limited before that, and . . ."

Rose was typing madly.

"Banana Republic," Maggie continued. "Macy's accessories,
Macy's fragrance, Cinnabon, Chik-fil-A, Baskin-Robbins . . ."

"What about that restaurant? The Canal House?"

Maggie winced. She'd been doing fine at the Canal House until
Conrad, the Sunday manager, had gotten all over her case.
MargarET, the salt shakers aren't full. MargarET, I need you to give
the busboy a hand. She'd told him over and over that her name
wasn't even Margaret—just Maggie—but he'd ignored her for an
entire month until she'd conceived of her revenge. Late one night in
May, she and her then-sort-of-boyfriend had scaled the roof and
wrenched the *C* free from the restaurant's sign. Which meant that
dozens of women in corsages had shown up for Mother's Day
brunch at the Anal House.

"I quit," said Maggie. *Before they could fire me,* she thought.

"Fine," said Rose, staring at the screen. "We're going to have to
edit."

"Whatever," said Maggie, and stomped into the bathroom,
where she washed the clay off her face. So her work history wasn't
the greatest, she thought furiously. It didn't mean she wasn't a hard
worker! It didn't mean she didn't try!

Her sister banged on the door. "Maggie, are you almost done in
there? I need to take a shower."

Maggie wiped off her face and went back to the living room,
flicked the television set back on, before sitting down in front of
the computer. While Rose took a shower, Maggie stored her
résumé, opened a new window, and started typing a list for Rose.
Exercise regularly (aerobics and weights), she typed. *Get regular
facials. Join Jenny Craig (they are running a special!)* She typed,
grinning, and then added a helpful link to an article about Carnie
Wilson's weight-loss surgery. She shoved a cigarette between her

lips and tripped out the door, leaving the printed-out list on Rose's seat and the article ("Star Sheds Half Her Body Weight!") on Rose's screen, so that it would be the first thing her sister saw when she came home from work.

"Lock the door behind you!" Rose called from her bedroom. Maggie ignored her. If she was so smart, let her lock her own door, she thought, and headed out into the hall.

"A lawyer?" The guy with the beard squinted at Rose. "Hey, what do you call six lawyers at the bottom of the ocean?"

Rose gave a small shrug and looked longingly toward Amy's front door, hoping that Jim would soon come through it.

"A good start!" the bearded guy bellowed.

Rose blinked at him. "I don't get it," she said.

He stared, unsure if she was kidding.

"I don't understand. I mean, why are the lawyers at the bottom of the ocean? Are they snorkeling or something?"

Now the guy was looking decidedly uncomfortable. Rose furrowed her forehead. "Wait . . . are they at the bottom of the ocean because they drowned?"

"Well, yeah," said the guy, using one fingernail to pry the label off his beer.

"Okay," said Rose slowly. "So there's six dead, drowned lawyers at the bottom of the ocean . . ." She paused and looked at the guy expectantly.

"It was just a joke," he said.

"But I don't understand why it's funny," she said.

The guy took two steps backward.

"Wait," said Rose. "Wait! You have to finish explaining this to me!"

"I'll be . . . um," said the guy. He sidled off toward the bar. Amy shot her a dirty look across the room and shook her head. *Bad girl,* Amy mouthed, wagging her index finger. Rose shrugged. She wasn't normally so mean, but Jim's tardiness—combined with Maggie's three-weeks-and-counting residence—had put her in a foul mood.

Rose stared at her best friend, thinking that at least one of them had changed since the misery of junior high. By ninth grade, Amy had grown to six feet tall, weighing in at perhaps a hundred and ten pounds, and the boys in the class called her Ichabod Crane—just Ick for short. But she'd gotten comfortable with her gangly frame. Now she wore her knobby wrists like expensive bracelets and wielded the fine bones of her face and hips like unusual pieces of art. She'd had dreadlocks in college, but after graduation she hacked her hair off and dyed it a dark red. She wore tight black tops and long black boot-cut jeans, and she looked fabulous. Exotic, and mysterious, and sexy, even when she opened her mouth and her thick, unreconstructed Jersey-girl accent came out. Amy always had at least half a dozen boyfriends, former boyfriends, and would-be boyfriends lining up for the privilege of buying her deep-dish pizza and listening to her dissect the state of hip-hop music in America.

Plus, Amy was a chemical engineer—an occupation that typically garnered at least a few interested questions from strangers she'd meet at parties—while Rose was a lawyer, which usually drew one of two responses: the first, typified by Mr. Lawyer Joke, and the second, Rose was pretty sure, soon to be elucidated by the tall, pale fellow in glasses who'd parked himself on the couch beside her, interrupting her special private time with the bowl of cheese curls.

"Amy tells me you're a lawyer," he began. "You know, I'm having a bit of a legal problem myself."

Of course you are, Rose thought, her smile spackled to her face. She glanced at the clock. Almost eleven. Where was Jim?

"There's this tree," the guy said. "It's growing on my property, see? But the leaves fall mostly into my neighbor's yard . . ."

Yeah, yeah, yeah, Rose thought. And you're both too lazy to rake the goddamn leaves. Or he chopped the tree down without your permission. And instead of just talking about the tree like normal people, or, God forbid, actually hiring a lawyer of your own, you want to unload on me.

"Excuse me," Rose murmured, cutting the guy off midway

through his saga, made her escape, and twisting through the crowd until she found Amy in the kitchen, leaning against the refrigerator, twirling a glass of wine in her fingers, head tilted back, laughing at whatever the guy in front of her was saying.

"Hey, Dan," Amy drawled. "This is my friend Rose."

Dan was tall, dark, and gorgeous. "Pleased to meet you," he said. Rose gave him a weak smile, clutching her purse—and within it, her cell phone—tightly to her side. She needed to talk to Jim. He was the only person that could soothe her and make her smile and convince her that life wasn't pointless and that the world wasn't full of joke-spouting idiots and litigious tree owners. Where was he?

She eased herself away from Dan and reached into her purse, but Amy was right behind her.

"Forget it," she said sternly. "Don't chase. It's not ladylike. Remember? Men like to be the hunters, not the prey." Amy took the cell phone from Rose's hand and replaced it with a slotted spoon. "Dumplings," she said, pointing Rose toward the stove, and a pot of steaming water.

"What have you got against Jim, anyhow?" Rose asked.

Amy gazed at the ceiling, then leveled her eyes at Rose. "It's not him, it's you. I'm worried about you."

"Why?"

"I'm worried that you're more into it than he is. I don't want you to get hurt."

Rose opened her mouth, then shut it fast. How could she convince Amy that Jim was just as into it as she was when he wasn't even here? And there was something else, something catching at the corner of her mind, something about the night he'd showed up late, with his arms full of flowers, and how he'd smelled of scotch, and rose blossoms, and, faintly, of something else. Perfume? she'd thought, and then stopped the thought in its tracks and built a wall around it, a wall composed largely of the word *no*.

"And isn't he your boss?"

"Not exactly," Rose said. Jim wasn't her boss any more than any

other partner was her boss. Which was to say, he was at least somewhat
her boss. Rose swallowed hard, shoved that thought to its accustomed
hiding place in the back of her head, and steamed a batch of shrimp
dumplings. When Amy's back was turned, she grabbed her purse
again, hurried down a hallway lined with African masks, ducked into
Amy's downstairs bathroom, and dialed Jim's work number. No
answer. She dialed her own number. Maybe he'd misunderstood her
and stopped by her house instead of heading straight to Amy's.

"Hello?"

Drat. Maggie. "Hi," said Rose. "It's me. Did Jim call?"

"Nuh-uh," said Maggie.

"Well, if he calls tell him . . . tell him I'll see him later."

"I probably won't be here. I'm on my way out," said Maggie.

"Oh," Rose said. There were a dozen things she wanted to ask:
Going where? With what friends? With what money? She bit down
hard. Asking Maggie would only infuriate her, and sending an
angry Maggie out on the town was a little like handing a loaded
gun to a two-year-old.

"Lock the door behind you," she said.

"I will."

"And please take off my shoes," Rose said.

There was a pause. "I'm not wearing your shoes," said Maggie.

Sure, because you just took them off, thought Rose. "Have fun," she
said instead. Maggie promised that she would. Rose splashed cool
water on her cheeks and wrists and stared at herself in the mirror.
She'd smeared her mascara. Her lipstick had evaporated. And she
was stuck at a party, steaming dumplings, alone. Where was he?

Rose opened the door and tried to edge past Amy, who was
standing in the doorway with her long arms crossed on her bony
chest. "Did you call him?" she demanded.

"Call who?" asked Rose.

Amy laughed. "You are just as crummy a liar as you were when
you had a crush on Hal Lindquist." She took a cocktail napkin and
wiped mascara from underneath Rose's eyes.

"I did not have a crush on Hal Lindquist!"

"Oh, sure. You just wrote down exactly what he was wearing every day in your math binder because you wanted future generations to have a record of what Hal Lindquist wore in 1984."

Rose smiled at herself. "So which one of these guys is your date?"

Amy made a face. "Don't ask. It was supposed to be Trevor."

Rose struggled to remember what Amy had told her about Trevor. "Is he here?"

"Indeed he is not," said Amy. "Check this out—we're at dinner."

"Where?" Rose asked dutifully.

"Tangerine. Very nice. And we're sitting there, and the lights are low, and the candles are flickering, and I haven't spilled any couscous on myself, and he tells me why he broke up with his last girlfriend. Evidently he'd developed certain interests."

"What interests?"

"Shit," said Amy, with an absolutely straight face.

"What?"

"You heard me. Consenting acts of defecation."

"You're kidding," Rose gasped.

"I shit you not," Amy deadpanned. "And so I'm sitting there, absolutely horrified. Needless to say, I couldn't eat another bite, plus I had to spend the rest of the meal making sure I didn't fart, because he'd think I was flirting . . ."

Rose started laughing.

"Come along," said Amy, pocketing the napkin and thrusting a beer into Rose's hand. "Join the party."

Rose went back to the kitchen, heated up artichoke dip, replenished the cracker basket, made conversation with another one of Amy's wannabes, although at the end of it she couldn't remember a word of what either one of them had said. She longed for Jim—who, based on the available evidence, was not longing for her.

TEN

Jim Danvers opened his eyes and thought the same thing that he thought every morning: today I will be good. *Lead me not into temptation,* he recited, dragging his razor over his jaw, staring at himself sternly in his bathroom mirror. *Get thee behind me, Satan,* he said, pulling on his pants.

The trouble was, Satan was everywhere. Temptation lurked around every corner. Here it was, leaning against a building, waiting for the bus. Jim slowed his Lexus and grabbed an eyeful of the blond in tight jeans, wondering what her body looked like beneath her bulky winter coat, wondering how she'd move in bed, how she'd smell, how she'd sound, and what it would take to find out.

Stop, he ordered himself, just stop, and punched the radio into life. Howard Stern filled the front seat, his tone leering, wise, and knowing. "Are those real, honey?" he inquired of the morning's starlet. "Real silicone," she giggled. Jim swallowed hard and switched to the classical station. It was so unfair. Ever since a wet dream on the third night of a Boy Scout camping trip at age twelve had heralded the advent of puberty, he'd dreamed of women with a concentrated fierceness, the abstract longing of a starving man stuck on an island with back issues of *Bon Appetit*. Blondes, brunettes, and redheads, small-breasted willowy girls and short bouncy curvy ones, black, Hispanic, Asian, white, young, old, and in between, and even, God help him, a cute girl in leg braces he'd glimpsed on the Jerry Lewis telethon—in his fantasy world, Jim Danvers was an equal opportunity employer.

And he'd never been able to have them. Not at age twelve, when he was short and pudgy and frequently out of breath. Not at fourteen, when he was still short and no longer pudgy but fat, and his face was riddled with what Dr. Guberman swore was the worst case of cystic acne he'd ever seen. At sixteen he shot up six inches, but the damage was done, and the nickname Fudgie the Whale unfortunately followed him to college. What followed was the classic vicious circle—he was miserable because of his weight. He ate to stanch his misery, feeding his pain with pizza and beer, which only made him bigger, which only pushed the women further away. He'd lost his virginity senior year to a prostitute who'd looked him up and down, cracking her gum in a meditative fashion before insisting that she be on top. "Not to criticize, hon," she'd said, "but I think what we've got here is a liability issue."

Law school could have been different, he thought to the soothing strains of Bach. He'd gotten even taller, and after the embarrassing ten minutes with the prostitute he'd taken up jogging, tracing Rocky's route through the Philadelphia streets (although he was pretty sure that even initially Rocky could make it farther than three blocks without having to stop and catch his breath). The weight came off. His skin cleared up, leaving behind only a fading webwork of interesting scars, and he'd gotten his teeth fixed. What remained was a crippling shyness, a paralytic lack of self-esteem. All through his twenties, through his years rising steadily through the ranks at Lewis, Dommel, and Fenick, whenever he'd heard women laughing he'd assumed they were laughing at, or about, him.

And then, somehow, everything had changed. He remembered the night he'd made partner, how he'd joined three of his recently elevated colleagues at an Irish bar on Walnut Street. "It's Nanny

Night," one of them had said, giving Jim a meaningful wink. Jim didn't know what he meant, but he soon found out. The bar was packed with Irish lasses, blue-eyed Swedes, Finnish girls with French braids. A half-dozen lilting accents chimed over the brass-and-mahogany bar. Jim was stunned into speechlessness and immobility. He stood frozen in a corner and downed champagne and stout and lager long after his colleagues went home, staring helplessly as the girls giggled and complained about their charges. On his way to the men's room, he'd bumped into a red-haired freckled girl with twinkling blue eyes. "Steady there!" she'd said, laughing as he mumbled an apology. Her name was Maeve, he'd learned, as she led him back to her table. "A partner!" she'd cooed, as her friends looked on approvingly. "Congratulations!" And somehow he'd wound up in her bed, spending a joyful six hours tasting her freckles, filling his hands with the crackling fire of her hair.

Since then he'd turned into a slut. There really was no other word for it. He wasn't a Don Juan or a Romeo; he wasn't a stud or a cocksman. He was a slut, living out every one of the fantasies of his frustrated adolescence in a city that suddenly seemed full of good-natured girls in their twenties, all of them just as eager for a no-strings-attached romp as he was. He'd turned some kind of magical corner where what he was (and what he earned) had some-how trumped the way he looked. Or his looks had improved. Or, to women, the words "I'm a partner" sounded exactly like "take off your panties." He couldn't explain it, but suddenly there were nannies and students and secretaries, bartenders and baby-sitters and waitresses, and he didn't even need to go to bars to find them. Why, right in the office there was a certain paralegal who'd be happy to stay late, to lock his office door behind her and take off everything except a lilac brassiere and a certain pair of sandals she had that laced around her calves, and . . .

Stop, Jim told himself. It was unseemly. It was embarrassing. It had to stop. He was thirty-five and a partner. He'd gorged himself at the all-you-can-eat flesh banquet for the past year and a half, and it should have been enough. Think of the risks, he instructed himself. Disease! Heartbreak! Angry fathers and boyfriends! The three guys who'd made partner when he had were already married, and two of them were fathers, and although nothing explicit had ever been said, it was clear that they'd chosen the kind of lifestyles the firm's powers approved of. Home and hearth, with possibly a discrete diversion on the side, that was the way to go, not these wild weekends of girls whose last names he didn't always catch. His colleagues' attitudes had already started to shift from awe to awed amusement. Soon they'd be looking at him with just amusement. And after that would come amused disgust.

And there was Rose. Jim felt himself soften as he thought of her. Rose wasn't the prettiest girl he'd ever been with, not the sexiest. She tended to dress like a repressed librarian, and her idea of sexy lingerie was when her cotton panties matched her cotton bra, but still, there was something about her that bypassed the hot wiring below his belt and grabbed directly at his heart. The way she looked at him! Like he was one of the coverboys from her romance novels come to life, like he'd left his white steed at a parking meter and had charged through a thicket of thorns to rescue her. He was surprised that the whole firm hadn't figured out what was going on between them, in spite of the rules about partners dating associates. Then again, maybe he was being blind. Maybe everyone had figured it out already. And here he was, tempted a hundred times a day to break her heart.

Sweet Rose. She deserved better than him, Jim thought, piloting his Lexus into the law firm's garage. And for her, he'd try to be as good as he could be. Already he'd swapped his hot secretary for a sixtysomething motherly type who smelled of lemon Luden's cough drops, and he'd stayed out of the bars for an unprecedented three weeks running. She was good for him, he told himself, stepping into the elevator that would take him to his office. She was sharp and smart and kindhearted; she was the kind of girl he could see growing old with, spending the rest of his life with. And for Rose he'd walk the straight and narrow, he vowed, looking over the trio of chattering secretaries who'd entered the elevator beside him before taking one last whiff of their mingled perfume, swallowing hard, and looking away.

ELEVEN

"Why do we have to do this again?" asked Maggie as she flung herself into the passenger's seat. It was the same question she asked as they set out for every home football game. They'd been going once a year for almost twenty years, Rose thought, and the answer never changed.

"Because our father is a very limited man," she said, and started driving toward the Vet. "Are you going to be warm enough? You remember we're playing Tampa, not going there." Maggie had dressed for the football game in a black catsuit, black boots with chunky heels, and a cropped leather jacket with a fake fur collar. Rose, on the other hand, had on jeans and a sweater, plus a hat, a scarf, mittens, and an oversized yellow down coat.

Maggie peered at Rose's jacket. "You look like a mattress that someone peed on," she said.

"Thanks for sharing," said Rose. "Fasten your seat belt."

"Fine," Maggie replied, pulling a flask out of one of the jacket's minuscule pockets. She took a swig and tilted it toward her sister. "Apricot brandy," she said.

"I'm driving," said Rose, her mouth set in a tight line.

"And I'm drinking," said Maggie, and giggled. The sound of her sister's laughter reminded Rose of every other football game they'd attended since her father, in a slightly misguided act of involved parenting, had bought the first set of season tickets in 1981.

"We hate football," Maggie had informed him with the absolute conviction of being ten years old and right about everything. Michael Feller's face had gotten pale.

"We do not!" Rose had said, and she'd given her sister a fast upper-arm pinch.

"Ow!" said Maggie.

"Really?" asked their father.

"Well, we don't like watching it on TV so much," said Rose, "but we'd love to see a real game!" She'd given her sister an insurance pinch to make sure she wouldn't say otherwise. And that was that. Every year, the three of them—eventually the four of them, once Sydelle appeared on the scene—would go to Eagles home games together. Maggie used to lay out her outfits days in advance, mittens trimmed with fake fur and hats with fluffy pompoms, and once, if Rose remembered right, a miniature pair of tasseled cheerleader's boots. Rose would make peanut butter and jelly sandwiches, and she'd put them in a lunch box, along with a thermos of hot chocolate. They'd bring blankets on the coldest days, and the three of them would huddle together, licking peanut butter off of their numb fingers, as their father would curse at every sack and fumble, then look guiltily at the girls and say, "Pardon my French."

"Pardon my French," Rose murmured. Maggie looked at her curiously, then took another slip of her brandy and hunched herself lower into the seat.

Their father and Sydelle were waiting for them by the ticket window. Michael Feller was dressed in jeans, an Eagles sweatshirt, and a down coat in the team colors of silver and green. Sydelle wore her customary look of icy discontent, a face full of makeup, and an ankle-length mink coat.

"Maggie! Rose!" their father called out, handing them their tickets.

"Girls," said Sydelle, kissing the air three inches to the right of their cheeks, then reapplying her lipstick. Rose followed her stepmother up toward their seats. Listening to the click of Sydelle's heels echo on the concrete, Rose wondered—and not for the first time—why in the world this woman had ever married her father. Sydelle Levine had been a divorcée in her mid-forties whose stockbroker husband had had the bad manners to leave her for his secretary. Très cliché, but Sydelle had survived the indignity, perhaps buoyed by the ample alimony payments her husband had eagerly agreed to (Rose imagined him thinking that even a million dollars a year was a small price to pay for years of Sydelle-free bliss). Michael Feller was eight years younger, a middle manager at a medium-sized bank. He'd be comfortable, but never rich. Plus, he had baggage—the dead wife, the daughters.

What could the attraction have been? Rose had spent hours of her adolescence trying to puzzle it out in the years after Michael Feller and Sydelle Levine met in the Beth Shalom lobby (Sydelle had been on her way in for a five-hundred-dollar-a-plate fund-raiser, and Michael had been on his way out of a Parents Without Partners meeting).

"Sex!" Maggie had said, cackling. And it was true that, objectively speaking, their father was a handsome man. But Rose wasn't sure. She thought that Sydelle had seen her father not just as handsome, or a good catch, but as her true love, her second chance. Rose always believed that Sydelle had really loved him—at least at the beginning. And she'd bet that her father hadn't been looking for anything more than a traveling companion—and, of course, a surrogate mother for Maggie and Rose, given Sydelle's success with My Marcia. Michael Feller had already found the love of his life, and buried her back in Connecticut. And every week that went by, Sydelle grew a little more aware of that truth, and became a little more disappointed—and a little meaner to Michael Feller's daughters.

It was sad, thought Rose, sitting down, pulling her hat over her ears, and wrapping her scarf tightly around her neck. Sad, and unlikely to change. Sydelle and her father were in it for the long haul.

"Want some?"

Startled, Rose jumped a little in her seat, and turned to face her sister, who'd flung her legs over the seat in front of her and was waggling her little flask of apricot brandy. "No thanks," said Rose, and turned to her father. "How have you been?" she asked.

"Oh, you know," he said. "Work's keeping me busy. My Vanguard 500 fund had a terrible quarter. I—RUN YOU BASTARD!"

Rose leaned past her sister to talk to Sydelle. "And what's new with you?" she asked, making her regular game-day effort to be nice to her stepmother.

Sydelle fluffed her mink. "My Marcia's redecorating."

"That's exciting," said Rose, trying to sound enthusiastic.

Sydelle nodded. "We're going to a spa," she continued. "In February," she said, and cast a meaningful glance toward Rose's midriff. "You know that when she got married, My Marcia bought a size six Vera Wang, and . . ."

". . . had it taken in," Rose recited silently to herself, just as Maggie said the same words, only out loud.

Sydelle narrowed her eyes. "I don't know why you feel compelled to be so rude."

Maggie ignored her and held out her hand for her father's binoculars as the cheerleaders took the field. "Fat, fat, old, fat," she recited, making her way down the line. "Bad dye job; ooh! bad boob job, old, fat, old. . . ."

Michael Feller waved at the beer vendor. Sydelle grabbed his hand, and put it back in his lap. "Ornish!" she hissed.

"Pardon me?" said Rose.

"Ornish," said Sydelle. "We're doing the Dean Ornish diet. Plant-based." She gave another sideways glance, this time at Rose's thighs. "You might want to try it."

I'm in hell, thought Rose bleakly. *Hell is an Eagles game, where the bleachers are always freezing, and the team is always losing, and my family is insane.*

Her father patted her shoulder and flipped open his wallet. "Want to get us hot chocolate?" he asked.

Maggie leaned over. "Can I have money, too?" she asked. Then she squinted at the wallet. "Who's that?"

"Oh," their father said, looking embarrassed, "it's just this article I cut out. I was meaning to give it to Rose . . ."

"Dad," said Rose. "That's Lou Dobbs."

"Right," said her father.

"You're carrying a picture of Lou Dobbs around in your wallet?"

"Not his picture," Michael Feller said. "This article. About preparing for retirement. It's very good."

"Do you have pictures of us in there?" Maggie demanded, grabbing for the wallet. "Or just Lou Whoever?" She flipped through the pictures. Rose looked, too. There were school pictures of her and Maggie that dated from sixth and fourth grade, respectively. A picture of Michael and Caroline, on their wedding day—a candid shot, with Caroline puffing out her lower lip to blow her veil off her forehead, and with Michael gazing at her. There was not, Rose noted, a shot of Michael and Sydelle. She wondered if Sydelle had noticed. Judging from her icy expression, the way her tiny eyes were fixed straight ahead, Rose guessed that the answer was yes.

"Go Birds!" the guy in the row behind them blatted into Rose's ear, and then belched as a finale. Rose got to her feet and headed into the echoing, windswept concourse, where she bought herself a cup of watery hot chocolate and a hot dog in a squishy white bun, which she devoured in four gigantic bites. Then she leaned against the railing, picking bits of relish off of her scarf, counting the minutes until eight o'clock when she was going to meet Jim for dinner. *Hold on,* she told herself. She bought three more cups of hot chocolate and carried them carefully back to the seats.

TWELVE

"Mrs. Lefkowitz?" Ella rapped hard on the aluminum door, balancing a lunch tray on her hip. "Hello?"

"Go to hell!" came the slurred voice from inside. Ella sighed and kept knocking.

"Lunchtime!" she called out, as cheerfully as she could.

"Fuck off!" yelled Mrs. Lefkowitz. Mrs. Lefkowitz had suffered a stroke, and her recuperation had unfortunately coincided with the week that Golden Acres had been getting free HBO. The free HBO had included a Margaret Cho stand-up special. Mrs. Lefkowitz had been calling Ella "Ass Master" ever since, and laughing uproariously each time she said it.

"I've got soup," Ella called.

There was a pause from the other side of the door. "Cream of mushroom?" Mrs. Lefkowitz asked hopefully.

"Split pea," Ella confessed.

Another pause, and then the door was flung open, and there was Mrs. Lefkowitz, four feet eleven inches, white hair rumpled and wild. She wore a pink sweatshirt and matching sweatpants and knitted pink-and-white booties—the kind of outfit you'd give a newborn, Ella thought, and tried not to smile, as her final Meals on Wheels client for the day glared at her furiously.

"Split pea sucks," said Mrs. Lefkowitz. The left corner of her mouth drooped slightly, and she held her left arm bent at an odd angle tightly against her side. She looked at Ella hopefully. "Maybe you could make cream of mushroom?"

"Do you have any?" asked Ella.

"Sure, sure," said Mrs. Lefkowitz, shuffling toward the kitchen, her tiny form swimming in all that pink yarn. Ella followed along, setting the tray down on the kitchen table. "Sorry I yelled at you. I thought you were someone else."

Who? Ella wanted to ask. As far as she could tell, she was the only one who ever saw Mrs. Lefkowitz, outside of her doctors and the home-care health aide who came three times a week.

"My son," Mrs. Lefkowitz supplied. She turned toward Ella with a can of Campbell's in her right hand.

"You tell your son to"— Ella couldn't bring herself to repeat it—"eff off?"

"Kids today," said Mrs. Lefkowitz complacently.

"Well, it's nice that he's visiting," said Ella, dumping the congealed grayish mass into a saucepan.

"I told him not to come," said Mrs. Lefkowitz. "But he said, 'Ma, you were on the verge of death.' I said, 'I'm eighty-seven years of age. What did you think I was on the verge of? Club Med?'"

"Well, that's lovely that he's visiting."

"Bullshit," said Mrs. Lefkowitz. "He just wants to get some sun. I'm convenient," she said, her drooping lip quivering. "Guess where he is right now. On the beach. Probably staring at the girls in the bikinis, and drinking a beer. Hah. He couldn't wait to get out of here."

"The beach sounds nice," Ella said as she stirred.

Mrs. Lefkowitz pulled a chair away from the table, carefully seated herself upon it, and waited until Ella pushed her chair close to the table's edge. "I guess," she said. Ella set the bowl in front of her. Mrs. Lefkowitz dipped her spoon and raised it toward her lips. Her wrist trembled, and half the soup wound up on the front of her sweatshirt. "Shit," she said, and her voice was small and wavering and defeated.

"Do you have plans for dinner?" asked Ella, handing Mrs. Lefkowitz a napkin and tipping the soup into a coffee mug.

"I told him I'd cook," she said. "Turkey. He likes turkey."

"I could help you," said Ella. "Maybe we could make a platter of different deli sandwiches. Easy to eat." She stood up, looking for a pen and a pad of paper so she could make a list. "We can go buy some brisket, and turkey and corned beef . . . cole slaw and potato salad, if he likes that . . ."

Mrs. Lefkowitz smiled with half of her mouth. "I used to buy it with caraway seeds, and at the end of dinner I'd find a little pile of caraway seeds on the side of his plate. He'd never complain . . . he'd just pick them all out and leave them there."

"My daughter was like that with raisins. She'd pick them out of anything," said Ella. Mrs. Lefkowitz looked at her sharply. Ella let her voice trail off.

Mrs. Lefkowitz maneuvered a spoonful of soup to her mouth and appeared not to notice Ella's silence. "So we'll go shopping?" she said.

"Sure," said Ella, bending to put the dishes in the dishwasher, turning her back to Mrs. Lefkowitz. Lewis was coming to pick her up tonight. They were going to a movie. And how soon before his questions came? *Do you have children? Do you have grandkids? Where are they? What happened? You don't see them? Well, why not?* "Sure."

THIRTEEN

"You're home!" said Maggie.

Rose entered the apartment warily. It had been a terrible day. She'd been at work for thirteen hours, and Jim's office door had been closed for all of them, and she was in no mood for Maggie's nonsense.

In the apartment's small living room, all the lights were blazing, something smelled like it was burning in the kitchen, and Maggie, dressed in ruffled red pajama shorts and a red T-shirt that read "SEX KITTEN" in silver letters, was perched on the couch, channel surfing. A bowl of singed-looking microwaved popcorn sat in the center of the table next to a bowl of reheated frozen corn, two celery sticks, and a jar of peanut butter. This, in Maggie's world, passed for a balanced meal.

"How's the job search going?" asked Rose, hanging up her coat and heading into the bedroom, where her bed was strewn with what appeared to be the entire contents of her closet. "What's this? What happened?"

Maggie plopped herself on top of the heap. "I decided to sort out your clothes."

Rose stared at the tangle of blouses and jackets and pants, now just as much a mess as Maggie's baggage out in the living room. "Why are you doing this?" she said. "Don't touch my things!"

"Rose, I'm trying to help you," said Maggie, sounding affronted. "I figure it's the least I can do, since you've been so generous." She stared at the floor. "Sorry I upset you," she said. "I just wanted to help."

Rose opened her mouth, then closed it. This was part of her sister's particular genius—just at the moment when you were ready to kill her, to throw her out on the street, to demand that she pay back your money and return your clothes and your shoes, she'd say something that would catch in your heart like a fishhook.

"Fine," she muttered. "Just put everything back when you're done."

"You're supposed to go through all of your stuff every six months," said Maggie. "I read it in *Vogue.* And you, obviously, have fallen behind. I found acid-wash jeans," she added with a shudder. "But not to worry. I threw them away."

"You should have taken them to Goodwill."

"Just because someone is poor," declared Maggie, "does not mean they must be unfashionable." She extended the bowl of corn toward her sister. "Niblet?"

Rose grabbed a spoon and helped herself. "How do you know what I'm wearing and what I'm not?"

Maggie shrugged. "Well, some of it's obvious. Like those size twelve pants from Ann Taylor?"

Rose knew the ones. She'd bought them on sale, and squeezed into them once four years ago after a week's worth of nothing but black coffee and Slim-Fast. They'd been hanging in her closet ever since, a silent reproach, a reminder of what was possible if she'd buckle down and stop eating french fries and pizza and . . . well, pretty much everything else she liked. "They're all yours," she said.

"They're way too big. But maybe I could have them taken in," Maggie said, and turned her attention to the television set.

"When are you going to put everything back?" asked Rose, imagining trying to sleep atop the litter of her wardrobe.

"Shh!" said Maggie, lifting one finger, and pointed toward the

TV, where a small, wheeled hunk of red-painted metal was menacing a bluish object that had a rotating blade protruding from its center.

"What is this?"

"Television," Maggie replied, stretching one leg out in front of her, and turning it this way and that, inspecting her calf. "It's this box, with pictures, and the pictures tell a delightful story!"

Rose thought about reaching for her wallet. *This is a paycheck,* she'd say, holding the object in question out for her sister's inspection. *It represents money, which you earn by holding a job.* Maggie took a swallow from the open bottle of champagne by her side. Rose opened her mouth to ask where she'd gotten champagne, then realized it was the bottle someone had given her when she'd passed the bar that had been reposing in a back corner of her refrigerator ever since.

"How's that champagne?" Rose asked.

Maggie took another gulp. "Delicious," she said. "Now, pay attention. Watch and learn. On this show, *BattleBots,* there are these guys who build robots . . ."

"That's a nice hobby," said Rose, who tried whenever she could to encourage Maggie in the pursuit of acceptable men.

Maggie waved a dismissive hand. "They're geeks. They build these robots, and the robots fight each other, and the winner gets . . . something. I'm not sure what. Look, look, there's my favorite," she said, pointing at what looked like a miniature trash truck with a spike welded to its middle. "That's the Philiminator," she said.

"Huh?" asked Rose.

"The guy who made it, his name is Phil, so it's the Philiminator." Sure enough, the camera had panned to a pale, lanky guy in a baseball cap reading "Philiminator." "He's undefeated in three rounds," Maggie said, as a second robot rolled into view. This one was a shiny green and looked like a souped-up Dustbuster. "Grendel," said the announcer.

"Okay," said Maggie. "You root for Grendel."

"Why?" asked Rose, but by then the match was starting. The two robots started off after each other, zipping around the concrete floor like small, crazed dogs.

"Go, Philiminator!" Maggie hollered, waving the champagne bottle exuberantly. She looked at her sister.

"Yay, Grendel," said Rose. Maggie's robot zipped in close. The spike from its center rose, and rose, and came crashing down like a guillotine, spearing Grendel through its center, as Maggie clapped and shouted her encouragement.

"Whew! Close one," said Maggie.

The robots wheeled around to face each other again.

"Come on, Philiminator. FUCK HIM UP!" Maggie bellowed.

Rose burst out laughing, as a spiked wheel on the front of Grendel started whirring. "Ooh, look out . . . here I come!"

Now Grendel advanced on his opponent. The Philiminator lifted its spike and speared its opponent through its center.

"Yeah!" Maggie cheered.

The two robots were locked together now, joined by the spike. Grendel twisted this way and that, unable to get free. "Come on . . . come on . . ." Rose muttered. Grendel's wheel whirred, striking sparks off the floor. The Philiminator raised its spike for the death blow, and Grendel zipped away.

"GO GRENDEL!" Rose hollered, and jumped to her feet. "Yes! YES!" Maggie sulked as Grendel charged at its opponent, wedged its nose underneath the much taller Philiminator, and flipped it on its back.

"Noooo," wailed Maggie as Rose's robot ran over hers once, and then again, until the thing was no more than a collection of crushed parts and broken pieces.

"Oh, yes. OH YES!" said Rose, pumping her fist in the air. "That's what I'm talking about!" she shouted, just the way she'd heard guys in the row behind her at Eagles games holler after particularly crucial touchdowns. Then she turned toward her sister, sure that Maggie would be smirking at her, doing a poor job of showing how pathetic she found Rose's excitement. Except Maggie wasn't smirking. Maggie, her cheeks flushed, was beaming at her sister, holding out her hand for a high five, laughing as she offered her sister the bottle of champagne. Rose hesitated, then took a swallow.

"Want to order a pizza?" Rose offered. She could envision the rest of the night—pizza and pajamas and fresh popcorn, the two of them on the couch beneath the blanket, watching TV.

Maggie did smirk then . . . but only a little. And her voice was almost kind. "You're really living now, aren't you?" she asked. "You should get out more."

"I get out enough," said Rose. "You should stay in more."

"I stay in plenty," said Maggie, rising gracefully to her feet. She padded into the bedroom, returning minutes later dressed in skintight faded jeans, slung low around her hips, a red top that left one shoulder and arm completely bare, and Rose's jalapeño leather cowboy boots. Rose's hand-stitched red leather cowboy boots, bought on a weekend in New Mexico, where Rose had gone once for a seminar about insurance law. "You don't mind, do you?" said Maggie, gathering her purse and her keys. "I found them in your closet. They looked lonely."

"Sure," said Rose. She stared at her sister and wondered what it must be to move through life being so thin and so pretty; what it would be like to have men look at you with unconditional approval, unmitigated desire. "Have fun."

"I always do," said Maggie, and breezed out the door, leaving Rose with the popcorn, the flat champagne, the ruin of clothes strewn across her bed. She flicked the television set into its customary silence, and started to clean up the mess.

FOURTEEN

"Can I help you?" asked Ella. It was Ella's afternoon at the thrift shop, where she passed a few pleasant, mostly uninterrupted hours sorting bags of clothing and putting price tags on furniture and dishes. A young woman in bright orange leggings and a stained T-shirt edged down the aisle that was decorated with fake pine swags and gold and silver tinsel, in preparation for the holidays.

"Sheets," the woman said, biting her lip nervously. Ella could see the faint remnant of a bruise high on her cheek. "I'm looking for sheets."

"Well, it's your lucky day," said Ella. "It just so happens we got a shipment in from Bullock's. Irregulars, of course, but I don't see a thing wrong with them, except the colors are a little . . . well, you'll see."

She started off down the aisle, walking briskly in her black pants and white blouse with her name tag clipped to the front. "Right here," said Ella, pointing to where the sheets were—a few dozen packets in all, some for queen-sized beds, some for twins. They were turquoise and hot pink, but they were new. "Now, they're five dollars each. How many will you need?"

"Um, two twins." The woman picked up the plastic-wrapped packages, turning them over in her hands. "Are the pillowcases extra?"

"Oh! Actually, no," said Ella. "It's five dollars for the set."

The woman looked relieved as she picked up a pair of pillow-cases and walked to the cash register. She pulled a five-dollar bill out of her pocket, and three crumpled singles. When she started rooting around for change, lining pennies up carefully on the counter, Ella slipped her sheets into a bag.

"That's fine," she said.

The woman looked up at her. "Are you sure?"

"It's fine," Ella repeated. "Take care of yourself, and come back . . . we're getting new stuff in all the time."

The woman smiled—politely, Ella thought—and walked out, her flip-flops slapping on the sidewalk. Ella stared at her back, wishing she'd found a way to slip some towels into the woman's bag along with the sheets. She sighed, and felt frustrated. It had been like that with Caroline—Ella always wanting to do more, to fix things for her daughter, to chase after her, with calls, with cards, with letters, with money, dangling the promise of vacations and trips, saying the same thing a dozen different ways: *Let me help you.* But Caroline hadn't wanted to be helped, because accepting help meant admitting that she couldn't do it herself. And look how that had turned out.

The door swung open again and Lewis walked into the thrift store with a bundle of newspapers under his arm.

"Hot off the presses!" he said. Ella tried for a smile and looked at her poem. "I AM NOT INVISIBLE," she read. Not invisible, she thought sadly. Just doomed.

Lewis was looking at her closely. "Still want lunch?" he asked, and when she nodded and closed the cash register, he offered her his arm. She walked out into the steamy sunshine, still wishing she'd done things differently. She wished she'd been able to start a con-versation, to maybe ask if the woman needed help, and then figured out how to help her. And, she thought, she wished that Lewis would never find out what kind of a person she really was. She hadn't brought up children and, so far, he hadn't asked . . . but someday soon he would, and what then? What would she say? What could she say, really, except that she used to be a mother, that she wasn't a mother anymore, and that it was her fault? And he'd stare at her, unable to make sense of it, and she wouldn't be able to explain it properly, even though she knew that it was true, and it was the stone she couldn't swallow, the river she couldn't cross. Her fault. And no matter how she tried to make up for it, what small acts of goodness she attempted, she would carry that around with her until the day she died.

FIFTEEN

"There's someone to see you," said Rose's secretary. Rose looked up from her computer and saw her sister, resplendent in black boot-cut leather pants, a cropped denim jacket, and the red cowboy boots, waltz into her office.

"Good news!" Maggie said, beaming.

Please let it be a job, Rose prayed. "What is it?"

"I had a job interview! At this great new bar!"

"Terrific!" said Rose, trying to match her enthusiasm to Maggie's. "That's great! When do you think they'll let you know?"

"I'm not sure," said Maggie, who was lifting and replacing books and folders from Rose's bookcase. "Maybe after the holidays."

"But wouldn't the holidays be their busy time?"

"Jesus, Rose, I don't know!" Maggie picked up the small plastic replica of Xena, Warrior Princess—one of Amy's birthday gifts—and stood it on its head. "Do you think you could maybe try to be happy for me?"

"Sure," said Rose. "And have you made any progress on putting my clothes back?" For the past several nights, the pile of clothing had shifted from her bed to the floor, but had not yet made it to the closet.

"I started," said Maggie, flopping into the seat across from Rose's desk. "I'll take care of it! It's not such a big deal."

"Sure, for you it isn't," said Rose.

"What is that supposed to mean?"

Rose got to her feet. "I mean, you're living with me rent-free, you haven't found a job . . ."

"I told you, I had an interview!"

"I don't think you're trying very hard."

"I am!" Maggie shouted. "What do you know about it?"

"Shh!"

Maggie slammed the door and glared at her sister.

"I know that it can't be that hard to find a job! " Rose said. "I see help-wanted signs all over the place! Every store, every restaurant . . ."

"I don't want to work in another store. I don't want to waitress."

"So what do you want to do?" Rose demanded. "Sit around like a princess, waiting for MTV to call?"

Maggie's face reddened as if she'd been slapped. "Why are you so mean?"

Rose bit her lip. They'd done this dance before, or, rather, Maggie had . . . with her father, with well-meaning boyfriends, the occasional concerned teacher or boss. Different partners, same steps. She could gauge the precise instant when Rose was going to apologize. And a heartbeat before Rose opened her mouth, the instant she began to inhale the air that would form the words *I'm sorry,* Maggie started talking again.

"I'm trying," she said, swiping at her eyes. "I'm trying very hard. It's not easy for me, Rose, you know? It's not easy for everyone the way it's easy for you."

"I know," Rose said gently. "I know you're trying."

"I try. Every day," said Maggie. "I'm not a freeloader. I don't sit around and feel sorry for myself. I go out and I look for a job . . . every . . . day. And I know I'm never going to be a lawyer like you . . ."

Rose made a protesting noise. Maggie cried a little louder. ". . . but that doesn't mean I just sit around and do nothing. I'm trying, Rose, I'm trying so h-h-h-hard . . ."

Rose crossed the room to hug her. Maggie shrugged away.

"Okay," said Rose. "Okay, don't worry about it. You'll find a job . . ."

"I always do," said Maggie, segueing seamlessly from her weepy Renee Zellweger into strength-through-adversity Sally Field. She wiped her eyes, blew her nose, straightened her back, and looked at her sister.

"I'm sorry," Rose said. "I'm really, really sorry." Wondering, even as she said the words, precisely what she was apologizing for. It had been over a month now. Maggie showed no signs of leaving. Her clothes and toiletries, compact disc cases and cigarette lighters, were still tossed all over Rose's apartment, which was feeling smaller by the day, and the night before Rose had burned her finger after dipping it in a saucepan that she thought held hot caramel sauce, which turned out to be Maggie's eyebrow wax. "Look," she said helplessly, "have you had dinner yet? We can go out, maybe see a movie . . ."

Maggie wiped her eyes again and squinted at her sister. "You know what we should do? We should go out. Like, really out. To a club or something."

"I don't know," said Rose. "You always have to wait to get into those places. And they're so smoky and loud . . ."

"Come on. Just once. I'll help you pick out an outfit . . ."

"Oh, fine," said Rose reluctantly. "I think there's some law firm thing going on at one of those places on Delaware Avenue."

"What kind of thing?" asked Maggie.

Rose rifled through her mail until she found the invitation. " 'A holiday cocktail party,' " she read. " 'Finger food, free games.' Maybe we can go there."

"To start with," said Maggie. She opened the door and bounced out of the office. "Let's go!"

Back at Rose's apartment, Maggie pulled a blue sweater and a black skirt from the pile beside the bed. "Go take a shower," she said, "and be sure to moisturize!"

When Rose got out of the shower, Maggie's multitiered makeup case was open, and she had a row of products lined up on the counter. Two kinds of foundation, three different concealers, a half-dozen discs of eye shadow and blush, brushes for eyes, for cheeks, for lips. . . . Rose sat on the toilet and stared, feeling dizzy.

"Where did all of this stuff come from?" she asked.

"Here and there," said Maggie, sharpening a gray eye pencil.

Rose studied the case again. "And how much do you think it all cost?"

"Dunno," said Maggie, smoothing lotion onto her sister's cheeks with quick, sure strokes. "But whatever it was, it was worth it. Just wait!"

Rose sat there, still as a mannequin, for the fifteen ticklish minutes Maggie spent on her eyelids alone. She got fidgety as Maggie blended foundation on the back of her hand, and brushed it on, then stood back, considering, then came forward again to brush on powder and blush, and she was downright bored by the time Maggie brought out the eyelash curler and the lip pencil, but she had to admit that the cumulative effect was . . . well, stunning.

"Is that me?" she asked, staring at herself in the mirror, at the new hollows underneath her cheekbones, and the way her eyes looked smoky and mysterious beneath the gold and cream eyeshadow Maggie had applied.

"Isn't it great? I'd do your makeup for you every day," Maggie said. "You'd have to start a serious skin-care regimen first, though. You *need* to exfoliate," she said, in the same tone another woman would have said, "You *need* to leave that burning building." She held up a black skirt and the blue top in one hand, a pair of thin-strapped high-heeled blue sandals in the other. "Here, try this."

Rose wriggled into the skirt and the low-cut top. Both of them were tighter than the things she normally wore, and together . . .

"I don't know," she said, forcing herself to stare at her body and not be distracted by her face. "Don't you think I look kind of . . ." The word *cheap* teetered on her lips. Her legs looked long and sleek in the blue shoes, and she had a veritable Grand Canyon of cleavage going on. Maggie approved.

"You look great!" she said, and spritzed her sister from her treasured bottle of Coco. Twenty minutes later, Rose's hair was up, her earrings were in place, and they were out the door.

"This party sucks," said Maggie, slurping her dirty martini.

Rose tugged at her top, squinting at the crowd. She couldn't see without her glasses, but of course Maggie wouldn't let her wear them. "Guys don't make passes at girls who wear glasses!" she'd singsonged, then spent five minutes pestering her sister about why she didn't just get the laser treatments already, like the newscasters and supermodels did.

They were at Dave and Buster's, a glorified arcade for grownups perched on the less-than-scenic bank of the Delaware River, where the law firm was, indeed, having its semi-annual Young Associates Social. Rose's name tag, perched next to her brand-new astonishing cleavage, read, "I AM Rose Feller," and then she'd added, in parentheses, "Litigation." Maggie's original name tag had read, "I AM drinking," until Rose made her take it off. Now it read, "I AM Monique," at which Rose had rolled her eyes but decided wasn't worth a fight.

The place was lousy with young lawyers, networking and sipping microbrewed beer, watching Don Dommel and his dreadlocked protégé show off their tricks on the Virtual Vert Ramp. There was a buffet laid out against one wall—Rose could make out what looked like a tray of vegetables and dips, and a stainless-steel pan of small fried chunks of something—but Maggie had pulled her away. "Mingle!" she'd said.

Now Maggie nudged her sister and pointed at a man-shaped blob standing by the foosball table. "Who's that?" she demanded.

Rose squinted. All she could make out was blond hair and broad shoulders. "Not sure," she said.

Maggie tossed her hair. Maggie, of course, looked unbelievable.

Maggie was wearing pink sandals and black leather pants that Rose knew for a fact cost two hundred dollars because she'd found the receipt on the kitchen counter, paired with a small, sparkly, silvery halter top that tied around her neck and left her entire back bare. She'd blown her hair out straight—a process that took the better part of an hour—and adorned her slender arms with rows of silver bangles. Maggie had done her lips in pale pink, loaded on the mascara, and rimmed her eyes in silvery pencil. She looked like a visitor from the future, or possibly from a television show.

"Well, I'm going to talk to him," she announced. She ran her fingers through her hair, which hung in a perfectly straight sheet of shimmering auburn, grimaced at Rose, asked whether she had lipstick on her teeth, and stalked into the crowd. Rose gave her top a final yank. Her feet hurt, but Maggie hadn't budged on the question of Rose's shoes.

"One must suffer to be beautiful," she had intoned, taking two steps back and surveying her sister carefully before wondering aloud whether Rose didn't have a pair of control-top panty hose that would offer a bit more control.

Rose peered across the room to see her sister assailing the unsuspecting barrister with the double whammy of her hair toss and bangle shake. Then she sidled toward the buffet table, glanced once, guiltily, over her shoulder, and loaded a small plate with dip, crackers, baby carrots, chunks of cheese, and a scoop of fried whatever-it-was. She found a table in the corner, kicked off her shoes, and started eating.

Another man-shaped blob—this one was short and pale, with tightly curled gingery hair—approached her. "Rose Feller?" he inquired.

Rose swallowed and nodded, peering at his name tag.

"Simon Stein," said the guy. "We were sitting next to each other at the pep rally."

"Ah," said Rose, and tried to nod in a manner that would give the impression that she recognized him.

"I gave you coffee," he said.

"Oh, right!" said Rose, remembering. "You saved my life! Thank you!"

Simon gave a modest nod. "So we're going to be travel buddies," he said.

Rose stared at him. The only travel she had planned was a recruiting trip to the University of Chicago Law School on Monday. Just her, and Jim.

"I'm subbing for Jim Danvers," Simon said. Rose felt her heart sink.

"Oh," she said.

"He got busy, so they asked me if I wanted to go."

"Oh," Rose said again.

"So, listen, do you live in Center City? I'll give you a ride to the airport."

"Oh," said Rose for the third time, and added another word just to change things up. "Sure."

Simon leaned closer to her. "Listen," he said, "you don't by any chance play softball, do you?"

Rose shook her head. Her one experience with the game had come during gym class her junior year of high school, when she'd failed to connect even once during the six-week session and dozens of at-bats, and she'd gotten hit in the chest with a foul ball. And there'd been nothing soft about it.

"We've got a team, you know. Motion Denied," said Simon, as if he hadn't noticed her head shake. "Co-ed. Only we don't have enough women on the roster. We'll have to forfeit if we can't find some more."

"Alas," said Rose.

"It's an easy game," said Simon. Rose figured he was probably a litigator. The men among them tended toward a terrierlike persistence. "Good exercise, fresh air . . ."

"Do I look like I need exercise and fresh air?" she asked, then looked down at herself ruefully. "Don't answer that."

Simon Stein continued his pitch. "It's fun. You'll meet lots of people."

She shook her head. "Really, you don't want me. I'm hopeless."

A woman came over and hooked one of her arms through Simon's. "Honey, come play pool with me!" she cooed. Rose winced. This was the girl she privately called Ninety-five, 1995 being the year she graduated from Harvard, a fact that she'd managed to drop into every single conversation Rose had ever had with her.

"Rose, this is Felice Russo," said Simon.

"We've actually met," Rose said. Felice reached up to smooth Simon's hair, which was not, in Rose's opinion, going to be improved by any amount of smoothing. Just then Maggie returned, with her cheeks flushed and a lit cigarette in her hand.

"This party still sucks," she announced, and looked around. "Introduce me."

"Maggie, this is Simon and Felice," said Rose. "We work together."

"Oh," said Maggie, taking a deep drag. "Great."

"What a beautiful bracelet," said Felice, pointing at one of Maggie's bangles. "It is indigenous?"

Maggie stared at her. "Huh? I got it on South Street."

"Oh," said Felice. "It's just that there was this little boutique in Boston that sold stuff like that, and I bought a few pieces there in college."

Here it comes, thought Rose.

"I went to Boston once," said Maggie. "I had a friend at Northeastern."

Three . . . two . . . one . . .

"Oh, really?" said Felice. "What year? I was at Harvard. . . ."

Rose grinned. And did she imagine it, or was Simon Stein smiling, too?

"Let's sit down," he said, and the four of them relocated to a spindly-legged cocktail table. Felice was still yammering about Cambridge in the wintertime. Maggie gulped her martini. Rose thought longingly of a return trip to the buffet.

"So you'll think about softball?" asked Simon.

"Oh, um . . . sure," she said.

"It's really fun," he said.

"Isn't it?" said Felice. "In college, I used to play intramural squash. Of course, not many schools have that, but luckily Harvard does."

And now she wasn't imagining it. Simon Stein had definitely rolled his eyes.

"We have happy hours, too," he said.

"Really?" asked Rose, just to be polite. "Where?"

While Simon was running through the roster of bars that Motion Denied had visited, Maggie and Felice had somehow gotten onto the topic of television.

"Oh, *The Simpsons*. I love *The Simpsons*! Do you know," Felice asked, leaning forward as if imparting some valuable secret, "in the episode about Homer's mother, where she has a fake driver's license?"

"No," said Simon.

"No," said Rose.

"I don't like cartoons," said Maggie.

Felice ignored them. "The address on the license was forty-four Bow Street, which is the actual address of *The Harvard Lampoon*!"

Maggie stared at Felice for a minute, then leaned toward her sister. "You know," she stage-whispered, "I think Felice went to Harvard."

Simon started coughing and took a large gulp of his beer. "Excuse us," Rose murmured, giving Maggie a swift kick, then dragging her toward the door.

"Not nice," Rose said.

"Oh, please," said Maggie. "Like she was such a treat."

"Not really," said Rose. "She's horrid."

"Horrid!" Maggie hooted. She tugged her sister toward the exit sign. "Come on, let's go away from all this horridness."

"Home?" Rose asked hopefully.

Maggie shook her head. "Somewhere much better than that."

• • •

Later—much, much later—the sisters sat across from each other in a booth at the International House of Pancakes.

They'd been to a club. Then an after-hours club. Then an after-party. And then, unless Rose was desperately mistaken, or enduring some sort of vodka-fueled hallucination, there'd been karaoke. She shook her head to clear it, but the memory remained—standing on stage, her shoes kicked off, a crowd chanting her name as she wailed a not-quite-on-key rendition of "Midnight Train to Georgia" while Maggie cavorted behind her, her own personal Pips.

"He's leaving . . ." Rose sang experimentally.

"All aboard! All aboard! All aboard!" Maggie chanted.

Oh, God, Rose thought, slumping in the booth. So it was true. *No more vodka,* she told herself sternly, and bit her lip, remembering what had caused her to get so drunk in the first place. Jim, canceling on their trip to Chicago, leaving her with Simon Stein. "I think you're more into this than he is," Amy had said, and the evidence was certainly suggesting that Amy was right. What had she done wrong? How could she win him back?

"You ladies ready?" asked the bored-looking waitress, pen poised over her pad.

Rose ran her fingertips over the menu as if it were braille. "Pancakes," she finally said.

"What kind?" asked the waitress.

"She'll have the buttermilk pancakes," said Maggie, taking the menu out of Rose's hands. "I'll have the same thing. And we'd like two large orange juices, and a pitcher of coffee, please."

The waitress walked away.

"I didn't know you could sing!" Maggie said as Rose began to hiccup.

"I don't sing," Rose said, "I litigate."

Maggie dumped four packets of Sweet'n Low into the cup of coffee that the waitress had set before her. "Wasn't that fun?"

"Fun," Rose repeated. She hiccupped again. The eyeliner and

mascara that Maggie had carefully applied the night before had run and smeared. She looked like a raccoon. "So what are you gonna do?" she asked.

"About what?" asked Maggie.

"About your life," said Rose.

Maggie scowled. "Now I remember why we never go out together. You have half of a wine cooler and decide to come up with a ten-step plan to improve me."

"I just wanna help," Rose said. "You need to have a goal."

The waitress arrived, dropped off the plates and a pitcher of hot maple syrup.

"Wait," asked Rose. She squinted tipsily at the waitress. "Are you guys hiring?"

"I think so," said the waitress. "I'll bring an application by with your check."

"Don't you think you're a little overqualified?" asked Maggie. "I mean, college, law degree . . . do you really just want to serve pancakes?"

"Not for me, for you," said Rose.

"Oh, you want me to serve pancakes," said Maggie.

"I want you to do something," said Rose, gesturing with drunken grandeur. "I want you to pay for your phone bill. And maybe gimme some money for groceries."

"I don't eat anything!" said Maggie, which was not quite true. She didn't eat much—an English muffin here, some milk and cereal there. It wouldn't add up to much. And it wasn't like Rose didn't have the money for it, either. She'd seen her sister's bank statements, which were kept in chronological order in a manila folder labeled "Bank Statements." Still, she could imagine Rose walking through the kitchen with a yellow legal pad, taking notes. *One Lean Cuisine Oriental Chicken dinner! One-half cup orange juice! Two packets microwave popcorn! Three teaspoons salt!*

Maggie felt her face heating up. "I'll give you some money," she said, biting off each syllable furiously.

"You don't have any money," said Rose.

"So I'll get some," Maggie said.

"When?" asked Rose. "When might this blessed event occur?"

"I've got an interview."

"Which is great, but it isn't a job."

"Fuck you. I'm leaving," Maggie said, throwing down her napkin.

"Sit down," said Rose wearily. "Eat your breakfast. I'm going to the bathroom."

Rose left the table. Maggie sat down, stabbed at her food, and didn't eat it. When the waitress came with the job application, Maggie filched a pen from her sister's purse, plus twenty dollars from her wallet, and filled the thing out with Rose's name, checking every possible "time available" slot and adding "I'll Do Anything!" in the comment section. Then she gave the application to the waitress, dumped boysenberry syrup on her sister's pancakes, knowing that Rose did not like colored syrups, and stomped out of the restaurant.

Rose came back to the table and gave a puzzled look at the ruin of her breakfast.

"Your friend left," said the waitress.

Rose shook her head slowly. "She's not my friend, she's my sister," she said. She paid the bill, pulled on her jacket, wincing at her blistered feet, and limped out the door.

SIXTEEN

"No more," said Ella, and passed her hand over the top of her wine-glass. It was their first dinner out, their first official dinner-date, which she'd finally consented to after weeks of effort on Lewis's part, and she'd agreed to share a bottle of wine with him, which was a mistake. It had been years—maybe even as long as a decade—since she'd had wine, and it had, predictably, gone straight to her head.

Lewis set the bottle down, and wiped his mouth. "I hate the holidays," he said, as casually as if he'd been telling her that he'd never liked artichokes.

"What?" she'd said.

"The holidays," he continued. "Can't stand them. Haven't been able to for years."

"Why?"

He poured himself another half-glass of wine. "Because my son doesn't come to visit me," he said shortly. "Which makes me the same as the rest of the yentas."

"He doesn't come ever?" Ella asked hesitantly. "Are you . . . Is there . . ."

"He spends the holidays with his in-laws," said Lewis, and from the halting way he spoke, Ella could tell that this was a painful topic. "They see me in February, when the kids have vacation from school."

"Well, that must be nice," said Ella.

"It's very nice," said Lewis. "I spoil them rotten. And I look forward to it, but the holidays are still not that great." He shrugged a little, as if to say that it wasn't the worst thing in the world, but Ella knew it had to be hard, being alone.

"So how about you?" Lewis asked, the way she knew he would, because as nice as he was and as well as they were getting along, she couldn't avoid this question forever. "Tell me about your family."

Ella forced herself to relax, reminding herself not to tense her shoulders or clench her hands into fists. She'd known that this was coming. It was only natural. "Well," she began. "My husband, Ira, was a college professor. The history of economics, that was his specialty. We lived in Michigan. He died fifteen years ago. Stroke." This was the acceptable Acres shorthand for a dead spouse: name, rank, how long they'd been gone, and what had carried them off, in generic terms (the ladies would, for example, not hesitate to whisper "cancer," but nothing could drag the prefix "prostate" from their lips).

"Was it a good marriage?" asked Lewis. "I know that it's none of my business . . ." And he trailed off and looked at Ella hopefully.

"It was . . ." she began, toying with her butter knife. "It was a marriage of the time, I suppose. He worked, and I ran the house. Cooked, cleaned, did the entertaining . . ."

"What was Ira like? What did he like to do?"

The funny thing was, Ella could barely remember. And what rose in her mind finally was the word *enough*. Ira had been nice enough, smart enough, had made enough money, had cared for her and for Caroline enough. He'd been a little cheap (frugal was how he'd put it), and more than a little vain (Ella couldn't help but cringe as she remembered the comb-over he'd maintained well past the point of plausibility), but for the most part he'd been . . . enough.

"He was fine," she said, knowing it was, at best, a tepid endorsement. "He was a good provider," she added, aware of how old-fashioned that sounded. "He was a good father," she concluded, although it hadn't been quite true. Ira, with his economics textbooks and smell of chalk dust, had been mostly bewildered by Caroline—beautiful, fragile, strange, furious Caroline, who'd insisted on wearing her tutu on the first day of kindergarten and had announced, at age eight, that she wouldn't answer to anything but Princess Maple Magnolia. Ira took her fishing and to ball games, and probably, secretly, wished that their one child had been a son, or at least a more normal sort of girl.

"So you have children?" Lewis asked.

Ella took a deep breath. "I had a daughter, Caroline. She died." She'd broken with protocol here. There was a name and the fact of a death, but nothing else: what Caroline had been, when she'd died, and what had killed her.

Lewis laid his hand on hers gently. "I'm sorry," he said. "I can't imagine what that must have been like."

Ella said nothing, because there were no words for what it was like. Being the mother of a dead child was worse than all of the clichés said it was. It was the worst thing. It was so bad she could only think of Caroline's death in snatches and snapshots, and not even many of those, a handful of memories, each one more painful than the last. She remembered the sleek mahogany stretch of the coffin, cool and solid under her hand. She could see the faces of Caroline's girls in their navy dresses, dark-brown hair swept into identical ponytails, and how the older girl had held the younger one's hand as they approached the coffin, and how the younger one was crying and the older one was not. "Say good-bye to Mommy," Ella remembered the older sister saying in her husky voice, and the little sister just shook her head and cried. She could remember standing there, feeling utterly empty, as if a giant hand had scooped out everything inside of her—her guts, her heart—and left her looking the same, but not being the same at all. She could remember Ira leading her around as if she were crippled, or blind, his hand on her elbow, helping her into the car, out of the car, up the funeral parlor steps past Maggie and Rose. They don't have a mother, she'd thought, and the thought had hit her like a bomb going off in her brain. She'd lost her daughter, which was a terrible thing and a tragedy, but these girls had lost a mother. And surely that was worse.

"We should move here," she'd told Ira that night, after he'd guided her into the chair in their hotel room. "We'll sell the house, rent an apartment . . ."

He'd stood beside the bed, polishing his glasses with the end of his tie, and looked at her with pity in his eyes. "Don't you think that would be locking the barn door after the horse has already gotten out?"

"Barn!" she'd screamed. "Horse! Ira, our daughter is dead! Our granddaughters have no mother! We have to help! We have to be here!"

He'd stared at her . . . and then, with the only piece of prescience she'd ever seen from him in almost thirty years of marriage, he'd said, "Maybe Michael doesn't want us here."

"Ella?" Lewis asked.

She swallowed hard, remembering how it had been raining the night she got the phone call, and how, days later, back at home, she'd dismantled the telephone: unscrewing the mouthpiece, detaching the coiled cord that joined the receiver to the phone itself, prying off the dial, unscrewing the bottom, and pulling out the telephone's wires and circuits, breaking the telephone that had brought her such horrible news into its component parts, and then staring at it, breathing hard, thinking, irrationally, *Can't hurt me now, can't hurt me now.* She could tell him how this had soothed her for about five minutes, until she'd found herself at Ira's dusty worktable in the basement, his hammer in her hand, smashing each of the pieces into a thousand shiny shards, and how she'd wanted to smash her own hands as punishment for believing what she'd wanted to believe—that Caroline was telling her the truth, that she was taking her medication, that everything was fine.

Lewis was looking at her. "You okay?"

Ella took a deep breath. "Fine," she said faintly. "Just fine."

Lewis studied her, then got to his feet, and helped Ella up. Once she'd risen, he kept one hand warm upon her elbow, steering her toward the door. "Let's go for a walk," he said.

SEVENTEEN

Maggie Feller spent Sunday afternoon in Sydelle's all-white fortress, playing Information.

She had woken up with the phone shrilling through her hangover. "Rose, the phone!" she'd moaned, except Rose wasn't answering. And Sydelle the Terrible kept calling until Maggie finally picked up and agreed to come over and get her things out of her bedroom. "We need the space," Sydelle said.

Stick it up your nose, Maggie thought. *There's plenty of room there.* "Well, where am I supposed to put everything?" she asked instead.

Sydelle had sighed. Maggie could practically see her stepmother—thin lips compressed to the width of a paper cut, nostrils flaring, strands of freshly colored ash-blond hair wagging stiffly as she shook her head. "You can move your things to the basement, I suppose," said Sydelle, her tone indicating that this was a concession akin to letting her wayward stepdaughter set up a roller coaster on the front lawn.

"That's very generous of you," Maggie said sarcastically. "I'll be over this afternoon."

"We'll be at a workshop," Sydelle had said. "Macrobiotic cooking." As if Maggie had asked. Maggie took a hot shower, helped herself to Rose's car keys, and made the drive to New Jersey. The house was empty, except for the idiot dog Chanel (whom Rose had nicknamed Knockoff), who, as usual, howled as if she were a burglar, then tried to hump her leg. Maggie shoved the dog outside and spent half an hour hauling boxes to the basement, which left her a whole hour for Information.

She started with Sydelle's desk, but didn't find anything interesting—some bills, stacks of stationery, a sheet of wallet-sized pictures of My Marcia in her wedding gown, a framed eight-by-ten of My Marcia's twins, Jason and Alexander—so she'd moved to the more fruitful hunting ground of the master bedroom's walk-in closet, which had previously yielded one of her prize finds—a jewelry box made of carved wood. The box was empty except for a pair of gold hoop earrings and a bracelet of narrow gold links that rattled inside it. Her mother's? Maybe, thought Maggie. It couldn't be Sydelle's because she knew where Sydelle kept her stuff. She'd considered pocketing the bracelets, but had decided not to. Maybe her father looked at these things, and would notice if they were gone, and Maggie didn't like the thought of him reaching for the jewelry box and finding nothing there.

She started at the first shelf. There was a rubber-banded stack of old tax returns that she picked up, flipped through, and replaced. My Marcia's cheerleading trophies, Sydelle's sweaters. Maggie stood on her tiptoes, reaching over rows of her father's summer shirts and brushing her fingertips along the top of the shelf until they stopped at what felt like a shoe box.

Maggie pulled the box off the shelf—it was pink, old-looking, crumpled around the corners. She brushed dust off the cover, carried it out of the closet, and sat down on the bed. It wasn't Sydelle's because Sydelle labeled her shoe boxes with a description of the shoes they contained (most of them very expensive, with painfully pointed toes). Plus, Sydelle wore a six narrow, and this box, according to the label, had once held a pair of pink Capezio ballet flats, girls' size four. Little kids' shoes. Maggie opened the box.

Letters. It was full of letters, at least two dozen of them. Cards, really, in colored envelopes, and the first one she pulled out was addressed to her, Miss Maggie Feller, at their old apartment, the two-bedroom place they'd lived in until her father had moved them all into Sydelle's house. The postmark read August 4, 1980, so it had been sent right around her eighth birthday (which, if she remembered right, had been a very glamorous affair at the local bowling alley, with pizza and ice cream afterward). There was a return-address sticker in the upper-left-hand corner. It said that the card came from someone named Ella Hirsch.

Hirsch, thought Maggie, feeling her heart beat faster at the prospect of this mystery. Hirsch had been their mother's maiden name.

She eased one edge of the envelope open. After almost twenty years, the glue let go easily. It was a birthday card, a little-kid's card with a pink frosted birthday cake and yellow candles on the front. "HAPPY BIRTHDAY!" it read. And inside, beneath the preprinted "WISHING YOU A VERY HAPPY DAY!" she read, "Dear Maggie, I hope you're well. I miss you very much and would love to hear from you." Then a telephone number and a signature that said "Grandma," with the words *Ella Hirsch* written in parenthesis beneath it. And a ten-dollar bill, which Maggie shoved in her pocket.

Interesting, Maggie thought, getting to her feet and walking to the bedroom window, checking out the street for signs of Sydelle's car. Maggie knew she had a grandmother; she had vague memories of sitting on someone's lap, smelling flowery perfume, and feeling a smooth cheek against her own while her mother took her picture. She vaguely remembered the same woman, this grandmother, at her mother's funeral. What had happened to the photograph was no mystery—after they moved in with Sydelle, all public evidence of their mother had disappeared. But what had happened to the grandmother? She remembered, years ago, on her first birthday in New Jersey, asking her father. "Where's Grandma Ella? Did she send me something?" A shadow had crossed her father's face. "I'm sorry," he'd said—or at least, that's what Maggie'd thought he'd said. "She can't come." And then, the next year, she remembered asking the same question and getting a different answer. "Grandma Ella's in a home."

"Well, so are we," said Maggie, who didn't understand what the big deal was.

But Rose knew. "Not this kind of home," she said, looking at her father, who gave her a nod. "In a home for old people." And that had been the end of that. But still, home or not, their grandmother had sent these cards. So why hadn't Maggie and Rose ever received them?

She wondered whether the cards were all the same, and selected another one from the stack, this one from 1982, addressed to Miss Rose Feller. This one wished Rose a happy Chanukah, and was signed the same way—"I love you, I miss you, I hope you're well, love, Grandma (Ella)." And another bill, a twenty, this time, which joined the ten in Maggie's pocket.

Grandma. Ella, she thought to herself. What had happened? Her mother had died, and there'd been a funeral. The grandmother would have been there for sure. Then they'd moved, from Connecticut to New Jersey, within a month of their mother's death, and as carefully as Maggie searched her memory, she couldn't remember seeing or hearing from the grandmother ever again.

Her eyes were still closed when she heard the garage-door opener churn into life, followed by car doors slamming. She added the Rose card to the money in her pocket and jumped to her feet.

"Maggie?" called Sydelle, her heels clicking on the kitchen floor.

"Almost done," Maggie yelled. She put the box back on the shelf and walked downstairs, where her father and Sydelle were unloading grocery bags full of various sprouts and whole grains.

"Stay for dinner," her father offered, kissing her cheek as she shrugged on her coat. "We're making . . ." He paused and squinted at one of the bags.

"Quinoa," said Sydelle, pronouncing the word with faux-Latino verve—*keen-wah!*

"No thanks," said Maggie, doing the buttons slowly, watching her father put groceries away. Hard to believe he'd once been handsome. But she'd seen pictures of him when he was younger, before his hairline had relocated to the center of his scalp and his face had sagged into a mass of wrinkles and resignation. And sometimes, from behind, or when he moved a certain way, she could look at the set of his shoulders and the shape of his face and see someone who'd been good-looking enough for a woman as beautiful as her mother to love. She wanted to ask her father about the cards, only not in front of Sydelle, because she knew that Sydelle would manage to change the subject from the mysterious grandmother to exactly what Maggie was doing going through their closet in the first place.

"Hey, Dad," she began. Sydelle zipped by her, heading toward the pantry with cans of the same brand of ultrabland, all-natural, salt-and-taste-free soup she'd found in Rose's kitchen. "Do you want to have lunch with me one day this week?"

"Sure," said her father—at the same instant when Sydelle asked, "How's that job hunt going, Maggie?"

"Fine!" she said brightly. *Bitch,* she thought.

Sydelle arranged her coral-painted lips into a bright, fake smile. "Glad to hear it," she said, turning her back on Maggie, heading back toward the pantry. "You know that we only want the best for you, Maggie, and we've been concerned . . ."

Maggie grabbed her purse. "Gotta go," she said. "Places to go, people to do!"

"Call me!" said her father. Maggie gave a brief, distracted wave and got into Rose's car, where she pulled out the card and the money and studied them to make sure that they were still there, that she hadn't made them up, that they'd said what she thought they'd said. *Grandma.* Rose would know what to do about it. Except when Maggie got home, Rose was packing. "I'm going to the office to finish up a brief. I'll be home late, and I'm leaving early in the morning. Business trip," she'd said, in her bossy, self-important way, rushing around with her suits and her laptop. Well, when Rose came home, they'd put their heads together and figure out the Mystery of the Missing Grandmother.

EIGHTEEN

On Monday morning, Simon Stein stood in the lobby of Rose's apartment building, wearing khaki pants and loafers, a Lewis, Dommel, and Fenick polo shirt with the firm's logo embossed on its chest, and a Lewis, Dommel, and Fenick baseball cap on his head. Rose hurried out of the elevator and walked right past him.

"Hey!" Simon said, waving.

"Oh," said Rose, running her hands through her wet hair. "Hi." The morning had gotten off to a terrible start. When she'd reached under the bathroom sink for her tampons, she'd found an empty box, bearing only plastic wrappers and the rattling remnants of a single tampon applicator. "Maggie!" she'd yelled. And Maggie, who'd been asleep, had rummaged through her purse and tossed Rose a single Slender Regular by way of consolation. "Where did all my Supers go?" Rose had demanded. Maggie had just shrugged. Rose would have to buy more at the airport, assuming she could shake Simon Stein for long enough, and . . .

". . . forward to this," Simon was saying, merging onto the highway.

"I'm sorry?"

"I said, I'm really looking forward to this," he said. "Aren't you?"

"Oh, I guess," said Rose. In fact, she wasn't looking forward to it at all. She'd spent weeks dreaming about being alone with Jim, in a city where nobody knew them, away from everyone at the firm. They'd have a wonderful romantic dinner somewhere . . . or maybe they'd just order room service. Stay in. Get reacquainted. And now she was stuck with Simon Stein, Boy Wonder.

"Do you think they picked us because we're good examples of young associates, or because they want to get rid of us?" she asked.

"Oh," said Simon, steering the car into the long-term parking lot, "me they picked because I'm a good example. You, they're just trying to get rid of."

"What?"

"Just kidding," he said, and gave her an impish smile. Revolting, thought Rose. Grown men should not look impish.

They got to the gate a full forty-five minutes before boarding would commence. *Perfect*, thought Rose, and dropped her stuff on a chair. "Listen, I'm just going to run to the newsstand," she said, and was relieved when Simon nodded and opened up a copy of *ESPN: The Magazine*. It was ridiculous, she knew, but she'd never been one of those women who could simply plop a box of Kotex Super Plus on top of her lettuce and turkey breast at the grocery store and stand, unflinching, as some teenage guy scanned her groceries. No indeed. Her tampons had to be purchased at the same CVS, and she'd lurk in the aisles until she could be guaranteed no line and a female clerk. It was no big deal, she knew (and certainly Amy and Maggie had told her), but for some reason she was always embarrassed buying them. Probably because when she got her period, her father had been so completely freaked out he'd left her in the bathroom, bleeding onto wadded-up toilet paper, for three hours, until Sydelle returned from her Jazzercise class with a box of sanitary napkins. Maggie, she remembered, had waited patiently on the other side of the door, pumping Rose for information.

"What's going on in there?" she'd asked.

"I've become a woman," Rose had replied from her perch on the edge of the bathtub. "Yay me."

"Oh," Maggie said. "Well, congratulations." And, Rose remembered, Maggie had tried to shove a *People* magazine underneath the door and had actually baked her a cake, thick with chocolate frosting, with "Congradulations Rose" written on top. True, their father had been too mortified to eat a bite, and Sydelle had made unpleasant noises about the fat grams and the misspelling, but it had been nice.

On the airplane, she shoved her bag into the overhead compartment, fastened her seat belt, and stared out the window, nibbling at her mixed nuts, trying to ignore her growling stomach, thinking that if she hadn't been so busy trying to make her brief as Jim-pressive as possible, or running around playing Guess What Maggie's Taken Now, she'd have had time to buy a bagel. Simon, meanwhile, had reached under his seat and retrieved a small box-shaped nylon pouch. He unzipped it with a flourish.

"Here," he said.

Rose glanced to her left and saw that he was holding a seed-studded roll.

"Nine-grain," he said. "From Le Bus. I've got an eleven-grain one."

"In case nine grains aren't enough?" Rose asked. She stared at him curiously, then accepted the roll, which was still warm and, all things considered, delicious. A minute later, he tapped her arm and offered her a wedge of cheese.

"What is this?" she finally asked. "Did your Mom pack you lunch?"

Simon shook his head. "My mother's lunches were nothing like this. She's not a morning person. So every morning, she'd, like, stagger down the stairs . . ."

"Stagger?" asked Rose, readying herself to produce the necessary sympathy if Simon started in on some dreary tale about his mother's drinking problem.

"She's not really graceful under the best circumstances, and especially not when she's half asleep. So she'd stagger downstairs and grab the economy-size loaf of generic white Wonder bread, and whatever lunch meat had been on sale, and a five-pound tub of margarine." Rose could almost picture his mother, in a ratty nightgown and bare feet, standing in front of the kitchen counter, performing this detested chore. "So she'd slap down the bread, and then she'd spread the margarine, or try to, but the margarine was cold, so usually it wasn't very spreadable, and the bread would rip, and you'd get these sandwiches with, like, lumps of margarine in them, and then she'd slap down a wad of lunch meat"—Simon performed the slapping motion—"and she'd put the other slice of bread on top, and shove the sandwich in a Baggie, and put it in a brown paper bag with some bruised fruit and a handful of peanuts in shells. And that was lunch. And that," he concluded, pulling a brownie from his bag and offering Rose half of it, "explains me."

"How does it explain you?"

"You grow up in a house where nobody cares about food, and you either end up not caring about food yourself, or probably caring too much." He gave his belly an affectionate pat. "Guess which one I am. How were your school lunches?"

"It would depend," Rose said.

"On what?"

Rose bit her lip. School lunches, for her, had fallen into three categories. Her mother's happy lunches were beautiful affairs—the sandwiches with crusts neatly cut off, the carrots peeled and cut into sticks of equal length, the apple washed, a paper napkin folded at the bottom of the bag, sometimes containing fifty cents for an ice-cream sandwich and a note reading "Have a treat on me." Then there were the deteriorating lunches. The crusts would stay on the bread. The carrots wouldn't be peeled—one time, her mother had put a whole carrot into her lunch bag, with the green fronds still on top. She'd forget napkins, forget milk money, sometimes forget the sandwich altogether. Once, Rose remembered, Maggie had caught her at her locker, looking dismayed. "Look," she'd said, and showed Rose that her lunch bag contained nothing except, inexplicably, her mother's checkbook. Rose had looked inside her own bag and found a crumpled leather glove.

"We got hot lunch, mostly," she told Simon. Which was true.

She'd had two years of her mother's lunches, good and bad, followed by the third category—ten years of steam-table pizza and mystery meat and Sydelle's offers of Lean Cuisine and chopped salad, which Rose usually turned down.

Simon sighed. "I would have killed for hot lunch. Anyhow," he said, his face brightening, "do you think this will be fun?"

"Do you remember what you were like as a first-year law student?"

Simon considered. "Insufferable," he said.

"Right. Me, too. So I think we can safely assume that the vast majority of these kids are going to be just as obnoxious as we were."

"Ah." said Simon. He reached into his briefcase and pulled out a handful of magazines. "Reading material?"

Rose considered a copy of *Cook's Illustrated,* then picked up something called *The Green Bag.* "What's this?"

"A fun legal journal," said Simon.

"As if," Rose said. She turned back toward the window, closed her eyes hoping that Simon would leave her alone, and feeling relieved when he did.

The first candidate blinked at Rose and Simon, repeating Simon's last question. "My goals?" she asked. She was disgustingly young and fresh-faced in her black suit as she stared at Rose and Simon in a way that was probably meant to be assertive but instead just made her look nearsighted. "I want to be sitting where you are five years from now."

Only with better feminine protection, Rose thought. For the past ten minutes she'd had the distinct feeling that the airport tampon wasn't getting the job done.

"Tell us why you're interested in Lewis, Dommel, and Fenick," Simon prompted.

"Well," she began confidently, "I'm very impressed by your firm's commitment to pro bono work . . ."

Simon glanced at Rose and made a check mark on the piece of paper they were using to keep score.

". . . and I respect the partners' understanding that there should be balance between work and family commitments . . ."

Simon made a second check mark.

"And," the young woman concluded, "I think Boston would be a wonderful city to work in."

Rose and Simon stared at each other, mid-check-mark. *Boston?*

The candidate stared at them uncertainly. "There's so much to do there! So much history!"

"True," said Simon, "but we're actually located in Philadelphia."

The young woman gulped. "Oh," she said.

"There's lots to do in Philadelphia, too," said Rose, thinking that this was something she would have done as a law student—scheduled so many interviews that all of the firms would have run together in one great big, family-friendly, committed-to-pro-bono blur.

"Tell us about yourself," Rose prompted the red-haired guy sitting across from her.

He sighed. "Well," he began, "I got married last year."

"That's great," said Simon.

"Yeah," the guy said bitterly, "except she told me last night that she's leaving me for our Criminal Law professor."

"Oh, dear," Rose murmured.

" 'He's advising me on my paper,' she told me. Okay, I wasn't suspicious. Would you have been suspicious?" he demanded, glaring at Simon and Rose.

"Um," said Simon. "Well, I'm not married."

The law student slumped in his suit. "Look, you've got my résumé," he said. "If you're interested, you know where to find me."

"Yeah," whispered Simon, as the guy left the room and the next candidate entered, "in the bushes outside the professor's apartment building with night-vision goggles and a mayonnaise jar to pee in."

•   •   •

"I began my legal career out of disgust," began the thin-lipped brunette. "Do you remember the case of the hot McNugget?"

"No," said Rose.

"Not really," said Simon.

The law student shook her head and stared at them scornfully. "A woman, through the drive-through of McDonald's, orders McNuggets. The McNuggets arrive, fresh from the fryer. They're hot. The woman bites into a McNugget, burns her lip, sues McDonald's for failing to inform her that the McNuggets would be dangerously hot, and wins hundreds of thousands of dollars. I was disgusted." She glared at them both to highlight her disgust. "Rewards like that create the cancer of litigiousness that's infecting America."

"You know, my uncle had that," Simon said sadly. "Cancer of litigiousness. Nothing much you can do for it, either."

The woman glared at them. "I'm serious!" she said. "Frivolous lawsuits are a terrible problem for the legal profession." Simon nodded attentively, and Rose stifled a yawn as the woman spent fifteen minutes giving them pertinent examples, cases, decisions, and footnotes, until she stood up abruptly, smoothing her skirt.

"Good day," she said, and marched out the door.

Rose and Simon stared at each other, then burst out laughing.

"Oh, dear," said Rose.

"I believe we have a winner," said Simon. "The Hot McNugget. That's what we're calling her. Agreed?"

"I don't know," said Rose. "What about the guy who spit when he talked? Or Miss Boston?"

"I was dying to tell her that she wouldn't like Boston, because it's not much of a college town, but she didn't look like someone who enjoyed *Spinal Tap,*" he said. "And now I'm feeling somewhat remiss, because we didn't ask any of them how they feel about alternative sports." He shook his head in mock despair. "I don't think we can go back to Philadelphia."

"The guy with the ex-wife looked like he's got a snowboard in his garage."

"Yeah," said Simon, "right next to his crossbow. And how about that blonde?"

Rose bit her lip. "That blonde" had been their second-to-last applicant. Mediocre grades and no experience to speak of, but she was gorgeous.

"I think some of the partners would have appreciated her," Simon said dryly. Rose winced. Did he mean Jim?

"Anyhow," said Simon, gathering his papers into the inevitable Lewis, Dommel, and Fenick folder. "What do you feel like for dinner?"

"Room service," said Rose, getting to her feet.

Simon looked dismayed. "Oh, no, no, we have to go out to eat somewhere! Chicago's got great restaurants!"

Rose gave him what she hoped was a kind look. "I'm really tired," she said, which was true. Also, she had cramps. And she wanted to be in her hotel room for Jim, who, in lieu of his presence, had offered her the consolation prize of a phone call. Was phone sex hard to do, she wondered? Could she pull it off, without sounding like one of those sleazy ads on late-night cable, or, alternately, like she was reading from the Clinton/Lewinsky depositions?

"Your loss," said Simon. He raised his hand in a salute, pushed his folder into a Lewis, Dommel, and Fenick tote bag (grown men, Rose thought, should not carry tote bags), and was gone, as Rose hurried off to the hotel room, and the telephone, and Jim.

NINETEEN

Maggie made a bet with herself that she could get a job before Rose came back from Chicago. If she had a job, she figured, Rose would be pleased with her, and willing to apply herself to the Case of the Missing Grandmother. So she gave up on the bartending gig and set out with her stack of résumés. Within a day she'd landed a job at the Elegant Paw, a chichi pet-grooming establishment around the corner from Rose's apartment, on a block that boasted two French bistros, a cigar bar, a women's clothing boutique, and a cosmetic store called Kiss and Make Up.

"You like dogs?" asked Bea, the manager, who was wearing overalls and smoking an unfiltered Marlboro as she worked on a shih tzu with a blow dryer.

"Absolutely," Maggie had said.

"And I can see that you like grooming," said Bea, taking in Maggie's tight jeans and tighter sweater. "You'll do fine. You wash the dogs, clip their nails and whiskers, condition their fur, blow them dry. It's eight bucks an hour," she added, picking the shih tzu up by its tail and its collar and depositing it into a plastic pet crate.

"Fine," said Maggie.

Bea handed her an apron, and a bottle of Johnson's baby shampoo, and nodded toward a small and dingy-looking poodle. "You know about the anal glands?"

Maggie stared at her, hoping she'd heard wrong. "Excuse me?"

Bea smiled. "Anal glands," she repeated. "Let me show you." Maggie had watched, revolted, as Bea lifted the dog's tail. "See here?" She pointed at the pertinent area. "Squeeze." She demonstrated. The smell was revolting. Maggie felt like throwing up. Even the poodle looked ashamed of itself.

"Do I have to do this for every dog?" she'd asked.

"Just the ones that need it," said Bea. Like that was some big consolation.

"And how do I tell which ones need it?" Maggie persisted.

Bea laughed. "Check to see if they're swollen," she said. Maggie shuddered, but swallowed hard and tentatively approached her first dog, who looked just as dubious about the whole enterprise as she was.

After eight hours, Maggie had washed sixteen dogs and had sixteen different kinds of dog fur clinging to her sweater.

"Good work," said Bea, nodding her approval as she tied a candy-cane-striped bandana around a sheltie's collar. "Next time wear better shoes. Flats, sneakers. You got shoes like that?"

Well, she didn't, but Rose did. Maggie limped onto the street, shoving her pruney hands into her pocket, glad that at least she'd have the place to herself for the night. She could make a bowl of popcorn and a drink, and there'd be no sister to complain that she was playing the music too loud or wearing too much perfume, or to ask pesky questions about where she was going, and when she'd be back.

Maggie squinted at the space on the street where Rose's car had been . . . a space that was presently occupied by only an iced-over puddle and a few dead leaves.

Okay, maybe it wasn't this space precisely, Maggie thought, trying to calm herself even as her heart started hammering in her chest. Pine Street. It had definitely been Pine Street. She walked to the stop sign by one of the French bistros, crossed at the corner, walked back down the length of the street, past the cigar bar and

Kiss and Make Up, which were both closed for the night, moving from streetlight to streetlight, from lamplit glow to absolute darkness, and still, no car.

She walked to the corner, then back again, underneath the streetlamps decorated with gold tinsel Christmas wreaths, feeling the icy air biting at her neck. It had been Pine Street, she was sure of it . . . except, what if she was wrong? That would be it for Rose, Maggie realized, imagining her sister coming home from Chicago to learn that her car had disappeared. She'd have Maggie out the door and on her way back to Sydelle's house before Maggie could even start explaining. And wasn't this the way her life always worked? One step forward, two steps back. Get an audition at MTV and get tripped up by the TelePrompTer. Get a job and find out that the car's been stolen. Get your foot in the door and have the thing swing shut on your toes. Fuck, she thought, turning in a circle. Fuck, fuck, fuck!

"They get you, too?" A man in a leather jacket was walking toward her. He cocked his thumb at the sign Maggie hadn't noticed until then. "Street cleaning," he said, and shook his head. "They used to just give tickets, but everyone ignored them, so they started towing last week."

Shit. "Where do they take the cars?"

"Impound lot," he said, shrugging. "I'd give you a ride, but . . ." And he looked at the space where his car had presumably been parked with such a mournful expression that Maggie had to laugh. "Come with me," he said. She looked at him, trying to puzzle out his features, but it was dark and he had the hood of his coat pulled up. "I'm just going to grab a quick beer while I wait for my buddy, and then he can run us over there. You got your checkbook?"

"Um . . ." said Maggie. "Will they take a credit card?"

The guy shrugged. "Guess we'll find out," he said.

The guy's name was Grant, and Tim was his buddy, and one beer was actually more like three, plus an Irish coffee that Maggie sipped slowly as she rocked her shoulders to the music and tried not to keep looking at the time while she performed the necessary motions. Cross your legs, lick your lips, twirl a lock of your hair around one finger. Look fascinated, yet somewhat mysterious. Look up from underneath your eyelashes, as if the guy is the most interesting guy you've ever seen, as if what he's saying is the most amazing thing you've ever heard. Pout like a model in an ad for panty hose or push-up bras. Toy with your swizzle stick. Stare at them, then drop your eyes shyly. Maggie could have done it in her sleep. And the guys, of course, had no clue. The guys never did.

"Hey, Monique, you want to come to a party with us once we get the cars back?"

She gave a rote nod, a tiny shrug, and crossed her legs again. Grant laid his hand on her knee, edging it up toward her thigh. "You're so soft," he said. She leaned into him for a second, then edged away. Forward, then back.

"Let's get the cars first. Then we'll see," she said, knowing that as soon as she got the car, she was going straight home. She was tired, and she just wanted to get the car, take a shower, collapse into the comfort of her sister's bed.

It was after ten o'clock when they finally stood up and shrugged into their coats. Grant held out his arm for her. Maggie breathed a quiet sigh of relief and smiled prettily as she let him help her off her barstool and up into Tim's truck. They were on the highway, then off, then on again, somewhere in South Philadelphia, Maggie thought. She thought she could see the Delaware River glimmering in the dark. Finally Tim turned onto a long, twisting road with no lights. Maggie felt an icy fingertip poke her in the chest as the men laughed and sang along to the radio and passed a bottle back and forth over her head. This could get bad, she thought. Where was she? Who were these guys? How could she have been so dumb?

She was trying to form a plan when Tim jerked the truck into a hard right turn, and they bounced alongside a lot full of cars, surrounded by a ghostly pale fence.

"Here we are," he said. Maggie peered into the darkness. There were cars upon cars upon cars . . . dozens of rows of them, burnt-out junkers and shiny new models, and there, right in front, was Rose's little silver Honda. And, at the far end, the dim shapes of guard dogs—German shepherds, Maggie thought—moving slowly along the fence.

Tim opened his door, crunching what sounded like half a roll of breath mints between his teeth. "Office is this way," he said, pointing to a cinderblock shack where light shone through the window. "You two coming?"

Maggie took another look. The gate was open. She could just walk to the car, get in, drive it right through the gate. She slid off the truck seat and onto the ground. "I'm going to get my car," she announced.

"Well, sure. That's what we brought you here for," said Tim.

Maggie bit her lip. The truth was, her license had expired six months ago, and she'd meant to get it renewed, but she kept forgetting. And of course the car was registered in Rose's name, not hers. Chances were, even if they did take her credit card they might not let her leave with the car. She'd have to think of something else.

She rocked her hips, settling her feet into the ground. It was so cold that her cheeks hurt, so cold that the inside of her nose was freezing, and every inch of her body was covered in goose bumps. And then she started walking, like she was walking on hot coals. Not too slow and not too fast.

"Hey!" said Grant, "hey!" She felt, rather then saw, him start to move, and she could see what he had in mind as if a movie screen had suddenly lowered before her eyes. First they'd get the cars, then go back to the bar, where one drink would become three or four or five. Then they'd tell her she couldn't drive, why didn't she come back to their apartment, sit for a while, have some coffee? And the apartment would smell like dirty laundry and underarms, and there'd be pizza boxes on the counter and dishes in the sink. Want to watch a movie? they'd ask, and it would be a naked-girl porno movie, and there'd be a bottle of something, and one of them would look at her with slow glazed eyes, *Hey sweetheart,* he'd say, grinning a slow glazed grin, *Hey, sweetheart, hey, baby, why don't you get comfortable? Why don't you come over here?*

Which was when Maggie started to run.

"Hey!" Grant yelled one more time, sounding seriously pissed. She could hear him panting behind her as her feet beat a swift tattoo on the frozen ground. She remembered a story, the story of Atalanta who did not want to be married, Atalanta who the gods let race for the golden apple, Atalanta who ran faster than all the men, who would have won the race, except she'd gotten tricked. Well, no one would trick her.

A-ta-lan-ta, A-ta-lan-ta, her feet pounded, and her breath came in silvery gasps. She was almost there, was almost there, was so close that if she'd stretched out her fingertips, she could have brushed the driver's side door handle, when Grant grabbed her around the waist and lifted her off of her feet.

"Where you going," he panted into her ear, his breath sour and moist, "where you going so fast?" He slipped one hand up her sweater.

"Hey!" she screamed, flailing her legs, as he held her away from him and laughed, hearing a dog howl in the distance. Tim was running toward them. "C'mon, man, put her down," he said.

"Put me down!" Maggie shrieked.

"Not yet," said Grant, his hand crawling over her chest. "Don't you want to have some fun with us before you go?"

Oh, God, Maggie thought. *Oh, no.* She remembered a night like this from long ago, a night in high school, a party in someone's big backyard. She'd had some beer, and then she'd had some pot, and then someone had given her a cup of sticky brown liquor, and she'd downed that, too, and things had started to get fuzzy. She'd hooked up with a guy, and they'd been lying on the grass, behind a tree, his pants unzipped, her sweater shoved up around her neck, and she'd looked up and there'd been two other guys standing there, staring down at them, holding cans of beer. Standing there, waiting their turns. And at that moment, Maggie had had a sense of how slippery a thing her own power was, how fast it could turn in her hands, like a knife in the sink, slick with soap, how quickly and deeply the blade could cut her. She'd staggered to her feet, making convincing gagging noises. "Sick," she'd gasped, and run into the house with her fingers laced over her mouth, and hidden in the bathroom until four in the morning, when everyone had passed out or gone home. But what would she do now, when there was no bathroom to run to, no party to disappear into, and no one around to save her?

Maggie kicked out as hard as she could and felt her heel connect with the soft muscle of Grant's thigh. He sucked in his breath, and she wriggled out of his arms.

"What the fuck!" she shouted, as Grant glared at her, looking sullen, and Tim stared at the ground. "What the FUCK?!?!" she repeated.

"Cocktease," Grant said.

"Asshole," Maggie jeered. Her hands were shaking so badly that she dropped the keys twice before she managed to get the car door unlocked.

"You've got to pay for that," said Tim, walking toward her slowly with his hands held open, palms up. "They've got your plate numbers . . . They'll send you a ticket in the mail, they'll make you pay all kinds of fines . . ."

"Fuck you," said Maggie. "Stay away from me. My sister's a lawyer. She'll sue you for assault."

"Look," said Tim, "I'm sorry. He had too much to drink . . ."

"Fuck you," said Maggie. She started the car and flicked on the high beams. Grant threw his arms over his eyes. Maggie revved the engine and thought for a minute about how it would feel to just stomp on the gas and squash him like a squirrel. Instead, she took a deep breath, tried to steady her hands on the wheel, and drove out of the gate.

TWENTY

If Maggie had been a regular roommate, the telephone bill would have been the beginning and the end of it, the straw that broke the camel's back. But Maggie was no regular roommate, Rose reminded herself. Maggie was her sister. But when she'd gotten home after two days in Chicago (the flight had been late, her luggage had been lost, the airport overheated and jammed with Christmas travelers) and found the phone bill sitting on the counter, she was astonished to see that it was more than three hundred dollars, a significant increase over her normal forty-dollar bill. The culprit: a two hundred and twenty-seven dollar phone call to New Mexico.

She vowed she wouldn't confront her sister with it as soon as Maggie walked in the door. She'd let Maggie hang her coat up, take her shoes off, and then she'd casually mention that the phone bill had come, and had Maggie made a new friend in Albuquerque? Except that when she went to the bedroom to put her things away she saw that her entire wardrobe was still in a pile on the floor, and that her sheets and pillows had been tossed on top of Mount Fashion. Which meant that Maggie had been sleeping in her bed. And wearing her shoes, Rose thought. And eating her porridge if she'd had porridge to eat.

Rose sat on the couch, fuming, until after midnight, when Maggie sauntered in, smelling like a barroom floor, with something wriggling stuck in her coat.

"You're here!" Maggie said.

"Yes, I am," said Rose. "And so is the phone bill," she said, as Maggie kicked her shoes into the corner and dropped her purse on the couch.

"I brought you something!" Maggie said. Her color was high and her pupils were enormous, and she smelled like whiskey. "Two things, actually," she said, holding two fingers up in the air and opening her coat with a flourish. "Honey Bun Two!" she announced, as a small, crumpet-shaped brown dog dropped to the floor. It had moist brown eyes and a brown leather collar and a face that looked as though somebody had smashed it in with a frying pan.

Rose stared. "Maggie . . . what is that?"

"Honey Bun Two," Maggie repeated, heading to the kitchen. "My gift to you!"

"I can't have dogs in here!" Rose shouted. Meanwhile, the little brown dog had taken a fast tour of Rose's apartment and was now standing in front of her coffee table, looking like a dowager who was displeased with her hotel room.

"You'll have to take it back," said Rose.

"Fine, fine," said Maggie, sauntering back into the living room. "She's just visiting, anyhow."

"Visiting from where?"

"My new job," said Maggie. "I'm now a dog groomer at the Elegant Paw." She sneered at her sister. "I'm employed. I've been working for two days. Are you happy?"

"We need to talk about the phone bill," said Rose, forgetting her plan to be calm and reasonable. "Did you make a phone call to New Mexico?"

Maggie shook her head. "Don't think so."

Rose shoved the bill toward her sister. Maggie stared at it. "Oh, yeah."

"Oh, yeah what?"

"I got my tarot cards read. But God, it was only like half an hour! I didn't think it would cost that much."

"Your tarot cards," Rose repeated.

"It was right before my audition," Maggie mumbled. "I had to find out whether it was an auspicious day for a new job."

"Unbelievable," Rose said to the ceiling.

"Rose, do we have to talk about this right now?" Maggie asked. "I'm really tired. I had a really hard night."

"Oh, sure," said Rose. "After two whole days of work, you must be exhausted."

"Whatever," Maggie said. "And I'll pay you back for the phone bill."

The little dog took one more look at her, then gave a dismissive snort and heaved itself onto the couch, where it began pawing at the pillow, scratching at it with its nails. "Cut that out!" Rose called. The dog ignored her, pawing and poking at the pillow until it was arranged to its satisfaction, then curling up on top of it and falling instantly asleep.

"Maggie!" Rose yelled. There was no answer. The bathroom door stayed closed, and she could hear the shower running and the little dog snoring. "What's the other surprise?" Rose asked. No answer. She stood outside the bathroom door, the phone bill clutched in her hand, before turning away in disgust. Tomorrow morning, she promised herself.

Except the next morning began with what had become a routine event at Rose's apartment—a call from a bill collector.

"Hello, may I speak to Maggie Feller?" the calls would begin. "This is Lisa calling from Lord and Taylor." Or Karen from Macy's, or Elaine from Victoria's Secret. Today, it was Bill from the Gap. At night, Rose would come home and find the answering machine crammed with messages: Strawbridge, Bloomingdale's, Citibank, American Express.

"Maggie!" Rose called. Her sister was curled up on the sofa, and the dog was curled up on a pillow on the floor—a pillow that Rose saw was now brocaded with drool. "Telephone!"

Maggie didn't turn over or open her eyes—she just extended one arm toward the phone. Rose shoved it into her hand and headed to the bathroom, closing the door on Maggie's irate voice spiraling higher and higher, saying, "Yes," and "No," and "I already sent you a check!" When she got out of the shower Maggie was still on the phone, and the dog was gnawing on what Rose was pretty sure was one of her red cowboy boots. "Jesus!" she hissed, and slammed the door as hard as she could.

Rose took the elevator to the lobby and crossed the street, hoping that her car would be in the same general area where she'd left it before her Chicago trip. And there it was, almost exactly where she'd left it. Thank God for small favors, she thought, sliding behind the wheel, when an old man tapped on the glass, startling her so badly that she let out a little scream.

"I wouldn't do that," he said.

"Huh?" said Rose.

"Booted," he said. "Take a look."

Rose got out of the car and walked around to the passenger's side. Sure enough, a bright yellow metal boot had been attached to the front wheel, along with a bright orange notice. "Delinquent?" Rose read. *Maggie,* she thought. *This is Maggie's fault.* She glanced at her watch, figuring she had enough time to run back up to the apartment and get some answers from Miss Maggie. She stormed back through the lobby ("Forget something?" the doorman called at her back), punched the button for the elevator, stared furiously at the mirrored ceiling as the elevator rose, and half-ran down the hall back to her apartment. "Maggie!" she called. No answer. The shower was running. "Maggie!" Rose yelled, pounding on the bathroom door. No answer. Rose turned the doorknob. It was unlocked. She stormed into the bathroom, intending to rip open the shower curtain, never mind that her sister was naked, and get some answers about what the hell was going on. She took one step into the steamy bathroom and stopped. She could make out her sister's silhouette through the plastic of the shower curtain. Her back was to the door, and her forehead was pressed against the tiled wall. More than that—worse than that—she could hear what Maggie was saying. One word, over and over.

"Stupid . . . stupid . . . stupid . . . stupid . . ."

Rose froze in her tracks. Maggie reminded her of a pigeon she'd once seen. She'd been walking to the Wawa on the corner and almost tripped over the pigeon, and instead of looking scared, the bird had glared at Rose with its tiny, hate-filled red eyes. She'd stumbled, almost falling, and when she started walking again, she saw the problem. One of the pigeon's feet was horribly mangled. It was hopping on its one good foot, with the injured one curled up tight against its body.

Rose had thought for a moment that she should try to help it. "Oh," she'd said, and reached out her hand, thinking . . . thinking what? That she'd scoop the filthy thing up, rush it to a vet? The bird had simply glared at her some more before hopping off with a terrible, pathetic wounded dignity.

Maggie was just like that, Rose thought. She was hurt, too, but you couldn't point that out, couldn't offer to help, couldn't say anything that would hint that you knew that Maggie was hurt or flawed or broken, that there were things she couldn't figure out, or fix on her own.

Rose backed out of the bathroom quietly, easing the door shut. *Maggie,* she thought, feeling the familiar mixture of pity and fury tangling in her heart. She walked back to the elevator, through the lobby, out into the sunshine, and caught a cab on the corner. The car, she thought. The phone bill. The bill collectors. The dog. The clothes on the floor, the cosmetics crowding her counter, the "Final Notice" envelopes jammed in her mailbox. Rose closed her eyes. This would have to end. But how?

TWENTY-ONE

Ella had sand in her shoes. She eased them off and rubbed the sole of her foot carefully against the floor of the car, trying to dislodge the grains before putting her shoes back on.

Lewis looked over at her when they pulled up to a red light. "Okay?" he asked.

"Yes," said Ella, and smiled to prove it. They'd gone for a late dinner (late in that it was after seven o'clock), and then they'd gone to a concert—and not one at the Acres Clubhouse, either, but at an honest-to-goodness club, in Miami, with Lewis driving his big car slowly through the steamy, sweet-smelling night.

Now, as Lewis pulled through the residents' gate at Golden Acres, Ella wondered what would happen. If she'd been a younger woman, she'd probably have counted their dates (six so far), calculated how long they'd been seeing each other, and come to the conclusion that Lewis probably wanted Something. Sixty years ago and she'd have been bracing herself for a half-hour of sweaty grappling and fumbling before curfew ended their fun. But what could happen, at her age? After what she'd been through? She'd thought her heart was dead; a withered stump of a thing, incapable of feeling anything, incapable of flowering. At least that was what she'd believed for the years after Caroline's death. But now . . .

Lewis pulled into a parking spot in front of his building. "Would you like to come up? Have some coffee?"

"Oh, I'll be up all night," she said, and giggled like a silly schoolgirl. They rode together in the elevator in silence. Ella thought that maybe she'd been misreading things. Maybe he just wanted to take her up to offer her tea and torment her with pictures of his grandchildren. Or, more likely, he was just looking for a friend, a sympathetic ear, someone who'd listen to stories about his dead wife. Sex was out of the question. He was probably on medication, like everyone else Ella knew. Only what if he had Viagra? Ella bit her lip. She was probably being silly. She was seventy-eight years old. Who'd be in a big hurry to take her to bed, all droopy and wrinkled and age-spotted the way she was?

Lewis was staring at her curiously as he unlocked his door. "You look like you're a million miles away," he said.

"Oh, I . . ." Ella began, unsure of exactly what she intended to say as she followed him inside. His apartment, she could tell, was much bigger than hers, and while hers overlooked the parking lot and the interstate highway beyond it, his faced the ocean.

"Have a seat," he said. Ella planted herself on the couch and felt a trilling note of—of what? Fear? Excitement? He hadn't turned on any lights.

He came back and sat beside her, pressed a warm mug of tea into her hands. Then he got up again and raised the blinds, and Ella saw the water shining in the moonlight. She could see the waves rolling up onto the pale sand. And the windows were so big, and she felt so close to the water, it was like . . .

"It's like being on a ship!" she said. And it was. Even though she hadn't been on a ship in years and years, this was what it had been like. She could almost feel motion, the rocking of the waves, taking her out to sea, far away from what she knew, far away from herself. And when Lewis took her hand, it felt as right as anything she could remember, as right and as natural as the motion of the water coming up onto the sand.

TWENTY-TWO

"She has to get out of my house," Rose said to Amy. They were sitting in a corner of Amy's favorite cafe, sipping iced tea and waiting for their lunches to arrive. Rose had taken a cab to work and spent most of her morning on the phone with the Philadelphia Parking Authority, trying to find out what had happened to her car and how much Maggie's latest stunt would cost her. Then she'd glanced at the clock, groaned, realized that she hadn't gotten any work done yet, and called her apartment. Maggie hadn't picked up. Rose had left a terse message—"Maggie, call me at the office when you get this." By one o'clock there'd been no response, and Rose had met Amy for salads and strategy.

"Remember when she stayed with me for three weeks that time? Remember how I thought that was a living hell? Remember how I swore never again?"

Amy gave a sympathetic nod. "I remember."

Rose winced. She remembered, too, how Amy had stopped by to watch a movie during the week of Maggie's visit, and had discovered the next day that two lipsticks and forty bucks were missing from her purse.

"Look," Amy said, "you've been a good sister to her. You've been more than patient. Has she found a job?"

"She says she has."

"She says," Amy repeated. "And is she giving you money for rent? For groceries? For anything?"

Rose shook her head. The tall, black, gorgeous waitress sauntered over with their plates, dropped them on the table, and sashayed away without appearing to notice Rose's empty water glass.

"Why do we keep coming here?" Rose asked, picking up her fork. "The service is horrible."

"I like to keep my money in the community," said Amy.

"Amy," Rose said patiently, "you aren't in the community." She ate a few bites of her salad, then pushed her plate away. "What am I going to do about Maggie?"

"Kick her to the curb," said Amy, through a mouthful of spinach. "Tell her she gots to get."

"And where's she going to go?"

"Not your problem," Amy said. "Look, I know that sounds cold, but Maggie's not going to starve on the street. And she's not your responsibility. You're her sister, not her mom."

Rose bit her lip. Amy sighed. "I'm sorry," she said. "I'm sorry Maggie's such a wreck. I'm sorry Sydelle's such a nightmare. I'm sorry about your mom. But, Rose, what you're trying to do here . . . it's not going to work. You can't be her mother."

"I know," Rose mumbled. "I just don't know what to do. I mean, I know what I'm supposed to do, I just don't know how to do it."

"Repeat after me: 'Maggie, you need to leave,' " Amy said. "Seriously. She'll go to your father and Sydelle's, and if that doesn't convince her to straighten up and fly right until she's got enough money for a place on her own, nothing will. You can even give her some money—and notice that I'm saying 'give' and not 'lend.' I'll help you, if you want."

"Thanks," said Rose, and got to her feet. "I've got to go."

"And so does Maggie," Amy said. "You need to take care of yourself here." Rose nodded miserably. "Call me if you need help. Call me if you need anything. Let me know what happens."

Rose promised that she would, and headed back to her office.

She checked her messages. Nothing from Maggie, but there was something from Sydelle. "Rose, please call us. Immediately."

So maybe that was where her sister had gone. Rose took a deep breath and dialed. "It's Rose," she said.

"You need to do something about your sister," said Sydelle, proceeding to launch into a recitation of the most recent and egregious of Maggie's abuses. "Do you know we've got bill collectors calling our house at eight in the morning?"

"Me, too," said Rose.

"Well, can't you do something?" Sydelle demanded. "You're a lawyer, can't you tell them it's illegal to call here? Honey, it's no good for your father . . ."

Rose wanted to say that it was no good for her, either—that nothing Maggie ever did was good for anyone but Maggie—but she kept her mouth shut and said she'd do what she could. She hung up the phone and called home again. Still no answer. Now she was getting worried. Maybe Maggie was at work. Sure, she thought sourly. And maybe the judges would be stopping by shortly to crown her Miss America. Rose logged on to her computer and checked her e-mail. Something from a partner asking, quite tersely, when Rose would be done with the draft of her brief. A group e-mail from Simon Stein entitled "Softball Pre-Season Meeting" that Rose deleted without reading.

She got to her feet and began pacing the length of her office. She needed to see Jim, she decided. She needed to see him now. She needed to see him whether he wanted to see her or not. She looked down and noticed with dismay that she was wearing two completely different black loafers—a natural consequence of having her sister dump every shoe she owned onto the floor. *Maggie!* she thought furiously, and, hurrying down the hallway, blew past Jim's secretary ("Hey! He's on a phone call, Rose!") and right into his office.

"Rose? What's going on?" he asked, hanging up the phone and closing the door behind her.

Rose stared down at her mismatched shoes. What was going on was that her apartment was a mess, her life was falling apart, she owed the Parking Authority two hundred dollars, there was a dog living illegally in her living room, and, evidently, she couldn't even dress herself anymore. She needed him to hold her, to cradle her head in his hands and tell her that the two of them were just starting out, and that it might have been a rocky start because of Maggie's omnipresence, but that soon they'd be together again.

"Hey," said Jim, leading her to the leather seat in front of his desk, the one for clients, the sloping Eames chair that canted their butts back and away from his own, assuring that he'd always be taller than they were, no matter what.

Rose stood instead, and took a deep breath. *Summarize,* she told herself. "I miss you," she said.

Jim looked rueful. "I'm sorry, Rose," he said, "but it's been just crazy around here."

Rose felt as if she were on a roller coaster that had just crested a hill that she hadn't seen coming, and now the bottom of her world was falling away. Couldn't he see that she needed him?

He wrapped his arms around her shoulders, but kept her body at a distance. "How can I help?" he murmured. "What can I do?"

"Come over tonight," she said, pressing her lips against his neck, knowing that she was doing the very thing that women were never ever under any circumstances supposed to do—namely, begging. "I need to see you. Please!"

"It might be late," he said. "Like, ten or so."

"It's okay if you're late. I'll wait for you." *I'll wait forever,* she thought, and let herself out of the office. His secretary glared at her.

"You can't just walk right *in,*" said the secretary. "You have to be *announced.*"

"I'm sorry," said Rose, feeling as though she'd done nothing but apologize all day long. "I am. I'm sorry."

TWENTY-THREE

Rose's phone was ringing again. Maggie ignored it. She dropped her towel on the living room floor and walked into the shower. It was her third shower of the morning. Maggie had taken lots of showers in the day following her up-close and personal encounter with the dynamic duo of Grant and Tim, spending ten, twenty, thirty minutes scrubbing herself with her loofah, washing her hair until it squeaked. And she still felt dirty. Dirty and furious. All these weeks on Rose's couch, and what did she have to show for herself? No money. No man. No head shots. Nothing, nothing, nothing. Just assholes who'd grab her in parking lots like she was nothing. Like she wasn't even real.

She heard her sister's voice blatting from the answering machine. "Maggie, are you there? Pick up if you're there. I really need to talk to you. Maggie . . ."

She wrapped herself in a towel, palmed the condensation off the mirror, ignoring her sister's voice on the answering machine, and looked at herself. Weapon One, as always, was her body, and it was finer than a gun, sharper than a knife. She'd find those guys again. She'd haunt the city until she found them, at a bar or on the bus. Somewhere. She'd walk over to them, head held high, chest thrust out, and smile. The smile would be the hardest part, but she was sure that she could manage it. She was an actress. She was a star. She would smile and lay her hand between Tim's shoulder blades, ask how he was doing. She'd sip her drink, leaving lipstick half-kisses on the rim, and brush her knee against his. She'd lean close and whisper that she'd had a great time that night, that she was sorry she'd run away, and could they maybe do it again? Were they free tonight? And they'd bring her back to the apartment. And then it would be Weapon Two. Maybe a knife. A gun, if she could find one. Something that would cause them permanent damage, something that would show them that she was not a girl to be fucked with.

The phone rang again. "Maggie, I know you're there. Would you please pick up the phone? I just got off the phone with the parking people again, and they say the car was taken out of an impound lot and there's a bunch of fines . . ."

Maggie ignored the phone and cranked up the stereo—Axl Rose wailing "Welcome to the Jungle." "Do you know where you are?" he squealed. She shoved her feet into Rose's newest acquisition, a pair of knee-high black leather boots that hugged her calves. Two hundred and sixty-eight dollar boots, and her sister could buy them without a second thought, because nothing ever went wrong for Rose. Oh, no. Rose wouldn't get tripped up by a TelePrompTer, Rose would never park on the wrong side of the street, Rose wouldn't have assholes groping at her in parking lots, and Rose certainly never would have to take a job that involved squeezing dogs' asses just to make ends meet. Rose had everything, and Maggie had nothing. Nothing at all, except for the little dog who'd been dumped at the Elegant Paw for months until Maggie had rescued her and taken her home.

Naked except for the boots, she paced back and forth from the bedroom to the living room to the kitchen and back again, hearing the squeak of the soles against the hardwood floors, smelling the leather and the soap and sweat from her body, seeing a red fog. Seeing the knife. Seeing herself flashing in the mirror as she stalked past the bathroom, flushed and wet and lovely—a clever disguise, a flower with creamy petals on long-stemmed legs. Nobody looking at her would ever suspect what she really was.

The intercom buzzed. The dog whined. "Don't worry," Maggie said, and yanked a T-shirt over her head. She thought about panties for a minute, then figured, why bother? It was eight o'clock—too early for Rose to be home and start lecturing her again. It was probably only the asshole next door telling her to turn her music down.

She turned out the lights and flung the door open, eyes blazing, prepared to give someone a piece of her mind, and saw Rose's boyfriend standing before her.

"Rose?" he said, squinting at her through the darkness. And Maggie laughed—a brief giggle at first, but the laughter kept rolling up her throat like poison, like throwing up in reverse. She wasn't Rose. She would never be Rose. She lacked her sister's abilities, her sister's easy successes. She'd never be the one to offer advice, to poke and prod and scold and lay down rules and offer cheesy sympathy laced with impatience. Rose. Hah! She threw back her head and let the laughter come. "Not hardly," she finally said.

He looked her up and down, his eyes lingering on her boots, on the span of bare thigh, on her breasts. "Is Rose home?" he asked.

Maggie shook her head and gave him a slow, saucy smile. A plan was forming in her brain. Revenge, she thought, the blood pounding in her temples. *Revenge.* "Would you like to come in and wait for her?" she asked. Jim stared at her, his eyes licking her up and down, and Maggie could practically read his mind. She was Rose, only improved, amplified, digitally perfected; Rose, only a thousand times better.

He shook his head. Maggie leaned against the doorframe insolently.

"Let me guess," she said in a rich, taunting voice. "You're looking to upgrade from ground chuck to filet."

Jim shook his head again, still staring at her.

"Or maybe," Maggie continued, "you want both of us. Is that it? A sister sandwich?"

He stared at her, trying to look outraged, but she could tell from the expression that had flickered across his face just how appealing he found that idea.

"Well, you'll have to wait," said Maggie. "Nobody home but little old me." She reached down, grabbed the hem of her T-shirt, pulled it up over her head, arching her back so that her breasts almost brushed his chest. He groaned. She took a short step forward, closing the distance between them. His hands closed over her breasts, and she was sucking at his neck with her hot, avid mouth.

"No," he whispered, even as his arms were wrapping around her.

"Don't," she said, and wrapped one naked leg around him, pressing herself against him.

"Don't what?"

And now she lifted her other leg so that she was twined around him like a snake, and he moaned as he lifted her and carried her inside. "Don't tell me no."

By the time she made it back to her apartment building, it was almost nine o'clock, and the elevator was crowded. Rose wedged herself into the last available bit of space and tried to ignore the suffocating perfume of the woman next to her.

"I swear, either I'm going crazy, or there's a dog in this building," the woman announced to the elevator at large.

Rose stared at her feet.

"I don't know who'd be inconsiderate enough to have a pet here," the woman continued. "There are people with terrible allergies."

Rose glanced up desperately at the floor indicator. Third floor. Thirteen to go.

"People are unbelievable," the woman continued. "They just don't care! Tell them what the rules are, and they say, 'Oh, well, those are rules for other people. Not for me. Because I'm *special.*'"

Finally, the scent-drenched lady got off the elevator, and Rose arrived at her floor. Walking down the hallway, she hoped that her sister would be home, and began rehearsing her speech. *Maggie, we need to discuss things. The dog has to go. The calls have to stop. I need my apartment back. I need my shoes back. I need my life back.*

She turned her key, opened the door, and walked into pitch darkness. She heard voices, a giggle, the little dog's whine.

"Maggie?" she called. There was a tie flung over the sofa. Oh, great, she thought bleakly. Now she's bringing guys home to my apartment. And doing God knows what with them on my bed. "Maggie!" she yelled, and walked into the bedroom. And there was her sister, on the bed, absolutely naked except for Rose's new Via Spiga boots, below a naked Jim Danvers.

"Oh, no," said Rose. She stood, staring, trying to make sense of what she was seeing. "No," she whispered. Maggie rolled out from beneath Jim and stretched languidly, giving her sister a long look at her slender back, her perfect little butt, her long, smooth legs rising from the black leather boots, before plucking Jim's T-shirt off the floor, pulling it over her head, and strutting out of the room, into the hall, as if it were a catwalk, as if there were an audience of thousands, with flashbulbs and notepads, all of them waiting for her. Jim shot Rose a desperately shamed look and yanked up the blankets.

Rose clapped her hand over her mouth, turned and ran to the bathroom, where she threw up into the sink. She ran water until she'd washed the remains of her lunch down the drain. Then she splashed her face, scrubbed her hair back with wet, shaking hands, and went back to the bedroom. Jim had his boxer shorts on, and was scrambling to pull on the rest of his clothes. Rose saw his retainer glinting on her bedside table.

"Get out," she said.

"Rose," he said, and reached for her hands.

"Get out and take her with you. I don't want to see either one of you ever again."

"Rose," he said.

"Get out! Get out! Get out!" She could hear her voice, spiraling up into a shriek. She reached for something to throw at him—a lamp, a candle, a book. Her hand wrapped around a bottle of massage oil, scented with sandalwood. Open. Capless. Recently used, no doubt, and bought with Maggie's credit card, another bill her sister would never pay. She threw it as hard as she could, wishing that it were glass, that it would break up and cut him. Instead, it bounced harmlessly off his shoulder and rolled on the floor, dribbling oil as it rolled beneath her bed.

"I'm sorry," Jim muttered, without meeting her eyes.

"I'm SAW-REE," Rose parroted. "Oh, you're sorry, huh? And so that makes it okay?" She stared at him, shaking. "How could you? How could you?"

She ran through the living room, where Maggie sat on the couch, channel surfing, and into the kitchen. She pulled out a trash bag and started filling it with everything she could find that belonged to either one of them. She snatched Maggie's lighter and cigarettes from the coffee table and threw them in. She picked up Jim's briefcase and hurled it against the wall as hard as she could, hearing a satisfying crack as something inside of it broke. She went to the bathroom and gathered up Maggie's stockings and bras, wisps of black and cream-colored synthetic satin, lined up on the shower curtain rack, and shoved them into the garbage bag, too. Back in the bedroom, Jim was pulling on his pants. Rose ignored him, grabbing Maggie's *Fifty Great Résumés* workbook. Maggie's nail polish and nail polish remover, her tubes and tins and pots of blush, foundation, mascara, hair mousse, her tiny tank tops and skintight jeans and knockoff Doc Martens from Payless. "Get out, get out, get out," she muttered under her breath, dragging the garbage bag behind her.

"Talking to yourself, Rosie Posey?" Maggie called. The words were ice-cold, but Maggie's voice was shaking. "You shouldn't do that. It makes you sound crazy."

Rose picked up a sneaker and threw it at her sister's head. Maggie ducked. The shoe bounced off the wall. "Get out of my house," Rose said. "You aren't welcome."

Maggie hooted. "Not welcome? Well, isn't that too bad."

She strolled into the bathroom. Breathing hard, sweating, Rose pulled the bag into her bedroom. Jim had gotten into his clothes, but his feet were still bare.

"I don't suppose it would do any good to say that I am sorry." He had gone from looking stricken to just plain sheepish.

"Save it for someone who cares," Rose snarled.

"Well, I want to say it anyhow." He cleared his throat. "I'm sorry, Rose. You deserve better."

"Asshole," she said, in a dead voice that surprised her, and scared her, and reminded her of someone else, from years and years ago. She felt as if this were all happening at a great distance, or to somebody else. "With my sister," she said. "My sister."

"I'm sorry," Jim said again. Maggie, who was now standing hip-sprung in the hallway, and who'd gotten herself dressed in painted-on jeans and spaghetti-strapped top, said nothing.

"You know the really pathetic part? I could have loved you. And Maggie won't even remember your name," she said to Jim. She felt the words, hateful forbidden words, words she'd never spoken before, bubbling up in her chest. She thought that maybe she should try to stop them, and then she thought, why? Had the two of them tried to stop themselves? "See, Maggie's very pretty, but she's not very bright." She turned, slowly, tucking her hair behind her ears. "In fact, Jim, if I were a betting woman, I'd say that she can't even spell it right now. Three letters long," she said, stabbing three fingers into the air. "And she can't do it. Want to ask her? Huh? Hey, Maggie, you want to give it a try?"

From behind her, she heard Maggie gasp.

"You're an asshole," she continued steadily, turning back to Jim, pinning him with her eyes. "And you," she said, turning to face her sister. Maggie's face was pale, her eyes were enormous. "I always knew you didn't have a brain. Now I know you don't have a heart."

"Fat pig," Maggie muttered.

Rose laughed. She dropped the bag and laughed. She rocked

back on her heels and laughed until tears spurted out of the corners of her eyes.

"She's crazy," Maggie said loudly.

"Fat . . . pig . . ." Rose gasped. "My God," she said, pointing at Jim. "You're a cheater, and you . . ." She pointed at Maggie, groping for the right word. "You're my sister," she finally said. "My *sister*. And the worst thing you can say about me is 'fat pig'?"

She lifted the bag, twirled it, tied the top into a knot, and heaved it as hard as she could at the door. "Get out," she said. "I never want to see either one of you again."

Rose spent most of the night on her hands and knees, scrubbing, trying to remove every trace of Maggie and Jim from her apartment. She yanked the sheets and pillowcases and comforters off her bed, dragged them to the laundry room, and doused them in two cups of detergent. She washed her kitchen and bathroom floors with Pine-Sol and warm water. She mopped the hardwood floors in her living room and bedroom and hall. She scrubbed the bathtub with Lysol, then scrubbed the tile shower walls with an antibacterial antimildew spray. The little dog watched for a while, following her from room to room, as if Rose were the new cleaning lady and the dog were a distrustful matron, then yawned and resumed its nap on the sofa. By four in the morning, Rose's mind was still whirling, and the one thing she could see clearly when she closed her eyes was a picture of her sister, in Rose's own new boots, churning her body up and down above Jim, who lay in the bed with a glazed, blissful look in his eyes.

She pulled on a clean nightgown, got into bed, and yanked the clean sheets up to her chin with an angry jerk of her wrists. Then she shut her eyes, breathing hard. She thought that she'd managed to tire herself out. She thought she might sleep.

Instead, she closed her eyes and fell headlong into the memory she knew was there, hiding, crouched and waiting for her. The memory of the worst night of her life, which had also starred Maggie.

• • •

It was an early day, a teachers' in-service, and it was just after noon on a late-May day when school let out. Rose had collected her books from her locker and met Maggie outside the first-grade classroom, checking to make sure that her sister had her own backpack. Maggie did. She also had a familiar-looking piece of pink paper in one hand.

"Again?" asked Rose, and held out her hand for the note from Maggie's teacher. She read it while Maggie walked ahead of her, toward the path behind the elementary school that would lead them home.

"Maggie, you can't bite people," Rose said.

"She started it," her sister called back sullenly.

"It doesn't matter," said Rose. "Remember what Mom said? You have to learn to use your words."

She hurried to catch up with her sister, huffing slightly beneath the weight of her backpack. "Did it bleed?" she asked Maggie.

Maggie nodded. "I could have bitten it off," she bragged, "if Miss Burdick wasn't looking."

"Why would you want to bite off someone's nose?"

Maggie pursed her lips even tighter. "She made me mad."

Rose shook her head. "Maggie, Maggie, Maggie," she said, the way she'd heard her mother saying it. "What are we going to do with you?"

Maggie rolled her eyes, then looked at her sister. "Will I be on punishment?" she asked.

"I don't know," said Rose.

Maggie pursed her lips. "It's Megan Sullivan's sleep-over party."

Rose shrugged. She knew all about the sleep-over party. Maggie had had her pink Barbie suitcase packed for days.

"Did you get any library books?" Rose asked, and Maggie nodded, and pulled *Goodnight Moon* from her backpack.

"That's a little kid book," Rose said.

Maggie glared at her sister. It was true, but she didn't care.

"Good night, mittens on the chair. Good night, people, everywhere," she whispered, and started skipping down the path.

The path ended behind the McIlheneys' yard. Rose and Maggie skirted the swimming pool and the deck, crossed the McIlheneys' front yard, then crossed the street to their house, which was a twin of the McIlheneys'—a twin, really, of every house on the street. Two stories, three bedrooms, red brick, and black shutters, and square green lawns, like houses in a little kid's coloring book.

"Wait up!" Rose yelled, as Maggie skipped across the street and dashed up their gravel driveway toward the front door. "You're not supposed to cross the street yourself! You're supposed to hold my hand!"

Maggie ignored her, hurrying ahead, pretending she couldn't hear. "Mom!" she called, setting her key down on the counter and sniffing to see what was for lunch. "Hey, Mom! We're home!"

Rose walked through the front door and set the backpack down. The house was silent, and she could tell even before Maggie told her that their mother wasn't home.

"Her car's not here!" Maggie reported breathlessly. "And I looked under the apple magnet, and there's no note."

"Maybe she forgot it was an early day," Rose said. Except she'd reminded her mother that morning, sneaking into the gloomy bedroom, whispering *Mom? Hey, Mom?* Her mother had nodded when Rose said they'd be home early, but she hadn't opened her eyes. *Be a good girl, Rose,* she'd said. *Take care of your sister.* It was the same thing she said every morning—when she said anything at all.

"Don't worry," said Rose. "She'll be back by three." Maggie looked worried. Rose took her hand. "Come on," she said. "I'll make you lunch."

Rose made eggs, which was nice, even though she wasn't supposed to, because they weren't allowed to turn on the stove. "Don't worry," Rose told Maggie. "You can double check me to make sure I turned it off."

Then it was one-thirty. Maggie wanted to cut through the backyard to play at her friend Natalie's house, but Rose thought it would be better if they stayed and waited for their Mom to come home. So they sat in front of the television and watched Heckle and Jeckle cartoons for half an hour (Maggie's choice), then educational *Sesame Street* (Rose's).

At three o'clock their mother still hadn't come home. "She probably just forgot," said Rose, but now she was starting to worry, too. The day before she'd heard her mother on the telephone. "Yes!" she was shouting at someone. "Yes!" Rose had edged right up to the closed bedroom door and pressed her ear against it. It had been months since she'd heard her mother speak in anything more than a drowsy, distracted mumble. But now she was yelling, each word hard and distinct as a pane of glass. "I. Am. Taking. My. Medication," her mother said. "For God's sake, let it go! Let me be! I'm fine! Fine!"

Rose closed her eyes. Her mother wasn't fine. She knew it, and her father did, too, and probably whoever her mother was screaming at knew it, too.

"It's okay," she told her sister again. "Can you find Mom's red phone book? We have to call Dad."

"Why?"

"Just find it, okay?"

Maggie came running with the book. Rose found her father's office number and dialed carefully. "Yes, may I speak to Mr. Feller, please?" she asked, in a voice at least an octave higher than her normal husky one. "This is his daughter Rose Feller calling." She waited, her face still, the telephone pressed to her ear, her little sister standing beside her. "Oh. I see. All right. No. Just tell him we'll see him later. Thank you. Okay. Good-bye."

She set the phone down.

"What?" asked Maggie. "What?"

"He's out," Rose said. "The lady she didn't know when he'd be back."

"But he'll be home for dinner. Right?" asked Maggie, her voice spiraling higher and higher and ending in a squeak. Her face was pale, her eyes were enormous, as if the prospect of having both parents go missing was more than she could take. "Right?"

"Of course," said Rose, and then did something that let Maggie know that there was really, actually something to be afraid of—she handed her sister the remote control and walked out of the room.

Maggie trailed her.

"Go away," said Rose. "I have to think."

"I can think, too," said Maggie. "I can help you think."

Rose took off her glasses and polished them on the edge of her shirt. "Maybe we should see if there's anything missing."

"Like a suitcase?"

Rose nodded. "Like that."

The girls hurried upstairs, opening their parents' bedroom door, and looking inside. Rose braced herself for the usual wreckage—tangled sheets, pillows on the floor, a collection of half-empty glasses and half-eaten pieces of toast on the bedside table. But the bed was neatly made. The dresser drawers were all closed. On the bedside table, Rose found a pair of earrings, a bracelet, a watch, and a plain gold band. She shuddered, then slipped the ring in her pocket before Maggie could see, and could start asking questions about why their mother had cleaned her room and taken off her wedding ring.

"Suitcase is here!" said Maggie, bounding happily out of the closet.

"Good," said Rose, through lips that felt frozen. She'd have to try calling her father again and telling him what she'd found, as soon as she could get her sister busy doing something else. "Come on," she said, and led Maggie out of the bedroom and back down the stairs.

Maggie worked the rolling pin back and forth over the plastic bag full of potato chips. Rose looked up at the clock for the third time in less than a minute. It was six o'clock. Rose was trying to pretend that everything was all right, even though nothing was all right at all. She hadn't been able to get her father on the phone, and their mother still wasn't home. Even if she'd forgotten about the early dismissal, she should have been home by three-thirty.

Think! Rose thought to herself, as her sister ground the potato chips into shards, then into dust. She had already pretty much decided that their mother had gone AWAY again. She and Maggie weren't supposed to know about AWAY—about where it was, about that her mother had been there. But Rose knew. Last summer, after their mother had come back from AWAY, Maggie had come to her with a crumpled brochure.

"What's this say?" she asked.

Rose read it carefully. " 'Institute of Living'," she said, staring at the drawing—a cupped palm holding the faces of a woman, a man, and a child.

"What's it mean?"

"I don't know," said Rose. "Where did you find it?"

"In Mom's suitcase."

Rose hadn't even asked what Maggie was doing looking in their mother's suitcase—even at six, Maggie was a notorious snoop. A few weeks later, Rose had been driving home from a Hebrew school field trip with the Schoens when they'd passed a bunch of buildings with a sign in front, and the sign had had the exact same picture on it as the brochure—same faces, same cupped hands.

"What's that?" she'd asked, trying to be casual, because the car had sped past the sign too fast for her to try to puzzle out.

Steven Schoen had snickered. "The loony bin," he'd said, and his mother had whirled around so fast her hair whipped against her cheeks, and Rose could smell Aqua Net. "Steven!" she'd scolded, and then turned to Rose, her voice soft and syrupy sweet. "That's a place called the Institute of Living," she'd explained. "It's a special kind of hospital for people who need help with their feelings."

So. That was AWAY. Rose wasn't too surprised, because anyone could tell that their mom had needed some kind of help. But where was she now? Had she gone back there?

Rose looked at the clock again. Five minutes past six. She called her father's office again, but the phone just rang and rang. She set the receiver down and walked into the family room, where Maggie was now sitting on the couch, looking out the window. She sat down next to her sister.

"Is it my fault?" Maggie whispered.

"What?"

"Is it my fault she went away? Did she get mad at me because I get in trouble at school?"

"No, no," Rose said. "It's not your fault. She's not away. She probably just got confused or something, or maybe she had car trouble. There's lots of things it could be!" But even as she reassured Maggie, Rose slipped her hand into her pocket and felt the cold gold ring. "Don't worry," she said.

"I'm scared," Maggie whispered.

"I know," said Rose. "Me, too." They sat on the couch, side by side, as the sun went down, waiting.

Michael Feller pulled into the driveway at just after seven o'clock, and Rose and Maggie hurried out the door to meet him.

"Daddy, Daddy!" Maggie said, catapulting herself toward her father's legs. "Mom's not here! She's gone! She didn't come back!"

Michael turned to his oldest daughter. "Rose? What's going on?"

"We got home from school early . . . it's a teachers in-service day, I brought home the notice about it last week . . ."

"She didn't leave a note?" asked their father, hurrying to the kitchen, so fast that Rose and Maggie had to run to keep up.

"No," said Rose.

"Where is she?" asked Maggie. "Do you know?"

Their father shook his head and reached for the red address book and the telephone. "Don't worry. I'm sure it's nothing to worry about."

Midnight. Rose had made Maggie eat some of the tuna noodle casserole, and tried to make their father eat some, too, but he'd waved her away, sitting hunched by the phone, making call after call after call. At ten, he'd noticed that they were still awake and he'd hurried them into their nightgowns and into their beds, forgetting to make them wash their faces or brush their teeth. "Go to sleep," he said. For the last two hours they'd been lying side by side in Rose's bed with their eyes wide open in the darkness. Rose had told Maggie stories—"Cinderella" and "Little Red Riding Hood," the story of the princess and the enchanted slippers who danced and danced and danced.

The doorbell rang. Rose and Maggie sat straight up at the exact same instant.

"We should get that," said Maggie.

"It might be her," said Rose.

They held hands as they ran down the stairs in bare feet. Their father was at the door already, and Rose could tell without even hearing a word that was said, that something very bad was happening, that their mother was not okay, that nothing would ever be okay again.

A tall man was at the door, a man in a green uniform and a broad-brimmed brown hat. "Mr. Feller?" he was asking. "Is this the residence of Caroline Feller?"

Her father swallowed hard and nodded. The tall man's hat dripped rainwater onto the floor. "I'm afraid I have some bad news, sir," he said.

"Did you find our mother?" Maggie asked in a tiny gasping voice.

The trooper looked at them sadly. His leather belt creaked as he reached to put his hand on their father's shoulder. Raindrops fell on Maggie's and Rose's bare feet. He looked down at them, then back up at their father.

"I think we should talk privately, sir," he said. And Michael Feller, shoulder slumped, face broken, led him away.

And after that . . .

After that was their father with his Stonehenge face. After that was "car accident," and packing up the house in Connecticut, leaving their school, their house, their friends, their familiar street. Their father piled their mother's things in boxes destined for Goodwill, and Rose and Maggie and their father got in a U-Haul truck and drove to New Jersey. "To start over," their father had said. Like that could ever happen. Like the past was something you could leave behind like a candy bar wrapper or a pair of shoes you'd outgrown.

In her bed in Philadelphia, Rose sat up in the darkness, knowing that she wouldn't be doing any sleeping that night. She remembered the funeral. She remembered the navy blue dress she'd worn, purchased for the first day of school, nine months before, and how it was already too short, and the elastic of the puffed sleeves had left red welts on her arms. She remembered her father's face over the grave, remote and distant, and an older woman with auburn hair, sitting in the back of the funeral parlor crying softly into a handkerchief. Her grandmother. Where had she gone? Rose didn't know. After the funeral, they'd rarely talked about their grandmother, or their mother. They lived far away from the policeman in the hat full of rain, and the driveway he'd parked his cruiser in, with the blue lights still flashing mutely through the darkness, and the road that had brought him to their house. The slick, wet road with its treacherous curves, a ribbon of black, like a lying tongue. They'd gone far away from the road, and the house, and the cemetery where their mother was buried, beneath a blanket of raw-looking sod and a headstone that had her name, the years of her birth and her death, and the words *Wife and Loving Mother* chiseled into it. And Rose had never once been back.

PART TWO

Continuing
Education

TWENTY-FOUR

What she needed, thought Maggie Feller, was a plan.

She sat on a bench inside Thirtieth Street Station, a grand, cavernous room littered with old newspapers and fast-food wrappers, smelling of grease and sweat and winter coats. It was almost midnight. Harried-looking mothers dragged their children along by their arms. Homeless people slept splayed out on the carved wooden benches. I could be one of them, thought Maggie, panic rising inside of her.

Think, she told herself. She had a garbage bag full of stuff, plus her purse, her backpack, and two hundred dollars, two crisp hundred-dollar bills Jim had given her before dropping her off. *Can I help you?* he'd asked, not unkindly, and she'd held out her hand without meeting his eyes. "I want two hundred dollars," she told him. "That's the going rate." He'd dug the money out of his wallet without a word of protest. "I'm sorry," he'd said . . . but sorry about what? And whom was he apologizing to? Not her. Maggie was sure of that. What she needed now was somewhere to stay . . . and then a job again, eventually.

Rose was out of the question. So was her father. Maggie shuddered, imagined herself dragging her bags across the lawn as the idiot dog howled, imagined the look of fake-o sympathy and barely disguised disgust as Sydelle opened the door, and how her eyes would say, *This is just what we expected of you,* even if her mouth was saying something else. Sydelle would want details, would want to know what had happened with Rose and with her job. Sydelle would needle her with dozens of questions, and her father would sit there, his eyes soft and defeated, not asking anything at all.

Where did that leave her? Maggie couldn't see herself in a homeless shelter. All those women, all those failed lives. She wasn't that way. She hadn't failed. Not like that. She was a star, if only someone could see it!

You're not a star, whispered a voice in her head, and the voice sounded like Rose's voice, only colder than Rose could ever sound. *You're not a star, you're a slut, a stupid slut. You can't even work the cash register! You can't balance your checkbook! Evicted! Practically homeless! And you slept with my boyfriend!*

Think, thought Maggie fiercely, trying to drown out the voice. What did she have? Her body. There was that. Jim had turned over the two hundred dollars easily enough. There were men who would pay her to sleep with them, certainly, and men who would pay to watch her dance with her clothes off. At least that was entertaining, performing. And plenty of the rising stars who'd gone before her had done it as a last-ditch measure, a stopgap thing.

So fine, Maggie thought, tightening her grip on her garbage bag as the homeless man two benches back moaned in his sleep. Stripping. Fine. It wasn't the end of the world. But that didn't solve the problem of where she'd stay. It was January, the cold, dead heart of winter. She'd planned on catching a SEPTA train to Trenton, then taking another train into New York City. But she wouldn't get there until two in the morning, and then what would she do? Where would she go?

She got to her feet, clutching her backpack tightly in one hand and her garbage bag in the other, and squinted at the New Jersey Transit board and the names of the towns the trains went to: Rahway. Westfield. Matawan. Metuchen. Red Bank. Little Silver.

That one sounded nice, but what if it wasn't? Newark. Too big. Elizabeth. The butt of Jersey jokes. Brick. Ugh. Princeton.

She'd visited Rose at Princeton a few times, when she was sixteen and seventeen. She could picture it if she closed her eyes— buildings made of carved gray stone, covered in ivy, with gargoyles leering from the ledges. She remembered dorm rooms with fireplaces in them, and wooden window seats that opened up to hold extra blankets and winter coats, and the many-paned leaded-glass windows. She remembered huge classrooms, sloping floors full of hard-edged wooden chairs with desks attached, and a party in a basement, with a keg of beer in the corner, and how vast the library had seemed—three floors up, and three floors down, each one long as a football field. The smell of burning wood and fall leaves, a borrowed red wool scarf warm around her neck, heading down one of the gray slate paths toward a party, knowing she'd never be able to find her way back by herself, because there were so many paths and all the buildings looked almost the same. "It's easy to get lost here," Rose had told her, so she wouldn't feel bad. "It happened to me all the time my freshman year."

Maybe she could get lost there now. She could take a train to Trenton, catch New Jersey Transit to Princeton, and stay there for a few days and regroup. Everyone always told her she looked younger than she was, and she had a backpack, the universal sign of students everywhere. "Princeton," she said out loud, and walked to the ticket window, where she paid seven dollars for a one-way ticket. She'd always meant to go back to college, she thought, heading up the ramp toward the trains. So what if this wasn't the most normal way to do it? When had she, Maggie Feller, ever been the most normal girl?

At two in the morning Maggie made her way across the darkened Princeton University campus. Her shoulder muscles were cramping from the weight of her backpack, and her hands were numb from towing the trash bag full of clothes, but she tried to walk briskly as she joined the crowds of students moving along the sidewalk, with her shoulders back and her head up, as if she knew exactly where she was going.

She'd gotten off the train at Princeton Junction in the middle of a vast parking lot, halogen lamps gleaming coldly in the dark. In an instant of panic, she turned around and sure enough, there were students—or at least people who looked like students—streaming across the platform, down into a tunnel below them. She followed them under the train tracks and then up the other side, where another, much smaller train waited. She bought a ticket on the train, and two minutes later arrived at the campus.

As she walked up the hill, Maggie made a quick but careful study of her fellow travelers—kids coming back from Christmas break, she figured, judging from the conversations and the amounts of luggage. Evidently, she decided, grooming was not a priority for these women, while purchasing the fashions of Abercrombie & Fitch was. None wore much more than lip gloss, and they were arrayed in some version of washed-out jeans, sweaters or sweatshirts, camel-colored overcoats, plus layers upon layers of hats, scarves, mittens, and winter boots. Well, that explains Rose, she thought and began mentally editing her wardrobe. Little halter top, no. Leather pants, probably not. Cashmere sweater set? Sure, if only she had one, she thought, and shivered as the icy wind bit at her bare neck. She'd need a scarf. Also, she needed a cigarette, though it seemed that none of the girls were smoking. Maybe because it was too cold, but probably because they just didn't. Probably because none of the girls in the Abercrombie & Fitch ads were smokers. Maggie sighed, and edged up as close as she could to a pack of chattering girls, looking for more information.

"I don't know," one of them said, giggling, as they walked past bulletin boards covered with fliers advertising everything from movies and concerts to used guitars for sale. "I think he likes me, and I gave him my number, but so far, nothing."

Then he doesn't like you, dummy, Maggie thought. If they liked

you, they called. It was as simple as that. And these were supposed
to be the smart girls?

"Maybe you should call him," one of her friends suggested. *Sure,*
thought Maggie, who hadn't telephoned a man since she gave up
crank calls at age thirteen. *And maybe you should wave a flag in front of
his room, too, in case he misses the point.*

The pack pulled up in front of a four-story stone building with
a heavy wood door. One of the girls pulled off her mittens and
punched a code into the doorknob. The door swung open, and
Maggie followed them inside.

She was in some kind of common area. There were half a dozen
couches covered in an indestructible industrial blue fabric, a few
scarred coffee tables scattered with newspapers and magazines, a
television set showing *It's a Wonderful Life*—which it wasn't, as far
as Maggie was concerned. Beyond them was a staircase that led,
presumably, to individual dorm rooms . . . and, from the sound of
it, there were parties going on. Maggie set down her bags, and her
fingers tingled as the blood started to come back. *I'm in,* she
thought, feeling triumph mixed with anxiety at what it would take
to pull off her next move.

The pack of girls tromped up the stairs, as graceful as a herd of
elephants in their heavy boots. Maggie followed them into the
bathroom ("So if I call him, what do I say?" the girl who hadn't gotten a phone call was asking plaintively). She waited until they'd
left, then she splashed warm water on her face and wiped off what
was left of her makeup. She tied her hair into a Rose-like ponytail
(the preferred Princeton hairdo, from what she'd seen so far), reapplied deodorant and a quick spritz of perfume, and rinsed her
mouth with water from the sink. For the next part of her plan to
work, she had to look her best, or as close to it as she could come
after what she'd been through.

Then she made her way back into the common room and scouted
it out. If she left the trash bags behind the couch, would anyone steal
them? No. Everyone here already had all of the clothes they could

want, Maggie figured, tucking herself into an armchair in the corner, where she wrapped her arms around her knees and watched, and waited.

She didn't have to wait long. A pack of guys—four, or maybe five of them, in sweatshirts and khakis, talking loud and smelling of beer—jostled their way past the guard at front, past Maggie, and headed toward the stairs. Maggie sidled behind them.

"Well, hey," said one of the guys, peering at her as if she was at the far end of a telescope. "Where are you going?"

Maggie smiled. "The party," she said, as if it were obvious. And he'd grinned at her blearily, one hand on the wall for balance, telling her that it must be his lucky day.

The party—and, of course, there was a party, because even though it was Ivy League, it was still a college, which meant that there would always be a party—was up four flights of stairs, in what Maggie took to be a suite. There was a living room with a couch and a stereo, two bedrooms with two bunk beds apiece, and, in between them, a tub full of ice and the inevitable keg resting atop it. "Get you a drink?" offered one of the stair guys—maybe the one who'd said it was his lucky day, maybe one of his friends. In the dim light, with all the noise and the press of bodies, she couldn't be sure, but she'd nodded just the same, leaning in close and letting her lips just brush his ear as she murmured, "Thanks."

By the time he wove his way back to her, sloshing half the beer on the floor as he progressed, she'd perched herself on a corner of the couch, long legs crossed.

"What's your name?" he asked. He was short and fine-boned with blond curls that would have been more fitting on one of those six-year-old beauty queens than on a college guy, and a watchful, foxy face.

She was ready for the question. "M," she said. She'd decided on the train not to be Maggie anymore. She had failed as a Maggie, had failed to find fame or fortune. From now on, she would just be M.

The guy squinted at her. "Em? Like Auntie Em?"

Maggie frowned. Did she have an Auntie Em? Did he? "It's just M," she said.

"Whatever," the guy said, giving her a shrug. "I haven't seen you around. What's your major?"

"Subterfuge," said Maggie.

The guy nodded as if he understood. Well, thought Maggie, maybe subterfuge was an actual major at this place. She'd have to check. "I'm poli sci," said the guy, and burped hugely. " 'Scuse me."

"No problem," said Maggie, as if she found intestinal gas the most fascinating and charming thing in the world. "What's your name?"

"Josh," said the guy.

"Josh," Maggie repeated, as if this, too, was fascinating.

"Wanna dance?" Josh asked. Maggie took a ladylike sip of her beer, and handed him the cup, which he drained obligingly. They stood, face-to-face, and danced . . . or, rather, Josh jerked back and forth as if his body was taking a low-grade electrical charge, while Maggie slowly ground her hips against him.

"Wow," he said appreciatively. He slid his hands around her waist and pressed her against the bulge in the front of his khakis. "You're a great dancer."

Maggie almost laughed. Twelve years of lessons, ballet and jazz and tap, and this was what passed for great dancing. Asshole. Instead, she tilted her head up to him, aiming her lips and warm breath toward his ear once more, letting her lips barely skim his neck. "Can we go somewhere quiet?" she asked. The words took a minute to register, but when they did, his eyes lit up.

"Sure!" he said. "I've got a single."

Bingo, thought Maggie. "One more beer first?" she asked, in a little-girl voice. He returned with two, and wound up drinking all of his own and almost all of Maggie's, too, before he wrapped his arm around her waist again, slung her backpack over his shoulder and led her back to the stairs and to the bliss he thought awaited back at his single in a dormitory called Blair. *Blair,* Maggie recited to herself, as she walked and he lurched. She'd have to start keeping a list—the names of places, the names of men. She'd have to be careful. She'd have to be smart. Smarter than Rose, even. Surviving a place like this when you were supposed to be here was one thing, but surviving here when you weren't would be a challenge worthy of all of her cunning, all of her skill, all of the intelligence that Mrs. Fried had promised her, long ago, that she had, no matter what the tests said.

Josh flung open the door like an emperor revealing the cedar walls and golden floors of his palace, and Maggie realized that this was where it could get tricky. She'd have to prepare herself for the possibility of actually having sex with this guy. Two guys in one night, she thought bleakly. Not a statistic she'd set out to achieve.

The dorm room was a tiny rectangle, littered with books and sneakers and tufts of unfolded laundry, smelling like sweat socks and old pizza. "Be it ever so humble," Josh said, giving her a sharp, appraising look, and flung himself onto the bed, shoving a chemistry book, a water bottle, a ten-pound barbell, and what Maggie thought was a fossilized half-eaten hoagie, to the floor. He spread his arms wide and gave her the cold smirk of a boy who's gotten every toy he's ever wanted and broken them just for spite. "Come to papa," he said.

Maggie instead gave him a slow, saucy smile and stood her ground at the foot of the bed. She traced one coy fingertip along her neckline. "Got anything to drink?" she whispered. Josh pointed. "On the desk," he said. Maggie found a flat brown bottle. Peach schnapps. Ugh. She took a swig, trying not to wince as the cloying taste of peaches filled her mouth, and tilted her head at Josh, daring him with her eyes. He was next to her in an instant, his lips cool and faintly repulsive against hers. She darted her tongue into his mouth to the beat of Cyndi Lauper's "Girls Just Want to Have Fun," which she played for herself in her head, and she let the heavy liquid slide from her mouth to his.

"When the work-ing day is done," she heard Cyndi wail in her head, as Josh gazed at her with a new drunken appreciation, clearly believing that he'd died and gone to heaven, or at least to the X-rated section of his internal video store.

She set one of her small hands in the center of his chest and pushed gently. He fell back on the bed like a tree. She took another gulp of schnapps and straddled him, grinding her crotch against him, smiling. *Courage,* she thought to herself. She leaned back on her haunches and pulled her top up over her head. Josh's eyes widened at the sight of her breasts in the faint glow from the lamps outside that filtered in through his window. She tried to put herself in his place, imagining what he saw—a lithe, half-naked girl, the spill of her hair over her shoulders, her white skin and slender midriff and hard brown nipples shining at him.

He reached for her. *Now,* she thought, and tilted the bottle of schnapps so that liquor flowed down her breasts, making a sticky trail toward the waistband of her jeans. "Oh, my God!" Josh groaned, "you are so hot!"

He was huffing and puffing, panting words she couldn't make out, as he snuffled at her skin and the schnapps, and his hands were fumbling uselessly at the waistband on her jeans. She'd counted on him being too drunk to operate a button fly, and it looked as though she'd guessed right.

"Wait," she whispered, flipping herself off of him and coming to lie by his side. "Let me take care of you."

"You're incredible," he said, and lay still with his eyes closed. Maggie leaned close and kissed his neck. He sighed. She planted a trail of tiny kisses from his earlobe to his collarbone, moving a little more slowly with each kiss. He sighed again, reaching down the front of his boxers. Maggie began trailing her tongue toward his chest. Slowly, she told herself, timing each lick and kiss to the beat of her heart. Slowly . . .

Each kiss was lighter than the one before it. Each one took longer to come. She held herself in check, and held her breath, tense beside him, until she heard his breathing slow to a regular rhythm, until she heard the first clotted rattle of a snore. She raised her head an inch and peeked at his face to make sure. His eyes were closed, his mouth was open, a bubble of spit expanded and retracted between his lips. Josh was asleep.

Asleep or passed out. She wasn't sure which, and it didn't matter. Her plan had worked so far. She eased one hand down into his pocket and came up with a plastic card. His student ID. Perfect. Then she crept out of his bed, located her tank top, and pulled it back on as Josh snored. She found a towel on the floor—it smelled sour and felt crusty, but no use looking for clean laundry in here, she thought, grabbing a plastic bucket that contained soap and shampoo.

His wallet was on the desk. She looked at it, considering, then picked it up and flipped it open. There were a half-dozen credit cards, a decent-sized wad of cash. She'd look through it later, she decided, and shoved the whole thing in her pocket before turning to the closet. Did she dare? She inched across the floor, and eased the door open by millimeters. Josh had not one but two leather jackets, plus all manner of shirts, sweaters, and khaki pants, sneakers and hiking boots, jeans and polo shirts, windbreakers, winter coats, and even a tuxedo wrapped in dry-cleaner's plastic. Maggie took two of the sweaters, and then looked in the corner. Bonus! There was a goosedown sleeping bag tucked neatly into a stuff sack, and an electric camping lantern next to it. He'd never miss them, and if he did, she was sure that whoever'd bought him all of his other stuff would just send a check for more.

Josh groaned thickly and rolled over, flinging one arm across the pillow where Maggie's head had been. Maggie felt her heart stop. She forced herself to count to a hundred before moving again, then gathered her spoils, cramming the sleeping bag and lantern into her backpack. She eased the door open, and headed into the hallway. It was four in the morning. Maggie could still hear stereos blaring, and the drunken whoops and shouts of people coming back from parties.

The bathrooms were at the end of the hall, and they had locks that required codes but, luckily, the ladies' room door was propped open by the prone body of a passed-out coed who'd succumbed half in and half out of one of the stalls. Maggie stepped over her legs and stripped, hanging her clothes neatly on one of the hooks, hanging the towel on top of them.

She stepped under the warm water and closed her eyes. Okay, she thought to herself. Okay. Next would come food and a place to regroup. She was thinking of the library, thinking how at every college she'd ever attended or visited the security guards never looked too closely at identification cards. If you looked like you belonged, they just waved you in. So first she'd get her clothes from behind the couch in the first dorm, and then she'd use his ID to sneak into a dining hall for some food, and then . . . .

Maggie looked down and saw a white plastic hair clip sitting in the soap dish. . . . the same kind of ugly thing that her sister used to shove her hair back off her face. *Rose,* she thought, and was suddenly caught in such a drowning wave of regret that her breath caught in her throat. *Rose,* she thought, *I'm sorry.* And in that instant, naked and alone, Maggie felt as wretched as she ever had in her life.

TWENTY-FIVE

Maybe this is what it feels like to go crazy, Rose thought, and rolled over and gave herself to sleep again.

In her dream, she was lost in a cave, and the cave kept getting smaller and smaller, the ceiling pressing lower and lower until she could feel the stalactites—or possibly the stalagmites, Rose had always gotten them confused—pushing wet against her face.

She woke up. The dog that Maggie had left behind was perched on a pillow beside her, licking her cheeks.

"Ugh," said Rose, burying her face in a pillow and rolling away. For a minute she didn't remember anything. Then it all came crashing back—Jim and Maggie. In bed. Together. "Oh, God," she groaned. The dog put its paw on top of her forehead, as if it were taking her temperature, and gave an inquisitive-sounding whine.

"Go away," Rose said. Instead, the dog turned in three circles on top of the pillow, curled itself into a graham-cracker-colored bundle and started to snore. Rose closed her eyes and followed the dog back into sleep.

When she woke up again, it was after eleven o'clock in the morning. She staggered to her feet and almost slipped in the warm, wet puddle outside of the bathroom. She stared at her wet foot dumbly, then back at the dog, still perched on the bed.

"Did you do this?" she asked. The dog just stared. Rose sighed, then dug out the Pine-Sol and a roll of paper towels and dealt with the mess. She couldn't blame the dog, she supposed . . . the poor thing hadn't been walked since yesterday.

She plodded to the kitchen, put on a pot of coffee, poured herself a bowl of bran flakes, and moved her spoon through them, back and forth. She didn't want bran flakes, she realized. She didn't want anything. She couldn't imagine ever feeling hungry again.

She stared at the telephone. What day was it? Saturday. Which gave her the weekend to get herself together. Or maybe she should just go ahead and call in sick right now, leave someone a message saying she wouldn't be in this week. But who? If Maggie were here, she'd know what to say. Maggie was the queen of white lies, half-truths, and mental-health days, which she felt completely justified in taking. Maggie.

"Oh, God," Rose groaned again. Maggie was back at her father's house, or lurking in the bushes or on a bench outside, certain that the morning would make Rose change her mind. Well, fat chance of that, she thought fiercely, giving up on breakfast and setting her bowl next to the sink.

The dog, evidently, did not share her black mood or lack of appetite. It had materialized by her feet and was staring at her cereal bowl with wet and avid eyes. Rose realized she had no idea what Maggie had fed the thing. She hadn't noticed any dog food around. Not that she'd been noticing much of anything. Except Jim. Or lack thereof. Tentatively, she lowered her cereal bowl to the floor. The dog sniffed it, lowered her nose, took a small lick of the milk, then snorted once, dismissively, and stared up at Rose.

"No good?" asked Rose. She rummaged through her cabinets. Pea soup. Probably not. Black beans . . . she didn't think so. Tuna fish! Or was that for cats? She decided to give it a go, mixing it with mayonnaise and setting it in front of the dog, along with a cup of water. The dog wolfed it down, making little grunts of happiness and nosing the bowl across the entire length of the kitchen floor, attempting to remove every last morsel of mayonnaise and flake of fish.

"Okay," said Rose. It was now the unimaginable hour of one in the afternoon. Her apartment was spotless, thanks to last night's cleaning. She wandered into the bathroom and stared at herself for a long moment. She was an ordinary girl, with ordinary hair and ordinary brown eyes. She had lips and cheeks and eyebrows, and there was nothing remarkable about any of them.

"What's wrong with me?" she asked the face in the mirror. The dog sat at the bathroom door, staring. Rose brushed her teeth, washed her face, made the bed, moving through the room on heavy, leaden legs. Go out? Stay in? Go back to sleep?

The dog was scratching at the front door.

"Hey, stop that!" She looked around, wondering whether Maggie had left a leash, then she pulled out a scarf she'd bought once during a single misguided afternoon when she'd thought she might actually become a scarf-wearing sort of person—the kind of woman who accessorized, instead of the kind of woman whose scarves inevitably wound up either slammed in the car door or trailing in her soup.

She knelt down and threaded the scarf through the dog's collar. The dog looked unhappy and put-upon, as if it—she?—realized that the scarf was polyester, not real silk. "A thousand pardons," Rose said sarcastically, finding her keys and sunglasses and mittens and a twenty-dollar bill to tuck into her pocket so that she could buy pet food. Then she headed to the elevator, scooped the dog up under her coat, slid past the doorman and headed out the door. There was, if she remembered right, a strip of grass at the corner of her street. The dog could do its business there, and then she'd cross the street to the Wawa, tie the dog to a parking meter the way she'd seen other people do, and buy dog food, and a doughnut, Rose decided. A jelly doughnut. Possibly two jelly doughnuts, and coffee with cream and three packets of sugar. She'd gain weight . . . but that didn't matter. Who'd be seeing her naked now? Who'd care? She could gain weight; she could let her leg hair grow until it was long enough for French braids; she could wear every single frayed, dingy, snapped-elastic pair of panties she had. None of it mattered anymore.

The dog shot Rose a grateful look as soon as they'd made it out of her building, trotted to the gutter, and squatted there, peeing for what felt like a very long time.

"Sorry about making you wait," Rose said. The dog snorted. Rose wasn't sure what that was supposed to mean. The dog certainly snorted a lot. Maybe it was just a . . . a breed thing. Maybe this was a particularly snorty breed of dog. Rose had no idea. After Honey Bun, their dog for a day, she and Maggie had never had so much as a goldfish. Too much extra responsibility for their father, who clearly found the two girls burden enough. And then after she and Maggie had left the house, Sydelle purchased her designer dog, a dog with a pedigree, and papers to prove it. "I'm allergic," her father had said. "Don't be silly," Sydelle had replied. And that was the end of that. Chanel the idiot golden retriever stayed. Her father suffered.

"What a cute little pug!" said a dark-haired woman, kneeling to let the dog sniff her hand. Pug, Rose said to herself. Okay, so the dog was a pug. That was a start.

"Come," Rose said, wrapping the scarf around her hand, and the dog walked sedately by her left heel as they made their way to the convenience store. "Stay," said Rose, and tied her scarf around a meter. The dog—the pug—looked up at her like a dinner guest waiting for the soup course. "I'll be back," said Rose. She went inside and spent ten minutes staring at the bewildering array of pet food before purchasing a bag of kibble for small adult dogs. She also bought a plastic bowl to pour the food into, two jelly doughnuts, coffee, two pints of ice cream, and a bag of cheese curls she'd grabbed from a display promising that they'd be the most CheeseRageous thing she'd ever eaten. The cashier raised his eyebrows at her haul. Rose came in here a lot, but all she ever purchased were newspapers, black coffee, and the occasional can of Slim-Fast.

"I'm on vacation," she explained, wondering why she felt the need to explain anything to a guy who worked the cash register at the Wawa. But he gave her a nice smile, and snuck a square of Bazooka gum into her bag, along with her receipt.

"Enjoy," he said. Rose returned his smile weakly, and went outside, where the dog was still sitting, tethered to its parking meter.

"What's your name?" Rose wondered out loud.

The dog just stared.

"I'm Rose," said Rose. "I'm a lawyer." The dog walked beside her. There was something in the set of her head, the way her ears were cocked, that suggested she might actually be listening. "I'm thirty years old. I graduated summa cum laude from Princeton, then I went to the University of Pennsylvania law school, where I was a *Law Review* editor, and . . ."

Why was she giving the dog her résumé? This was silly. The dog wasn't going to hire her. Probably neither was anyone else. Word would get out about her and Jim. It had probably started already, Rose realized bleakly. It was probably going on while she was at the firm and she was too dumb and doped up with love to see it.

"I was having an affair," said Rose, as she and the dog paused for a red light. The teenage girl with the gold hoop through her lip standing next to her on the sidewalk stared at Rose curiously, then started walking faster. "There was this guy." She paused. "Well, isn't there always. He was kind of my boss, actually, and he turned out to be . . ." She swallowed hard. "Bad. Very, very bad."

The dog gave a single sharp bark—of despair? Affirmation? Rose wasn't sure. She wanted to call Amy, but she didn't think she could cope with the sting of having to tell her best friend that she'd been right, that Jim had been as big a jerk as Amy had imagined . . . and that Maggie, her sister, who she'd opened her house to, her sister who she'd tried to help, had been worse still. The light turned green. The dog barked again, and tugged gently against the scarf. "It's over," said Rose—just to say something, just to end the story somehow, even if she was just talking to a dog, and the dog wasn't listening. "Over," she repeated, and crossed the street. The dog looked at her, then looked back down.

"So the girl who was taking care of you. That was Maggie. My sister," she continued, as they walked closer to her apartment building. "We'll have to feed you, and get you a leash, and figure out where you came from. Have to take you back." She stopped at a corner and considered the dog again—small, coffee-colored, harmless, she supposed. The dog looked up at her, then gave a brisk and, Rose thought, dismissive snort. "Fine," she said, "don't be grateful." She crossed the street and walked herself home.

TWENTY-SIX

Who ever told the truth about a marriage? Certainly Ella never had. She and her friends would talk about their husbands like they were children, or pets—some strange species responsible for bad smells and strange noises and messes they'd have to clean up. They turned their husbands into punch lines. They spoke of them in shorthand, a code of rolled eyes and pronouns. He. Him. *He doesn't eat green vegetables, so how am I supposed to make the kids do it? I'd love to go on that cruise, but of course I'll have to ask him.*

Ella used to contribute from her own small stock of anecdotes, the stories that would make Ira appear as simple as a child's cartoon drawn in broad lines. She'd have the ladies howling around the bridge table with stories of how he wouldn't go on a trip longer than twenty miles without a mayonnaise jar in case he didn't like the looks of the gas station rest rooms, or the eighty dollars he'd spent on a do-it-yourself yogurt-making kit. Not ice cream, not beer, she'd say, as the ladies laughed so hard they had to wipe tears from their cheeks, not something you'd actually want, but yogurt. Ira the yogurt king.

Those were the stories she told, but she never told the truth about her marriage. Never told the ladies how it felt to live with someone who'd become more like a roommate than a husband, like someone who'd been assigned to share your living quarters for the duration of a trip. Never told them about the bruising politeness, the way Ira would thank her when she poured his coffee, or the way he'd take her arm when they were out in public, at weddings or his company's Christmas party, how he'd hold her arm and guide her from the car out to the sidewalk, as if she were made of glass. As if she were a stranger. And she'd certainly never mentioned the way they'd quietly moved into separate beds after Caroline started school, and how Ira had relocated to the guest room the week their daughter had gone off to college. Things like that were never spoken of, and Ella wouldn't have even known how to begin the conversation.

The sound of banging startled her from her reverie. Mrs. Lefkowitz was pounding at the door. "Ass Master? You in there?" Ella hurried to let her in, hoping that none of her neighbors had overheard. Mrs. Lefkowitz shuffled into Ella's kitchen, reaching into her oversized pink crocheted purse and setting a glass bottle on the countertop.

"Pickles," she announced. Ella stifled a smile and emptied the jar of Claussen's finest into a serving dish, as her guest peered into her living room and sniffed. "He's not here yet?"

"Not yet," Ella called, peering into the oven. She'd never figured out Florida cuisine, if there was such a thing, and on the infrequent occasions when she had to cook for someone other than herself, she found herself relying on the same handful of company meals she'd cooked during her years of marriage. Tonight she'd be serving a brisket, potato pancakes, a tsimmes of carrots and prunes, with challah from the bakery, and Mrs. Lefkowitz's pickles, and two kinds of cake and a pie. Too much food, she thought, too much for just the three of them, and too heavy for these hot Florida nights, but when she'd been running to the grocery store or bustling around in her too-small kitchen, the work had kept her mind off how nervous she was.

"I'd like to meet your friends," Lewis had said, and how could Ella tell him that she didn't really have friends here? He'd think that she was crazy, or that there was something wrong with her.

And Mrs. Lefkowitz had been, if anything, even more insistent. "A gentleman caller!" she'd cackled, after Ella had made the mistake of letting Lewis drop her off for Meals on Wheels duty, and she'd followed Ella around the kitchen, thumping the floors with her cane. "Is he handsome? Good income? A widower, or divorced? Toupee? Pacemaker? Does he drive? Does he drive at night?"

"Enough!" Ella had said, laughing, with her hands in the air in the universal gesture of surrender.

"Then it's settled," said Mrs. Lefkowitz, with a crooked grin that made her look like a lopsided Cheshire cat.

"What's settled?" Ella asked.

"You'll have me over for dinner. It'll be good for me to get out," Mrs. Lefkowitz said airily. "My doctor says so." She picked up what she'd told Ella was a PalmPilot from the coffee table. "Should we say five o'clock?"

That had been three days ago. Ella glanced at her watch. It was five after five. "Late!" Mrs. Lefkowitz observed helpfully from the living room couch. Lewis knocked on the door.

"Hello, ladies," he said. He had an armful of tulips, a bottle of wine, and something in a square cardboard box tucked underneath his arm. "Smells delicious!"

"I made too much," Ella said weakly.

"So you'll have leftovers," he said, and held out his hands to Mrs. Lefkowitz, who, Ella saw, had applied a fresh streak of geranium pink lipstick.

"Hello, hello!" she cooed, looking him over as he helped her to her feet.

"You must be Mrs. Lefkowitz," he said. In the kitchen, Ella held her breath, hoping that she'd finally learn Mrs. Lefkowitz's first name. Instead, Mrs. Lefkowitz gave a coquettish giggle and allowed Lewis to walk her to the table.

After dinner and dessert and coffee in the living room, Mrs. Lefkowitz gave a contented sigh and a small burp. "My trolley's coming," she announced, and limped out into the night. Lewis and Ella exchanged a smile.

"I brought you something," Lewis said.

"Oh, you shouldn't have," Ella said reflexively, as Lewis retrieved his cardboard box. She felt her heart contract into an icy ball as she saw what he'd brought. A photo album.

"I was telling you about my family the other night, so I thought maybe you'd want to see some pictures," Lewis said, settling himself on her couch as if this wasn't unusual or terrifying at all. As if anyone could do this—open a photo album, look the past right in the face. Ella's face felt frozen, but she made herself smile, and sit next to him.

Lewis flipped his album open. There were pictures of his parents, first, standing stiffly in their old-fashioned clothes, and Lewis and his brothers. And here was Sharla, wearing orange or bright pink or turquoise (and, sometimes, all three together), and their son. There were shots of Lewis and Sharla's house in Utica, a ranch with pots of roses beside the front door. "That was John's high-school graduation, or was it college? . . . there we are at the Grand Canyon, which you probably could recognize without me. . . . That was my retirement dinner." Wedding pictures, bar mitzvah parties, the beach, the mountains; the babies. Ella endured them all, smiling and nodding and saying the right things until finally, blessedly, Lewis closed the book.

"How about you?"

"How about me what?" she asked.

"Could I see pictures of you?"

She shook her head. "I don't have many," she told him. And it was the truth. When she and Ira had sold their house in Michigan and moved down here, they'd put all kinds of things into storage— furniture and winter coats, boxes and boxes of books. And all of their pictures. It hurt too much to see them. But maybe . . .

"Wait here," Ella said. She went to the closet in the back bedroom and reached past the boxes of clothes and extra towels, and felt for an old purse that contained a plain white envelope, with a handful of snapshots inside. She came back to the couch and showed Lewis the first in the stack, a shot of her and Ira, standing in the spray of Niagara Falls on their honeymoon.

Lewis studied the photograph carefully, tilting it from side to side beneath the lamp on the side table.

"You look worried," he finally said.

"Maybe I was," said Ella, shuffling through the snapshots. There was Ira, posing beside a "Sold" sign in front of their house in Michigan, Ira behind the wheel of their first new car. And finally, at the bottom of the stack, was a shot of Ella and Caroline.

"Here," she said, and passed Lewis the picture. Their next-door neighbor had taken it the day they'd come home from the hospital. Ella was in the background, with her small suitcase, and Ira was by the door, with Caroline, three days old, wrapped in a pink blanket, peering out suspiciously from his arms. "My daughter," she said, steeling herself for what was coming next. "Caroline."

"She was a beautiful baby," said Lewis.

"She had black hair. A head full of black hair," Ella remembered. "And she cried for what felt like a year, nonstop."

She flipped to the last two pictures. Caroline and her father, posing in a rowboat, wearing matching caps and fisherman's vests. And finally, Caroline on her wedding day, with Ella standing above her, arranging the folds of her veil.

"What a beautiful girl," said Lewis. Ella said nothing. There was silence. "I didn't want to talk about Sharla for months," Lewis said. "So I'll understand if you don't. But sometimes it's nice just to talk. To remember the good times."

Had there been good times with Caroline? It felt as if all she could remember was the heartache and endless nights of worry, waiting wide-eyed in the dark listening for the door (or the window, if Caroline had been grounded) to creak open. She remembered sitting on the gold velvet love seat in the living room, a tiny coffin too narrow to lie down in, waiting for her daughter to come home.

"She was," Ella began. "She was so beautiful. Tall, with brown hair, lovely skin, and she was . . . lively. Funny." *Crazy,* her mind whispered. "Mentally ill," she said instead. "She was manic-depressive. Bipolar, they call it now. We found out when she was in high school. She'd been having . . . episodes." Ella shut her eyes, remembering how Caroline had barricaded herself in her bedroom for three days, refusing to eat, screaming through the door that there were ants in her hair and she could feel them when she slept.

Lewis made a sympathetic noise. Ella kept talking, the words spilling out over each other like she'd kept them dammed up too long.

"We saw doctors. All kinds of doctors. And they gave her medicine, and it made her better in some ways, but it slowed her down, too. It was hard for her to think, she said." Ella could remember Caroline on lithium, how her face had bloated into a pale circle, and how her hands had swollen like cartoon mittens, how she'd yawned all day long. "She'd take it sometimes, and stop taking it, and tell us she was taking it. She went to college, and did all right for a while, and then . . ." Ella drew a shuddering breath. "She got married, and seemed to be doing well. She had two daughters. And she died when she was twenty-nine."

Lewis's voice was gentle. "What happened?"

"Car accident," said Ella. Which was the truth. Or a truth. Caroline was in a car. The car had crashed. She had died. But what had happened before that was also the truth, which was that Ella hadn't stepped in when she should have. She had given in to her daughter's repeated pleas to be left alone, to live her life, feeling resignation and sadness and also a great, shameful relief that she couldn't ever talk about—not to Ira, not to anyone. She'd called Caroline every week, but she'd visited only twice a year, for weekends. In the place of facts, she'd created fiction—the Daughter, to go along with the Husband. She'd display her snapshots like a winning poker hand—Caroline and her husband, Caroline and Rose, Caroline and Maggie. Her lady friends would ooh and aah, and all along, Ella knew the truth—the pictures were pretty, but the reality of Caroline's life was something else. It was jagged rocks hiding beneath the pretty curls of the waves, it was black ice on the pavement.

"Car accident," she said again, as if Lewis had questioned her, because "car accident" was enough of the truth, and never mind the letter that had come in the mail the day after the funeral, the letter sent from Hartford the day Caroline had died, the letter that was two lines long, written on a wide-ruled page ripped out of a schoolgirl's notebook in faint, wavering letters. "I Can't Anymore. Take Care of my Girls."

"And the granddaughters?" he asked gently.

Ella pressed her hands against her eyes. "I don't know them," she said.

Lewis's hand moved in warm circles on her back. "We don't have to talk about it anymore," he said. Oh, but he didn't know, and she couldn't explain it. How could he ever understand Caroline's dying wish, and how over the years avoidance became easier and easier. Caroline said, "Leave me alone," so she'd left her alone, and Michael Feller had said, "We're better off without you," and Ella had let him push her away, feeling sadness mixed with that secret, shameful relief. And now she'd never know her own granddaughters. And it was exactly what she deserved.

TWENTY-SEVEN

Rose woke up on Monday morning, then on Tuesday, and on Wednesday and Thursday, too, thinking that this would be the day—the day she took a shower, brushed her teeth, snuck the dog out the front door for her walk, came back home, then donned her suit and panty hose, pulled her briefcase out of the hall closet, and went to work like the rest of the world.

Every morning she'd wake up, full of good intentions and high energy. She'd lecture herself in the shower about how the Chinese symbol for crisis was the same as the one for opportunity. She'd walk the dog to Rittenhouse Square, and she'd look to the south, to where the gleaming glass face of the high-rise that housed Dommel, Lewis, and Fenick stood like a fifty-two story reproach, and her heart would sink. Really, everything would sink—all of her internal organs, kidney and liver and whatever else was down there, all of it joining in a universal cringe, all of it thinking, "No" and "Can't" and "Not today."

So she'd go home and call Lisa, her secretary, and explain that she was still sick. "I think it's the flu," she'd croaked on Monday.

"No prob," Lisa had said—Lisa, who never wasted an entire word on Rose when a portion of a word would do. But by the end of the week Lisa wasn't sounding quite so tolerant, and had actually granted Rose a full sentence. "You'll be back Monday, right?"

"Right," Rose had said, trying to sound crisp and competent and sure of herself. "Certainly," she said. "Of course." Then she'd plopped down on the couch and watched *A Wedding Story*. In her week away from work, Rose had become completely addicted to the show. *A Wedding Story* lasted half an hour and was as carefully structured as a sonnet, or a geometry proof. First segment: Meet the Bride and Groom (yesterday the bride had been Fern, a clerk at a drugstore, and the groom had been Dave, a heavily bearded long-distance trucker twenty years her senior). Second segment: How They Met ("I walked in for Pepto-Bismol," Dave had rumbled, "and there she was, behind the counter. Prettiest girl I'd ever seen.") Part Three: Wedding Plans (Fern and Dave were getting hitched at the Radisson. Dinner and dancing to follow, with Dave's two sons from two previous marriages serving as best men.) Final segment: The Big Day. (Fern walked down the aisle, a vision in off-white. Dave had cried. Rose had, too).

It had been like that for four days running. She'd eat doughnuts and cry at every bride, every groom, every dress, every mother and mother-in-law, every first kiss and first dance; at dumpy social workers from Alabama, schoolteachers from New Jersey, tech-support assistants from San Jose with actual, visible mustaches, girls with bad skin and bad perms and bad grammar. Everyone else in the world can do this, she'd think, as the dog wedged herself onto her lap and licked at her tears. Everyone but me.

On Saturday morning the telephone started ringing. Rose ignored it, hitching the dog to the leash she'd finally purchased and hurrying out the door before noticing she was still in her slippers. Her fuzzy bunny slippers. Oh, well. A homeless guy eyed her appreciatively. "You looking good, baby!" he yelled. Well, that was encouraging, Rose thought. "You heavy-set, but you still looking good!" Okay, she amended, maybe not so encouraging. She spent twenty minutes letting the dog sniff hedges, hydrants, the bases of parking meters and other dogs' butts, and when she came home, the phone was still ringing, as if it hadn't ever stopped. The phone rang while she stood like a lump of lead in the shower, letting the water thunder down on her head, trying to muster the energy to wash her hair. At five o'clock, Rose finally yanked it to her ear.

"What?" she said.

"Where the hell have you been?" Amy demanded. "I left you fourteen voice-mail messages at work; I sent you six e-mails; I stopped by the other night . . ." Her voice trailed off.

Rose vaguely remembered knocking, and how she'd pulled her pillow over her head until it stopped.

"Your secretary says you're sick, and my friend Karen saw you wandering around Rittenhouse Square in your pajamas and slippers."

"I was not wandering. And I wasn't wearing pajamas," Rose said haughtily, ignoring the matter of the slippers for the time being. "They were sweatpants."

"Whatever," said Amy. "What's going on? Are you sick?"

Rose glanced longingly at the television set, then forced herself to look away. "I need to talk to you," she finally said.

"Meet me at La Cigale in fifteen minutes," said Amy. "No, half an hour. You'll need to find some regular clothes. I don't think you'd be welcome in your jammies."

"They weren't pajamas!" Rose repeated, but Amy had hung up. She set the phone back on the counter and set off to find some shoes.

"Okay," said Amy, who'd already ordered coffee and a pair of scones as big as baseball mitts. "What'd he do?"

"Huh?" Rose asked.

"Jim," Amy said impatiently. "I know this is all that son of a bitch's fault. Tell me what he did, and we'll figure out what to do to repay him."

Rose smiled a tiny smile. Amy had honed her philosophy of failed relationships, and how to behave in their wake, over years of bad boyfriends. Step one: Mourn for a month (two weeks if the relationship hadn't involved sex). Step two: If you'd been dumped or cheated on, permit yourself one scandalous act of revenge (her last boyfriend, a hard-core vegan, had doubtlessly been shocked and horrified to find himself enrolled in the Organ Meat of the Month Club). Step three: Get over it. No regrets, no moping, no late-night drive-bys or dialing while drunk. Just on to the next adventure.

"So what did he do?"

"He cheated on me," Rose said.

Amy shook her head. "I knew it." She narrowed her eyes. "Now, how are we going to make him pay? Professional humiliation? Anonymous letter to the law firm? Something disgusting left in his car?"

"Like what?" Rose asked.

"Anchovy paste," Amy said. "A few squirts inside the glove compartment, and his Lexus will never be the same."

"Well, it wasn't just him," said Rose.

"What do you mean?"

"It was Maggie," said Rose.

Amy spat out a chunk of her scone. "What?"

"Maggie," Rose repeated. "I walked in on them." She'd said it so many times in her head, and to the little dog, that when she finally gave voice to the story, she felt as if she were reciting a poem she'd memorized years ago. "I walked in and they were in bed. And she had my new boots on."

"The Via Spigas?" Amy was sounding more horrified by the minute. "Oh, Rose. I am so sorry."

But not surprised, thought Rose.

"Oh, God," said Amy, looking stricken. "That little bitch."

Rose nodded.

"How could she?"

Rose shrugged.

"After you gave her a place to live, and probably money, and tried to help her . . ." Amy rolled her eyes toward the ceiling. "What are we going to do?"

"Never see her again," Rose said.

"Yeah," said Amy, "I imagine this might make Thanksgivings pretty awkward. So where is Little Miss Hot Pants?"

"I don't know," Rose said dully. "With my father and Sydelle, I guess."

"Well, then she's already suffering," said Amy. "Now, how about you?"

"Oh, I'm suffering plenty," Rose said, and sighed, and poked at her scone.

"What can I do?" Amy asked.

Rose shrugged. "Nothing to give it but time, I guess," she said.

"And retail therapy," said Amy, pulling Rose to her feet. "The mall beckons. It'll cheer you up. Come along."

All afternoon, Amy and Rose walked through the King of Prussia Mall. Rose eventually managed to fill three shopping bags with things she didn't need, with anything that caught her eye and gave her even a second's hope that her life—that she herself—could be repaired. She bought exfoliating scrubs and moisturizing creams. She bought candles scented with lavender and a beef-basted rawhide bone and a two-hundred-dollar beaded evening bag. She bought lipsticks and lip glosses and lip liners, three pairs of shoes, and a red cashmere ankle-length skirt that she couldn't imagine ever actually wearing. Finally, she headed to the bookstore.

"Self-help?" Amy asked. *"Better Sex through Yoga? How to Snare Mr. Fabulous in Ten Sneaky Steps?"* Rose laughed a little, shook her head, and located Current Fiction. Ten minutes later she'd amassed a stack of ten glossy paperbacks about women who found love, lost love, and then found it again.

"Just remember, I've still got that anchovy paste, in case you change your mind," Amy said as they walked through the parking lot. "And if you want an impartial third party to give Miss Maggie May a talking-to."

"You aren't impartial," said Rose.

"Well, no," said Amy. "But I play impartial on TV." She looked at her watch. "Do you want me to come home with you? Or do you want to come with me? I'm going to my mom's house for dinner . . ."

Rose shook her head. "I'm okay," she said, thinking she could do without a night at Amy's mom's house—the inevitable pasta supper, followed by a few hours indulging Amy's mom's passion for the posable dolls and jewelry from QVC.

"Call me," said Amy. "I'm serious."

Rose said she would. As her first step toward normal living, she presented the pug with the rawhide bone and forced herself to listen to all forty-three of her voice-mail messages. Sixteen from Amy, a dozen from work, three from her father, a handful from telemarketers, a half-dozen from bill collectors, and a single inexplicable call from a manager at the International House of Pancakes telling Rose to come in for an interview whenever she liked. She left her father a message saying she was alive and well, deleted the rest, and slept for eighteen hours straight. On Sunday morning—the day she had decided would be her absolute final day of moping—she called Amy to let her know that she was still alive, if not well. She put on lipstick and the red cashmere skirt, tucked one of the books into her pocket, leashed the little dog, and walked to her customary bench in the park. It was time for a decision.

"Pro," she whispered to herself. "I'm a lawyer, and it's a good job. Con," she said, as the dog snuffled at her feet. "It makes me sick to even think of going there."

She opened her book, pulled a pen out of her pocket, and started writing next to the breathless quotes that decorated the first few pages of all the books she'd purchased ("A witty, sexy romp!"). "Pro," she wrote on the book's inside cover, "if I go to work I'll have money. Con . . ." The little dog at her feet gave a short bark. Rose looked at her side and saw that a second dog, a strange, spotted, quivery-looking thing the size of a cat, had hopped on the bench and was now sitting beside her, regarding her with fearless black eyes.

"Hello," she said, and allowed the dog to sniff her mitten.

"Who are you?" She squinted at the tag around the dog's neck and wondered what kind of name Nifkin was. Foreign, probably. "Go home," she urged the spotted dog, whose whiskers trembled with each breath. "Go find your people." The dog merely stared at Rose and showed no signs of moving. Rose decided to ignore it.

"Con," she continued. She closed her eyes again and felt a wave of sickness wash over her as she imagined walking into the lobby, getting onto the elevator, and stepping onto the floor and walking the hallways where she'd fallen in love with Jim and imagined that he was in love with her.

"Con," she repeated, and opened her eyes. Nifkin was still sitting next to her on the bench, and now there was a little girl in a red coat standing in front of her. She had on red mittens and red rubber boots, and hair the color of maple syrup pulled into a thin carrot-shaped ponytail. Jesus, Rose thought, what am I? Snow friggin' White?

"Dog!" the girl announced, and waved one mittened fist.

"That's right," said Rose, as the pug gave a small, excited snort.

The girl bent down and stroked the pug's head. The pug wriggled in pleasure. Meanwhile, quivery little Nifkin had hopped off the bench and was sitting next to the little girl, so both of them were staring up at Rose. "I'm Joy," the little girl announced.

"Hi!" said Rose in a loud, cheerful voice. "This is . . ." Oh, dear. She still had no idea what the dog's name was. "This is the dog I walk!"

The little girl nodded as if this made perfect sense, pulled on Nifkin's leash, and toddled across the park. Meanwhile, a white-haired woman in sunglasses was looking at them. "Petunia?" she called. "Is that Petunia?"

Petunia, Rose thought. The pug looked back at her. Rose thought she could detect a hint of embarrassment on her squashed features.

"Hi, Petunia!" the woman said, as Petunia gave a regal snort.

"So is Shirley back from Europe already?" the woman asked.

"Um," said Rose weakly. She hadn't counted on running into any of the dog's intimates.

"I thought she was boarding her until next month," the woman continued.

Rose saw a lifeline, and seized it with all her might.

"That's right," she said. "This is actually a new service . . . a daily walk. So the dogs can, you know, get some fresh air, visit their neighborhoods, see their friends . . ."

"What a great idea!" said the woman, as two other dogs—a large chocolate-colored dog with a broad, snaky tail, and a prancing black poodle with its red tongue lolling—came over to them. "So you work for the kennel?"

"Actually, I'm . . . freelance," said Rose. She remembered reading a fairy tale where a princess was cursed, and every time she opened her mouth, frogs and toads would leap out. Rose decided that she had been similarly afflicted—when she opened her mouth, out came not warty amphibians, but lies. "I walk dogs for the kennel, but I also do, you know, house calls for individual pets . . ."

"Do you have a card?" asked an old guy at the end of the poodle's leash.

Rose made a show of groping in her pockets and coming up empty-handed. "I'm sorry," she said. "I seem to have left them at home . . ."

The guy pulled a pen and paper out of his pocket, and Rose scribbled her home telephone number, then added the words *Rose Feller, Dog Care* beneath them. And soon she was standing at the center of a mad Maypole of leashes and fur and fast-talking owners, all, it seemed, in search of responsible pet care.

Yes, Rose told them, she'd watch cats, too. No, she said, she didn't do obedience training, but she'd be more than happy to escort dogs to classes.

"Pet sitter!" called a woman in a droopy green sweater. Her dog was as low to the ground as Petunia, but perhaps twice her size, with a deeply wrinkled face and drool dripping from his ponderous jowls. "Memorial Day weekend?" she said.

"I'll be here," Rose said. Petunia and the wrinkly dog gave each other grave and solemn sniffs, as if they were members of the same club and giving each other the secret handshake.

"Are you licensed?" the woman asked, in the quick staccato rhythms of a former drill sergeant. "Licensed? Bonded? Insurance?"

"Um . . ." said Rose. The crowd held its breath. "Just finishing the paperwork. By next week I'll be good to go," she concluded, making a mental note to figure out what it would take to get licensed and insured as a pet walker.

"And your rates?"

Rates, thought Rose. "Um . . . ten dollars per walk, twenty-five dollars for a full day's care." From the look on the pet owners' faces, Rose determined that she'd offered them a bargain. "It's my new-customer special," she added. "And of course, if you'd rather your dog stayed in the kennel, I can pick them up there and take them for a walk in the park every day. Kind of the best of both worlds. Just give me a call!" She gave a jaunty wave and hurried out of the park. "Who's Shirley?" she asked the pug, who made no reply. "Is your name really Petunia?" she inquired. The pug continued to ignore her as Rose made her way toward the Elegant Paw. The bells jangled as she pushed the door open, and the woman behind the desk leapt to her feet.

"Petunia!" she cried, stubbing out her cigarette. Petunia barked once and began wagging not just her tail but her entire backside. "Oh, thank God! We've been going crazy!"

"Hi," said Rose, as the woman rushed around the counter, knelt on the floor, and rubbed Petunia from head to tail.

"Where'd you find her?" asked the woman. "God, we've been frantic! Her owner isn't due back for three weeks, but we didn't want to call her . . . I mean, can you imagine? You drop your dog off at the kennel and fly to Europe, and you get a call saying that the dog's been lost?" The woman straightened up, smoothing her denim overalls, and stared at Rose through her tangle of frizzy gray curls. "So where'd you find her?" she repeated.

"In the park," said Rose, who decided that she'd do all of her lying for the month—for the year, even—in this single day. "She didn't look lost or anything, but I know her . . . I mean, I don't know her, but I've seen her in the park before, and I figured that maybe you knew her, too . . ."

"Thank God," the woman said again, and scooped Petunia into her arms. "We were really worried. Pugs are very delicate, you know . . . they get all kinds of colds, respiratory infections, anything going around . . . I don't know who's been taking care of her for the last few weeks, but it looks like they've done a good job." She turned her eyes back to Rose. "There's a reward, of course . . ."

"No, no," said Rose, "I'm just happy she's back where she belongs . . ."

"I insist," said the woman, scooting back around the counter and opening the cash register. "So what's your name? Do you live around here?"

"I, um," said Rose. "I do, actually. I live in the Dorchester, and I'm an associate at Lewis, Dommel, and Fenick. But here's the thing. I'm starting a new business. A dog-walking company."

"Well, there's a bunch of those in town already," said the woman, tossing Petunia a biscuit, which she caught on the fly and munched noisily.

"I know," said Rose. "But here's the difference. I'll walk dogs who are being boarded. So they can get some fresh air and exercise."

Now the woman was looking mildly interested. "How much?"

"I'm going to charge ten dollars a walk," she said. And, just as the woman's face started to draw itself into a frown, she said, "which I'd split with you. Because it would be good for new business."

"So they'd pay ten dollars for a walk, and you'd give me five?"

"That's right," said Rose. "For the first month's worth of business. Then we'll see where I am." She was already starting to do the math, running calculations through her head—five dollars a walk times, maybe, ten dogs a day at the kennel, plus perhaps another three or four at ten dollars per walk . . .

"I do errands for the owners, too," said Rose, thinking quickly of all the things she'd always meant to make time for in her previous life as a lawyer. "Dry cleaning, groceries, making doctor's and dentist appointments, picking up gifts . . . If you want to try me out, I'll walk Petunia for free."

"Tell you what," said the woman. "I'll give it a try, as long as we keep Petunia's little adventure just between us."

"Deal," said Rose, and the woman came out from behind the register to shake her hand.

"I'm Bea Maddox."

"I'm Rose Feller."

The woman squinted at her. "Any relation to Maggie?"

Rose felt her smile freeze on her face. "Maggie's my sister. But I'm not like her," she said. She could feel Bea's eyes on her. Rose drew herself up straight and squared her shoulders and tried to look responsible, dependable, mature—in short, un-Maggie-like.

"You know, she's still got my keys," Bea said.

"I don't know where she is right now," said Rose. "I'll pay you back for them, though."

The woman stared at her, then shrugged. "I guess we could give it a try. It doesn't look like I've got anything to lose. And you did find this one." She gave Rose her card and directed Rose to the copy shop on the corner to make up a few signs with her name and her rates and the services she offered.

Rose went to the copy shop, dropped a freshly printed flyer at the Elegant Paw, then hurried home, where she changed her outgoing voice mail message to say, "You've reached Rose Feller at Rose's Pet Care. Please leave me a message, including your name, number, pet's name, and the dates you'll require service, and I will get back to you as soon as possible." *Taking a break,* she told herself, listening to the message again. She felt as though her life had turned into a movie, with a stranger playing the part of her. Taking a break, she repeated sternly. She'd never taken off more than a week at a time. She'd gone straight from college to law school with barely time to do her laundry in between. She was due, she decided.

Next stop, the law firm. First thing Monday morning, Rose sat on the couch, took a deep breath, and dialed not Lisa but Don Dommel himself. His secretary put her right through. Rose wasn't sure whether that was a good sign or a very bad one. She braced herself for his bluster, for the suggestions he was bound to have: Drink wheat grass! Toss a medicine ball around! Take up BMX biking!

"Rose!" said Don heartily. "How are you feeling?"

"Actually, much better," she said. She sat on the couch, pushing the stack of *Dog Fancy* magazine and *Dogs for Dummies* aside and realizing how empty the apartment felt without Petunia. "Listen, I'm wondering . . . I'm going through some personal difficulties right now . . ."

"Would you like to take a leave of absence?" Don asked, so hastily that Rose was sure he'd been thinking about it since the first day when Jim had shown up for work and she hadn't. "The firm's got a very flexible policy . . . unpaid leave, of course, but you'll keep all of your benefits, and you'll be free to pick up right where you left off. When you feel ready, of course. Or if not . . ." His voice trailed off. Rose could read volumes into the short silence that ensued. *Go away,* Don Dommel was thinking, so hard she could practically hear the words. *You're a problem, you're a scandal, you're a piece of juicy gossip, you're egg yolk on our collective tie. Go away and don't come back.*

"Six months?" she asked, figuring that in six months she'd have her head on straight, and she'd be ready to pick up where she'd left off.

"Excellent!" Don agreed. "Now, you should certainly feel free to get in touch should you need references . . ."

"Of course," said Rose. She was astonished at how easy this was, how easy it was to let go once she'd made up her mind. All the work she'd been obsessed with . . . reassigned, she supposed, to some other hungry young associate. It was completely unfair. Jim was as much to blame as she was. She knew that. But Jim would stay; he'd get his equity, his raises, his holiday bonus, his corner office with a view of City Hall. And she would get unpaid leave and pro forma letters of recommendation. Whatever, she thought. Fine. She'd be fine. Somehow, she would.

". . . happens," said Don, who was, evidently, not through with her.

"I'm sorry?" said Rose.

"It happens," said Don, and now he'd dropped the bluster and bombast of the pep rallies, and his voice was actually kind. "Not every firm is a perfect fit."

"That's very true," Rose said gravely.

"Keep in touch," said Don. Rose promised she would, and hung up the phone. Then she sat back and considered. No more law, she thought. "At least for now," she said out loud, and found that the words didn't even cause her a momentary pang of unhappiness. "Pets," she said, and laughed a little, because it was strange to think of herself this way—Rose Feller, a creature of pure ambition, Rose Feller, the eternal striver, bypassing the fast track for a pooper-scooper. "I'm just taking a break," she told herself. Then she put on a pot of water for tea, settled herself on the couch, closed her eyes, and wondered what on earth she'd done.

TWENTY-EIGHT

Maggie remembered once overhearing her sister on the telephone when she'd come back from college for Thanksgiving. "I live at the library," she'd declared melodramatically. Well, Rose should get a look at her little sister now.

For her first week at Princeton, Maggie slept in different places—snatching a few hours' shut-eye on a couch in a dorm's common room, a bench in a basement laundry room—while carefully casing the lower levels of Firestone Library, looking for more permanent accommodations. She found them on C floor, the third level down, in the far southeast corner, a place Maggie came to think of as the Hurt Book Room. These were books with torn pages and broken bindings, books whose spines had snapped and whose glue had given way, a stack of ancient *National Geographic*s in one corner, a pile of books written in some curlicued alphabet she'd never seen before, and three chemistry textbooks in which the tables appeared to be missing a few of the more recently discovered elements. Over an afternoon, Maggie watched the door carefully. As far as she could tell, no book ever left the Hurt Book Room . . . and no new books came in. Even better, there was a hardly used ladies' room right around the corner, which boasted not only toilets and sinks, but a shower. The marble tiles were coated in dust, but when Maggie eased the taps open, the water ran clear.

And so, on her seventh day on campus, in the windowless room of forgotten books, Maggie set up her base camp. She hid in the bathroom's handicapped stall until the last student had been shooed out of the library, and the doors were locked behind them. Then she crept into the room, spread her sleeping bag between two tall shelves of dusty old books, flicked on the stolen lantern, and lay down on top of the bag. There. Cozy. And safe, too, with the door locked, and with all of her stuff stowed neatly under one of the bookshelves. Casual passers-by wouldn't even know that anyone was there, unless they knew exactly where to look, and what to look for. It was exactly the effect that Maggie was seeking for herself. To be there, but not really there, to be present but invisible at the same time.

She reached into the pocket of the jeans she'd been wearing since she arrived. There was the wad of bills, the three different student IDs she'd acquired during her days of sticky-fingered scavenging in the library. There were Josh's credit cards, and one of Rose's, too, a key she'd found and kept even though she'd probably never know what door it unlocked. And an old birthday card. *Wishing you a very happy day,* she read, and then she set the card on a shelf where she'd be able to see it.

She crossed her arms over her chest, and breathed in the darkness. It was quiet down there, three floors below the ground, beneath the weight of thousands of books, quiet as she imagined a tomb would be. She could hear every click of her tongue against her teeth, the rustle of the sleeping bag every time she moved.

Well, she thought, at least she'd be able to sleep. But she wasn't tired yet. She rifled through her backpack until she found the paperback she'd picked up after someone had left it unfolded across an armchair. *Their Eyes Were Watching God,* it said, but the drawing on the cover didn't make it look like a religious book. It was a picture of a black woman (actually, she was sort of purplish on the cover, but Maggie assumed she was meant to be black), and she was lying on her back under a green tree, looking up at it with a pleased, dreamy expression. Not as good as *People*, she figured, but certainly better than those legal magazines Rose had lying around, or the antiquated medical textbooks on the shelf closest to her sleeping bag. Maggie opened the book up and started to read.

TWENTY-NINE

"Ella?" Lewis asked. "Are you okay?"

"Sure," she said, and nodded for emphasis.

"You got kind of quiet," he said.

"I'm fine," she said, and smiled at him. They were sitting together on Ella's screened-in porch, listening to the crickets chirp and the frogs croak and Mavis Gold discussing last night's episode of *Everybody Loves Raymond*.

"So tell me this," Lewis began. "What do you regret?"

"That's a strange question," said Ella.

"That's not an answer," Lewis replied.

Ella thought about it. Where could she start? Not with the real regrets, she decided. "You know what I regret? I've never been swimming in the ocean."

"Really? Never?"

"Not since I've moved here. Not since I was a little girl. I went one day, I had my towel and my bathing cap and everything, but it just seemed too . . ." It had taken her half an hour just to find a parking space, and the beach had been crowded with girls in shockingly small bikinis and boys in brightly colored bathing trunks. There'd been a dozen different songs blaring from a dozen different radios, and the air was full with loud teenager voices, and the sun seemed too bright, and the ocean seemed too big, and she'd turned around and gotten back in her car before even setting foot on the sand. "I think I'm too old," she said.

He got to his feet, shaking his head. "No such thing. Let's go."

"Lewis! Now? But it's so late!"

"I don't think the beach has hours," he said.

She'd stared up at him, a million reasons why not to go running through her head. It was late, she had an early-morning appointment, it was dark, and who knew who they'd find out there? Midnight drives to the beach were something for teenagers or newlyweds, not senior citizens with arthritis and hearing aids.

"Come on," he said, tugging at her hands. "You'll like it."

"I don't think so," she said. "Another time, maybe." But somehow she was on her feet, and out the door, and the two of them were tiptoeing past Mavis Gold's quiet apartment like coconspirators, or kids on a dare.

The beach was just ten minutes away. Lewis pulled into a spot right by the sandy edge, held her door, and helped her out of the car. "Leave your shoes," he said.

And there it was, the water that she'd seen a hundred times, from her car, from his high windows, from the postcards and the glossy brochures that had lured her to Golden Acres in the first place. There it was, moving restlessly, with waves swelling and foaming and running up onto the sand, close enough to tickle her bare feet.

"Oh!" she said, and jumped a little. "It's cold!"

Lewis bent down and rolled up his cuffs, and then rolled hers. He held her hand and they waded out until the water was past their ankles, almost at their knees. Ella held still, feeling the pull and suck of the water as the waves rearranged the sand. She could hear the roar of the waves, and she could smell smoke from a fisherman's bonfire, far off down the beach. She let go of Lewis's hand.

"Ella?" he asked.

She waded out further, two steps, then three, and the water was past her knees, past her thighs. Her loose cotton shirt floated out around her, billowing each time the waves rolled in. The water was shockingly cold, colder than the lakes of her girlhood, and her teeth chattered until her body adjusted to the temperature.

"Hey, be careful!" he called.

"I will," she called back. Suddenly, she was afraid. Did she even remember how to swim? Was it the kind of thing you could forget? Oh, she should have waited until daytime, or at least brought a towel . . .

No more, she thought. No more. She'd been afraid for twenty years—longer even, if you counted all of those terrible nights when Caroline was out and she didn't know where—but she didn't want to be afraid here. Not now. And swimming had been her favorite thing for years of her girlhood, her young-woman-hood. She'd felt invincible in the water, and free, as if she could do anything, as if she could go forever, could swim to China. *No more,* she thought again, and pushed off with her feet, propelling herself forward. A wave hit her full in the face. She spluttered, spat out salt water, and moved through it, her hands reaching through the dark water, feet churning unsteadily before finding their rhythm. And there it was. The water held her, and she was swimming again.

"Hey!" Lewis called. Ella half expected to turn around and see her little sister, Emily, standing at the edge of the water, pale and goose-pimpled, crying, "Ella! You're out too far! Ella, come back!"

She turned, and almost laughed to see Lewis paddling after her, his teeth clenched and head held high (to protect his hearing aid, she figured). She floated on her back, her hair streaming out with each wave until he'd caught up with her, and then she'd reached for him, brushing his hand with her fingertips and setting her feet back on the sand.

"If I'd known we were going to be swimming," he panted, "I would have worn my trunks."

"I didn't know!" she said. "It was an impulse!"

"Well, have you had enough?"

She lifted her feet, tucked her legs against her chest, and let the water hold her. She felt like an egg in a pot of warm water, buoyed and surrounded entirely. "Yes," she finally said, and paddled with her arms until she'd turned around, and by Lewis's side she paddled back toward the shore.

Later, sitting on top of a picnic table on the beach, wrapped in a musty blanket Lewis had unearthed from the trunk of his car, she said, "You asked me before what I regret."

"This was before our dip?" he asked, as if the salt water had obliterated his memory.

"Yes," said Ella. "Before. But I want to tell you the truth now." She breathed deeply, remembering the feeling of the water all around her, holding her up, making her brave. She remembered being a little girl and swimming out farther then any of the other kids, farther than any of the grownups, so far that Emily would later swear that she was barely a speck in the water. "I regret that my granddaughters are lost to me."

"Lost to you," Lewis repeated. "Why?"

"When Caroline died, their father took them away. He moved them to New Jersey, and he didn't want me to keep in touch. He was very angry . . . at me, at Ira, at everyone. Angry at Caroline, too, but she wasn't there to be angry at, and we were. I was." She wrapped the blanket around her more tightly. "I don't blame him for that." She looked down at her hands. "There was a part of me that was . . ." She breathed again. "Relieved, I guess. Caroline was so hard to deal with, and Michael was so angry, and it just felt safer not to have to deal with any of them. So I took the easy way out. I stopped trying. Now they're lost."

"Maybe you should try again," said Lewis. "Maybe they'd be glad to hear from you. How old are they?"

Ella didn't respond, even though she knew the answer. Maggie would be twenty-eight, and Rose would be thirty. They could both be married, with husbands and children and different last names and no use for an old woman, a stranger, barging in with a heart full of sad memories, and their dead mother's name on her lips. "Maybe," she repeated, because Lewis was looking at her, sitting cross-legged on top of the picnic bench with his hair still damp from the water. And Lewis had nodded, and smiled at her, and she knew she wouldn't have to answer any other questions that night.

THIRTY

Princeton was not going to be a problem. But money was. Maggie realized that her math skills weren't the greatest, but two hundred bucks, minus the twenty or so she'd spent on food at the Wawa during the days she hadn't been able to sneak into a dining hall or a study break offering free pizza or Thomas Sweet ice cream, plus stolen credit cards that she was too afraid to use, did not equal enough to fund a new life. It wouldn't even be enough for a plane ticket to California, let alone a deposit on an apartment, and head shots.

There must be more money, Maggie whispered to herself. It was a line from a short story she'd read in another abandoned book, a story about a little boy who could ride a rocking horse and see the winners of real horse races; and the more urgently he rode, the louder his house seemed to whisper. *There must be more money.*

She considered her options as she sat inside the Student Center, nursing a ninety-cent cup of tea. She needed a job that paid cash, and the only possibility she'd seen was printed on a flier that she'd pulled down from the library wall. She set her mug aside and carefully unfolded the sheet of yellowing paper. "Housekeeper Needed," it read. "Light cleaning, some errands, once a week." Then there was a telephone number starting with 609.

Maggie pulled out her cell phone—the one her father had bought her, the one where the bills for the charges went directly to his office—and dialed. Yes, an old-woman-sounding voice informed her, the job was still open. Once a week, easy work, but if Maggie was interested, she'd have to provide her own transportation. "You could take the bus," she said. "Right from Nassau Street."

"Would you mind paying me in cash?" asked Maggie. "It's just that I haven't gotten my checking account set up here. I've got an account at home . . ." She let her voice trail off.

"Cash will be fine," the woman said crisply. "Assuming you work out."

So Thursday morning Maggie got up extra early, creeping like a mouse through the silence of the library before any of the lights came on, making sure her things were tucked out of sight. She hid in the first-floor bathroom and listened to the security guards unlock the front doors. Ten minutes after the library opened for business, she walked out the door, and was on her way to Nassau Street.

"Hello there," called the woman on the porch. She was short and thin with white hair flowing past her shoulders, and she wore what looked like a man's oxford shirt with a pair of leggings underneath it, and sunglasses, even though it was cloudy outside.

"You must be Maggie," she said, tilting her head in Maggie's direction. She put one hand on the railing for balance and held out the other one for Maggie to shake. Blind, Maggie realized, and shook the woman's hand carefully. "I'm Corinne. Come on in," she said, leading the way into a large Victorian house that already seemed scrupulously clean, and precisely organized. In the entryway hall, there was a stark wooden bench to the right and a series of cubbyholes hanging above it and a pair of shoes in each cubbyhole. A raincoat and a winter coat hung on adjoining hooks; an umbrella and hat and mittens were laid neatly on a shelf above them. And next to the empty coat rack was a white cane.

"I don't think you'll find the work too difficult," said Corinne, taking careful birdlike sips from a cup of coffee in a lemon-yellow mug. "The floors need to be swept and mopped," she began, ticking off the tasks on her fingers. "I'd like you to organize the recycling, the glass and paper in particular. The laundry should be sorted, the dishwasher needs to be emptied, and . . ."

Maggie waited. "Yes?" she finally asked.

"Flowers," said Corinne, and tilted her chin up defiantly. "I'd like you to buy some flowers."

"Okay," said Maggie.

"I'm sure you're wondering why I want them," said Corinne.

Maggie, who hadn't been wondering, said nothing.

"Because I can't see them," said Corinne. "But I know what flowers look like. And I can smell them, too."

"Oh," said Maggie. And then, because "Oh" seemed somehow insufficient, "Wow."

"The last girl said she brought flowers," said Corinne, pursing her lips. "But they weren't real ones." Her lip curled. "Plastic. She thought it wouldn't matter."

"I'll find some real flowers," said Maggie.

Corinne nodded. "I would appreciate that," she said.

It took Maggie less than four hours to do everything Corinne had asked. She wasn't an experienced housekeeper, because Sydelle had never trusted the girls to do anything right and had employed an anonymous army of housekeepers to maintain the pristine state of her glass-and-metal-filled rooms. But Maggie did a good job, sweeping every mote of dust from the floors, then folding the laundry and returning dishes and silverware to their shelves and drawers.

"My parents left me this house," Corinne said while Maggie worked. "It's the house I grew up in."

"It's beautiful," said Maggie, which was true. But it was also sad. Six bedrooms, three bathrooms, a vast staircase that curved through the center of the house, and the only resident a blind woman who slept in a single narrow bed with a single flat pillow, who would never appreciate all of the space or how the sun looked as it spilled through the wide windows and pooled on the hardwood floors.

"Are you ready to go to the market?" Corinne asked.

Maggie nodded, then remembered that nodding would do her no good. "All set," she said.

Corinne used her fingertips to extract a single bill from her wallet. "This is twenty dollars?" she asked.

Maggie inspected the bill and said that yes, it was a twenty.

"That's all the money machine gives out," said Corinne. *Then why are you asking me?* thought Maggie. Then she realized that it was possibly a test. And, for once, she'd managed to pass on her first try. "You can go to Davidson's market. It's right up the street."

"Do you want a flower with a smell?" asked Maggie. "Like lilacs or something?"

Corinne shook her head. "No smell will be necessary," she said. "Use your discretion."

"Do you need anything else while I'm there?"

Corinne seemed to consider this. "Yes. You can surprise me," she said.

Maggie walked to the market, thinking of what she might buy. Daisies, for starters, and she was lucky to find bunches of them clustered in a green plastic tub out front. She wandered the aisles, considering and rejecting plums, a pint of strawberries, a bundle of green-smelling spinach, a half-gallon of milk in a heavy glass bottle. What would Corinne like? Something that smelled seemed too obvious, especially since she'd been so quick to reject scented flowers, but Maggie wanted something . . . She groped for the word, and grinned when she found it—*sensual.* Something that had a feel to it, a weight, a heft, like the glass milk bottle, or the satiny feel of the daisy's petals. And suddenly, there it was, right in front of her, another glass jar, only this one glowing amber. Honey. "Orange Blossom Honey. Locally Produced," read the label. And even though it was $6.99 for even the smallest jar, Maggie added it to her basket, along with a bumpy-looking loaf of twelve-grain bread. Later, back in the large, clean house, when Corinne sat across from Maggie at the kitchen table, slowly munching a slice of the toasted bread spread thick with honey and then pronouncing it perfect, Maggie knew that she wasn't just paying her an empty compliment. She'd passed her second test of the day by finding exactly the right thing.

THIRTY-ONE

"I'm worried about your sister," Michael Feller said without preamble. Rose sighed and stared at her cup of coffee, as if Maggie's face might appear inside of it. So what else was new?

"It's been eight weeks," her father continued, as if Rose had somehow lost track of time. His face looked as pale and vulnerable as a peeled hard-boiled egg, all high, wide forehead and sad little eyes above his standard-issue gray banker's suit and subdued maroon tie. "We haven't heard from her. You haven't heard from her," he said, his voice rising at the end of the sentence, turning it into a question.

"No, Dad, I haven't," said Rose.

Her father sighed—a typical Michael Feller sigh—and poked at his dish of melting ice cream. "Well, what do you think we should do?"

Meaning, what do you think I should do, thought Rose. "Did you try all of her ex-boyfriends? That should have taken you a week or two," she said. Her father was silent, but Rose could hear reproach in what he wasn't saying.

"Did you call her cell phone?" she asked.

"Of course," said Michael. "Her voice mail's working. I leave messages, but she doesn't call back."

Rose rolled her eyes. Her father pretended not to notice.

"I'm really worried," Michael continued. "This is a long time for us not to hear anything. I wonder . . ." His voice trailed off.

"If she's dead?" Rose supplied. "I don't think we're going to get that lucky."

"Rose!"

"Sorry," she said, not very sincerely. She didn't care if Maggie was dead. Well . . . Rose pulled a handful of napkins out of the dispensers. That wasn't true. She didn't want her awful little sister to be dead, but she thought she'd be perfectly happy if she never saw or heard from her again.

"And, Rose, I'm worried about you, too."

"Nothing to worry about," Rose said, and started to fold one of the napkins into a pleated fan. "Everything's fine."

Her father's voice was dubious as he raised his gray eyebrows. "Are you sure? You're okay? You're not having . . ."

"Having what?"

Her father paused. Rose waited. "Having what?" she asked again.

"Some kind of trouble? You don't want to, um, talk to someone or something?"

"I'm not nuts," Rose said bluntly. "You don't have to worry about that."

Her father raised his hands, looking helpless and upset. "Rose, that wasn't what I meant . . ."

But of course, Rose thought, it was exactly what he meant. Their father never talked about it, but she knew it had been on his mind as he'd watched his daughters—especially Maggie—make their way toward womanhood. *Are you cracking up, are you losing your mind, are those bad strands of DNA starting to speak up, are you looking into taking a short fast drive around a tight, slippery curve?* "I'm fine," Rose said. "I just wasn't happy at that particular law firm, so I'm taking some time to figure out what I want to do next. Lots of people do it. It's very common."

"Well, if you're sure," her father said, and turned his attention back to his ice cream—a special treat, Rose knew, as Sydelle hadn't allowed anything more caloric than ice milk and Tofutti into their house since the early 1990s.

"I'm fine," said Rose. "You don't have to worry about me." With heavy emphasis on the *me,* to make it clear who her father did have to worry about.

"Could you call her?" Michael asked.

"And say what?"

"She won't talk to me," he said sadly. "Maybe she'll talk to you."

"I don't have anything to say to her."

"Rose. Please?"

"Fine," Rose grumbled. That night, she set her alarm for one in the morning, and when it went off she groped through the darkness for her telephone and punched in Maggie's cell phone number.

One ring. Two. And then her sister's voice, loud and cheerful. "Hello?"

Jesus! Rose made a disgusted noise. She could hear party sounds in the background—music, other voices. "Hel-lo!" Maggie trilled. "Who's this?"

Rose hung up. Her sister was like a fucking Weeble, she thought. She'd wobble, she'd screw up, she'd steal your shoes and your cash and your guy, but she'd absolutely never fall down.

The next morning, after her first round of dog walks, she called her father at his office. "She's alive," she reported.

"Oh, thank goodness!" her father said, sounding absurdly relieved. "Where is she? What did she say?"

"I didn't speak to her," Rose said. "I just heard her voice. The prodigal daughter is alive and well, and has lived to party another day."

Her father was silent. "We should try to find her," he said.

"Feel free," said Rose. "And give her my best when you do." She hung up the phone. Let her father try to track down his wayward daughter. Let Michael and Sydelle try to sucker her into coming home. Let Maggie Feller be someone else's problem for once.

She walked out the door and into a world she'd only discovered since defecting from full-time employment and spending her days traversing the city's streets, often with a bouquet of leashes in her hands. The city from nine to five was hardly the ghost world she'd been imagining. There was an entirely different population, a secret city of mothers and babies, shift workers, students and deliverymen, the retired and unemployed, moving through streets and corners of the city that she'd never even known about, in spite of her years at law school and her years at the firm. Why would an unmarried, childless lawyer have known about Three Bears Park, a tiny pocket of a playground between Spruce and Pine Streets? Would a woman who took the same route to work every day have known that on the five hundred block of Delancey every house flew a different flag? How could she have suspected that the shops and grocery stores would be bustling at one in the afternoon, filled with people in khakis and sweaters instead of business suits and briefcases? Who knew that she could easily fill her hours with the stuff she used to cram into mere minutes of spare time?

Her days began with dogs. She had her own key to the Elegant Paw, and each morning at the time she'd normally be buying her large black coffee and heading to the office, she'd be unlocking the door to the kennel, leashing two or three or four dogs, stuffing her pockets with biscuits and plastic poop bags, and heading toward Rittenhouse Square. She'd spend forty-five minutes there, in the square of the park, surrounded by dress shops and bookstores and fancy restaurants and high-rise apartment buildings, letting her charges sniff at bushes and hedges and other dogs. Then she'd spend her morning running errands. Drop-offs at the drugstore, pickups at the dry cleaners, zipping along sidewalks and side streets with her pockets heavy with keys, opening up doors for decorators, landscapers, exterminators, personal chefs, even chimney sweeps.

In the afternoons, she'd go on another round of walks, heading back to Rittenhouse Square for her daily date with the little girl, the spotted dog, and the woman who was with them.

Over her eight weeks as a dog-walker she'd become fascinated with the little girl, Joy, the dog Nifkin, and the woman she guessed was the girl's mother. They came to the park between four and four-thirty every afternoon. Rose would spend an hour tossing the tennis ball for her afternoon dogs and inventing a life for the woman and the girl and the dog. She imagined a husband, handsome in a regular-guy kind of way. She gave them a big house with fireplaces and bright woven rugs, a wooden chest full of every kind of toy and stuffed animal for the little girl. She sent them on family trips to the shore, hiking in the Poconos. She imagined them getting off an airplane—the father pulling a big wheeled suitcase, the mother pulling a medium one, the little girl with an appropriately small bag. Papa Bear, Mama Bear, Baby Bear, and the dog trotting jauntily behind them. In her mind, she gave them a quiet, happy life—good jobs, enough money, dinners at home on weeknights, just the three of them, the parents urging the little girl to drink her milk, the little girl surreptitiously sneaking her vegetables to the dog named Nifkin.

She'd already progressed from nodding hello to waving hello to actually saying "Hi." Given enough time, Rose thought, things might blossom into actual conversation. She sat and watched as the little girl chased the spotted dog toward the fountain, and the mother, who was tall, broad-shouldered, and heavy hipped, talked on her cell phone.

"No, I don't like liverwurst," she overheard the woman saying. "That's Lucy. Remember? The other daughter?" She rolled her eyes at Rose and mouthed *My mother.* Rose gave what she hoped was an understanding nod and a little wave. "No, I don't think Joy likes liverwurst either, Ma." She paused, listening, then shook her head. "No, Peter does not like liverwurst. In fact, I don't think anyone really likes liverwurst. I don't even know why they make it anymore." Rose laughed. The woman smiled at her, still listening. "Nifkin likes liverwurst," she said. "We can give it to him!" Another pause. "Well, I don't know what you should do with it. That was my one suggestion. Put it on crackers or something. Tell your book club it's paté. Okay. Right. We'll see you then. Okay. Bye."

She hung up the phone and put it in her pocket. "My mother thinks I'm unemployed," she began.

"Oh," said Rose, and cursed her rusty conversational skills.

"I'm not," said the woman. "But I work at home. Which, to my mother, seems to mean that I don't work at all, so she can call me whenever she wants to and ask me about liverwurst."

Rose laughed. "I'm Rose Feller," she said.

The woman extended her hand. "I'm Candace Shapiro. Cannie."

"Mom!" The little girl had suddenly reappeared, holding Nifkin's leash.

Cannie laughed. "Excuse me," she said. "I'm Candace Shapiro soon-to-be Krushelevansky." She made a funny face. "Try fitting that on a business card."

"So you're married?" asked Rose. She winced, shut her mouth, and wondered what had happened to her. Two months out of the office, two months with mostly dogs and deliverymen, and she'd forgotten how to talk to people.

But Cannie didn't act as though she'd noticed anything strange. "Engaged," she said. "We're doing the deed in June."

Huh, Rose thought. Well, if Hollywood stars could have babies before they got married, she supposed regular Philadelphians could, too. "Are you having a big wedding?"

Cannie shook her head. "Nope. Small. In our living room. Rabbi, family, a few friends, my mother, her life partner, their softball team. Nifkin's going to be the ring dog, and Joy will be the best baby."

"Oh," said Rose. "Um . . ." That didn't sound like any of the nuptials she'd seen on TV. "How," Rose began, and then stopped, unsure of herself, before starting again with the most banal of cocktail-party questions. "How did you meet your husband-to-be?"

Cannie laughed and flipped her hair over her shoulders. "Now that," she said, "is a long and involved story. It started with a diet."

Rose snuck a glance at Cannie and decided that it couldn't have been a very successful diet.

"I actually met Peter when I was pregnant with Joy, but I didn't know I was pregnant yet. He was running this weight-loss study, and I thought that if I lost weight this guy who I'd broken up with would want me back." She smiled at Rose. "But you know how it goes. You chase after the wrong guy until the final reel and then find out the right one was there waiting all along. Love works in mysterious ways. Or is that the Lord? I can never remember."

"The Lord, I think," said Rose.

"If you say so," said Cannie. "So how about you? Are you married?"

"No!" said Rose emphatically. "I mean, no," she said, in a more modulated tone. "It's just that . . . well, I just ended a relationship. Well, I didn't end it exactly. My sister . . . anyhow. Long story." She looked down at her hands, then at Petunia, curled at her feet, then over at Joy and Nifkin, who were playing fetch with a red mitten, then over at half a dozen dogs standing in the middle of a triangle of grass. "I guess I'm trying to figure out what's next."

"Do you like what you're doing now?" Cannie asked.

Rose looked at Petunia, at the other dogs in the park, at the grayish tennis ball in her hand, and the bunch of plastic poop bags beside her. "Yes," she said. It was true. She liked all of her dogs— the disdainful, snorty Petunia; the golden retriever who was always so glad to see her that he whirled in circles of joy when he heard her key in the door; the grave bulldogs; the fractious schnauzers; the narcoleptic cocker spaniel named Sport who'd occasionally fall asleep at red lights.

"And what else do you like?" Cannie prompted.

Rose shook her head, smiling ruefully. She knew what made her sister happy—size two leather pants, sixty-dollar French skin cream, men telling her she was beautiful. She knew what made her father happy—a bear market, dividend checks, a crisp new copy of *The Wall Street Journal,* the infrequent occasions when Maggie'd managed to hold a job. And what made Amy happy—Jill Scott records, Sean Jean pants, and the movie *Fear of a Black Hat.* She knew what Sydelle Feller loved—My Marcia, organic grains, Botox shots, and feeding fourteen-year-old Rose dietetic Jell-O for dessert while everyone else got ice cream. Once upon a time, she'd even known the things that made her mother happy, like clean sheets and bright red lipstick, and the costume-jewelry pins that she and Maggie would pick out for her birthday. But what did Rose herself like, besides shoes, and Jim, and foods that were bad for her?

Cannie smiled at Rose, and got to her feet. "You'll figure it out," she said cheerfully. She whistled for Nifkin, and the dog came running, with Joy trailing behind him, her cheeks pink and her hair coming loose from its ponytail. "Will we see you tomorrow?"

"Sure," said Rose. She pocketed the tennis ball and began gathering her charges, holding five leashes in her left hand and the leash of a single renegade greyhound in her right. She dropped dogs off until she was left with just Petunia. The pug trotted a few steps ahead of her like a plump croissant with legs. Petunia made her happy, even though she'd had to relinquish Petunia to her owner, Shirley, a no-nonsense seventy-two-year-old woman who lived downtown and who luckily consented to let Rose walk the pug every day. What else? Not clothes, really. Not money, because all she'd ever done with her exorbitant six-figure salary was pay her rent and her student loans, sock away a prudent percentage for her retirement, and let the rest gather interest in a money market account, per Michael Feller's explicit instructions.

So what?

"Yo!" called a bicycle messenger. Rose scooped Petunia into her arms and jumped aside as the bike whizzed past them. Its rider had a bag slung over his shoulder and a walkie-talkie, bleating static, on his hip. Rose watched him pedal off down the street, remembering that she'd had a bike, when she was a girl. A blue Schwinn, with a blue-and-white seat and a white straw basket and pink and white plastic tassels on the handlebars. There had been a bike path that ran behind her parents' house in Connecticut, a trail that led to the town golf course and soccer fields. It also wove through a crab apple orchard, and in the fall, Rose used to ride her bike there, her wheels crunching through the fallen crab apples, whispering over the red and gold leaves. Sometimes her mother would come with her, on her own bike, which was the grown-up version of Rose's, a Schwinn three-speed with a baby seat over the rear wheel, a seat that had once held Rose and Maggie.

What had happened to her bike? Rose tried to remember. When they'd moved to New Jersey, they'd lived in a rented condominium just off the highway, which meant parking lots and roads with no sidewalks or shoulders. She'd probably outgrown the bike while they'd lived there, and when they'd moved to Sydelle's, she'd never gotten a new one. She'd gotten her driver's license instead, three days after she turned sixteen, and she'd been excited, at first, about the prospect of freedom, until she realized that most of her driving would consist of dropping her sister off at parties, picking her up after dance lessons, and going grocery shopping.

She dropped Petunia off in Shirley's apartment and decided that over the weekend she'd buy herself a bike—a used one, to start with, so she could see if she liked it. She'd buy one, and maybe put a Petunia-sized basket on the handlebars, and she'd ride it . . . somewhere. She'd heard that there were bike trails in Fairmount Park and a towpath that ran all the way from the art museum out to Valley Forge. She'd buy a bike, she thought, smiling now and walking with a bounce to her step. She'd buy a bike, she'd get a map, she'd pack a picnic of bread and cheese and grapes and brownies and a can of gourmet dog food for Petunia. She'd have an adventure.

THIRTY-TWO

Mrs. Lefkowitz hadn't wanted to go for their weekly walk. "I can get my exercise in here," she'd told Ella, waving her cane at the ten-by-sixteen-foot expanse of her living room, into which she had crammed a couch, two love seats, an armchair with doilies decorating the arms, and an enormous wide-screen TV.

"Not the way you need to," Ella had said patiently.

"*The View* is on," she said, gesturing at the television set, where four women on the television screen were yelling at each other. "Don't you like *The View?*"

"You mean the ocean?" Ella asked innocently. "I love the view of the ocean. Let's go outside and have a look."

"Also, I've got a proposal for you," said Mrs. Lefkowitz, playing what was clearly her last card. "I've been thinking about you. Your predicament."

"Later," Ella said firmly.

"Agh, I give up," Mrs. Lefkowitz said. She put on gigantic square-lensed sunglasses, smeared zinc over her nose, and knotted the laces of her Nikes. "Come on, Bruce Jenner. Let's get this over with."

They walked down the drive toward the tennis courts, where, last month, someone had hit *Drive* instead of *Reverse* and plowed right through the fence, right through the net, and right into an unfortunate woman named Frieda Mandell, who'd been playing a desultory game of doubles and ended up splayed on the hood of a Cadillac, with her racquet still in hand. This, Mrs. Lefkowitz had announced mordantly, was clear evidence that sports and exercise— tennis in particular—could kill you if you weren't careful.

But her doctor had insisted she walk, and so every Tuesday at ten, Ella and her charge walked slowly to the clubhouse, had lunch, and took the trolley back home. Somewhere along the line, Ella had even started to enjoy the older woman's company.

Mrs. Lefkowitz's walk had a rhythm. She'd plant the cane, sigh, step forward with her right foot, then drag her left foot behind it. Plant, sigh, stomp, shuffle. It was soothing, really, Ella thought.

"So what's new?" asked Mrs. Lefkowitz. "You still seeing that one?"

"Lewis," said Ella.

Mrs. Lefkowitz nodded. "He's a good one. Reminds me of my first husband."

Ella was puzzled. "Your first husband? Did you have two?"

Plant, sigh, stomp, shuffle. "Oh, no. I just call Leonard my first husband. It makes me sound more worldly."

Ella bit back her laughter and kept a light hand on Mrs. Lefkowitz's elbow as she negotiated a crack in the sidewalk.

"Does Lewis have a good income?"

"Fine, I think," said Ella.

"You think? You think?" Mrs. Lefkowitz demanded. "Don't think. Find out! You could be left with nothing! Like that Charles Kuralt!"

Ella was confused. "He was left with nothing?"

"No, no, no. Not him. But he had, remember, the other girl-friend. And she was left with nothing."

"Not even the Winnebago?"

"Sure. Laugh," said Mrs. Lefkowitz darkly. "You won't be laugh-ing when you're eating the cheese the government gives out."

"Keep walking," said Ella.

"And his children," Ella said. "Do they know about you?"

"I think so," said Ella.

"Make sure," said Mrs. Lefkowitz. "You know about Florence Goodstein, right?'

Ella shook her head.

"Well," Mrs. Lefkowitz began, "she and Abe Meltzer were keeping company. They'd go to movies, and dinner, and Flo would drive Abe to his doctors' appointments. One day his kids called her to check up on their father, see how he was doing, and Flo happened to mention that she was tired. Well, they heard 'tired' and thought she didn't want to take care of him anymore. And the very next day," said Mrs. Lefkowitz, pausing as the story reached its crescendo, "they flew down here, packed up his apartment, and moved him to assisted living in New York."

"Oh, my," said Ella.

"Flo was beside herself," said Mrs. Lefkowitz. "It was like the raid on Entebbe."

"I'm sorry for her. Keep walking," Ella said.

Mrs. Lefkowitz lifted her sunglasses and peered at Ella. "Are you ready to hear my proposal?"

"Sure," said Ella. "What's it about?"

"Your granddaughters," said Mrs. Lefkowitz, and resumed her shuffling walk.

Ella groaned inwardly. She couldn't believe she'd told Mrs. Lefkowitz about her lost granddaughters. Then again, a year ago she'd never have believed she'd be able to tell the story to anyone. Now, it seemed, she couldn't keep her mouth shut.

"Do they have the Emil?" Mrs. Lefkowitz asked.

"Emil?" Ella repeated.

"Emil, Emil," said Mrs. Lefkowitz impatiently. "On the computer."

"Oh, e-mail," said Ella.

"What I said," said Mrs. Lefkowitz, with a long-suffering sigh.

"I don't know."

"Well, we could find out. On the Internet. We could find out all kinds of things about them."

Ella's heart lurched. "Do you have a computer?" she asked, barely daring to hope.

Mrs. Lefkowitz gave a dismissive wave with her good hand. "Sure, who doesn't?" she asked. "My son got me an iMac for my birthday. Tangerine. Guilt," she said, apparently in response to Ella's unspoken questions of *What color?* and *Why?* "He doesn't visit too much, so he sends the computer, e-mails me pictures of my grandbabies. You want we should go back and look up your granddaughters?" she asked hopefully.

Ella bit her lip. She could hear the voice inside of her crying, *Look them up!* at war with the much more familiar, much more insistent voice that said, *Let them go,* could feel anticipation and fragile hope shot through with pure terror. "Let me think about it," she finally said.

"Don't think," said Mrs. Lefkowitz, drawing herself up to her four feet eleven inches and whacking at the ground with her cane, narrowly missing Ella's left foot. "There is no think, only do."

"What?"

"Yoda," said Mrs. Lefkowitz, and began the laborious process of turning herself around. "Let's go."

THIRTY-THREE

"Step out the front door like a ghost into the fog," said a guy in a rumpled white linen shirt, as Maggie walked through Firestone Library's doors at ten o'clock on a not-at-all foggy morning.

Maggie looked at him as he fell into step beside her, his own backpack slung loosely—slung stylishly, somehow—over his shoulders. He had a long, pale face, brown hair curling past his ears, and what he wore—the linen shirt with pressed oatmeal-colored linen pants—was a significant deviation from the unofficial campus uniform of jeans and a T-shirt.

"It's not foggy out," she said. "And isn't that from a song?"

"Notwithstanding," he said. He pointed at the copy of *My Antonia* that Maggie had tucked under her arm. "Women in Literature?"

Maggie gave a shrug that could have been either a yes or a no, figuring the less she said, the better. In her weeks on campus, excepting her first night at the party, she hadn't been saying much more than "Thank you" or "Excuse me" to the other students. Which was fine, Maggie thought. She had Corinne to talk to. She had books. She had a comfortable chair in the library's sunny reading room staked out, a favorite little table in the Student Center when she felt like a change of scenery. She'd finished the Zora Neale

Hurston, finished *Great Expectations,* and was now working her way through *A Tale of Two Cities,* rereading *My Antonia,* and plowing through *Romeo and Juliet,* which was much harder going than the Baz Luhrmann movie had made it out to be. Conversation with students could only lead to questions, and questions could only lead to trouble.

"I'll walk you," said the guy.

"That's okay," said Maggie, and tried to edge away.

"Not a problem," the guy said cheerfully. "It's in McCosh, right?"

Maggie had no idea where Women in Literature met or where McCosh might be located, but she nodded again, and picked up her pace. The guy kept up with her easily. Long legs, Maggie observed with dismay.

"I'm Charles," said the guy.

"I'm sorry," she finally said, "I'm not interested, okay?"

Charles stopped and smiled at her. He looked a little bit like a picture of Lord Byron that Maggie'd seen in one of her purloined books—a long blade of a nose, an amused curl to his lips. No six-pack, she was sure, no biceps to hang on to. Not her type. "You haven't even heard my pitch yet," he said.

"There's a pitch?" asked Maggie unhappily.

"Absolutely," said Charles. "I. Um. This is awkward. But it happens that I have need of a woman."

"Don't you all," said Maggie, slowing her pace so that her feet were practically dragging, figuring that if she couldn't run away from him, she could perhaps make him hurry away from her and off to his own class.

"No, no, not like that," he said, smiling and matching her pace again. "I'm in a playwriting class, and we have to present scenes, and I need a woman—an ingenue type—to do my scene for me."

Maggie looked at him. "You mean acting?" She stopped walking and stared up at him. He was tall, she saw. With nice gray eyes, too.

Charles nodded. "The very thing. I'm hoping," he said, as he and Maggie continued toward McCosh Hall, "to do a one-act at

Theatre Intime in the spring." He pronounced it *Ohn-Team*, and for a moment Maggie wasn't sure what he meant. She'd walked by that building a hundred times and she'd always figured it sounded like it was spelled: *In Time*. Which scared her—how many other things had she been getting wrong, even if she was only getting them wrong in the privacy of her own head? "So if the scene goes well, it'll be, you know, a good first step. So," he concluded, "want to help a brother out?"

"You're not my brother," said Maggie. "And how do you even know that I can act?"

"You can, though, can't you?" asked Charles. "You have that look."

"What look is that?"

"Dramatic," he said promptly. "But I'm getting ahead of myself. I don't even know your name."

"It's Maggie," said Maggie, momentarily forgetting her desire to be known as M.

"I'm Charles Vilinch. And I'm right, aren't I?" asked the guy. "You're an actress, right?"

Maggie simply nodded, hoping he wouldn't ask for specifics, as she didn't think that either her stint singing backup for Whiskered Biscuit or her hip's appearance in the Will Smith video would impress him much. "Look, I'd like to help you, but . . . well, I don't think I can," said Maggie, with real regret, because starring in a play—even if it was just some lousy student one-act—was extremely appealing. It could, she thought, be a start. Princeton wasn't that far from New York. Maybe word of the play, and its star, would reach the city. Maybe a casting agent or director would take a train down for a look. Maybe . . .

"Why don't you take today to think about it?" said Charles. "I'll call you tonight."

"No," said Maggie, thinking quickly. "No, um, my phone's not working."

"Then meet me for coffee," he said easily.

"I can't . . ."

"Decaffeinated tea, then," said Charles. "Nine o'clock in the Student Center. I'll see you there." And he loped off, leaving Maggie at the entrance to the lecture hall, where students—women, mostly, with a few holding her very same *My Antonia*—were streaming through the doors. Maggie stood for a minute, thinking *Why not?* as the bodies poured around her. It would be more trouble to turn around than to simply follow the crowd inside. She'd sit in the back, she figured. Nobody would notice. Plus, she was curious as to what the professor would say about the book. Maybe she'd even learn something.

THIRTY-FOUR

"Are you doing okay?" Amy had asked Rose one morning over blueberry pancakes at the Morning Glory Diner. Amy, in fitted black pants and a midnight-blue blouse, was on her way to the airport and a business trip that would take her to rural Georgia and deepest Kentucky, where she'd be lecturing at waste-water treatment facilities ("which smell," she'd told Rose, "about how you'd imagine they would"). Rose, in her now-customary loose-fitting Army-Navy surplus khaki pants, was on her way to take ten recently read romances to the Book Trader, in exchange for ten more, and then walk a schipperke named Skip.

Rose chewed and thought about it. "I'm good," she answered slowly, as Amy's spidery fingers snagged a piece of bacon off her plate.

"You don't miss work?"

"I miss Maggie," Rose mumbled into a mouthful of pancake. It was the truth. The Morning Glory was in Maggie's old neighborhood, right around the corner from the apartment she'd been kicked out of just before she'd moved in with Rose. While Rose was in college, and then in law school, Maggie would come to stay for a weekend once or twice a semester, and then, once Rose started working, she'd come to South Philadelphia and meet Maggie for

brunch, or drinks, or pick her sister up for a trip to the King of
Prussia Mall. Rose had fond memories of Maggie's series of apartments. No matter where she was living, the walls would wind up
painted pink, and Maggie would park her antique hair dryer in the
corner, set up a makeshift bar somewhere, with a thrift-shop martini shaker standing perpetually at the ready.

"So where is she?" asked Amy, wiping a butter knife with a
napkin and using it to inspect her lipstick.

Rose shook her head, feeling the familiar Maggie-induced sen-
sations of anger, frustration, fury, and sympathy rising up in her
throat. "I don't know," she said. "I don't know if I want to know."

"Well, knowing Maggie, she'll turn up," said Amy. "She'll need
money, or a car, or a car full of money. Your phone will ring and
there she'll be."

"I know," said Rose, and sighed. She did miss her sister . . .
except *miss* wasn't quite the right word. Sure, she missed having a
companion, having someone to share breakfasts and pedicures and
trips to the mall with. She even found that she missed Maggie's
noise, Maggie's clutter, the way she'd turned the thermostat up to
eighty degrees, until her apartment felt like a trip to the tropics,
and how, in Maggie's hands, even the most mundane story would
turn into a three-act adventure. She remembered Maggie trying
to flush a wad of makeup-caked Kleenex down Rose's recalcitrant
toilet, yelling, "Take it all, bitch!" at the bowl; Maggie throwing
a fit in the Shampoo and Soap aisle of the drugstore because they
were out of her particular-colored-hair-specific brand of conditioner; the flicking, go-away motion she'd make with her fingertips when she wanted Rose to give her more room on the couch;
the song her sister would sing in the shower. "It had to be me . . .
it had to be me . . ."

Amy drummed her knife impatiently on the edge of her plate.
"Earth to Rose."

"Right here," said Rose, and waved weakly. Later that morning,
she pulled her bike up to a pay phone, dug a fistful of change out of

her pocket, and dialed her sister's cell phone again. One ring, then two. "Hello?" Maggie demanded, her voice brash and bossy. "Hello, who's this?"

Rose hung up, wondering if Maggie would see the 215 area code and wonder if it was her, and if she'd care.

THIRTY-FIVE

If Maggie Feller had learned one thing in her fourteen years of deal-ing with members of the opposite sex, it was this: your bad hookups will always come back to haunt you. There could be a guy you'd never seen before in your life, and all you had to do in order to guarantee that you'd be seeing him everywhere was spend a few quality minutes alone with him in the backseat, the bedroom, or behind a locked bathroom door. Then he'd be popping up in the cafeteria, in the halls, sitting behind the counter of the diner where you'd just started work, and holding some other girl's hand at the next Friday night party. It was the Murphy's Law of relationships— the guy you never want to see again was the guy you'd never be able to avoid. And Josh, from her first night on campus, was, unfortu-nately, no exception.

She wasn't sure he'd even recognize her—he'd been so com-pletely drunk, and it had been late, and she'd been fresh off the train, without a chance to perfect her Princeton camouflage. But Josh was everywhere, looking as if he was just on the verge of attaching her face to his missing money, sleeping bag, camping lantern, and clothes.

She'd look up from her book in the library and catch a glimpse of his sweatshirt, and the side of his face. She'd be refilling her mug

with coffee in the dining hall and he'd be standing behind the salad
bar, studying her. He actually started talking to her the Saturday
night she dragged a stolen pillowcase full of her laundry into the
laundry room, operating under the mistaken assumption that
absolutely nobody would be doing their laundry on a Saturday
night.

"Hey," he said casually, while peering at her bras and panties as
she stuffed them into the machine.

"Hi," she said, keeping her head down.

"What's going on?" he asked. Maggie gave a small shrug,
dumping detergent on top of the laundry from one of those little
cardboard packets she'd bought from the vending machine.

"You want some fabric softener?" He lofted his jug at her, and
smiled. But his eyes weren't smiling. His eyes were taking a careful
inventory of her face, her hair, her body, measuring what he saw
against what he remembered from that one night in his bed.

"No thanks. I'm fine," she said. She pushed her quarters into
the slot. Just then, her cell phone rang. Her father, she figured—
he'd called before, and she'd never answered, but now she grabbed
at the phone as if it were a life buoy and she was drowning. "Hello!"
she said cheerfully, turning her face and her body away from Josh's
scrutiny.

There was no answer, just breathing. "Hello!" Maggie said
again, hurrying up the stairs, past a group of students who were
passing around a bottle of champagne and singing some kind of
football fight song. "Who's this?" No answer. Just a click, then
silence. She shrugged, put the phone in her pocket, and hurried out
into the cool spring air. There were lamps illuminating the path at
regular intervals, and there were carved wooden benches along the
path and alongside the buildings. Maggie selected a bench away
from the light, and sat down in a corner. Time to go, she was thinking. It's not a big campus, and you're seeing that guy everywhere,
and it's only a matter of time before he figures out who you are and
what you did, if he hasn't figured it out already. Time to cash in

your chips, time to put the cards down, time to get on the next bus to somewhere.

Except, the weird thing was, she didn't want to leave. She was having . . . what? Maggie tucked her legs up against her chest and stared up at the tree branches, heavy with tight green buds, and the starry night sky. Fun. Well, not fun exactly, not fun like a party was fun, not fun like getting dressed up and looking great and feeling people's jealous eyes moving over her was fun. It was a challenge— the kind of challenge that her series of dead-end minimum-wage jobs never gave her. It was like being the star of her own detective show.

And it wasn't just a question of not letting anyone notice. These were the smart kids, the honors-course kids, the National Merit Finalist kids, the cream of the crop, the pick of the litter. If Maggie could move invisibly among them, didn't it prove what Mrs. Fried had always told her? If she could survive Princeton, if she could sit in the back row of a dozen different classes and actually follow what was being taught, didn't it mean that she was smart, too?

Maggie brushed dew off the seat of her jeans and got to her feet. Plus, there was Charles's play, his directorial debut, a Beckett one-act at Theatre Intime. And she was the star. She'd been meeting with him every few days for rehearsal, running her lines in the Student Center, or in an empty classroom in the arts building down on Nassau Street.

"I'm over in Lockhart," he'd told her the last time they'd met, walking her back from 185 Nassau. "I stay up late. I've got two roommates," he added, before Maggie had a chance to lift an eyebrow. "I guarantee that your virtue is safe with me."

Well, it was late now. She wondered if he'd be up. She wondered, wrapping her arms around herself, if he'd possibly be willing to lend her a sweatshirt. She hurried across the campus. Lockhart, if she remembered right, was right next to the University Store. Charles's room was on the first floor, and when Maggie tapped on the window, he pulled back the shade and smiled, and hurried around to let her in.

Charles's room was like nothing she could have imagined. It was like walking into another country. Every inch of wall space, and the ceiling, too, was covered with Indian-print tapestries and dozens of silver-framed mirrors. An Oriental rug, crimson and gold and blue, covered the floor, and instead of a coffee table in the center, there was an old, battered trunk—a treasure chest, Maggie thought. He and his roommates had pushed their desks against the walls and surrounded the chest with piles of cushions—red with gold fringe, purple with red fringe, a sage-green one embroidered with gold thread and beads.

"Have a seat," said Charles, indicating the cushions. "Do you want something to drink?" There was a tiny refrigerator in the corner, a cappuccino machine on top of it.

"Wow," said Maggie. "Are you running a harem?"

Charles laughed and shook his head. "Nah," he said. "We just like to play around. Last semester Jasper went to Africa, and we had kind of a safari theme going, but the animal heads on the walls freaked me out. This is better."

"Very nice," said Maggie, walking a slow circle of the room, checking it out. There was a small, fancy-looking stereo in the corner, with compact discs organized by genre—jazz, rock, world beat, classical—and then alphabetically. In another corner there was a small, high table stacked with travel books—Tibet, Senegal, Machu Picchu. When she breathed deeply, she could catch the scent of incense and cologne and cigarettes. The half-sized refrigerator contained bottled water, lemons, apples, and apricot jam. Not a single beer or bottle of condiment.

Gay, Maggie decided, closing the refrigerator door. Gay, she thought, with a certain degree of relief. Gay without a doubt. She picked up a framed photograph from Charles's desk. It was him, with his arm slung over the shoulders of a laughing girl.

"Your sister?" she asked.

"Ex-girlfriend," he said. *Huh,* Maggie thought.

"I'm not gay," Charles said. Then he laughed a little apologetically. "It's just that everyone who comes over here thinks that. And then I have to spend three months acting as heterosexual as possible."

"So what, you have to scratch yourself every five minutes instead of every ten? That's not hard work," said Maggie, plopping herself back onto the cushions, and flipping through a book about Mexico. Whitewashed houses stark against that piercing blue sky, weeping Madonnas in tiled courtyards, white-tipped waves curling onto golden sand. She was disappointed. She'd only known three kinds of guys in her entire life—those who were gay, those who were old, and the third category, a hundred times larger than the first two, those who wanted her. If Charles wasn't gay, and he certainly wasn't old, then he probably wanted her. Which made Maggie feel sad, and a little cheated. She'd never had a guy who was just a friend before, and she'd spent enough time with Charles that he liked her for her brains and her quickness, her resourcefulness, instead of the one thing that every other guy in the world usually liked her for.

"Well, I'm glad we got that cleared up. And I'm glad you're here. I've got a poem for you."

"For me? Did you write it?"

"No. We had it last week in my History of Poetry class." He flipped open a *Norton Anthology* and began to read:

> " 'Márgarét, áre you gríeving
> Over Goldengrove unleaving?
> Leáves, líke the things of man, you
> With your fresh thoughts care for, can you?
> Áh! ás the heart grows older
> It will come to such sights colder
> By and by, nor spare a sigh
> Though worlds of wanwood leafmeal lie;

And yet you *will* weep and know why.
Now no matter, child, the name:
Sórrow's spríngs áre the same.
Nor mouth had, no nor mind, expressed
What heart heard of, ghost guessed:
It ís the blight man was born for,
It is Margaret you mourn for.' "

He closed the book. Maggie took a deep breath. Her arms had broken out into goose bumps. "Whoa," she said. "Dark. But I'm not Margaret."

"Oh, no?"

"No," she said. "I'm just Maggie. Maggie May, actually." She gave an embarrassed laugh. "From the noted poet, Rod Stewart. My mother liked the song."

"What's your mother like?" Charles asked.

Maggie looked at him, then away. Usually, at this moment of the back-and-forth with her guy of the hour, this would be the point where Maggie would produce her own version of the tragic tale of her mother's death, and lay it in the guy's lap like a gaily wrapped package. Sometimes she'd have her mother dying of breast cancer, and sometimes she'd stick to car wreck, but always she'd lavish the story with detail and drama. The chemotherapy! The cop at the door! The funeral, with the two little girls crying over the coffin! But she didn't feel like telling Charles that version of the story. She felt like telling him something closer to the truth, which scared her, because if she told him the truth about this, what else would she be tempted to blurt out?

"Not much to tell," she said lightly.

"Oh, I know that's not true," he said. She felt his eyes on her. She knew what was coming. *Why don't you come a little closer? Or, Can I pour you a drink?* And soon she'd feel his lips on her neck or his arm around her shoulders, with his hand edging toward her breast. It was a dance she'd done too many times.

Except the words never came, and his lips never came. Instead, Charles stayed just where he was. "Fine. Hold out on me," he said, and smiled at her—a friendly smile, she thought, and felt relieved. Maggie glanced at the antique-looking clock on his desk. It was after one. "I should go," she said. "Got to get my laundry."

"I'll walk you," said Charles.

"No, that's okay."

But he was shaking his head and picking up his backpack. "It isn't safe to walk around by yourself."

Maggie almost laughed at him. Princeton was the safest place she'd ever been. It was safer than a kiddie pool, safer than a child's car seat. The only thing she'd ever seen go wrong was when somebody dropped their tray in the dining hall.

"No, really. I'm actually hungry. Have you ever been to P.J.'s?"

Maggie shook her head. Charles affected a look of absolute horror. "It's a Princeton tradition. Excellent chocolate chip pancakes. Come on," he said, holding the door for her, "my treat."

THIRTY-SIX

Rose Feller figured that the day would come.

After three months of dog-walking and dry-cleaning pickups, trips to the drugstore and the grocery store and the video store, she figured she was overdue to run into some of the familiar faces from her less-than-halcyon days at Lewis, Dommel, and Fenick. So on a sunny, sixty-degree day in April, when Shirley, Petunia's owner, handed her an envelope with the familiar address printed on the outside and said, like it was no big deal, "Could you drop this off at my attorney's office?" Rose had just swallowed hard, tucked the envelope into her shoulder bag, and got on her bike, pedaling toward Arch Street and the tall, gleaming tower where she'd once worked.

It could be, she reasoned as she rode, that nobody would even recognize her. She'd spent her days at Lewis, Dommel, and Fenick in pantsuits and heels (*and in love,* her tattletale brain insisted on reminding her). Today she was wearing shorts, a pair of ankle-high socks decorated with skillets, fried eggs, and coffee cups (a little something Maggie had left behind), and hard-soled bicycling shoes. Her hair had grown out past her shoulders and was braided in two pigtails—Rose had learned through trial and error that it was one of the only styles that worked underneath a bicycle helmet. And although she hadn't lost any weight since her untoward departure from the world of litigation, her body looked different. Days of biking and walking had given her muscles in her arms and legs, and her office-drone pallor had been replaced by a tan. Her cheeks glowed pink, her hair, bound in its pigtails, was shiny. So she had that going for her, at least. *Get through it,* she told herself, as she walked off the elevator and over to the reception desk, her bare brown calves flashing, her shoes clattering on the tiled floor. *Get through it.* It wouldn't be hard. She'd drop off the package, get a signature, and . . .

"Rose?"

She held her breath, half hoping that what she'd heard had issued from her imagination rather than from an office across the lobby. She turned, and standing there was Simon Stein, instigator of intramural softball, his gingery hair garish under the overhead lights, and his muted red-and-gold tie highlighting the gentle swell of his belly.

"Rose Feller?"

Well, she thought, giving him a half-smile and a quick wave, it could be worse. It could be Jim. Now, if she could just dump her envelope and get out of here . . .

"How are you?" asked Simon, who'd hustled across the lobby and was now standing right beside her, looking her up and down as if she'd mutated into some previously unknown species. Maybe she had, she thought grimly. The Former Lawyer. How many of those had Simon Stein ever seen?

"I'm fine," she said quietly, and handed the envelope to the receptionist, who was looking at Rose with undisguised curiosity, trying to match the tanned girl in shorts with the sober young woman in suits.

"They told us you were on leave," said Simon.

"I am," she said shortly, collecting the signed receipt from the receptionist and turning toward the door. Simon followed after her, even as Rose willed him to go away.

"Hey," he said, "have you had lunch?"

"I should really get going," she said, as one of the elevators opened and a crowd of partners came pouring out. Rose peeked up surreptitiously, looking for Jim's face, and didn't start breathing again until she didn't see it.

"Free food," said Simon Stein, and gave her a charming grin. "Come on. You've got to eat anyhow. We'll go somewhere fancy and pretend that we're important."

Rose laughed. "Not with me dressed like this, we can't."

"Nobody's going to say anything," said Simon, and followed Rose onto the elevator as if he was one of the dogs she walked each day. "It's going to be fine."

Ten minutes later, they were sitting at a table for two at the Sansom Street Oyster House, where, just as Rose had feared, she was the only woman who wasn't wearing hose and heels. "Two iced teas," said Simon Stein, loosening his tie and rolling his sleeves up over his freckled forearms. "Do you like clam chowder? Do you eat fried food?"

"Sure and sometimes," said Rose, who'd unfastened her pigtails and was trying to casually rearrange her hair.

"Two bowls of New England clam chowder, and the mixed seafood platter," he said to the waitress, who nodded approvingly.

"Do you always order for strangers?" asked Rose, who'd decided that her hair was a lost cause and was now trying to tug her shorts down over the scabs on her right knee.

Simon Stein nodded and looked pleased with himself. "Whenever I can," he said. "Did you ever get food envy?"

"What's that?" asked Rose.

"When you go to a restaurant and order something, and then you'll see them bring someone else's food and it'll look, like, ten times better than what you ordered?"

Rose nodded. "Of course. Happens all the time."

Simon looked smug. Actually, given his curly red hair and his grin, he looked sort of like Ronald McDonald. "Well, it never happens to me," he said.

Rose stared at him. "Never?"

"Well, hardly ever," said Simon. "I'm an expert orderer. A master of the menu."

"A master of the menu," Rose repeated. "You should be on TV. Cable, at least."

"I know it sounds crazy," said Simon, "but it's true. Ask anyone I've ever been out with. I'm never wrong."

"Okay," said Rose, rising to the challenge, and thinking of the best restaurant she'd been to recently, with 'recently' defined as six months ago, when she'd gone with Jim late one night after work, when they were both certain they wouldn't see anyone he knew. "London."

"The city or the restaurant?"

Rose resisted the urge to roll her eyes. "The restaurant. It's in the art museum neighborhood."

"Of course," said Simon. "You'd get the salt and pepper squid, roast duck with sweet ginger, and the white chocolate cheesecake for dessert."

"That's amazing," Rose said, only half-sarcastically.

Simon shrugged his shoulders and raised his small hands to the heavens. "Look, lady, it's not my fault if all you ever eat is a baked potato and broiled fish."

"How do you know that?" asked Rose, who had, if she remembered it right, ordered the broiled salmon at London.

"Lucky guess," said Simon. "Also, that's all most women ever eat. Which is a pity. Try me again."

"Brunch at Striped Bass," said Rose, naming one of the best restaurants in town. Her father had taken her and Maggie as a special treat. Rose had gotten the turbot. Maggie, she remembered, had gotten three rum and Cokes and, eventually, the sommelier's phone number.

Simon Stein closed his eyes. "Do they have the eggs Benedict with poached lobster on the menu?"

"I don't know. I've never actually been for brunch."

"We should go," said Simon.

We? thought Rose.

"Because that's what you get," he continued. "You start with the oysters, if you like oysters . . . you do like oysters, don't you?"

"Sure," said Rose, who'd never had oysters.

"And then you get the eggs Benedict with poached lobster. It's really good." He smiled at her. "Next?"

"Penang," said Rose. Penang was the new, hot, Malaysian fusion spot that had just opened in Chinatown. She'd only read about it, but Simon Stein didn't know that.

"Coconut sticky rice, roast chicken wings, beef rendang, and those summer rolls with the fresh shrimp."

"Wow," said Rose, as the waitress set their soup in front of them. She dipped her spoon in, tasted, and closed her eyes as her mouth filled with the texture of heavy cream and the faint salty tang of the ocean, of fresh, sweet clams and potatoes cooked until they dissolved on her tongue. "My fat grams for the week," she said once she'd recovered.

"It doesn't count if someone else is paying," said Simon Stein, offering Rose the oyster crackers. "Try some of these."

Rose ate half her cup of soup before it occurred to her to speak again. "This is delicious," she said.

Simon nodded, as if he expected nothing else but her praise for the soup. "So can you tell me a little bit more about this leave?"

Rose swallowed hard against a lump of clam and potato. "It . . . um . . ."

Simon Stein was looking at her quizzically. "Are you sick?" he asked. "Because that was one of the rumors."

"One of the rumors?" Rose repeated.

Simon nodded, and pushed his own empty soup cup aside. "Rumor one was mysterious illness. Rumor two was that you'd been head-hunted by Pepper, Hamilton. Rumor three . . ."

Just then the waitress reappeared with a platter heaping with golden-brown strips and filets. Simon busied himself squeezing lemon over everything and giving the french fries a judicious sprinkle of salt.

"What was Rumor Three?" Rose demanded.

Simon Stein stuffed two fried scallops into his mouth, and looked at her with wide blue eyes, guileless beneath his curly, strawberry-blond lashes. "Mmhph oo er narphing mm mhmphair."

"What?" said Rose.

Simon swallowed. "That you were having an affair," he said. "With one of the partners."

Rose's mouth fell open. "I . . ."

Simon raised one hand. "You don't have to say anything. I shouldn't have even brought it up."

"Does everyone think that?" Rose said, trying not to sound shocked.

Simon helped himself to tartar sauce and shook his head. "No. Most people are betting on either lupus or lower back trouble."

Rose ate a few clam strips and tried to look nonchalant, and feel like she wasn't ridiculous. But she was ridiculous, of course. She'd ditched her job, her boyfriend had ditched her, she was dressed like an overgrown schoolgirl, and now a guy who was practically a stranger was salting her fries. Worst of all, everyone knew about her and Jim. And she'd thought it was a secret. How dumb could you get? "Was there a specific partner's name attached to this rumor?" she asked, trying to sound as if it didn't even matter, dipping a shrimp into the tartar sauce and hoping against hope that at least part of her secret was still safe.

Simon Stein shrugged. "I didn't listen," he said. "It was just gossip, that's all. You know how lawyers are. They've got to have answers for everything, so when someone just disappears, you know, they want an explanation."

"I didn't disappear. I'm on leave. As you know," Rose said stubbornly, and ate a piece of flounder, which was, all things considered, very tasty. She swallowed and cleared her throat. "So. Um. What else is going on at the firm. How are you?"

He shrugged. "The same. I've got a case of my own now. Unfortunately, it's the Stupid Bentley Case."

Rose gave him a sympathetic nod. The Stupid Bentley Case involved a client who'd inherited his father's millions and, apparently, none of his father's brains. The client had bought a used Bentley, then had spent the two years subsequent to the purchase trying to get his money back from the dealership. His contention was that the car had produced a cloud of oily black smoke since the first time he'd taken it on the highway. The dealership's belief—which was, unfortunately for the client, supported by the client's now ex-wife—was that the smoke was the result of the client driving the Bentley with its emergency brakes on. As Simon told some of the details, Rose could hear him trying to sound bored and cynical—disgusted that the firm's client was such a boob, disgusted with a process that had allowed the case to go as far in the system as it had—but the boredom and cynicism were a thin and easily cracked patina over Simon Stein's obvious enthusiasm for his work. Sure, it was a small case, and sure, the client was an ass, and no, his sparkling eyes and waving hands said, this case wasn't going to set legal precedent, but still, she could tell that he was having fun as he described the depositions, the discovery, the subpoenaing of the subliterate mechanic named Vitale. Rose sighed, listening, wishing she still felt that way about the legal life, and wondering if, really, she ever had.

"But enough about the Bentley," Simon concluded, popping the second-to-last fried shrimp into his mouth and tossing the last one to Rose. "You look terrific, by the way. Very rested."

Rose looked down at herself ruefully, from her slightly sweaty T-shirt down to the calves that were tattooed with grease from her bicycle chain. "You're too kind."

"Would you like to have dinner with me on Friday?" asked Simon. Rose stared.

"I know that was kind of abrupt," said Simon. "It's the result of billing by the hour, I think. You just blurt out what you have to say, because the meter's running."

"Don't you have a girlfriend?" asked Rose. "And didn't she go to Harvard?"

"Gone," said Simon. "It wasn't working out."

"Why not?"

Simon thought it over. "She didn't have much of a sense of humor, and the Harvard stuff . . . well, I guess I just couldn't see spending my future with a woman who referred to her period as the Crimson Tide."

Rose snorted. The waitress took their plates and put dessert menus in front of them. He barely spared it a glance. "Hot apple cobbler," he said. "Want to split it?"

He smiled at her, and she saw that even though he was shortish, and vaguely egg-shaped, and about as far from Jim looks-wise as Saks Fifth Avenue was from Kmart, she had to admit that he was funny. Nice, too. Sort of appealing. Not to her, of course, she thought hastily, but still . . .

Simon, meanwhile, was staring at her expectantly, and humming the chorus of what Rose recognized as "Lawyers In Love." "So are we on for dinner?"

"Why not?" said Rose.

"I was hoping for a more enthusiastic response than that," Simon Stein said dryly.

Rose smiled at him. "Yes, then."

"She smiles!" said Simon; and when the waitress brought the cobbler, he said, "Let's put some ice cream on top of that. We're celebrating."

THIRTY-SEVEN

Ella sat in front of the keyboard at Mrs. Lefkowitz's computer, took a deep breath, and stared at the blank screen. "I don't think I can do this," she said.

"What?" Mrs. Lefkowitz called from the kitchen. "Did it freeze up again? Just restart the computer. You'll be fine."

Ella shook her head. She didn't think that she would be fine at all. She was in Mrs. Lefkowitz's spare bedroom, which served as a sort of office-cum-storage area, with the tangerine iMac perched on top of a ponderous claw-footed walnut desk, aside a red velvet couch with the stuffing leaking out, beneath a stuffed elk's head, flanked by a copper-and-bamboo umbrella stand, which housed Mrs. Lefkowitz's cane. "I don't think I can do this," Ella said again . . . but nobody heard her. Lewis and Mrs. Lefkowitz were in the kitchen, slicing up muffins and fresh fruit, and in the living room the television set was blaring *Days of Our Lives.*

Ella squeezed her eyes shut, typed in "ROSE FELLER" and hit the "enter" key before she lost her nerve.

When she opened her eyes, Mrs. Lefkowitz and Lewis were standing behind her, and the screen was full of words.

"Wow," Lewis said.

"Popular name," observed Mrs. Lefkowitz.

"How do I know which one's her?" Ella asked.

"Just try one," said Lewis. Ella clicked one of the links, and discovered that the words "Rose" and "Feller" had brought her to Feller Florals in Tucscon, Arizona. She sighed, returned to the search page, and clicked another link. This one was a record of marriage licenses from Wellville, New York, for a Rose Feller born in 1957. Not her Rose. She backed up, clicked once more, and finally, her granddaughter's face, twenty-two years older than when Ella had seen it last, filled the screen.

"Oh!" she gasped, and read through each word on the page as fast as she could. "She's a lawyer," she said, in a voice that didn't sound like it belonged to her.

"Well, that's not the worst thing she could be," said Mrs. Lefkowitz, and cackled. "At least she's not in jail!"

Ella stared. It was Rose. It had to be. She had the same eyes, the same serious expression, the same eyebrows that followed a straight line across her forehead that Ella remembered from when she'd been a little girl. Ella got up and collapsed on Mrs. Lefkowitz's loveseat. Lewis took her place and starting scrolling through the text. "Princeton University . . . University of Pennsylvania law school . . . specialty in commercial litigation . . . lives in Philadelphia . . ."

"She was so smart," Ella murmured.

"You can e-mail her," said Lewis.

Ella buried her face in her hands. "I can't," she said. "Not yet. I'm not ready. What would I say?"

"You'd start with 'hello,' " said Mrs. Lefkowitz, and laughed at her own wit.

"Where's her sister?" Ella managed to ask. "Where's Maggie?"

Lewis gave her a reassuring look that felt like his hand, warm on her shoulder. "I'm looking," he said. "Haven't found anything yet."

But he would, Ella knew. The girls were out there, living lives she couldn't imagine. And they were grown-ups now. They could make their own decisions about whether to let her into their lives or not. She could write to them. She could call. But what would she say?

Mrs. Lefkowitz plopped down beside her. "You can do it!" she said. "Come on, Ella. What do you have to lose?"

Nothing, Ella thought. *Everything.* She shook her head and shut her eyes. "Not today," she said. "Not yet."

THIRTY-EIGHT

Much to her surprise, Maggie Feller found that she was actually getting a strange sort of education at Princeton.

She'd certainly never planned on it, she thought as she walked across campus with an armload of books. But the truth was, that first class had hooked her. And Charles had hooked her, too, with his books of monologues, his conversations about things no guy had ever wanted to discuss with her—character arcs, moods and motivation, books and real life and how they were the same and how they were different. Even the one fly in her ointment, Josh, the unfortunate and suddenly ubiquitous hookup, felt like a distraction instead of a real danger. She liked being a student, she thought ruefully. She should have given it more of a chance ten years ago.

Take poetry. For Maggie, reading anything from the simplest sentence on up involved a sort of detective work. First, she'd have to sound out and decipher each individual letter of every single word. Once she had them individually, she'd have to string them together, nouns and verbs and the gaudy baubles of adjectives, and read it over and over and over again before she could extract the meaning, like a chunk of walnut tucked into a gnarled shell.

She knew this wasn't how it worked for most people. She knew that Rose could glance at a paragraph or a page and know what it meant as if she'd soaked the knowledge of it in through her skin, which was why she could devour thick romance novels, while Maggie stuck to magazines. But poetry, Maggie had found, was the great equalizer, because poetry wasn't made to be obvious on its surface, and every reader, whether they were Princeton smarties or community-college dropouts, had to go through the process of deciphering the words, then the sentences, then the stanzas, pulling the poem apart and putting it back together before it would yield its meaning.

Three and a half months into her campus camp-out, Maggie walked into "her" Modern Poets class and settled herself in the back row, making sure to leave an empty seat on either side of her. Most of the students clustered near the front, hanging breathlessly on Professor Clapham's every word, practically dislocating their shoulders when they threw their hands into the air to volunteer an answer, which meant that Maggie was fine in the back. She sat, opened her notebook, and copied the day's poem from the blackboard, whispering each word to herself as she wrote it.

One Art

> The art of losing isn't hard to master;
> so many things seem filled with the intent
> to be lost that their loss is no disaster.
>
> Lose something every day. Accept the fluster
> of lost door keys, the hour badly spent.
> The art of losing isn't hard to master.
>
> Then practice losing farther, losing faster:
> places, and names, and where it was you meant
> to travel. None of these will bring disaster.

I lost my mother's watch. And look! my last, or
next-to-last, of three loved houses went.
The art of losing isn't hard to master.

I lost two cities, lovely ones. And, vaster,
some realms I owned, two rivers, a continent.
I miss them, but it wasn't a disaster.

—Even losing you (the joking voice, a gesture
I love) I shan't have lied. It's evident
the art of losing's not too hard to master
though it may look like *(Write* it!) like disaster.

"I lost my mother's watch," Maggie whispered as she scribbled down the poem. The art of losing. She could write a book about that. The things she found in the school's various lost-and-found boxes continued to boggle her mind—and keep her very well outfitted. With her textbooks and sweatshirts, hats and mittens from J.Crew or the Gap, she looked the part of a Princetonian. And she was starting to believe her own fiction. The semester was drawing to a close, and Maggie felt like she was close to becoming an actual, honest-to-God student. Except the summer was coming. And what did students do during the summer? They went home. And she couldn't. Not yet.

"The art of losing's not too hard to master," she wrote, as Professor Clapham, blond, in her late thirties, and enormously pregnant, waddled to the front of the room.

"This is a villanelle," she said, settling her books on the desk and herself, gingerly, into a chair, and flicking her laser pointer on. "One of the most demanding rhyme schemes. Why do you think Elizabeth Bishop matched this particular form to her subject matter? Why was this a good fit?"

Silence. Professor Clapham heaved a sigh. "Okay," she said, not unkindly, "let's start at the very beginning. Who can tell me what this poem's about?"

Hands shot up. "Loss?" offered a sleek blond girl in the front row. *Duh,* thought Maggie.

"Of course," said the professor, in a tone only marginally kinder than Maggie's mental *Duh* had been. "But the loss of what, exactly?"

"Losing love," ventured a boy with bare, hairy legs exposed by his shorts, and a sweatshirt bearing the bleach stains of someone not yet used to managing his own laundry.

"Whose love?" Professor Clapham demanded. She put her hands at the small of her back and stretched as if her back hurt or, maybe, as if her students' ignorance was causing her physical pain. "And is the love lost already, or does the poet place that loss, out of all the others, in the realm of the theoretical? Is she talking about this loss as a possibility? A probability?"

Blank stares and bowed heads.

"A probability," Maggie blurted, and then sat, crimson, as embarrassed as if she'd farted.

But the professor gave her an encouraging look. "Why?"

Maggie's hands and knees were trembling. "Ummm," she said, in a faint and fading voice. And then she thought of Mrs. Fried, bending over her, her glasses swinging on a beaded chain, whispering, *Just try, Maggie. It doesn't matter if you're wrong. Just try.*

"Well," Maggie began, "at the beginning of the poem, she's talking about real things, stuff that everybody loses, like keys, or people's names."

"And then what happens?" the professor prompted. Maggie got it, almost as if she'd plucked a kite out of the sky.

"It shifts from the tangible to the intangible," she said, the long words rolling off her lips as if she'd been saying them all her life. "And then the poet starts getting . . ." Shit. There was a word for this. What was the word for this? "Grandiose," Maggie finally managed. "Like, she lost a house—okay, lots of people move; but then she says she's lost a whole continent . . ."

"Which, we can assume, would not be hers to lose," Professor Clapham said dryly. "So we see another shift."

"Right," Maggie agreed, her words coming faster, tumbling over one another. "And the way she writes about it, like it doesn't even matter that much . . ."

"You're talking about Bishop's tone," the professor said. "Would you call it ironic? Detached?"

Maggie thought about it as two girls in the front row raised their hands. Professor Clapham ignored them. "I think," Maggie said slowly, staring at the words on the page, "I think she wants to sound detached. Like it doesn't matter to her, right? Like the words she's using. *Fluster*. A fluster isn't a big deal. Or even the line that repeats, about how the art of losing isn't hard to master. It's like she's making fun of herself by even calling it an art." In fact, the tone's poem reminded Maggie of the way her sister talked about herself. She remembered watching the Miss America Pageant with Rose, asking Rose what her talent would be, and how Rose had thought about it and then said, very thoughtfully, "Parallel parking." "So she's trying to, like, turn it into a joke. But then, by the end . . ."

"Let's consider the structure again," the professor said, and while her words were intended for the rest of the class, her eyes were still on Maggie's. "A B A. A B A. Stanzas of three lines, until we reach the end, the final quatrain, and what happens?" She nodded at Maggie.

"Well, it's four lines, not three, so it's different. And there's that interruption—'write it!'—it's like she wants to be distant, she wants to be apart from it, but she's thinking of what's going to happen when she loses . . ."

"Loses what?" Professor Clapham asked. "Or loses who? Is this a poem about a lover, do you think? Who is the 'you' of this poem?"

Maggie bit her lip. "I don't think so," she said. "But I don't know why. I think that it's more a poem about losing . . ." *A sister,* she thought. *A mother.* "A friend, maybe," she said out loud.

"Very good," said the professor, as Maggie flushed crimson again, this time in pleasure, rather than shame. "Very good,"

Professor Clapham repeated, and then she turned back to the board, back to the class, back to the rhyme scheme and the formal demands of a villanelle. Maggie barely heard a word of it. She was still blushing. She, who never blushed, not even when she'd had to dress up like a gorilla for the three-day stint as a singing telegram girl, had turned the rich ripe red of a Jersey tomato.

That night, she curled up on top of her sleeping bag, thinking about her sister, wondering if Rose had taken that particular poetry class and had read that particular poem, and whether Rose would ever believe that it was Maggie, Maggie above all of the other students, who'd understood the poem best. She wondered when she'd get to tell Rose about it, and turned restlessly in the dark, trying to puzzle out what she'd have to do in order to get her sister to even speak to her again; what she'd have to do to get Rose to forgive her.

By the next morning, riding the bus to Corinne's through the bright spring sunshine, she was starting to feel regret. The whole point of being at Princeton was try to be . . . what was the word? . . . *interstitial.* It wasn't a word she'd learned on campus, it was a word she'd gotten from Rose. She could close her eyes and see Rose pointing out the commercials crammed onto half of the TV screen while the credits for the show that had just ended ran beside them. *Interstitial* meant, basically, the thing between the thing—the stuff that happened alongside the main event, while you were paying attention to something else.

And now she'd gone and shouted out answers in class. What was she thinking? Someone was going to notice her. Someone was going to remember. Someone was going to start wondering exactly where she lived, what her major was, what year she was, and what she was doing there.

Swirling the mop over Corinne's already gleaming floors, she wondered if maybe she wanted to be discovered, if she was tired of being invisible. She was doing something . . . well, not important, exactly, but something that required a certain level of daring, and cunning, and skill, and she wanted to be acknowledged for it. She wanted to tell Charles, or Rose, or someone, everything she'd figured out. How she'd learned to be careful never to fall into regular, detectable patterns. How she'd figured out no fewer than six different places to take showers (Dillon gym, the basement shower in the library, and four dormitories where the locks were reliably broken), how she knew the only washing machine that would run without quarters and the single soda machine that would routinely disgorge a free can of Coke if you hit it just right.

She wanted to tell them how she'd figured out the dining halls—how, if you sneaked in through the steamy dish room in the early morning hours, dressed as if you were working there, in grungy sneakers and jeans and a sweatshirt, everyone assumed that you were one of the student employees, just grabbing a bite before taking your place behind the steam tables or on the dish line. She wanted to explain how easy it was to slip food into her backpack—peanut butter sandwiches, pieces of fruit, layered between napkins.

She wanted to tell them about Thursday lunches at the International Student Center, where for two dollars she could get a giant plate heaping with rice and stir-fried vegetables and chicken curried in coconut milk—the best food she'd ever had, she thought sometimes—with the tea they served that tasted like cinnamon, how she'd drink cup after cup with teaspoonfuls of honey, and it would chase the heat of the food out of her mouth, and how nobody ever asked her anything because most of the other lunchgoers were graduate students and new to English, so the most she ever got was a shy smile, and a nod, and change for her five-dollar bill.

She used Windex to clean Corinne's glass cabinets and imagined introducing Rose to Charles and seeing her sister nod her approval. "I'm fine," she imagined telling her sister; "you shouldn't have been so worried about me, because I'm fine." And then she would say that she was sorry . . . and, well, after that, who knew? Maybe Rose could find a way for Maggie to get credit for the classes she'd listened in on. Maybe Maggie could even get a degree some day, if she kept plugging away, because she'd found that if she took her time, even the thickest books weren't so awful. And she'd star in all of Charles's plays, and give her sister tickets to the premiere, and also something great to wear, because Lord knew that if left to her own devices Rose would just show up in something frumpy, like one of her shoulder-padded sweaters that made her look like small bear, and . . .

"Hello?" Corinne said. Maggie jumped and practically fell off the step stool.

"Hi," she said. "I'm up here. I didn't hear you come in."

"I move on little cat feet. Like the fog."

"Carl Sandburg," said Maggie.

"Very good!" said Corinne. She ran her fingertips along the countertops, then eased herself into a seat at the dining room table that Maggie had wiped clean. "How's school?"

"It's very good," said Maggie. She hopped off the step stool, folded it up, and stowed it on its hook inside the closet. And it was good. Except for the fact that she didn't really belong here. Except for the fact of Rose, the terrible thing she'd done to her, and her sense that nothing she'd learned in college would help her figure out how to make that right again.

THIRTY-NINE

In the week since her walk with Mrs. Lefkowitz, Ella had managed to learn a great deal about her granddaughter Rose, and almost nothing about Maggie.

"This one, this Rose," Mrs. Lefkowitz had said. "She's everywhere!"

Indeed, cyberspace was littered with references to Rose, from the directory of her high school's National Honor Society to an article in the *Daily Princetonian* about on-campus recruiting. Ella learned where Rose had gone to school, what area of law she was practicing, even extrapolated her telephone number from an on-line search engine.

"She's done all right for herself," said Mrs. Lefkowitz, as they plodded past the tennis courts.

"It said she's on indefinite leave," Ella noted, remembering her granddaughter's stern face flickering on the computer screen. "That doesn't sound good."

"Feh," said Mrs. Lefkowitz. "She's probably on vacation."

Maggie, meanwhile, proved much harder to pin down. Mrs. Lefkowitz, Ella, and Lewis had tried every possible combination of MAGGIE FELLER and MAGGIE MAY FELLER and even MARGARET FELLER, even though it wasn't right, and found not a single reference to her younger granddaughter, not so much as a mention, not even a telephone number. "It's like she doesn't exist," Ella had said, frowning. "Maybe . . ." She let her voice trail off, unwilling to give voice to the horrible thought that had seized her.

Mrs. Lefkowitz shook her head. "If she was dead, there'd be an obituary."

"Are you sure?" asked Ella.

"How do you think I keep up with my friends?" Mrs. Lefkowitz asked. She reached into her pink fanny pack and pulled out an orange cell phone. "Here. You should call the Rose one. Quick, before you lose your nerve."

Ella shook her head, thinking of her granddaughter's face. "I don't know," she said. "I want to, but . . . I have to think about it. I want to do it just right."

"Think, think," said Mrs. Lefkowitz. "You're taking too long. Just do it! Some of us are not planning to live forever."

Ella stayed awake all night, lying alone on top of her comforter as the frogs croaked and the horns honked and the sky finally got light. When she pushed herself out of bed, she made herself say it out loud. "Today," she announced to her empty apartment. "I'm going to call her today."

That morning, at the hospital, Ella set a sleeping baby back into its Isolette and hurried down the hall. There was a bank of pay phones right across from the surgical lounge. Ella stationed herself in front of the phone the farthest from the doors and fumbled for her calling card. She poked at the keyboard, punched in her calling card number, then Rose's law-firm number. Voice mail, she thought—she, who hadn't prayed since the last night her daughter had gone missing, had suddenly become God's intimate companion. Please, Lord, let it be voice mail.

And it was . . . but it wasn't what she'd expected to hear. "You have reached a nonworking number at Lewis, Dommel, and Fenick," said the disembodied computerized voice. "Please press zero to be connected with an operator." Ella pressed zero, and after a minute a receptionist said, "It's an outrageous day at Lewis, Dommel, and Fenick!"

"Excuse me?" said Ella.

"They make us say that instead of 'hello,' " said the receptionist in a hushed whisper. "How can I help you?"

"I'm trying to reach Rose Feller," said Ella.

"I'll connect you," the receptionist singsonged. Ella's heart leapt in her chest . . . but the woman who answered the phone wasn't Rose, just a bored-sounding woman who identified herself as Lisa, Rose's former assistant.

"She's on leave," Lisa said.

"I know," said Ella, "but I was wondering if I could leave her a message? This is her grandmother," she said, feeling herself swell with fear, and pride, the instant she'd spoken the words *her grandmother.*

"Sorry," said Lisa. "She doesn't call in for her messages. She hasn't been here in months."

"Oh," said Ella. "Well, I've got her home number, so I'll try her there."

"Fine," said Lisa.

"Thank you," said Ella. She hung up the phone and sank into a chair outside the lounge, feeling exhilarated and terrified at the same time. She'd taken the first step, and what was the corny thing that Ira, of all people, used to say? *The greatest journey begins with a single step.* True, he'd usually say it before starting on a fresh batch of yogurt, but still, Ella thought. It was true, and she'd done it. She hadn't chickened out, she thought, reaching for the telephone again, hurrying to call Lewis and give him the amazing news. She'd jumped into the water. She'd begun.

FORTY

Rose had to give Simon Stein this—he was nothing if not persistent.

The day after they'd had lunch, a dozen red roses had arrived at her apartment, with a card saying, "Looking forward to seeing you again. PS: Don't eat a big lunch." She'd rolled her eyes at that, hoping he wasn't getting the wrong idea, as she loaded the roses into an inadequate vase and set them on her kitchen counter, where they promptly began making the rest of her belongings look shabby and unromantic in comparison. He was a nice enough guy, certainly, but nobody she'd ever be attracted to. Besides, she thought later, swinging one leg over her bicycle and heading down Pine Street to begin her morning rounds, she was through with love, and it would take more than a man who styled himself a walking Zagat's guide to change her mind.

"I'm on hiatus from romance," she told Petunia, as they strolled through the morning sunshine on their daily walk. Rose had to admit that while she liked all of the dogs she cared for, she'd always have a soft spot for the scowling little pug.

Petunia squatted, peed briefly into the gutter, snorted a few times, and began her pursuit of street sushi—pizza crusts, puddle beer, discarded chicken bones. "I think it's a good idea to take a break every once in a while," Rose said. "So I'm taking a little break."

That evening, Rose shaved her legs carefully, toweled herself off, and surveyed the outfits she'd laid out on her bed. Of course, none of them looked right. The red skirt that had looked adorable in the mall bunched up oddly around her hips. The green sundress was hopelessly wrinkled, the denim skirt was missing a button, and the long black skirt made her look as if either she'd come straight from the office or she was in mourning, or as if she'd been in mourning at the office. God, where was Maggie when she needed her?

"Shit!" Rose said. She was sweating, in spite of her freshly applied deodorant, and already five minutes late. "Shit, shit, shit!" She pulled on the red skirt, yanked a white T-shirt over her head, and reached into her closet for her snakeskin slides, figuring that even if the outfit was a near-disaster, her shoes would be, as always, without fault.

She groped along the shelf. Boots, boots, loafers, heels, pink slides, black slides, the ill-advised pair of Tevas she'd purchased the week she thought she might become one of those fresh-faced, rosy-cheeked L.L. Bean girls who hiked the Appalachian Trail during spring break . . . where the hell was the pair she was looking for?

"Maggie," she moaned, with her hands still rooting through the tangle of straps and buckles. "Maggie, if you took my shoes, I swear to God . . ." And then, before she could decide what she was vowing to do to her sister, if she ever saw her sister again, Rose's fingertips brushed the tops of the slides in question. She snatched them off the shelf, shoved her bare feet inside of them, grabbed her purse, and headed for the door. She stabbed the elevator button, then rocked from leg to leg, making sure her keys were in her purse, trying to avoid her reflection in the elevator doors, certain that she wouldn't like what she'd see. The Former Lawyer, she thought, glancing rue-fully at her legs, freshly shaved but still scabby.

Simon Stein was waiting outside her building, wearing a but-ton-down blue shirt, khakis, and brown loafers, the uniform at

Lewis, Dommel, and Fenick on the days that didn't require a team jersey. Unfortunately, he hadn't grown eight inches and become handsome and broad-shouldered since she'd seen him last. But he was holding open a cab door in a very polite manner. "Hi," he said, and looked her over approvingly. "Pretty dress."

"It's a skirt," said Rose. "Where are we off to?"

"Surprise," said Simon, and gave her a confident nod. A practiced, lawyerly, brisk little *everything's fine* nod. A nod that Rose herself had once deployed to great effect. "Don't worry. I'm not going to kidnap you or anything."

"Or anything," Rose repeated, still shocked at the sight of seeing her nod performed by Simon Stein. The cab pulled to the curb on a suspect-looking block of South Street. There was a chain-link fence holding back an overgrown tangle of weeds and grass on one side of the street, a burned-looking house with boarded-up windows on the other, and at the corner, a little concrete storefront, painted green, with the words *Jerk Hut* in neon over the window.

"So this is where all my boyfriends have been coming from!" said Rose. Simon Stein, to his credit, gave a Petunia-ish snort, and held the door open for Rose to climb out, his blue eyes alight with amusement—or maybe just excitement about dinner, Rose thought. He had a brown paper bag tucked under one arm, Rose noticed. She glanced around uneasily, noticing a cluster of men leaning against the boarded-up building, passing a bottle back and forth, and the litter of broken glass on the sidewalk.

"Not to fear," said Simon, holding her elbow and steering her toward the storefront . . . then past it, where there was a painted wooden door, standing in the center of the sidewalk, with nothing on either side of it but the ratty-looking tangle of green. He put his hand on the door and looked at Rose. "Do you like Jamaican food?"

"Do I have a choice?" asked Rose, glancing back over her shoulder at the men as their cab pulled away.

If it wasn't for the square glittering mica-flecked gray stones that formed a path through the tangle of city growth—empty bottles, half-rotted newspaper, something that looked a lot like a used condom—Rose would have been certain they were wandering toward another vacant lot. The grass was knee-high, seemingly untended, and she could hear what sounded like steel drums in the distance.

Then they rounded a corner, and Rose could see a multilayered deck behind the tiny storefront, a deck tented in orange cloth, and lined with tiny white lights like stars. The edges of the deck were ringed with lit torches, and there was a three-piece band on one of the platforms. She could smell cloves and chilies and wood smoke curling from the grill, and above her head, even on this lousy block of South Street, the sky was full of stars.

Simon led Rose to a wooden table on the deck and pulled out Rose's chair. "Isn't this great?" he asked, looking pleased with himself. "You'd never know it was back here."

"How'd you find it?" asked Rose faintly. She was still looking at the sky.

"Instinct," Simon said. "And it was reviewed in the paper." He pulled a six-pack out of the brown paper bag and peppered her with questions. Did she like spicy food? Was she allergic to nuts or shellfish? Did she have any philosophical or gustatory objection to eating goat? It was like giving a medical history, centered solely on food, Rose thought, smiling and telling him that yes, she liked spicy, no, she wasn't allergic, and that she supposed she could taste the goat.

"Good," said Simon, closing the menu. Rose felt relieved, as if she'd passed some kind of test. Which was ridiculous, she thought. Who was Simon Stein to be giving her tests, and what did it matter whether she passed them?

After the curried goat and the spicy shrimp, after the beef patties and jerk chicken wings and coconut rice, and after Rose had an unprecedented three beers, plus a swallow of a fourth, Simon asked Rose a question.

"Tell me something you like," he said.

Rose hiccupped. "A person?" she asked coyly, "or a thing?" She was thinking that he would say, "a person," and she would say, "you," at which point, she figured, he would decide that it was okay to kiss her. She'd played the kissing-Simon scenario in her mind somewhere after the third beer, and had decided that if the night ended with her being kissed by Simon Stein, it would be okay. There were worse things, she reasoned, than sitting underneath the stars on a warm spring Saturday night, being kissed by a man, even if the man was a good three inches shorter than she was, and obsessed with food and the law firm's softball team. He was nice. Really nice. So she'd kiss him.

But Simon Stein surprised her. "A thing," he said. "A thing you like."

Rose considered her options. Your smile? This place? The beer? Instead she fished in her purse and produced her key chain, her new key chain that she purchased at the dollar store on Chestnut Street after she started acquiring people's keys. "I like this," she said, and showed him that at the end of the key chain there was a tiny flashlight, no bigger than a wine cork. It took her a few tries, because her fingers were thick and somewhat clumsy from the beer, but she managed to turn it on and flash it at his face. "This cost a dollar."

"A bargain," said Simon Stein. Rose frowned. Was he making fun of her? She took another swallow of beer and tossed her hair.

"Sometimes," she said, "I think about getting on my bike and riding across the country."

"By yourself?"

Rose nodded. She could picture it, too—getting a set of panniers to clip over her back wheel, and one of those little trailers that long-distance cyclists tow behind their bikes, getting a one-person tent and a sleeping bag, and sticking Petunia in the trailer and . . . going. Riding in the morning, stopping for lunch at a diner or café, pedaling a few more hours, then setting her tent up by a stream, writing in a journal (in this fantasy, she kept a journal, though she didn't in real life), reading one of her romance novels, and falling asleep under the stars.

It was like the fantasy she'd had in the years after her mother had died, of getting a motor home, one of those Winnebagos a lane and a half wide with all of the modern conveniences built right in. She must have seen a picture somewhere, or maybe even been inside of one. She remembered how they were like little self-contained worlds, with the beds that folded out of the walls, and the tiny two-burner stoves, the shower stalls barely big enough to fit into, TV sets hidden in the ceilings. Her dream had been to get her father and Maggie and just drive away. They'd leave their place in New Jersey and go somewhere warmer, somewhere where there was no wet road, no gray headstone, no trooper at the door. Phoenix, Arizona; San Diego, California; Albuquerque, New Mexico. Someplace sunny, where it was always summer, where it smelled like oranges.

She'd lie awake in bed and roll those names on her tongue, imagining the trailer, imagining Maggie tucked tight into the bottom bunk bed, imagining herself brave enough to sleep on top, and their father at the wheel, his face handsome and happy in the light of the dashboard. They'd get their dog, Honey Bun, back, and their father would stop being allergic, and Honey Bun would sleep on a pillow in the passenger's seat, and their father wouldn't cry anymore. They'd drive and drive until they were far away, until they'd outrun the memory of her mother, and the kids who'd tormented her on the playground and the teachers who shook their heads at Maggie. Then they'd find somewhere to stay by the ocean. She and Maggie would be best friends. They'd swim every day, and cook their food on a campfire, and sleep snug in the mobile home every night.

"Thank you," her father would say. "This was such a good idea, Rose. You saved us." Rose would feel the truth of it, like sunshine, like the feel of her own skin, the weight of her own bones. She would save all three of them, she'd think, and finally fall asleep, dreaming of bunk beds and turning wheels and the ocean she'd never seen.

"Would you be lonely?" asked Simon.

"Lonely?" Rose repeated. For a moment, she wasn't sure what

he was talking about. She was still lost in the fantasy of the mobile home, which she'd embroidered and amplified over the years, even when she realized it would never come true. The one time she'd come across an ad for a used Winnebago in the neighborhood shopping circular and hesitantly pointed it out to her father, he'd squinted at her as if she'd started speaking Martian, then said, kindly, "I don't think so."

"Don't you think you'd miss people?" asked Simon.

Rose shook her head instantly. "I don't need . . ." She took a deep breath, stopping herself before she said it. Suddenly she felt hot, unbearably hot and uncomfortable. The music was too loud, and her face was flushed, and the spicy food was forming an excruciating knot in her stomach. She gulped at her glass of water and started again. "I'm very independent," she said. "I like being alone."

"What's wrong?" he asked. "Are you okay? Do you want some ginger ale? They make their own here; it's great if your stomach's upset. . . ."

Rose waved him away, then buried her face in her hands. With her eyes closed she could still see the Winnebago the way she'd imagined it, the three of them beneath an awning that would extend from the wall, holding hot dogs over a campfire on a beach, sitting up in their sleeping bags, safe and snug in their perfect little home like caterpillars in a cocoon. She'd wanted so badly for it to be true, and instead she'd lost her father to Sydelle, and to a world of box scores and stock tickers, where the only subjects he could safely discuss were free-throw percentages and the stability of the bond market, where the only things he let himself feel were excitement when the Eagles won and disappointment when his investments lost. And Maggie . . .

"Oh," she moaned, aware that she was probably scaring Simon Stein, but unable to help herself. Maggie. She thought she'd be able to save Maggie. And look how that had turned out. She didn't even know where her sister, her own sister, was living.

"Oh," she said again, softly, and now Simon Stein's arm was wrapped around her shoulder.

"What is it?" he asked. "Do you think you've got food poisoning?" He sounded so solicitous that Rose started to laugh. "Can you drink some water?" He reached for his pocket. "I've got Pepcid, Alka-Seltzer . . ."

Rose raised her head. "Does this happen a lot to you on dates?"

Simon Stein pursed his lips. "I wouldn't say it happens frequently," he finally said. "But maybe on occasion." He looked at her carefully. "Are you okay?"

"Insofar as I don't have food poisoning, I'm fine," said Rose.

"Then what is it?" he asked.

"I just . . . I was thinking of someone."

"Who?"

And Rose blurted the first thing that came into her head. "Petunia. This dog that I take care of." And Simon Stein, to his eternal credit, did not laugh or so much as snicker, or look at her like she was crazy. He simply stood up, folded his napkin, left a ten-dollar tip on the table, and said, "So let's go get her."

"This is crazy," Rose whispered.

"Shh," said Simon Stein.

"We could get in trouble," Rose insisted.

"Why?" Simon asked. "You're supposed to walk the dog on Saturday. Well, it's Saturday."

"It's Friday night."

"It is," said Simon, consulting his watch, "five minutes after midnight."

Rose rolled her eyes. They were in the elevator of Petunia's apartment building, which was empty except for the two of them. "Do you always have to be right?"

"I prefer it," Simon said, and this struck Rose as hysterically funny. She started laughing. Simon put his hand over her mouth.

"Shh," he whispered. Rose fumbled with her flashlight key chain, found the key whose masking-tape label read, "Petunia," and handed it to Simon.

"Okay," said Simon, "here's how we're going to pull this off. I'll unlock the door. You turn off the alarm. I'll grab the dog. Where do you think she'll be?"

Rose considered this. Her brain felt fogged. After all of the beers at the Jerk Hut, they'd gone to a bar to perfect Operation Petunia; there had been some vodka involved. "I don't know," she finally answered. "When I come get her, she's usually on the couch, but I don't know where she sleeps when her people are home."

"Well, leave that to me," he said. Rose was inclined to do just that. She hadn't been keeping score, but she was almost positive that he hadn't had as much vodka as she'd had.

"Leash?" asked Simon, and Rose reached into her pocket and pulled out the two shoelaces that they'd pulled out of Simon's shoes and tied together at the bar. "Treat?" Rose fished in her purse and came up with a napkin-wrapped beef patty, the grease staining the napkin. "Note?" Rose produced another napkin. After three drafts, they'd decided that "Dear Shirley, I was in the neighborhood and thought I'd give Petunia an early walk," sounded the most plausible.

"Are you ready?" asked Simon, grasping Rose by the shoulders and looking deeply into her eyes, smiling at her. "Are you set?" asked Simon, and Rose nodded again. Simon leaned forward and gave her a kiss on the lips. "Let's do it," he said, only Rose was so shocked by the intensity of the kiss that she stood there, frozen, as Simon unlocked the door and the alarm started howling into the night.

"Rose!" he hissed. She rushed into the apartment, stabbing at the alarm keypad, as Petunia scuttled into the living room, barking frantically before she slid to a stop on the hardwood floors and started wagging her tail.

Shirley hurried behind the dog, portable phone at the ready. "Oh," she said, peering at the two of them. "Simon. You don't knock anymore?"

Rose gaped, staring from Simon to Shirley to Petunia, who was currently trying to launch herself into Simon's arms. And Simon was smiling at her. "Rose," he said, "this is my grandmother. Nanna, you know Rose, right?"

"Of course I know Rose," Shirley said impatiently. "Petunia, cut that out!" A chastened Petunia stopped jumping and sat on the floor, her stump of a tail moving in frantic circles, her pink tongue lolling. Rose stood as if she'd been frozen, staring and trying to make sense of it, but sense was not forthcoming.

"So . . . you know Petunia?" she finally asked.

Simon nodded. "I've known Petunia since she was this big," he said, holding his hands in the shape of a teacup.

"And you know Simon," said Shirley.

"We used to work together," said Rose.

"Great," said Shirley. "So now that everyone knows everyone, can I go to sleep?"

Simon walked over and kissed his grandmother's forehead. "Thanks, Nanna," he said sweetly. "Sorry we woke you up."

Shirley nodded, said something that Rose couldn't quite hear, and left them alone in the hallway. Petunia, still on her haunches, still with her tail wagging happily, looked from Simon's face to Rose's face and back again.

"What did she say?" Rose asked faintly.

Simon smiled at her. "I think she said, 'It took you long enough.'"

"What did . . . How did . . ."

Simon pulled Petunia's leash out of the drawer where Shirley kept it, and smiled at Rose. "Let's go for a walk," he said. He held Petunia's leash in one hand, and Rose's hand in the other, and led them up to his apartment, where Petunia curled up at the foot of the bed, and Rose and Simon lay together on top of his blue comforter, whispering and kissing and sometimes laughing so hard that Petunia woke up and snorted at them, until the sun came up.

FORTY-ONE

Maggie stepped out of the shower, dried off quickly, and pulled on her clean clothes as fast as she could. She brushed her hair into a ponytail, took one last look behind her, then eased the door shut, moving fast, before she could lose her nerve. She was going to tell Charles her story. She'd pitch it as a play she was thinking about writing. *Once upon a time, a girl ran away to college.* She'd hear what he said, she'd watch his face as she told him, and if he seemed receptive, she'd tell him that it was true. She pushed the door open and ran into a man. Josh. Josh from her first night at Princeton, who was standing there in the darkness, glaring at her, with her backpack dangling from his hands.

Her breath froze in her throat as she reeled backward against a wall. Josh didn't look drunk or dazed or flirtatious and besotted. He looked like he wanted to kill her, and that he might be convinced to settle for hurting her instead. *Bad hookups always come back,* Maggie thought, and inched backward, wondering what he wanted, wondering how he'd even gotten in here, because the library was closed. He must have waited for her, which meant that they were alone in the library basement together . . .

Oh, God, thought Maggie, inching backward, trying to melt into the wall. This was going to be bad. This was going to be so bad.

"Well, hello," he said softly, and rubbed his thumb over her tattoo, the one that said "Mother," the one she figured he'd finally remembered from that one night in his bed. "Little M. You owe me something, I think."

"I'll give the money back," Maggie whispered, as he pressed so close to her that his nose brushed hers. "It's in my bag; I never even spent it; I'll give it back to you right now . . ." She shuddered as he held her, and bit back hard against a scream. *Disaster,* she thought bleakly. Just like the poem said. *Like disaster.* She squirmed against him, thinking that she could run, that maybe she'd have a chance then, but he was holding on too tightly, and kept whispering horrible things at her.

"What are you doing here?" he asked her. "You don't belong. You're not supposed to be here. So what's your story?"

"I'll give you your money. Just let me go," said Maggie, and tried to wriggle away, but he had her cornered, pushed up against the icy granite of the library wall. He kept talking to her—talking at her, really, pushing words into her face as she twisted. His voice was constant, but as he talked, his tone shifted from hectoring and accusatory to an oily wheedle.

"Maybe I should let you make it up to me some other way," he said, running his eyes over her body in a way that made her feel like he'd just dumped acid down her shirt. "I don't remember exactly what happened that night, but I don't think we finished what we started. And we're all alone here. We could finish up now."

Maggie moaned and writhed desperately. "Let me go," she begged.

"Why should I?" asked Josh. His pale face was flushed. His blond hair hung over his forehead, and he sprayed her with spit as he talked. "You're in trouble. A lot of trouble. I went through your backpack. Three IDs. Very nice. My credit cards, of course, and plenty of cash. Who's that from? How many other guys? And are you living down here? Do you have any idea what would happen if I told campus security? Or the cops?"

Maggie turned her face down and started to cry silently. She couldn't help it. In a way, this talking, his hands binding her wrists, was every bit as bad as it had been when the guys had grabbed at her in the impound lot . . . and she was as frightened as she'd been there. It was the shame of it, his words raining down on her like a hailstorm, scalding her skin. And it was so unfair. What was her crime? What had she taken? Some food, when there was plenty to go around. Some books, which their owners were stupid or lazy or rich enough to just leave lying around, unattended. Some clothes from lost-and-found baskets, some empty seats in lecture halls where the professors were going to talk anyhow.

Maggie lifted her chin and widened her eyes. "Okay," she said. "That's enough." She forced herself to smile, forced herself to pull her hair free from her ponytail and flick it over her shoulders. "You got me," she murmured. "You got me right where you want me." She summoned every ounce of charm she had, all of the sex appeal she'd kept buried under sweatshirts for the semester, and gave him a smile as rich and inviting as a dollop of caramel on a scoop of vanilla ice cream. "Want to go exploring?" she asked, hearing the quiver in her voice and praying that he missed it, praying that her body would be a sufficient distraction.

Josh wiped his hands on his jeans. It was all the opening Maggie needed. She grabbed her backpack by a strap and whirled it at him, whacking him on the side of his face. He stumbled backward. She kicked him in the shin as hard as she could. He gasped and doubled over, and Maggie took off.

She bolted up three flights of stairs, pushed through the heavy glass doors, hearing alarms blaring behind her, as she sprinted across the courtyard, holding her backpack by the strap that had broken when he grabbed her, her mind blank, her feet flying, her blood singing with adrenaline. It was a gorgeous spring night. Students in shorts and T-shirts drifted along the walkways, lounged under the weeping willows, called each other's names through open windows. Maggie felt as if she were naked, or wearing a sign that read, "I DON'T BELONG HERE." She ran faster and faster, a cramp stabbing at her rib cage, out of the campus, onto the sidewalk, over to the bus station on Nassau Street. *Please God please God please,* she prayed, and a bus rolled into view. She jumped on board, grabbed change from her pocket and shoved it in the till, then sat down, wrapping her arms around her backpack. Her heart was still thundering in her chest.

Get to Corinne's, she thought. Get to Corinne's and think of something that will make her let me in, even though it's the middle of the night and I'm not supposed to be there until the morning. She sat back in the seat and squeezed her eyes shut, thinking that she was in a box, another box, same as when she'd started out here, and she'd have to think her way out of it, same as she had before. Then she pulled her cell phone out of her pocket, swallowed hard, and dialed her sister's number. It was late. It was a school night. Rose would be home. She'd know what to do.

Except Rose wasn't home. "Hello, you've reached Rose Feller, and Feller Pet Care," said the machine. What? "Please leave me a message with your name, number, the name of your pet, and the dates you require service, and I will return your call as soon as possible." Wrong number, Maggie thought. It had to be. She dialed again and got the same thing, only this time after the beep she opened her mouth. "Rose," she croaked. "I'm . . ." I'm what? I'm in trouble—again? I need you to bail me out—again? Maggie closed her eyes and her telephone. She'd figure it out herself.

"Maggie?" asked Corinne, looking off-balance as she stood at her door. "What time is it? What are you doing here?"

"It's late," said Maggie. "There's been . . . I have . . ." She took a deep breath. "I was wondering if I could stay for a few days. I'll pay you rent, or I'll clean for you for free . . ."

Corinne held the door open with her hip. "What happened?"

Maggie ran through the possibilities. Could she tell Corinne she'd had a fight with a roommate? Had she told Corinne that she had roommates? She couldn't remember. And what if the terrible boy had followed her here? If he knew she was staying in the library, maybe he knew she was working here, too.

"Maggie?" Corinne's forehead was wrinkled. She didn't have her sunglasses on, and Maggie could see her blue eyes darting back and forth like lost fish.

"Something happened," Maggie said.

"I think we've established that," said Corinne, letting Maggie in and walking toward the kitchen with her fingertips brushing along the wall. Maggie sat at the table while Corinne filled the kettle, flicked on the gas, took two mugs and two tea bags down from the shelf beside the stove. "Can you tell me what?"

Maggie bowed her head. "Not really," she whispered.

"Is it drugs?" Corinne asked sharply, and Maggie was so startled that she laughed.

"No," she said. "Not drugs. I just need to lay low for a while." Which, she realized, made her sound like a complete criminal, but it was all she could think of on short notice. "I'm just kind of stressed," she added lamely. "And it's so peaceful here."

Clearly, she'd said the magic words. Corinne beamed. She spooned sugar into the tea and brought the cups to the table. "Finals are hard, aren't they?" she said. "I remember trying to study for mine. The dorms were so noisy, and the library got so crowded! Don't worry," she told Maggie. "You can stay in any of the rooms on the third floor. They're all clean, right?"

"Right," said Maggie. She'd cleaned them herself. She sipped her tea and tried to stop her heart from racing. Plan. Plan. She needed another plan. She'd stay here a few days. She'd have to buy herself some new things; she had a change of clothes and some underwear in her backpack, but the rest of her stuff was in the library and she couldn't go get it. And then where? Could she go back to her father, back to Rose? Would they take her back? Would she want to go?

She closed her eyes and saw herself sitting in the back row of the poetry class, telling the professor what "One Art" meant. She saw Charles's face, his hair falling over his forehead as he talked about Shakespeare and Strindberg and how he'd seen John Malkovich on stage once. Nobody at Princeton had known she was a failure or a fuckup, her family's shame, the black mark on their report card. Nobody at Princeton knew she was any different than they were. Until the boy in the library. Until now.

She blinked hard. She wouldn't cry. She'd figure this out. Lay low, she thought. Then get out. She couldn't stay here while that guy was still on campus, and after the students went home, she wouldn't be able to stay, because there'd be no one left for her to blend in with. So then what?

"Maggie?" Corinne asked. Maggie stared at her. "Do you have family? Is there someone I should call?"

Maggie sniffed and bit her lip. She wanted to cry, but what good would crying do? "No," she said. Her voice was wobbly. "I don't. I don't have anyone."

Corinne cocked her head. "Are you sure?"

Maggie thought of her backpack, the money she kept wrapped in a rubber band, snug in one of the inside zippered pockets. She heard Josh's voice. *I went through your backpack.* She grabbed for it, yanking it open. The money was gone. Her IDs and credit cards were gone. There was nothing except clothes, and books, and . . . Her fingers brushed the softened paper of the birthday card. She pulled it out, opened it up, reading it for the hundredth time, the birthday greetings, and the signature, and the phone number.

"A grandmother," she said, in a quivery voice. "I have a grandmother."

Corinne gave a well-that's-settled nod. "Go to sleep," she said. "Take whichever bedroom you want. You can call her in the morning."

And so, the next morning, Maggie stood in the center of Corinne's sun-washed kitchen, with her cell phone in her hand, and dialed the number that the grandmother had written on the card almost twenty years before. The phone rang and rang. Maggie crossed the fingers of both hands. *Please,* she thought, unsure of what she wishing for, except for someone to answer.

And somebody did.

Rose Feller woke up at five in the morning in a strange bed with her heart pounding. *Maggie,* she thought. She'd been dreaming of Maggie.

"Maggie," she said out loud, but even as she was saying it, even as she was swimming up through sleep toward wakefulness, she wasn't sure that it was Maggie she'd seen. A woman running through a forest. That had been all. A woman with terrified eyes, her mouth stretched into a scream, running through green branches that reached out like arms to trap her.

"Maggie," she said again. Petunia stared up at Rose, before deciding that there was neither an emergency nor food at hand, and closed her eyes again. Rose swung her legs out of the bed. Simon put his hand on her hip.

"Shh," he said, pulling her back toward him, curling his body around hers and kissing the back of her neck. "What's wrong?" He nuzzled her, and she felt the crisp curls of his hair brush against her neck. "Did you have a bad dream?"

"I dreamed about my mother," said Rose, in a low voice, slower and deeper than her own, an underwater sleeping voice. But was that right, either? Her mother. Maggie. Or maybe it was here, running through those trees, tripping over roots, falling down on her knees and splayed hands, then getting up, running some more. But running from whom? And toward what? "My mother's dead, you know. Did I tell you that? I can't remember. She died when I was little."

"I'll be right back," Simon whispered, and got up from the bed. She heard him padding through the kitchen, returning in his silly striped pajamas a minute later with a glass of water in his hand. She drank it gratefully as he got back into bed and turned off the lights. Then he curled around her again, with one hand snug across her forehead and the other cupping the base of her head as if she were something delicate and rare.

"I'm sorry about your mom," he said. "Do you want to talk about it?"

Rose shook her head.

"You can tell me anything," said Simon. "I'll take care of you. I promise." But Rose told him nothing that night. She just closed her eyes, let herself lean against him, and let herself fall into asleep.

Ella was sitting at her table, staring at her notebook, working on compiling a list of free health screenings for the upcoming week's *Golden Acres Gazette* when the telephone rang.

"Hello?" she said.

No answer . . . just breathing.

"Hello," she repeated. "Mrs. Lefkowitz, is that you? Are you all right?"

A young woman's voice answered her question. "Is this Ella Hirsch?"

Telemarketer, thought Ella. "Yes, it is."

The voice paused. "Did you have a daughter named Caroline?"

Ella drew a breath. "I do," she said without thinking. "That is, I did."

"Well," said the young woman. "You don't know me. My name is Maggie Feller."

"Maggie," Ella said instantly, feeling the familiar mixture of hope and relief and exhilaration and terror flooding through her as she said her granddaughter's name again. "Maggie. I called. That is, I called your sister . . . did she get my message? Did she tell you?"

"No," said Maggie, and paused. "Look," she started again. "You don't know me, and you don't have any reason to help me out, but I'm in trouble right now, I'm in a lot of trouble . . ."

"I'll help you," Ella answered immediately, and squeezed her eyes shut, hoping fiercely as Maggie told her how.

PART THREE

I Carry Your Heart

FORTY-TWO

Rose Feller had never wished for a mother as much as she did during her engagement to Simon Stein. Their first date had been in April. By May they were seeing each other four and five days a week. By July Simon had all but moved into Rose's apartment. And in September he'd taken her back to the Jerk Hut, ducked under the table, ostensibly to retrieve a dropped napkin, and reappeared with a black velvet box in his hand. "It's too soon," Rose had said, still not quite believing that this was happening, and Simon had looked at her steadily and said, "I'm sure about you."

The wedding was set for May, and it was already October, which meant, as the salesladies this afternoon had been quick to point out, that Rose was late in selecting a wedding dress. "Do you know how long it takes for the dresses to arrive?" the woman at the first shop had asked. Rose had thought of retorting, "Do you know how long it took me to find a guy to marry?" but decided to keep her mouth shut.

"This is torture," she said, struggling to haul up the panty hose that had developed an inch-thick run the instant she'd poked one foot inside.

"Shall I call Amnesty International?" Amy asked. Rose shook her head and tossed her sneakers into a corner of the peach-painted, lace-curtained dressing room of a bridal shop (or "shoppe," as Rose had learned to think of them), where the air smelled like lavender potpourri and the Muzak played only love songs. She was strapped into a bustier that hoisted her breasts to practically chin level and, as she would later discover, left nasty welts in her side, plus a girdle that the saleslady had tried to tell her was really a "shaper brief," except Rose knew a girdle when she saw one—and when she felt one cutting off her air supply. But the saleslady had insisted. "The proper foundation garments are crucial," she'd said, looking at Rose as if to say, *and the rest of my brides-to-be have already figured that out.*

"You don't know what I'm going through," Rose moaned. The saleslady bundled a dress in her arms and held it open for Rose. "Dive," she ordered. Rose tucked her arms by her sides, bent at the waist, wincing at the pinch of her double-barreled girdle, and shoved her head through the opening, groping. The dress's full skirt fell down to her ankles as Rose poked her arms through the sleeves and the saleslady started attempting to work the zipper up her back.

"What are you going through?" asked Amy.

Rose closed her eyes and uttered the name that had haunted her during the two months of her engagement, and who would, she felt certain, continue to bedevil her as the wedding date drew closer. "Sydelle," she said.

"Oy," said Amy.

"Oy is not the half of it," said Rose. "My wicked stepmother has now decided that she wants to be my best friend." And it was true. When she and Simon had driven to New Jersey to tell Michael Feller and his wife the good news, Michael had hugged his daughter and clapped Simon on the back, while Sydelle sat on the couch looking stricken. "How wonderful," she finally managed, the words squeezing through her thin, perfectly-painted lips while her jumbo nostrils flared as if she was trying to inhale the coffee table. "How wonderful for you both!" And the very next day she'd called Rose at home to insist that they have tea to celebrate, and to offer her services as a wedding planner. "Not to toot my own horn, dear, but people are still talking about My Marcia's wedding," she'd said. Rose thought that was understandable, given Sydelle's penchant for mentioning Marcia's wedding in every conversation, but she was caught so completely off guard by Sydelle's doing something that didn't involve criticism of her clothes, hair, or diet, that she agreed. With her brand-new ring still feeling strange on her finger, she'd gone off to the Ritz-Carlton to meet Sydelle for tea.

"It was wretched," she remembered as Amy nodded and smoothed the elbow-length lace gloves she'd tried on. Rose had spotted her step-mother instantly. Sydelle sat alone at a table set with a teapot and two gold-rimmed cups. She looked as formidable as always. Her hair was blow-dried into immobility, and her skin looked as shiny and taut as shrink-wrap. She wore immaculate makeup, imposing gold accessories, and the brown leather jacket that Rose had ogled in the window of Joan Shepp on her way to the hotel.

"Rose," she'd cooed, "you look marvelous." The glance she gave to Rose's khaki skirt and ponytail suggested otherwise. "Now," she said, once they'd made a few minutes of small talk, "let's get to the details. Do you have a color scheme in mind?"

"Um," said Rose. Which was all the opening that Sydelle Feller required.

"Navy," she decreed. "Navy's the latest. Very, very chic. Very now. I'm seeing . . ." And she closed her eyes, allowing Rose a moment to marvel at the shades of brown, taupe, and putty eyeshadow cleverly blended on her lids. ". . . bridesmaids in simple navy sheaths . . ."

"I'm not having bridesmaids. Just Amy. She'll be my maid of honor," said Rose. Sydelle raised one perfectly plucked eyebrow.

"What about Maggie?"

Rose stared at the pink linen tablecloth. She'd gotten a very strange message from Maggie months before. A one-word message, consisting of only Rose's name, and the word *I'm.* No word since then, although every few weeks Rose would call the cell phone and hang up after her sister had said "Hello." "I'm not sure," she said.

Sydelle sighed. "Let's talk tables," she said. "I'm seeing navy tablecloths with white napkins, very nautical, very crisp, and we'll want delphiniums, of course, and those gorgeous gerbera daisies . . . or, no. No," said Sydelle, shaking her head once, as if Rose had contradicted to her. "Pink roses. Can you see it? Masses and masses of pink roses, overflowing from silver bowls!" She smiled, looking pleased with herself. "Roses for Rose! Of course!"

"Sounds beautiful!" said Rose. And it did, she guessed. "But, um, with the bridesmaids . . ."

"And of course," Sydelle continued, as if Rose hadn't spoken, "you'll want My Marcia, too."

Rose gulped. She didn't want My Marcia. At all.

"I know she'd be honored," Sydelle said sweetly.

Rose bit her lip. "Um," she began. "I really . . . I think . . ." *Come on!* she urged herself. "Just Amy, really. That's all I want."

Sydelle pursed her lips and flared her nostrils.

"Maybe Marcia could do a reading," Rose said, groping desperately for a bone to throw her stepmother.

"Whatever you like, dear," Sydelle said icily. "It's your wedding, of course." Which was the line Rose had repeated to Simon that night.

"It's our wedding. Of course," she said, and buried her head in her hands. "I just have this horrible feeling that I'm going to wind up with My Marcia and five of her best friends in matching navy sheaths walking me down the aisle."

"You don't want My Marcia?" Simon asked innocently. "But she's so classy! You know, I heard that when she was married, she bought a size six Vera Wang and had it taken in."

"I've heard that rumor, too," Rose muttered.

Simon took her hands. "My beloved," he said, "it's our wedding. It will be just the way we want it. As many bridesmaids as you want. Or none at all."

That night, Rose and Simon wrote out the short list of what

they wanted (great food, a kick-ass band), and what they didn't ("Celebration," a garter toss, My Marcia).

"And no chicken dance!" Simon said the next morning.

"We're having roses!" Rose yelled toward his departing blue-suited back. "Silver bowls overflowing with pink roses! Doesn't that sound beautiful!"

Simon shouted a word that sounded alarmingly like "allergic" over his shoulder, and hurried toward the bus. Rose sighed, and went inside to call Sydelle. By the end of their conversation, she'd agreed to outfit her wedding party in navy, to dress the tables in white, to let My Marcia read a poem of her choosing, and to meet with Sydelle's preferred florist the following week.

"What kind of women talk about 'my florist'?" Rose asked Amy, as Amy cruised the glass case full of headpieces, finally selecting a pearl-studded pouf and plopping it on her own head.

"Pretentious ones," Amy said, affixing an ankle-length veil shimmering with tiny crystals to Rose's head. "Ooh, pretty!" She found a matching veil and put it on her own head. "Come along," she said, and tugged Rose toward a mirror.

Rose looked at herself in the seventh and final dress she'd selected. Yards of lace swirled around her legs. A glittering bodice, stiff with sparkling crystals, encased approximately two-thirds of her midriff and gaped open in back. Stiff embroidered sleeves choked her arms. Rose stared at herself miserably. "Oh, God," she said, "I'm a Mardi Gras float!"

Amy burst out laughing. The saleslady stared at both of them. "Would shoes help?" she asked.

"I think a lighter would help," Amy murmured.

"I think," Rose began. God, she needed a mother. A mother would be able to take the situation in hand, to look at the dress and dismiss it with a brief but undeniable shake of her head. A mother would say, "My daughter likes things that are simple," or, "I see her in an A-line"—or a ballgown, a basque waist, one of those bewildering types of dresses. Even after weeks of study, Rose hadn't been able to puzzle out the differences between them, let alone figure out which one would look best on her. A mother would get her out of this itchy tornado of a dress, out of the iron-lung girdle, out of the showers and teas and cocktail parties and dinners that Rose could no more navigate than she could paddle single-handed up the Schuylkill. And surely a mother would know how to politely tell Sydelle Feller to take her two dozen suggestions and shove them up her tiny, tight ass.

"It's awful," Rose finally blurted.

"Well, I'm sorry," said the saleslady, whose feelings Rose had obviously hurt.

"Maybe something a little less fussy?" Amy suggested. The saleslady pursed her lips and disappeared into the store's back room. Rose slumped into a chair, hearing a sighing noise as the dress deflated around her.

"We should elope," she said.

"Well, I have always loved you, but not in that way," said Amy. "And there's no way I'm letting you elope. You'd deprive me of my butt bow." The day after Rose had told her best friend that she was getting married—before Sydelle had issued her edict on navy— Amy had made a pilgrimage to Philadelphia's premiere thrift shop and procured a frothy salmon-colored frock with tiered layers of tulle, oversized rhinestone buckles at the shoulder, and a butt bow as wide as a city bus, plus, as an engagement gift, a six-inch-thick ivory candle studded with fake plastic pearls and the words *Today I Marry My Best Friend* curling around the sides in gold gilt. "You're not serious," Rose had said, and Amy had shrugged and said that she understood her role as maid of honor, that it was the bride's day to shine, and that if she bought this dress (with shoes dyed salmon to match), she'd be the shoo-in victor at Philadelphia's annual Bridesmaids' Ball, where the women competed to see who had the worst dress. "Plus, as it happens," she'd said, "I look *fierce* in a butt bow."

Now she wrapped her arms around Rose's shoulders. "Don't

worry," she said. "We'll find it. We're just getting started! If it was supposed to be easy, do you think they'd publish thirty million magazines about how to find the dress?"

Rose sighed and got to her feet. Out of the corner of her eye she saw the saleslady approaching, her arms overflowing with silk and satin. "Maybe this dress isn't so bad," she muttered.

"No," said Amy, looking her up and down, "no, it is indeed awful."

"In here, please," the saleslady said curtly, and Rose picked up her skirt and dragged her train in behind her.

FORTY-THREE

Ella Hirsh had endured almost an entire summer of her grand-daughter's silence before deciding that she wouldn't take one moment more.

Maggie had arrived in May, the day after that first tortured, stop-and-start conversation, during which Ella had to keep asking her to repeat herself to make sure that she understood what her long-lost granddaughter was telling her, that this was Maggie, not Rose, and that she was at Princeton, but not really there. Yes, said Maggie, Rose and her father were fine, but she couldn't call them. No, she wasn't hurt, or sick, but she needed a place to go. She didn't have a job at the moment, but she was a hard worker, and she'd find something. Ella wouldn't have to worry about supporting her. There were a thousand things more that Ella wanted to ask her, but she stuck to the basics, the who and what and where, and the mechanics of how to get Maggie from the New Jersey supermarket parking lot down to Florida. "Can you get to Newark?" she asked, somehow extracting the name of New Jersey's major airport from her head. "Call me when you get there. I'll call the airlines, figure out who's got a direct flight, and there'll be a ticket waiting for you at the gate."

Eight hours later, Ella and Lewis had driven to the Fort Lauderdale airport, and there, clutching a backpack and looking weary and bedraggled and scared, was Caroline.

Ella had gasped and squeezed her eyes shut, and when she'd opened them, she saw that she was wrong. This girl wasn't Caroline, not really. Ella saw that as soon as she blinked . . . but the resemblance was very strong. This girl's brown eyes, the way her hair fell over her forehead, her cheeks and her hands and even, somehow, her collarbones, were all Caroline's. But the determined look on her face, the pugnacious set of her chin, the way her eyes had moved over them quickly, sizing them up, told a different story, and certainly forecast a different ending than the one her own daughter had come to. This girl, Ella saw, would not succumb to the lure of a rain-slicked road. This girl would keep her hands on the wheel.

There was an early awkward moment—would they hug?— which Maggie had solved by shifting her backpack into her arms and holding it like a baby, as Ella stumbled through the introductions. Maggie hadn't said much on the way out to short-term parking. She'd refused Ella's offer of the front seat, and sat up straight in the backseat as Lewis drove and Ella tried hard not to pester her with too many questions. Still, she had to know, for her own safety, her own peace of mind, if nothing else. "If you'll tell me what kind of trouble you're in, I'm sure we can figure it out," said Ella.

Maggie had sighed. "I was . . ." She paused. Ella stared at her in the rearview mirror as Maggie groped for the name of her transgression. "I was living with Rose, and it didn't work out, and I've been staying on campus for a few months . . ."

"Staying with friends?" Lewis guessed.

"Staying in the library," said Maggie. "Living there. I was . . ." She stared out the window. "I was like a stowaway. Stowaway," she repeated, which made her sound like she'd been having a grand adventure on the high seas. "Only there was someone watching me, and he was going to get me in a lot of trouble. So I had to leave."

"Do you want to go back to Philadelphia?" asked Ella. "Back to Rose?"

"No!" said Maggie, so vehemently that Ella jumped a little in her seat, and Lewis accidentally hit the horn. "No," she repeated. "I don't know where I want to go. I don't really have a place in Philadelphia. I was in an apartment, but I got evicted from there, and I can't go back with my father, because his wife hates me, and I can't go back with Rose . . ." And she'd sighed a piteous sigh and wrapped her arms around her knees, throwing in a small shiver for dramatic effect. "I guess maybe I could go to New York. I'll get a job and save up my money, and I'll go New York. Find a roommate or . . . something," she'd concluded.

"You can stay with me as long as you need to," said Ella. The words were out of her mouth before she'd considered them, before she'd thought to wonder whether it was a good idea or not. Judging from the look on Lewis's face, the answer was probably "not." Maggie had been evicted. Then she'd been living with her sister, which, for some reason, hadn't worked out. She didn't feel welcome at her father's house. She was stowing away—whatever that meant—in a school where she wasn't enrolled, living in the library. How could that add up to anything but trouble?

As Lewis steered them through the airport traffic, back toward Golden Acres, Maggie had sighed, cupped her chin in her palm, staring out the window as the palm trees and traffic rolled by. "Florida," she said. "I've never been here before."

"How is . . ." Ella began. "Can you tell me about your sister?"

Maggie was quiet. Ella pressed on. "I looked Rose up on the Internet, at her law firm . . ."

Maggie shook her head, staring out the window, as if envisioning her sister's face reflected in the glass. "Is that, like, the worst picture in the world? I kept telling her to make them take another one, and she kept saying, 'It doesn't matter, Maggie. Don't be so superficial.' And I said, 'That picture's out there for the whole world to see, and it isn't superficial to want to look your best,' but of course she didn't listen. She never listens to me," said Maggie, and then closed her mouth as if worried that she'd said too much. "Where are we going, exactly? Where do you live?"

"We live in a place called Golden Acres. It's . . ."

". . . a retirement community for active seniors," she and Lewis recited together.

In the rearview mirror, Maggie's eyes widened in alarm. "A nursing home?"

"No, no," said Lewis. "Don't worry. It's just a place for older people."

"Condominiums," added Ella. "And there are stores, and a club-house, and a trolley that runs for people who don't drive anymore . . ."

"Sounds great," said Maggie, obviously not meaning it. "So what do you do all day?"

"I volunteer," said Ella.

"Where?"

"Oh, all over. The hospital, the pet shelter, the thrift store, Meals on Wheels, and there's this woman I'm helping, she had a stroke last year. . . . I keep busy."

"Do you think I could find a job here?"

"What kind of job?" asked Ella.

"I've done everything," said Maggie. "Waitressing, dog groom-ing, hostessing . . ."

Hostessing? Ella wondered what that meant.

"Barista, bartender," Maggie continued, "baby-sitting, working in an ice-cream shop, working at a fried-dough stand . . ."

"Wow," said Ella. Maggie wasn't through.

"I sang in a band for a while." Maggie thought better of telling the grandmother the name of the band, on the off chance that she'd know what a whiskered biscuit even was. "Telemarketing, spraying people with perfume, T.J.Maxx, the Gap, the Limited : . ." Maggie paused and yawned hugely. "And at Princeton I helped out this blind lady. I cleaned her house. I brought her things."

"That's . . ." Again, Ella was out of words.

"So I guess this will be okay," Maggie said. She yawned, redid her ponytail, then curled up on the backseat and fell instantly asleep. At the next red light, Lewis looked over at Ella.

"Okay?" he asked.

Ella gave him a small shrug, then a smile. Maggie was here, and no matter what the truth turned out to be, that was something.

When Lewis pulled into his parking space, Maggie was still asleep in the backseat, with a lock of brown hair stuck to her sweaty cheek. Her bitten fingernails were so precisely like Caroline's fingers that Ella felt her heart lurch hard against her rib cage. Maggie opened her eyes, stretched, grabbed her backpack, and stepped out of the car, blinking. Ella followed her gaze. There was Irene Siegel, pushing her walker across the parking lot, and Albert Gantz, slowly unloading an oxygen tank from his trunk.

"It is the blight man was born for," Maggie said in a low, resigned voice.

"What was that, dear?" asked Lewis.

"Nothing," Maggie said. She shouldered her backpack and followed Ella inside.

True to her word, Maggie got a job at a bagel shop half a mile from Golden Acres. She'd work the early shift, creeping out of the apartment at five in the morning, working through breakfast and lunch. And then what? Ella had asked, because Maggie rarely reappeared at the apartment before eight or nine. Her granddaughter had shrugged. "I go to the beach," she said. "Or the movies. Or the library." For weeks, Ella had offered dinner. Each time, Maggie refused. "I already ate," she'd say—although, skinny as she was, Ella sometimes wondered whether Maggie ate anything at all. She'd decline Ella's offers to watch TV, to go to a movie, to join her at the Clubhouse for a bingo game. The only thing that had gotten even a flicker of interest was Ella's offer of a library card. Maggie had accompanied her grandmother to the small, one-story library, filled out her forms with Ella's address, then disappeared into the Fiction and Literature shelves, emerging an hour later with her arms full of poetry books.

And that was that. For May. For June. For July and August. At night, Maggie would come home, nod hello, and disappear. She'd emerge for a shower, then slip silently into the back bedroom, easing the door closed behind her, carrying her single towel, her shampoo, her toothbrush and toothpaste, with her as if she were an overnight guest, even though Ella had told her that she was welcome to leave her things wherever she wanted. There was a small television set in Maggie's bedroom, but Ella never heard it go on. There was a telephone, too, but Maggie never called anyone. She read, Ella knew—every three or four days she'd notice a new library book in Maggie's bag, thick novels, biographies, books of poetry, the kind of odd, fragmented, non-rhyming poems that never made sense to Ella—but Maggie never seemed to talk to anyone, and Ella was starting to worry that she never would.

"I don't know what I'm going to do," she said. It was eight in the morning, almost eighty-five degrees, and she'd fled to Lewis's apartment after Maggie had glided past her and out the door again.

"About the weather? Just wait. It can't last."

"About her," said Ella. "Maggie. She doesn't talk to me! She doesn't even look at me. She pads around on her bare feet . . . I never hear her coming. . . . She's out until all hours, she's gone when I wake up. . . ." Ella paused, took a deep breath, and shook her head.

"Well, normally I'd say to give her time . . ."

"Lewis, it's been months, and I don't even know the story with her sister, or her father. I don't even know what she likes for dinner! You've got grandchildren . . ."

"Grandsons," Lewis said. "But I think you're right. This calls for drastic measures." He nodded, and got to his feet. "We need to call in the big guns."

Luckily, Mrs. Lefkowitz was home. "Let's start out with a few questions," she said, moving back and forth across her cluttered living room in her familiar plant, sigh, shuffle, stomp. "Do you have prunes in your refrigerator?"

Ella stared at her.

"Prunes," Mrs. Lefkowitz prompted.

"Yes," said Ella.

Mrs. Lefkowitz nodded. "You got Metamucil on the kitchen counter?"

Ella nodded. Didn't everyone?

"What magazines do you subscribe to?"

Ella thought. "*Prevention*, the thing the AARP sends . . ."

"Do you get the HBO and the MTV?"

Ella shook her head. "I don't have cable."

Mrs. Lefkowitz rolled her eyes and plopped down on an overstuffed armchair, on top of a needlepoint pillow that announced, "I'm the Princess." "Young people have their own things. Their own music, their own TV programs, their own . . ."

"Culture?" Lewis supplied.

Mrs. Lefkowitz nodded. "There's nobody here for her," she said. "Nobody her own age. How'd you like to be twenty-eight and stuck in a place like this?"

"She didn't have anywhere else to go," said Ella.

"Neither do prisoners," said Mrs. Lefkowitz. "It doesn't mean they have to like being in jail."

"So what should we do?" Ella asked.

Mrs. Lefkowitz struggled to her feet. "You got money?" she demanded.

Ella nodded.

"Then let's go," she said. "You drive," she said, pointing her chin at Lewis. "We're going shopping."

• • •

Coaxing Maggie out of her room proved to be a costly proposition. First, there were the magazines, almost fifty dollars' worth, each one fatter and glossier and more crammed with perfume samples and subscription-card come-ons than the last. "How do you know about all of this?" Ella asked, as Mrs. Lefkowitz stacked an issue of *Movieline* on top of the latest *Vanity Fair.* Her friend waved her good arm carelessly. "What's to know?" she asked.

Their next stop was a gigantic electronics store. "Flat screen, flat screen," Mrs. Lefkowitz recited as she zipped down the aisles in the motorized scooter she used for her shopping expeditions. Two hours and several thousand dollars later, Lewis's car was packed with a flat-screen TV, a DVD player, and a dozen videos, including the first season of *Sex and the City,* which Mrs. Lefkowitz guaranteed that all the young women were raving about. "I read about it in *Time,"* she boasted, lifting herself into the passenger's seat. "Turn left up here," she told Lewis. "We're going to the supermarket and liquor store," she said, and smiled to herself. "We're going to have a party." At the liquor store, she accosted the pimply-faced clerk in a polyester pinny. "Do you know how to make a cosmopolitan?" she demanded.

"Cointreau . . ." the clerk ventured.

Mrs. Lefkowitz pointed at Lewis. "You heard the man!" she said.

Later, their arms laden with cointreau and vodka, cheese puffs and corn chips, miniature hot dogs and frozen egg rolls, plus two bottles of nail polish (one red, one pink), and cardboard boxes full of electronics. Ella and Lewis and Mrs. Lefkowitz piled into the elevator up to Ella's apartment.

"Do you really think this will work?" she asked, as Lewis put the frozen foods in her freezer.

Mrs. Lefkowitz pulled up a seat at the kitchen table and shook her head. "No guarantees," she said, pulling a hot-pink piece of paper out of her purse. "You're Invited!" it read in silver letters across the top.

"Where's that from?" Ella asked, peering over her shoulder.

"My computer," said Mrs. Lefkowitz, tilting the invitation so that Ella could read that Miss Maggie Feller was invited to a *Sex and the City* party on Friday night at Ella's house. "I can do anything. Invitations, calendars, parking permits . . ."

"What's that?" asked Lewis, who'd been putting snack foods away.

Mrs. Lefkowitz suddenly became very interested in the contents of her purse. "Oh, nothing. Never mind."

Lewis stared at her. "You know, one of my reporters told me that there were people printing up fake parking permits. He wants to do an investigative series."

Mrs. Lefkowitz lifted her chin defiantly. "You're not going to turn me in, are you?"

"Not if this works, I won't," he promised.

Mrs. Lefkowitz nodded, then handed Ella the invitation. "Slip it under her door when she's gone."

"But, if it's a party . . . who's coming?"

Mrs. Lefkowitz stared at her. "Well, your friends, of course."

Ella looked helplessly at Lewis. Mrs. Lefkowitz squinted at her. "You do have friends here, don't you?"

"I—" Ella began. "I have coworkers."

"Coworkers," Mrs. Lefkowitz said to the ceiling. "Well, never mind. It'll just be the three of us, then." She pushed herself up from the table. "See you Friday!" she said, and thumped her way out the door.

"I feel like the witch in 'Hansel and Gretel,'" Ella said, sliding a tray of miniature egg rolls into the oven. It was Friday night, after nine, which meant that Maggie could appear at any moment—if she came home at all. "Did you get your invitation?" Ella had called toward the closing door as Maggie left for work in the morning. The girl had responded with a vaguely affirmative-sounding grunt as the door had closed behind her.

"Why?" Lewis asked. Ella pointed at the lures—the piles of

magazines, the bowls of chips and dips, the platters of deviled eggs and chicken wings and half a dozen other treats that she knew would give her devastating heartburn if she risked more than a bite.

Mrs. Lefkowitz tugged at her sleeve. "One more thing," she said. "The secret weapon."

"What?" Ella asked, glancing at her watch.

"Your daughter," said Mrs. Lefkowitz.

Ella stared. "What?"

"Your daughter. Caroline, right?" Mrs. Lefkowitz said. "All of this"—she swept her hand toward Ella's living room, where Lewis was fiddling with the DVD player and contentedly eating his way through a platter of spinach puffs—"will probably work. But if it doesn't, what's the one thing you've got that Maggie wants?"

"Money?" Ella guessed.

"Well, that, maybe," said Mrs. Lefkowitz. "But there's lots of places she can get money. How many places can she get the story of her mother?"

The story of her mother, Ella thought to herself, wishing with all her heart that it was a longer, happier tale.

"Information," Mrs. Lefkowitz said. "That's what we have that the young people want. Information." She considered. "And some Microsoft stock, in my case. But for you, information ought to be enough." She nodded as Maggie's key turned in the lock. "Showtime!" she whispered. Ella held her breath. Maggie walked into the apartment as if she had blinders on, looking not to the left, and the kitchen stocked with tempting goodies, nor to the right, with the new television set on which a woman was talking about . . . no. She must be hearing it wrong, Ella thought, as the actress burbled, "I don't want to be the up-the-butt girl!" and Mrs. Lefkowitz laughed into her cosmopolitan. Halfway down the hall, Maggie paused.

"Maggie?" Ella called. She could almost feel how torn her granddaughter was—wanting to stay, wanting to go. *Please don't let me mess this up,* Ella prayed. Maggie turned around. "Do you want . . ." What? What could she offer this wary girl with her watchful brown eyes, so similar to and so different from her own lost daughter's eyes? She held out her hand, and the drink she was holding. "It's a cosmopolitan. It has vodka and cranberry juice . . ."

"I know," Maggie said scornfully, "what's in a cosmopolitan." It was one of the longer sentences Ella had gotten out of her granddaughter. Maggie took the drink and swallowed half of it in one mouthful. "Not bad," she said, turned on her heel and strode into the living room. Mrs. Lefkowitz handed her the bowl of Fritos. Maggie plopped herself on the couch, swallowed the remaining half of her drink, and picked up a copy of *Entertainment Weekly.* "I've seen this episode," she said.

"Oh," said Ella. On the one hand, that was bad news. On the other hand, it was a second unsolicited sentence from her granddaughter. And Maggie was there, wasn't she? That was something, right?

"But it's a good one," said Maggie. She flipped the magazine back onto the coffee table and looked around. Ella glanced desperately at Lewis, who hurried out of the kitchen with the pitcher full of drinks. He refilled Maggie's glass. Maggie daintily selected a chicken wing from the platter and sat back with her eyes on the screen. Ella felt herself relax in increments. It wasn't a victory, she told herself, through four straight episodes of women saying things that would have gotten her mouth washed out with soap sixty years ago. But it was a start. She glanced over at her granddaughter. Maggie's eyes had slipped shut. Her eyelashes lay like a spiky fringe on top of her cheek. There was a dusting of Cheetos debris on her chin. And her lips were pursed, as if she were awaiting a kiss in her dreams.

After four cosmopolitans, three chicken wings, and a fistful of Fritos, Maggie had bid Ella and Company good night. She lay on the thin mattress of the pullout couch and closed her eyes, thinking that she might have to reconsider her plan for handling Florida.

Initially, she'd decided to simply watch, wait, stay out of the way, until she could figure things out. That might take some time, Maggie'd acknowledged. Everything she knew about old people she'd learned from TV, from commercials, mostly, which told her that they had high blood sugar and overactive bladders, and were in need of panic buttons to press when they'd fallen and couldn't get up. She'd sit back and focus on the grandmother, who clearly had money. And guilt. Whatever Ella Hirsch had done or hadn't done, she clearly felt beyond awful about it. Which meant that if Maggie was patient, she'd be able to convert those awful feelings into cash—cash she could add to the pile growing slowly in the box beneath her bed. She was earning just minimum wage at Bagel Bay, but Maggie figured that with a few tearful scenes, a few sad stories about how much she missed her mother and how much she would have welcomed the love of a grandmother, or any woman, really, in her short but troubled life, she'd be waltzing out of death's waiting room—aka Golden Acres—with enough money to buy whatever she wanted.

The problem was that getting things from Ella would be almost too easy. It wasn't enough of a challenge, after all of the challenges Maggie had been through. It felt . . . disappointing, somehow. Like gearing up to power your fist through a cinderblock wall and winding up punching a marshmallow instead. The grandmother was so absolutely pathetic that Maggie, who didn't feel bad about much, felt the tiniest bit lousy about planning to separate her from her money. She ate up scraps of Maggie's company, her attention, every word she said, as if she'd been starving in the desert and Maggie were a dish of good ice cream. Now there was the new television set, the DVD player, all of the food, in addition to Ella's constant offers of dinner, movies, day trips to Miami or the beach. Ella was trying so hard that it made Maggie's stomach twist. And the only thing she'd asked for was that Maggie

call her father and tell him that she was all right. There'd been no
mention made of rent, or of giving Ella money for gas or car insurance, or groceries, or anything at all. So why should she be in a
hurry to leave?

Watch and wait, she thought, tucking the pillow more firmly
under her cheek. Maybe she'd get Ella to take her to Disney World.
Ride the teacups. Send home a postcard. *Wish you were here.*

FORTY·FOUR

"Tell me why we're doing this again?" Rose whispered.

"Because generally, when two people decide to get married, it's traditional for their parents to meet," Simon whispered back. "And it's going to be fine," he said. "My parents love you, and I'm sure they'll like your father, and as for Sydelle . . . what's the worst that could happen here?"

In the kitchen, Simon's mother, Elizabeth, was scowling at a cookbook. She was a short, plump woman with silvery-blond hair and the same milky skin as her son. Dressed in a long, flower-patterned skirt, a ruffled white blouse, and a yellow apron whose wide pockets were accented with fabric roses, she looked sort of like a domestic, Jewish Tammy Faye Bakker, minus the eyelashes. In her case, though, looks were deceiving. She taught philosophy at Bryn Mawr in the same flowery skirts and cashmere cardigans that she wore around the house. She was sweet, and funny, and easygoing . . . but wherever Simon had gotten his talents for cooking, and food appreciation, it hadn't been from her. "Shallot," she murmured. "I don't think I have that. In fact," she said, smiling as her son walked in and kissed her cheek, "I'm not sure I know what it is."

"It's sort of a cross between an onion and a clove of garlic," said Simon. "Why? Was it in your crossword puzzle?"

"Simon, I'm cooking," she said firmly. "I can, you know," she added, sounding mildly offended. "I'm a very fine cook, when I do it. It's just that I usually don't."

"And you decided to give it a go tonight?"

"It's the least I can do to welcome the *mishpochah*," she said, beaming at Rose, who smiled back and relaxed, leaning against a counter. Simon, meanwhile, was sniffing the air suspiciously.

"What are you making?"

She tilted the cookbook so he could read it.

"Roast chicken with wild rice and apricot stuffing," said Simon, looking impressed. "Did you remember to clean the chickens?"

"They're from the organic grocery store," she said. "I'm sure they're fine."

"Yeah, but did you take out the innards? The neck and the liver and all? The stuff that they put inside the cavity? Wrapped in plastic?"

Now Rose sniffed, too . . . and noticed that the kitchen smelled a great deal like burning plastic. Mrs. Stein looked worried. "They felt kind of crowded when I was stuffing them," she said, bending to open the oven.

"Nothing to worry about," said Simon, deftly extracting the pan of smoking, raw-looking chicken.

"Towel's on fire," Simon's father remarked, strolling into the kitchen.

"What?" asked Simon, whose attention was focused on the chicken. Tall and thin, with tufts of the same gingery hair that Simon had, Mr. Stein calmly swallowed the mouthful of cheese and crackers he'd been eating and pointed to a dish towel on top of the stove that had indeed burst into flames.

"Towel," he said. "Fire." He walked to the stove, flicked the flaming towel neatly into the sink, where it hissed and smoked, and gave his wife a squeeze. "Calamity Jane," he said affectionately. She swatted at him, still studying her cookbook.

"You're not eating up all the cheese and crackers, are you?"

"Not at all," said Mr. Stein, "I've moved on to the cashews." He turned to Rose, offering the plate of cheese and crackers. "My advice," he said, his voice low and his tone conspiratorial, "fill up on this."

Rose smiled at him. "Thanks," she said.

Simon's mother rolled her eyes and wiped her hands. "So is your, um, Sydelle a good cook?"

"She's usually got my father on some kind of weird diet," said Rose. "High-carb, low-fat, high-protein, vegetarian . . ."

"Oh," said Elizabeth, frowning, "do you think this will be okay? I probably should have asked . . ."

"This will be fine," said Rose, knowing that as soon as Sydelle arrived, food would be the last thing on her mind. The Steins, as it turned out, lived in a large, sprawling, somewhat messy mansion set on two acres of shaggy green grass on a street full of similarly impressive domiciles. Mr. Stein was an engineer who invented parts for airplanes. He'd patented two of them years ago, Simon had told her, which was where a lot of the money came from. Now he was almost seventy, semiretired, and he spent a lot of his time at home looking for his glasses, the cordless telephone, the remote control, and his car keys. Which was probably because Mrs. Stein seemed to spend a lot of her time at home moving things from one pile of stuff to another. That, and working in her overgrown vegetable garden and reading the kind of bodice-ripping novels that Rose had always read in secret, books that always had three words in their titles. *Her Forbidden Desire* was currently perched on top of the microwave, and Rose had also glimpsed *Passion's Tawny Flame* facedown on the living room sofa. Simon told Rose that in high school he'd given his mother a fake gift certificate for a nonexistent book he'd entitled *Love's Moist Panties*. "Was she mad?" Rose had asked. Simon thought about it. "I think she was actually disappointed that the book didn't exist."

Now Simon sniffed the air again, looking worried. "Ma, the walnuts," he said.

"They're fine," said Elizabeth Stein serenely, and shook dinner rolls out of a paper bag and into a napkin-lined basket that looked as if it had been kicked in on one side. "Oh, dear," she murmured. "Lopsided."

This, too, was typical. Simon's parents tended to be unconcerned with formality when it came to tableware. Rose wasn't surprised to see the table covered with a handmade linen tablecloth, set with mismatched plates. She counted three plates from the Steins' set of good china, rimmed with gold, and three from their everyday plates, bought in bulk from Ikea. There were four water glasses and two coffee mugs for drinking water, three wineglasses, two brandy snifters, and a single champagne flute for wine, and a different paper napkin, one of which read, "HAPPY ANNIVERSARY," at each of the plates. Sydelle was going to shit, Rose decided, and smiled to herself, thinking that it suited her just fine.

Simon walked up behind her, carrying a pitcher full of ice water and two bottles of wine. "My advice to you," he said, handing her a glass, "is start drinking heavily."

A car turned into the driveway. Rose glimpsed her father's face, his familiar high forehead and bald spot, and Sydelle sitting beside him, resplendent in lipstick and pearls. She grabbed her fiancé's hand. "I love you," she whispered.

Simon stared at her curiously. "I know."

The car doors slammed. Rose listened to the sounds of polite "hellos" and the sound of Sydelle's heels tap-tapping on the Steins' scuffed hardwood floors. Family, she thought. She swallowed hard, squeezed Simon's hand, wishing for something she couldn't name, for ease and comfort, for a fast joke and a breezy manner, for the absolute right outfit. In other words, for Maggie. To be Maggie for one night, or at least have the benefit of her sister's advice and presence. This was her family, old and new, and Maggie should be here.

Simon stared at her curiously. "You okay?"

Rose poured herself a half-glass of red wine and drank it quickly. "Fine," she said, and followed him into the kitchen. "Fine."

FORTYFIVE

"Rosenfarb!" Maggie shouted at the guard. The guard nodded slowly (no surprise—Maggie had quickly figured out that everyone at Golden Acres did everything slowly), and she stomped on the gas as the parking gate wavered up into the sky. In the months she'd been at Golden Acres, Maggie had privately been conducting an experiment to see whether simply shouting any Jewish-sounding last name at the security guards would be enough to gain admittance. So far, she'd run through *Rosen, Rosenstein, Rosenblum, Rosenfeld, Rosenbluth,* and, once, late at night, *Rosenpenis,* in her personal homage to *Fletch.* The guards (if you could call antiques in old polyester uniforms guards at all) had not so much as batted a gray eyelash as they waved her through.

Maggie piloted Lewis's school-bus-sized Lincoln toward her grandmother's apartment building, parked it in the designated slot, and climbed up the stairs, heading for her bedroom, a room with blank walls and a beige pullout couch that could have been the little sister of the one Maggie remembered from Rose's apartment. The room was so spare and so clean that Maggie wondered whether Ella had ever used it, whether she'd ever had anyone stay overnight.

It was three in the afternoon. She figured that she'd go upstairs, grab the bathing suit she'd found in Ella's closet, go to the beach, kill some time before dinner. Maybe she'd eat with Ella. Maybe they'd pop in another one of the DVDs that Ella had come home with the week before. Except when she opened the door, she was surprised to see her grandmother sitting at the kitchen table, hands folded in front of her, like she'd been waiting.

"Hi," said Maggie. "Aren't you supposed to be at the hospital? Or the hospice? Or someplace that starts with 'hosp'?"

Ella shook her head, smiling faintly. In black slacks and a white blouse, her hair twined around her head as usual, her grandmother looked shabby and small, a monochrome mouse crumpled in a corner.

"We need to talk," Ella said.

Oh boy, thought Maggie. *Here it comes.* She'd gotten this speech, or a version of it, from roommates and boyfriends—and, of course, from Sydelle. *Maggie, you're taking advantage. Maggie, you need to contribute. Maggie, your father shouldn't have to take care of you his whole life.*

But Ella had a different speech in mind. "I owe you an explanation. I've been meaning to talk to you for a long time, but . . ." Her voice trailed off. "I know you're probably wondering where I was, all those years. . . ."

Ah, Maggie thought. So this was what Ella was getting at. Not Maggie's dependence, but Ella's own guilt. "You sent cards," she said.

"That's right," said Ella, nodding. "And I called, too. You never knew?" She asked the question, even though she knew the answer. "Your father was very angry at us. At me and my husband. Then, after Ira died, just at me."

Maggie pulled up a chair and sat down at the table. "Why angry?" she asked.

"He thought I did a terrible thing to him," the grandmother said. "He thought that I—well, my husband and I—should have told him more about Caroline. Your mother."

"I know what her name is," Maggie said irritably. The subject of her mother—her mother's name in this old woman's mouth—

flared like an old wound. She wasn't ready for this. She didn't want to hear about her mother; she didn't want to think about her mother; she didn't want to know the truth, or whatever the grandmother's version of the truth was. Her mother was dead, the first of her life's losses, and that was more truth than any daughter should have to handle.

Ella kept talking. "I should have told your father that she was . . ." Ella stumbled over the words. "Mentally ill . . ."

"You're lying," said Maggie sharply. "She wasn't crazy, she was fine, I remember."

"But she wasn't always fine, right?" asked Ella. Maggie closed her eyes, hearing only snatches of what her grandmother was saying: *manic episodes* and *clinical depression, medication,* and *shock treatment.*

"So if she was crazy like that, why'd you let her get married?" Maggie demanded. "Why'd you let her have kids?"

Ella sighed. "We couldn't stop her," she said. "Whatever her problems were, Caroline was a grown woman. She made her own decisions."

"You were probably glad to get rid of her," Maggie muttered, voicing one of her own worst fears, because it was easy for her to imagine how happy her father and Sydelle and Rose, and her father too, would be to get rid of her, to foist her off on some unsuspecting love-struck guy so that she'd be his problem, not theirs.

Ella looked shocked. "Of course not! I was never glad to get rid of her! And when I lost her . . ." She swallowed hard. "It was the worst thing I could imagine. Because I lost her, and I lost you and Rose, too." She looked down at her hands, folded on the table. "I lost everything," she said. And she lifted her tear-filled eyes and stared at Maggie. "But now you're here. And I hope . . ."

She reached down next to the table. "Here," she said, and pushed a box across the table. "These were in Michigan, in storage. I sent for them. I thought maybe you'd like to see."

Maggie reached inside the box. It was full of photo albums, old ones. She opened the one on top, and there she was—Caroline.

Caroline as a teenager, in a tight black sweater and lots of black eye-liner. Caroline on her wedding day, in a fitted lace dress and a long sweep of veil. Caroline on the beach in a blue bathing suit, squinting in the sunshine, with Rose clutching her leg and baby Maggie in her arms.

Maggie flipped through the pages faster and faster, watching her mother get older, watching herself grow up, knowing that the pictures would stop, that her mother never got older than thirty, that in this world she and Rose would be forever frozen as little girls. *The art of losing isn't hard to master.* Her grandmother was staring at her, her old eyes full of hope. *No,* Maggie thought. *Not this.* She couldn't stand this. She didn't want to be anyone's hope. She didn't want to stand in for anyone's dead daughter. She didn't want anything, she told herself sternly, not anything, not anything at all except some money and a plane ticket out of this place. She didn't want to see the grandmother as anything but a means to an end, a pocketbook and a sad story. She didn't want sympathy extended toward her, and she sure as hell didn't want to feel sorry for anyone else.

She closed the book with a snap, rubbing her palms against her shorts as if they were dirty. "I'm going for a walk," she said, shoving past Ella's chair, heading for the bedroom, grabbing the old-lady bathing suit she'd found in the back bedroom's closet, her towel and sunblock, and an empty notebook and hurrying out the door.

"Maggie, wait," Ella called. Maggie didn't break stride. "Maggie, please!" Ella called, but Maggie was already gone.

Maggie walked through Golden Acres, past Crestwood and Farmington and Lawndale, past all the streets with made-up English-village-sounding names and the buildings that looked exactly identical to the ones standing next to them. *Make her pay,* she whispered to herself.

People owed her—everyone who'd mocked her in high school,

everyone who'd made her less than she was, who'd conspired to keep her invisible, undiscovered. She was almost thirty, for chrissake, and still without a part to her credit, and the closest she'd come to a 90210 address was when she'd watched reruns on TV.

Make her pay, she told herself. She got to the swimming pool, which was deserted except for a handful of old people sunning themselves, reading, playing quiet games of cards. Maggie put on the old-lady swimsuit in the bathroom, then dragged one of the lounge chairs into prime tanning position, spread her towel on the chair, spread herself on top of the towel, and stared at her notebook. How much money would it take to get her out of here? Five hundred dollars for plane fare, she wrote. Another two thousand for security deposit, first and last month's rent. That was more than she'd saved right there. Maggie groaned to herself, tore out the page, crumpled it, and laid it by the side of the chair.

"Hey!" called an old man in a shirt unbuttoned to display a bathmat's worth of frothing white chest hair, "no littering!"

Maggie glared at him, shoved the crumpled piece of paper under her shorts, and resumed writing.

"Head shots," she wrote. How much would those cost?

"Miss!" called a strange voice. "Oh, miss!"

Maggie looked up. This time, it was an old woman in a fringed pink bathing cap.

"I'm sorry to bother you," she said, edging toward Maggie. The loose flesh of her thighs and upper arms wobbled with each step. "But you're going to get a very bad sunburn unless you wear sunblock."

Maggie silently brandished her tube of Bain de Soleil at the old woman, who did not appear to be at all deterred. And was it her imagination, or were the other old people moving toward her, inching their chairs closer each time she closed her eyes, like some kind of senior-citizen *Dawn of the Dead?* "Oh, I see, I see," said the woman, "SPF fifteen, that's good, very good, of course thirty would be better, or even forty-five, and it should be waterproof, really. . . ."

She paused, waiting for a response. Maggie ignored her. The woman kept talking. "And I notice that you haven't put any on your back. Do you need some help?" she inquired, leaning toward Maggie. The thought of having some strange old saggy creature actually touching her caused Maggie to recoil, shaking her head and saying, "No, thank you, but I'll be fine."

"Well, if you need me," the old woman said cheerfully, wobbling back toward her chair, "I'm right here. My name's Dora," she said, in answer to the question that Maggie hadn't asked. "What's your name, dear?"

Maggie sighed. "Maggie," she said, figuring that a fake name might be too much trouble to remember. Back to Maggie, she thought grimly, and returned to her notebook, underlining the words "head shots." She would explain to the grandmother what they were and why she needed them, how much she wanted to be an actress, how she'd always wanted to be an actress, and how, without a loving mother to make those dreams come true, she'd been forced to rely on her wits and her luck, only now . . .

"Excuse me!"

Oh, for chrissake, Maggie thought, and squinted through the sunlight at a pair of old guys in shorts. With sandals. And socks.

"We were hoping you could help us settle a dispute," the leader of the pair began. He was a tall, skinny, bald man, sunburned to the color of a salmon.

"I'm kind of busy," said Maggie, indicating her notebook, hoping that they'd leave her alone.

"Don't bother the girl, Jack," said the other man—he was short and barrel-shaped, with a fringe of white hair and atrocious black-and-red plaid shorts.

"It's just a quick question," said the man who was probably Jack. "I was just wondering—well, we were just discussing . . ." Maggie stared at him impatiently. "You look so familiar," he said. "Are you an actress?"

Maggie tossed her hair over her shoulders and favored the

geezers with her most dazzling smile. "I was in a music video," she said. "Will Smith."

The tall man stared at her, eyes wide. "Really? Did you meet him?"

"Well, not exactly," Maggie said, propping herself up on her elbows. "But I saw him at lunch. At craft services," she said, tossing out the terminology and shaking her auburn curls. And suddenly there were four old people gathered around her, Jack and his friend, the blabbering woman Dora, and the guy who'd yelled at her about the trash. Maggie saw liver spots and sunblock, mothball-smelling shorts, wrinkles and whiskers and flyaway white hair.

"An actress. My goodness," said Jack.

"Wow," echoed the barrel-shaped guy.

"Who do you belong to?" burbled Dora, who'd reappeared. "Oh, your grandparents must be so proud of you!"

"Do you live in Hollywood?"

"Do you have an agent?"

"When you got that tattoo," rasped Jack's barrel-shaped friend, "did it hurt?"

Dora shot him a sharp look. "Herman, who cares?"

"I care," said Herman, looking truculent.

Jack jiggled the edge of Maggie's chair impatiently and said what to Maggie were the magic words. "Tell us all about yourself," he said. "We want to hear everything."

FORTY-SIX

Simon set his briefcase on the floor of Rose's apartment and held his arms open. "Bride-elect!" he called. He'd come across the term in a small-town newspaper when he had to drive out to central Pennsylvania for a deposition, and had been using it on Rose ever since.

"Just a minute!" called Rose from the kitchen, where she was sitting at the table flipping through the folders from three different catering companies that had arrived in the mail that day. Simon wrapped his arms around her. "How serious are you about baby lamb chops?" she murmured into his neck. "Because I have to tell you, they're expensive."

"Money is no object," Simon declared grandly. "Our love must be celebrated with all the proper pomp and circumstance. And lamb chops."

Rose set a gift-wrapped box in front of him. "This came today, and I can't figure out what it is."

"An engagement gift!" said Simon, rubbing his hands together and reading the return address. "From Aunt Melissa and Uncle Steve!" He opened the box, and together they stared at the gift inside. After a minute, Simon glanced at Rose, and cleared his throat. "I think it's a candleholder."

Rose pulled the block of glass out of its nest of tissue paper and held it up toward the light. "There's no candle."

"Well, but there's a place for a candle," said Simon, pointing out the shallow indentation on one of its sides.

"I don't think that's deep enough for a candle," said Rose. "And if it was a candleholder, wouldn't they have sent it with a candle? So we'd know?"

"It has to be a candleholder," said Simon, without conviction. "What else could it be?"

Rose stared at the glass block some more. "I was thinking maybe a serving piece?"

"For very small meals?" asked Simon.

"No, no, for, like, nuts or candy or something."

"The hole's not big enough for nuts or candy."

"Oh, but it's big enough for a candle?"

They stared at each other for a minute. Then Simon picked up a thank-you note and started writing. "Dear Aunt Melissa and Uncle Steve. Thank you for the lovely gift. It will look . . ." He paused, staring at the ceiling. "Lovely?"

"You just said lovely," said Rose.

"Wonderful!" Simon amended. "It will look wonderful in our home, and will provide hours of entertainment for years to come as we try to figure out what in God's name it is. Thank you for thinking of us, and we look forward to seeing you soon." Simon signed their names, capped the pen, and turned to Rose, beaming. "There!"

"You didn't really write that," said Rose.

"No," said Simon. "I didn't. How many left?"

Rose consulted the list. "Fifty-one."

"Are you kidding?"

"It's your fault," Rose said. "I blame you."

"Just because my family buys us gifts . . ."

"Just because my family's not ridiculously enormous . . ."

Simon stood up, grabbed Rose around the waist, and blew a

raspberry against the side of her neck. "Take it back," he said.

"Ridiculously enormous!"

"Take it back," he whispered into her ear, "or I will force you to do my every bidding."

Rose twisted around to face him. "I am not," she said breathlessly, "writing those thank-you notes myself!"

Simon pulled her close and kissed her, running his hands through her hair. "The notes can wait," he said.

Later, lying in bed, warm and naked beneath the down comforter, Rose rolled onto her side and finally started talking about the thing she'd been holding off on from the moment he'd come home. "There's something else," she said. "My father called today. About Maggie."

Simon's face was neutral. "Oh?" he asked.

Rose flipped onto her back and stared at the ceiling. "She's resurfaced," she said. "All my father would tell me over the phone was that she's fine. He wants to see me, he says. To tell me the rest."

"Okay," said Simon.

Rose shut her eyes and shook her head. "I'm not sure I want to know the rest. Whatever the rest is. I just don't . . ." Her voice trailed off. "The thing about Maggie is, she's horrible."

"What do you mean?" Simon asked.

"She's . . . I mean, she . . ." Rose grimaced. How was she supposed to explain to the man she loved about her sister? Her sister, who stole money and stole shoes and even stole boyfriends, and then went missing for months on end? "Just take my word for it. She's very bad news. She has learning disabilities . . ." And then she stopped. The learning disabilities, really, were just the tip of the Maggie iceberg. And wasn't it just like her sister to reappear as soon as Rose got engaged, as soon as there was a chance that she'd be the center of attention, for a change? "She's going to ruin our wedding," she said.

"I thought Sydelle was going to ruin our wedding," said Simon.

Rose smiled in spite of herself. "Well, Maggie's going to ruin it more." God, she thought. Things had been so calm with Maggie gone off to who-knows-where. No bill collectors blasting at the morning's silence with their phone calls, no former or potential boyfriends disrupting Rose and Simon's sleep. Things stayed where Rose put them. None of her shoes, or her clothes, or her cash, ever went wandering. The car stayed where she parked it. "I'll tell you one thing," Rose continued. "She's not going to be a bridesmaid. She'll be lucky if she gets an invitation."

"Okay," said Simon.

"She'll be lucky if she gets dinner," said Rose.

"More food for me," said Simon.

Rose stared at the ceiling some more. "I still think that glass thing was some kind of serving dish."

"I already licked the envelope," said Simon. "Let it go."

"Agh," said Rose. She closed her eyes and wished for a normal family, like Simon's. No dead mother, no vanished little sister, no father who reserved most of his passion for the morning market reports, and certainly no Sydelle. She rested her face against the cool cotton of the pillowcase for a minute, then got up and went to the living room and picked up a thank-you note—a card of heavy cream paper that had their names, *Rose* and *Simon,* set on either side of a gigantic *S,* to stand for *Stein,* which was not going to be Rose's last name. But even though she'd pointed that out to the Stepmonster, Sydelle had gone ahead and ordered them monogrammed thank-you cards that suggested that Rose was going to be Rose Stein, like it or not.

Dear Maggie, thought Rose. *How could you do what you did to me? And when are you coming home?*

FORTY-SEVEN

Ella walked up to the fence surrounding the swimming pool and pressed her face against it. "There," she said, giving the single word all of the sadness and disappointment she felt. "There she is."

Lewis stepped next to her, and Mrs. Lefkowitz zipped up in her new scooter. Together, the three of them stood at the fence, looking through the diamond-shaped holes. Looking at Maggie.

Her granddaughter lay on a chaise lounge beside the deep end, resplendent in a brand-new pink bikini, with a silver chain, thin as a filament of hair, clinging to her belly. Her skin shone with suntan lotion. Her hair was arranged in a soft pile of loose curls on top of her head, and her eyes were hidden behind small round sunglasses. And around her were four people—an old woman in a faded pink rubber bathing cap, and three old men in shorts. As Ella watched, one of the old men leaned forward, toward Maggie, as if he was asking her a question. Her granddaughter propped herself up on one elbow, looking thoughtful. When her lips moved, her audience burst into laughter.

"Oh," said Lewis. "It looks like she's made some new friends."

Ella felt her heart give a painful twist, as Maggie continued to amuse her new acquaintances, looking more relaxed and at ease than Ella had ever seen her, as the Water Babies aerobics class splashed energetically to a wavery tape recording of "Runaround Sue." Every day for the past week—every day since Ella had tried to tell Maggie about her mother—this had been her granddaughter's routine. Maggie would come home from work, dash into the back bedroom, swap her Bagel Bay uniform for her bathing suit and shorts, and come here. "I'm going swimming," she'd say. Ella was never invited. And Ella could see where this was going. Maggie would move out—into an apartment of her own, or maybe in with one of her new friends, some pleasant old woman who'd offer all of the benefits of being a grandmother with none of the messy complications or painful history. Oh, she thought, it wasn't fair! She'd waited for so long, she'd hoped for so much, and now, to see Maggie slipping away from her like this!

"What should I do?" she whispered.

Mrs. Lefkowitz backed up her scooter and drove it, full speed ahead, toward the entrance to the pool.

"Wait!" Ella cried. "Where are you going?"

Mrs. Lefkowitz didn't turn, didn't stop, and didn't answer. Ella shot a helpless glance at Lewis.

"I'll go . . ." he began.

"We better . . ." she said.

Ella's pulse beat in her throat as she hurried after Mrs. Lefkowitz, who was speeding through the gates, straight toward Maggie, and didn't show any signs of slowing down.

"Hey!" one of the old guys called as Mrs. Lefkowitz zipped past him, bumping into the table on which he'd spread a hand of cards. She ignored him and pulled her scooter up to Maggie's lounge chair. Maggie lowered her sunglasses and stared. Breathing hard, Ella and Lewis hurried after Mrs. Lefkowitz, and for one bizarre moment Ella was reminded of a dozen spaghetti westerns and the scene each one of them had, where the good guys made their stand against the enemy on a conveniently deserted street or in the middle of an empty corral. All the scene needed, she thought, was for some tumbleweed to blow past Mrs. Lefkowitz's scooter. Even the

Water Babies had ceased their splashing and stood quietly in the shallow end, water dripping from their tanned, wrinkled arms, watching to see what would happen next.

Maggie stared at Mrs. Lefkowitz, and Maggie's new friends eyeballed Ella and Lewis, and Ella made a careful study of the cracked concrete beneath her feet, wishing for a cowboy hat and, even more desperately, for a script. Was she the good guy or the bad guy here? Was she the hero, come to rescue the damsel in distress, or the villain, come to lash her to the train tracks?

Hero, she decided, just as Mrs. Lefkowitz rolled the scooter forward another six inches, nudging the edge of Maggie's lounge. Ella was reminded of a puppy pushing its nose against a closed door.

"Maggie, dear," Mrs. Lefkowitz said, "there's something that maybe you can help me with."

Maggie raised her eyebrows as one of the old men glared at Mrs. Lefkowitz.

"She's tired," he said belligerently, gripping his cane with two hands. "She had a very long day. And she was just getting ready to tell us about how she almost got a job at MTV."

Mrs. Lefkowitz wasn't moving. "So go ahead. Tell."

Maggie looked over Mrs. Lefkowitz's head and addressed herself to Ella. "What do you want?"

The words rose up, unbidden, to Ella's mouth and threatened to spill over. *I want you to love me. I want you to like me. I want you to stop running away.* "I . . ." she managed.

"She's busy," the short, round, barrel-shaped man said, stepping in front of Maggie's lounge chair protectively.

"Are you Maggie's grandmother?" asked the woman in the pink bathing cap. "Oh, you must be so proud of her! Such a beautiful girl, and so accomplished . . ."

Maggie bit her lip, and the old man with the cane made an unpleasant noise as Lewis quietly pulled two chairs over to Maggie's circle and motioned for Ella to sit.

"MTV?" Mrs. Lefkowitz asked, nodding knowledgeably, as if

she'd invented the station. "Were you going to be a contestant on one of their game shows?"

"On-air talent," Maggie muttered.

"Like the Carson Daly," said Mrs. Lefkowitz, crossing her hands over her lumpy waist and tilting her square sunglasses toward the sun. "So handsome, that one."

The two groups arranged themselves in an uneasy half-circle around Maggie's lounge chair. Ella and Lewis and Mrs. Lefkowitz were on one side, Maggie's new friends on the other. Maggie stared at one group, then the other. Then she gave an almost invisible shrug, reached into her backpack, and pulled out a notebook. Ella felt herself relax the tiniest bit. It wasn't progress, exactly, but at least Maggie hadn't bolted, or asked them to leave.

"It's Jack, isn't it?" Lewis asked the man who'd been gripping the cane. The man—Jack—gave an affirmative grunt. Lewis offered him his hand. The talkative woman began quizzing Mrs. Lefkowitz about her scooter. The two other men went back to their game of cards. Ella closed her eyes, and breathed quietly, and hoped.

In her lounge chair, Maggie also had her eyes closed, thinking about what to do and how to make things right, even when part of her protested that it wasn't her job to fix things. Except nobody in Florida knew what was her job and what wasn't. Nobody here knew what a mess she'd made of her life. Nobody here knew Rose, and how she was the one who took care of things, the same way they didn't know that Maggie was always the one who needed saving, or fixing, or help. She had a job, a place to live, people who cared about her. Now it was time for her to start repairing the damage, starting with the one she'd hurt the worst—starting with Rose.

She squeezed her eyes shut, feeling afraid, part of her wanting to jump to her feet, hurry through the gate, jump behind the wheel of Lewis's long car, and drive off someplace where nobody knew her, where nobody knew who she was, or what she'd done, or where she'd come from. But she'd already run to Princeton, and then she'd run here. She didn't want to run anymore.

In the shallow end, the Water Babies began their cool-down. In the chair beside her, her grandmother cleared her throat. "I bet you miss people your age," Ella said. "It must be hard for you, being the only young person here."

"I'm okay," said Maggie.

"She's fine," growled Jack.

Maggie opened her eyes, then opened her notebook. "*Dear Rose,*" she wrote. Ella looked at the page, then very quickly looked away. Dora, the woman in the pink bathing cap, had no such compunctions.

"Who's Rose?" she asked.

"My sister," said Maggie.

"You've got a sister? What's she like?" Jack put down his cards, and Herman set aside his *Mother Jones.* "She's got a sister!"

"She's a lawyer in Philadelphia," said Ella, and then closed her mouth and looked at Maggie for help. Maggie ignored her, closing her notebook, getting up and walking through the gauntlet of senior citizens to the edge of the pool, where she dangled her legs in the water.

"Is she married?" asked Dora.

"What kind of law?" asked Jack. "Does she do wills, by any chance?"

"Is she coming to visit?" demanded Herman. "Does she look like you? Does she have any tattoos?"

"She's not married," said Maggie. "She has a boyfriend . . ." *Or at least, she used to have a boyfriend, until I fucked that up that for her.* Maggie stared unhappily into the chlorinated depths of the deep end.

"Tell us more!" urged Dora.

"Does she have anything pierced?" asked Herman.

Maggie smiled and shook her head. "She doesn't look like me. Well, a little bit, maybe. We have the same color eyes and hair, but she's bigger than I am. And no tattoos, either. She's very conservative. She wears her hair twisted up all the time."

"Like you!" Ella said.

Maggie started to protest, then touched her ponytail and realized that it was true. She hopped into the water, flipped onto her back, and floated.

"Rose can be funny," she said. Ella hurried to the edge of the pool to listen. The rest of Maggie's pool friends followed after her, jostling for prime position along the deep end's ledge. "And mean, sometimes. When we were girls, we had to share a room. We had twin beds, and there was a space in between them, and she'd lie there, reading, and I used to jump over her." Maggie started to smile as she remembered. "She'd be lying there, and I'd jump back and forth, from one bed to the other, and I'd say, 'The quick brown fox jumped over the lazy dog!'"

"So you were the quick brown fox," said Ella.

Maggie gave her a "duh" look that was quickly repeated by Jack, Dora, and Herman. "I'd do it until she hit me," she said.

"She hit you?" asked Ella.

"I'd jump back and forth, and I could see that she was getting really irritated, but I'd keep doing it until she'd stick her arm up in the air and bat me down when I was jumping." Maggie nodded and pulled herself out of the water, looking strangely pleased with the memory of being hit by her sister, mid-leap.

"Tell us more about Rose," Dora said, as Jack handed her a towel and her tube of Bain de Soleil.

"She doesn't care that much about looks. And stuff," said Maggie, resuming her sprawling position on her lounge chair, remembering Rose squinting at herself in the mirror, or Rose clumping mascara onto her lids, then heading out the door with half-moons of black on her cheeks.

"Oh, I'd like to meet her," said Dora.

"Invite her for a visit," said Jack, cutting his eyes toward Ella. "I'm sure your grandmother would love to have both of you."

Maggie knew that he was right. Ella would love to meet Rose. What grandmother wouldn't? A smart, successful granddaughter with a law degree. But Maggie wasn't sure whether she was ready to see Rose again, even if Rose was willing to forgive her. Things were going better for her than they ever had, ever since she'd left Philadelphia that terrible night. For once in her life, she wasn't in Rose's shadow, she wasn't the second sister, the one who wasn't as smart, wasn't as successful, the one who was just pretty in a time when pretty felt as if it mattered less and less. Corinne and Charles hadn't known about her history, her struggles, the remedial classes, all the jobs she'd quit or been fired from, all the girls who used to be her friends. Dora and Jack and Herman didn't think she was stupid or a slut. They liked her. They admired her. They listened to what she had to say. And Rose would show up and ruin everything. "A bagel shop?" she'd ask, in a tone suggesting that a bagel shop was the best Maggie could hope for—a bagel shop, a spare bedroom, a borrowed car, the kindness of strangers.

Maggie opened her notebook again. "Dear Rose," she wrote once more, and then stopped. She couldn't think of how to do this, of what she was going to say next.

"This is Maggie, in case you can't tell from the handwriting," she wrote. "I am in Florida with our grandmother. Her name is Ella Hirsch, and she was . . ." Agh. This was so hard. There was a word for what she wanted to say here. Maggie could almost catch it, could practically taste it on her tongue, and the feeling caused her heart to quicken, the way it had during the classes at Princeton, when she'd sat in the back with the right answers waiting to burst from her mouth. "What's the word that means that someone wants to be with someone else, but they're not, because of a fight or something?" she called.

"The Yiddish word?" asked Jack.

"Who's she gonna write to in Yiddish?" asked Herman, returning his attention to *Mother Jones*.

"Not Yiddish," said Maggie. "The word for where there's two

relatives, or something, but other people in the family are angry at each other about stuff, so the relatives never meet."

"*Estranged*," said Lewis. Jack glared at him. Maggie appeared not to notice.

"Thanks," she said.

"Glad to be of use in my golden years," said Lewis.

"Her name is Ella Hirsch, and she was estranged from us," Maggie wrote, and stared at the page. This was the hard part . . . but she'd had practice at Princeton, working with words, picking out the best ones the way a careful cook chooses the best apples from the basket, the plumpest chicken from the butcher's case.

"I'm sorry for what happened last winter," she wrote, deciding that this was probably the best way to handle it—flat out, in the open. "I am sorry I hurt you. I want . . ." And she paused again, aware that everyone was staring at her, as if she were some rare aquatic creature recently brought into captivity, some animal at the zoo who'd just learned an amusing new trick.

"What's the word for when you want to make something right?"

"*Reconciliation*," Ella said quietly, and spelled it, and Maggie wrote it twice, just to be sure she got it right.

FORTY-EIGHT

"Okay," said Rose, as she got into the passenger's seat of her car, "okay, so you swear and affirm under penalty of perjury as defined by the Pennsylvania Code that there will be absolutely nobody else from Lewis, Dommel, and Fenick at this wedding?" This was important information. Of all the things she'd covered with Simon—dead mother, vanished sister, unspeakable stepmother—they'd never gotten around to the topic of Mr. Jim Danvers. And Rose was determined not to have to do it at the nuptials of two of Simon's law-school classmates mere months before their own wedding.

"As far as I know," said Simon, straightening his tie and starting the car.

"As far as you know," Rose repeated. She flipped down the mirror, glanced at her makeup, and began swiping at an unblended patch of concealer beneath her right eye. "So I'll just have to keep my eyes open for skateboards."

"I didn't tell you?" Simon asked innocently. "Don Dommel fell off his board and hit his head on a railing and saw God. No more extreme anything. He's into meditation now. There's yoga every afternoon at lunchtime. The whole place smells like incense, and the secretaries have to say *Namaste* when they answer the phone.'"

"Heh," said Rose.

"Rose," said Simon, "it's a wedding, not a mob hit. Calm down."

Rose began rooting in her purse for a lipstick, thinking that it was easy for Simon to say. He wasn't the one who had to explain himself. She was starting to understand why Maggie had been so defensive. Moving through the world with a title—doctor, lawyer, college student—gave you armor. Having to continually try to find a way to tell people who you were—which really meant telling them what you did—was difficult when you didn't fit into one of the world's neat little cubes. *Well, I'm an aspiring actress, but I'm waitressing right now,* or, *I used to be a lawyer, but for the last ten months I've been walking dogs.*

"You'll be fine, Rose," said Simon. "You just have to be happy for my friends, and drink champagne, and dance with me . . ."

"You didn't mention dancing," said Rose, and gazed dismally at her feet, currently cramped in the first pair of high-heeled shoes she'd worn since her defection from big firm life. *Courage,* she told herself. "I'm sure this is going to be great!" She swallowed hard. She was sure it was going to be awful. She didn't do well at large functions, which was one of the reasons she was semi-dreading her own nuptials. She had too many memories of bar and bat mitzvah parties, afternoons like these in synagogues and country-club ballrooms, where she'd always felt like the tallest, ugliest girl, and how she'd station herself in a corner close to the chopped liver and miniature hot dogs in puff pastry, reasoning that if nobody could see her, it wouldn't hurt when nobody asked her to dance, and she'd spend hours alone, eating, and watching Maggie win the limbo contest.

Flash forward eighteen years, add one fiancé, and here she was again, she thought, following Simon through church doors festooned with giant tufts of lilies and white satin ribbons. Except instead of chopped liver and teeny weenies, there'd be crudités and champagne, and there'd be no limbo-ing little sister to distract her. Rose picked up a program. "The bride's name is Penelope?"

"We actually call her Lopey," said Simon.

"Lopey. Right," said Rose.

"I'll introduce you to some people," Simon said. And, in short order, Rose met James, and Aidan, and Leslie, and Heather. James and Aidan were also law-school classmates of Simon's. Leslie worked in publicity; Heather was a buyer at Macy's. Both of them were tiny little things wearing linen sheaths (Heather's was cream, Leslie's was yellow) and cashmere wraps slung loosely over their shoulders. Rose looked around the room, despair welling in her chest as she realized that every single other woman—every single one of them!—was wearing a simply cut dress and a wrap, and delicate little sandals, and here she was, in the wrong outfit, in the wrong color, with pumps, not sandals, and chunky beads, not pearls, and her hair was probably a frizzy mess staging a jailbreak from the tortoiseshell combs she'd carefully positioned an hour ago. Shit. Maggie would have known what she was supposed to wear, Rose thought dismally. Where was her sister when she needed her?

"And what do you do?" asked Heather. Or maybe it was Leslie. They were both blondes; only, one of them had a pageboy and the other had her hair pinned into a graceful chignon; and they both had the kind of translucent skin that comes from excellent breeding and regular exposure to the air inside of Talbots' dressing rooms.

Rose fiddled with her beads, wondering if anyone would notice if she slipped them into her purse during the service. "I'm an attorney."

"Oh!" said Leslie. Or possibly Heather. "So do you work with Simon?"

"I'm . . . I'm actually . . ." Rose shot Simon a desperate look, but he was deep in conversation with the guys. She wiped at her damp forehead, realizing that she'd probably just removed her foundation. "I used to work at Lewis, Dommel, and Fenick, but I'm sort of taking a break for the time being."

"Oh," said Leslie.

"That's nice," said Heather. "And you're getting married, right?"

"Right!" Rose agreed, too loudly, and wrapped her fingers around Simon's forearm, taking care to make sure that her engagement ring was front and center, in case they'd think that she was lying.

"I took three months' leave from work to plan my wedding," said Heather. "Oh, I remember that time. All those meetings . . . the menus, the flowers . . ."

"I just worked part time," chimed in Leslie. "I'd keep busy, of course, with the Junior League, but mostly it was all wedding, all the time."

"Would you excuse me?" Rose murmured, knowing that any minute they were going to start talking dresses, and she'd be forced to reveal the truth, which was that she hadn't been looking since her one disastrous afternoon with Amy. *No dress, no job,* their eyes would say, *and no membership to the Junior League. What kind of a bride are you?*

Rose hurried out into the aisle, back through the foyer, and out onto the brick path, where a tall man in a suit was standing as if he were waiting for her. Rose stopped, and stared up at his crisp white shirt, red-and-gold patterned tie, square jaw, tanned skin, sparkling blue eyes. Jim Danvers.

"Hello, Rose," he said.

He looked exactly the same. But what had she expected? That he'd wither up and die without her? That he'd go bald, that he'd develop adult acne, that hair would sprout out of his ears?

Rose nodded at him, hoping he couldn't tell that her knees were shaking, her hands were trembling, that even her neck was wobbling, too. Come to think of it, she saw, he did have hair coming out of his ears. Not much, really, not the kind of disgusting bristly growth she'd noticed coming out of other men's ears, but still . . . there it was. Ear hair. The incontrovertible evidence that he wasn't perfect. Then again, sleeping with her sister could also be interpreted as evidence of his lack of perfection, but still, she found the ear hair comforting.

"What brings you here?" he asked. His voice sounded higher than she remembered it. Could it be that Jim Danvers was nervous?

Rose tossed her hair. "Oh, Lopey and I go way back. We rode horses together, and then we were in that a capella singing group together in college. We were sorority sisters, we went on double dates . . ."

Jim shook his head. "Lopey's a vegetarian, and I think she believes that riding horses would be exploitative. Also, she was a pretty hard-core lesbian in college, so any double-dating you did would have to be of the all-female variety."

"Ah," said Rose, "I must have been thinking of the groom, then."

Jim gave a short, uncomfortable laugh. "Rose," he began. "I've been meaning to talk to you."

"Lucky me," said Rose.

"I've missed you," he said.

"What's not to miss?" she said. "Come meet my fiancé."

His eyes widened almost imperceptibly. "Take a walk with me first," he said.

"I don't think so."

"Come on. It's a beautiful day."

She shook her head.

"You look so beautiful," he murmured.

She whirled, glaring at him. "Look, Jim. You've had your fun with me, so why don't you give it a rest? I'm sure there's plenty of women here who'd be impressed with your talents."

Now Jim looked distressed. "Rose, I'm sorry. I'm sorry if I offended you."

"You slept with my sister," she said. "I'm a little past offended."

He took her arm and tugged her toward a wooden bench, sat down beside her, and looked earnestly into her eyes. "I've been wanting to talk to you for a while. The way it ended . . . What I did . . ." He clutched her hands. "I wanted to be good for you," he said in a choked voice. "I was weak. I was an idiot. I threw away everything we could have had, and I've felt horrible about myself for months . . ."

"Please," she said. "I've felt horrible about myself for practically my entire life. You think I'm going to feel sorry for you?"

"I want to make it up to you," he said. "I want to make it right."

"Forget it," she said. "It's over. I've moved on. I'm engaged now. . . ."

"Congratulations," he said sadly.

"Oh, come on," she said. "Don't tell me you even thought for a minute that you and I were . . . that we would . . ."

He blinked. And were those tears in his eyes? *Amazing,* thought Rose, who felt as if she were observing a specimen on a slide through a microscope. *I wonder if he can make himself cry whenever he wants to?*

Now he was taking her hands, and she could predict every single one of his moves, every word that he'd say.

"Rose, I'm sorry," he began, and she nodded, because she'd figured that would be his lead-in. "What I did was unforgivable," he said, "and if there was any way to make it up to you . . ."

She shook her head and got to her feet. "There's not," she said. "You're sorry for what happened. I'm sorry, too. Not only because you're the kind of guy you turned out to be, but . . ." And suddenly her throat felt thick, as if she were trying to swallow a sweat sock. "Because you ruined . . ." *My life?* she thought. No, that wasn't true. Her life was fine, or it would probably be fine, once she got the whole career thing back on track, and she was with Simon now, Simon who was so kind, who called forth all of the goodness in her own heart, who made her laugh. The short, spectacularly failed romance she'd had with Jim felt like nothing more than a far-off bad dream. He hadn't ruined her, but he'd damaged something else, hurt it possibly beyond repair. "Because of Maggie," she finally said.

And now he was pulling her back to the bench, and he was talking about her future, how terrible he'd felt when she'd left Lewis, Dommel, and Fenick, and how that had been unnecessary—he was a cad, yes, he'd admit to that, but at least he was discreet, and nothing would have happened to her at work—and where had she landed? Did she need help? Because he could help her, it was the least he could do in light of what had happened, and . . .

"Stop! Please!" said Rose. She could hear the strains of a string quartet filtering through the garden, and the church doors creaking shut. "We need to get back."

"I'm sorry," he said.

"I accept your apology," Rose said formally. And then, because he looked so sad—and because, in spite of her absent sister, wicked stepmother, and lack of a legal career, she was so happy—she leaned close to him and kissed his cheek lightly. "It's okay," she said. "I hope you'll be happy."

"Oh, Rose," he groaned, and wrapped his arms around her.

And suddenly, there was Simon, his eyes wide and shocked. "They're starting," he said quietly. "We should go."

Rose looked at him. His pale face was even paler than it usually was. "Simon," she said. Oh, God.

"Come on," he said, in a soft, toneless voice, and he walked her up toward the wedding, where the flower girls had already started their trip down the aisle, strewing pale-peach rose petals as they went.

Simon sat quietly through the service. He was silent during dinner. When the band started to play, he made a beeline for the bar, and stood there, drinking beer, until Rose finally convinced him that they should talk, and they should do it in private. He held the car door open for her—a gesture that had always seemed kind, but now seemed ironic, even cruel. "Well," he began. "Interesting after-noon." His eyes were straight ahead, and there were splotches of hectic red high on his pale cheeks.

"Simon, I'm sorry you saw that," Rose said.

"Sorry that it happened, or sorry that I saw?" Simon asked.

"Let me explain," she said. "I've been meaning to tell you about this. . . ."

"You kissed him," Simon said.

"It was a kiss good-bye," said Rose.

"Good-bye for what?" Simon asked. "What was going on with you two?"

Rose sighed. "We dated."

"A partner dating an associate? How daring," Simon said.

Rose squeezed her eyes shut. "I know. It was really stupid. A big mistake for both of us."

"When did your association begin?"

"Our association?" Rose repeated. "Simon, it wasn't a corporate merger!"

"Not a corporate one, evidently," he said. "Why didn't it work out?"

"Infidelity," Rose said quietly.

"Yours or his?" Simon shot back.

"His! Of course his! Come on, Simon, you know me better than that." Rose took a look at him. He ignored her. "Don't you?"

Simon said nothing. Rose stared out the window, at the blur of trees and buildings, at other cars. How many couples in how many cars were fighting? she wondered. And how many of the women were doing a better job of explaining themselves than she was?

"Look, the important thing is that it's over," she said, as he parked the car in front of their apartment. "It's really, truly, genuinely, absolutely over, and I'm sorry that you saw what you saw, but it doesn't mean anything. Believe me, Jim Danvers is the last thing I want in my life. Which is what I was telling him when you showed up."

Simon exhaled. "I believe you," he said, "but I want to know what happened. I want to understand it."

"Why? I don't want to know about your old girlfriends."

"This is different."

"Why?" Rose followed him into the bedroom, finally pulling her beads over her head.

"Because whatever happened between you two, it was bad

enough to make you never want to see the inside of a law office again."

"Not every law office," Rose said. "It's really that particular one that presented a problem."

"Don't change the subject. You have this . . . this history. And I don't know anything about it."

"Everyone's got a history! You're friends with people named Lopey, which could have been pointed out to me earlier . . ."

"But I don't know any of your history!"

"What do you want to know?" she asked him. "Why is it so important?"

"Because I want to know who you are!"

Rose shook her head. "Simon, it's not like I'm some huge mystery. I had a . . ." she searched for the least offensive word. "A relationship with this guy. It didn't end well. And it's over. And that's all!"

"How did it end?" Simon asked again.

"He did something," Rose began. "Something with someone . . ." She swallowed hard.

"When you're ready to tell me," Simon said coolly, "I'll be happy to listen."

He walked into the bathroom. Rose listened to him slamming the door and starting the shower. She walked back to the living room, bending to scoop up the pile of mail they'd both stepped over when they'd come home. Bill, bill, credit-card offer, actual card with her name on it, her name written in very familiar, large, looping handwriting.

Rose sank onto the couch. Her hands were shaking as she opened the envelope and unfolded the single sheet of notebook paper inside.

Dear Rose, she read. Words jumped out at her. *Grandmother. Sorry. Florida. Ella. Reconciliation.*

"Oh, my God," Rose breathed. She forced herself to read the whole thing twice, then hurried into the bedroom. Simon was standing in front of the bed with a towel wrapped around his waist and a serious look on his face. Wordlessly, Rose handed him the letter.

"My . . . grandmother," she said. The word felt strange in her mouth. "It's from Maggie. She's staying with my grandmother."

Now Simon looked even more upset. "You have a grandmother? You see what I mean, Rose? I didn't even know you had a grandmother!"

"I didn't know either," Rose said. "I mean, I guess I knew I had one, but I don't know anything about her." She felt like she'd suddenly been plunged underwater, like everything was slow and strange. "I have to . . ." she said. "I should call them." She sank onto the bed, feeling dizzy. A grandmother. Her mother's mother. Who, evidently, wasn't living in some old-age home, the way Rose had always believed, unless they were letting twentysomething vagabonds stay in those places, too. "I should call them. I should . . ."

Simon was staring at her. "You really didn't know you had a grandmother?"

"Well, I mean, I knew that my mother came from somewhere. But I thought she was . . . I don't know. Old, or sick. In a home. My father said that she was in a home." Rose stared at the letter, feeling her stomach clench. Her father had lied to her. Why had her father lied about something as important as this?

"Where's the phone?" she asked, jumping to her feet.

"Hey, hold on. Who are you going to call? What are you going to say?"

Rose set down the telephone and picked up her car keys. "I've got to go."

"Go where?"

Rose ignored him, hurrying to the door, running for the elevator, her heart thrumming in her chest as she ran down the street to her car.

Twenty minutes later, Rose found herself in the same place where she and her sister had stood almost a year ago—on Sydelle's doorstep, waiting for admission. She leaned against the doorbell. The dog howled. Finally, the lights flicked on.

"Rose?" Sydelle stood in the front door, blinking at her. "What are you doing here?" Her stepmother's face looked strange somehow beneath the glare of the light. Rose looked carefully before deciding that it was just the usual—another eye lift. She shoved Maggie's letter at her stepmother. "You tell me," she said.

"I don't have my glasses," Sydelle parried, pulling her lace-trimmed bathrobe tightly around her and pursing her lips at the blank spot on her walkway where Maggie had yanked out the shrub back in November.

"Then let me fill you in," said Rose. "This is from Maggie. She moved in with my grandmother. My grandmother who I didn't know was still making sense."

"Oh," said Sydelle. "Oh. Um . . ."

Rose stared. If her stepmother had ever been at a loss for words, she sure couldn't remember it. But there she was, nonplussed and twitching uncomfortably underneath her face cream and stitches.

"Let me in," said Rose.

"Of course!" Sydelle said in a strange, twittery voice, and stepped aside.

Rose strode past her and stood at the foot of the stairs. "Dad!" she yelled.

Sydelle put her hand on Rose's shoulder. Rose jerked away. "This was your idea, wasn't it?" she said, glaring at her stepmother. " 'Oh, Michael, they don't need a grandmother. They've got me!' "

Sydelle stepped back as if Rose had slapped her. "That's not how it happened," she said in a quivering voice. "I never thought I could be a substitute for . . . for everything you'd lost."

"Oh? Then how did it happen?" Rose demanded. She felt as if every cell of her body had been pumped to the bursting point with rage, as if she were going to explode. "Fill me in!"

Michael Feller hurried down the stairs, dressed in sweatpants and a white T-shirt, polishing his glasses with his handkerchief. His fine hair floating like a mist over his bald head. "Rose? What's going on?"

"Well, what's going on is that I've got a grandmother, she's not in a home, Maggie's living with her, and nobody saw fit to mention any of this to me," Rose said.

"Rose," said Sydelle, reaching toward her.

Rose whirled toward her. "Don't touch me," she said. Sydelle flinched.

"That's enough!" said Michael.

"No," said Rose. Her hands were shaking, her face was on fire. "No, it's not enough. It's not even a good start. How could you?" she yelled, as Sydelle cringed into a corner of her freshly wallpapered foyer. "I know you never liked us. But hiding a grandmother? Even for you, Sydelle, that's a stretch."

"It wasn't her," said Michael Feller taking Rose by the shoulders. "It wasn't her idea. It was mine."

Rose gaped at him. "Bullshit," she said. "You wouldn't . . ." She stared at her father, his faint gray eyes and high white forehead, her sad, kind-hearted, lost dog of a father. "You wouldn't . . ."

"Let's sit down," Michael Feller said.

Sydelle looked at Rose. "It wasn't me," she said, in a flat, dull voice. "And I'm sorry . . ." Her voice trailed off. Rose stared at her stepmother, who had never looked less monstrous, had never seemed more pathetic. Her face looked small and vulnerable, in spite of the tattooed lipstick and taut skin. Rose stared at her, trying to remember whether she'd ever heard those words before, whether Sydelle had ever been sorry for anything. She decided that if her stepmother had ever apologized to her, she couldn't remember it.

"You don't know . . ." Sydelle drew a whispery breath. "You don't know what it was like to live in this house. You don't know what it was like to spend years never being good enough. Never being the first choice, never being the one anyone really wanted. Never being able to put a foot right."

"Gee, I'm sorry," Rose said, in a snotty voice she could have borrowed from her little sister.

Sydelle lifted her eyes and glared at Rose. "Nothing I did was ever what you wanted," she said, and blinked her freshly-stitched eyelashes. "I never had a chance with you or Maggie. Not with any of you."

"Sydelle," Michael said gently.

"Go on," Sydelle said. "You tell her. Tell her the whole thing. It's time she knew."

Rose stared at her stepmother seeing, for the first time, the vulnerability that lay beneath the makeup, the Botox, the diet tips and condescension. She looked and saw a woman who'd left sixty behind her, whose thin body was stringy and unwelcoming, and whose face looked like a cruel caricature, a harshly etched drawing of a woman instead of the real thing. She looked and saw the sadness Sydelle had lived with every day—a husband still in love with his dead first wife, an ex-husband who'd left her, a daughter grown and gone.

"Rose," her father said. Rose followed him into Sydelle's living room. The leather couches had been replaced by slipcovered suede, but they were still a blinding white. She sat down on one end, her father sat on the other.

"I'm sorry about Sydelle," he began, and looked out into the foyer. He was waiting for her, Rose thought. Waiting for her to come and do his dirty work.

"She's going through a really bad time right now," her father said. "Marcia's giving her mother a very hard time."

Rose shrugged, not feeling terribly sympathetic toward either Sydelle or My Marcia, who'd never had much time for or interest in her stepsisters, other than making sure they weren't touching her things while she was off at college.

"She's joined Jews for Jesus," he said, and looked away.

"You can't be serious."

"Well, that's what we thought at first, that she was kidding."

"Oh, God," Rose said, thinking that Sydelle, who had mezuzahs on every door of the house, including the bathrooms, and scowled at every shopping-mall Santa she saw, had to be in agony. "So she's Christian?"

Her father shook his head. "We drove up to visit last weekend and she had a big wreath on the door."

"Ho ho ho," said Rose cheerlessly.

"Rose," her father said, a warning tone in his voice. Rose lifted her head and glared at him.

"Now, moving on to more pertinent topics. My grandmother."

Michael Feller swallowed hard. "She called you? Ella?"

"Maggie wrote to me," said Rose. "She said she's living with this . . . with Ella. So what's the story?"

Her father said nothing.

"Dad?"

"I'm ashamed of myself," Michael finally said. "I should have told you about this—about Ella—a long time ago. He laced his hands around his knees and rocked back and forth, clearly wishing for an annual report or at the very least a *Wall Street Journal* to get him through this. "Your mother's mother," he began. "Ella Hirsch. She moved to Florida a long time ago. After . . ." He paused. "After your mother died."

"You told us she was in a home," Rose prompted.

Michael Feller curled his hands into fists, planted them on his thighs. "She was," he said. "Just not the kind of home you probably thought."

Rose stared at her father. "What do you mean?"

"Well, she was in a home. Her home." He swallowed hard. "With Ira, I guess."

"You lied to us," Rose said flatly.

"It was a lie of omission," her father said. Clearly, this was a line he'd thought of long ago, a line he'd been rehearsing in his head for years. Michael took a deep breath. "After your mother . . ." His voice trailed off.

"Died," Rose supplied.

"Died," said Michael. "After she died I was angry. I felt . . ." He paused, and stared at Sydelle's glass-and-metal coffee table.

"Angry at Mom's parents? Angry at Ella?"

"They tried to tell me about Caroline, but I didn't want to listen. I was so in love with her . . ." Rose winced at the pain in her father's voice. "I was so in love with her. And I was so angry at them. Your mother was on lithium when I met her. She was stable. But she hated the way the medicine made her feel. And I'd try to make her take it, and Ella, her mother, would, too, and for a while she'd be fine, and then . . ." He exhaled, pulling off his glasses as if he couldn't bear their weight on his face. "She loved you. She loved all of us. But she couldn't . . ." Michael's voice caught in his throat. "And it didn't matter. It didn't change how I felt about her."

"What was she like?" asked Rose.

Her father looked surprised. "You don't remember?"

"You didn't exactly keep a shrine to her in our house or anything." She swept her hands around Sydelle's spotless living room— the white walls and white carpet, the bookshelves that had never held books, only glass objets and an eight-by-eleven framed shot of My Marcia's wedding. "There aren't any pictures of her. You never talked about her."

"It hurt." said Michael. "It hurt to remember. It hurt to see her face. I thought it would hurt you and Maggie, too."

"I don't know," said Rose. "I wish . . ." She looked down at her feet in the woven white carpet. "I wish she hadn't been a secret."

Michael was quiet. "I remember the first time I saw her. She was walking across the campus at the University of Michigan, pushing her bike, and she was laughing, and it was like a bell going off in my head. She was the most beautiful thing I'd ever seen. She had a pink scarf tied in her hair . . ." Her father's voice drifted off.

Rose could remember glimpses, snatches, pieces of stories, a sweet, chiming voice, a smooth cheek pressed against hers. *Sweet dreams, dream girl. Sleep tight, honey bun.* And everyone had lied by the things they'd told and the things they'd kept secret. Ella had lied to her father about Caroline—or, rather, she'd told him the truth, but he hadn't wanted to listen. And her father had lied to the girls about Ella—or he'd told them a tiny piece of the truth and left the rest of it unsaid.

She got to her feet, her hands clenched into fists. Lies, lies, lies, and where was the truth in all of this? Her mother had been crazy, then dead. Her father had yoked himself to a wicked witch and had given his daughters over to her care. Her grandmother had vanished down a rabbit hole, and Maggie had gone chasing after her. And Rose didn't know anything, not anything at all.

"You just got rid of her. All the time growing up, I don't remember a single picture of her, or any of her things . . ."

"It hurt too much," Michael said simply. "It was bad enough having to look at the two of you."

"Gee, thanks."

"Oh, no, I didn't mean . . ." He took Rose's hand, a move that shocked her into speechlessness. She couldn't remember her father touching her at all except for the occasional peck on the cheek since that disastrous day when she was twelve and came out of the bathroom and whispered that her period had started. "It was just that you two reminded me of her so much. Everything you did, it was like having to remember Caroline all over again."

"And then you married her," said Rose, nodding toward the foyer where, presumably, her stepmother lingered.

Her father sighed. "Sydelle meant well."

Rose gave a short, barking laugh. "Oh, sure. She's wonderful. She just hated me and Maggie."

"She was jealous," said Michael.

Rose was flabbergasted. "Jealous of what? Jealous of me? You have to be kidding. When My Marcia is superior in every way. And even if she was jealous, she was horrible. And you let her get away with it!"

Her father cringed. "Rose . . ."

"Rose, what?"

"There's something I need to give you. It's too late, but still. . . ."

He hurried upstairs and came down with a shoe box in his hands. "These are from her. Your grandmother," he said. "She's in Florida," he said. "She tried to get in touch with me—with you and Maggie—for years. But I didn't let her." He reached into the box and pulled out a creased and faded envelope with "Miss Rose Feller" written on the outside. "This was the last card she sent."

Rose ran her thumb under the flap, which came loose easily from glue that was fifteen years old. Inside was a card with a bouquet of flowers on the front. The flowers were pink and purple, dusted with gold glitter that sparkled dimly on Rose's fingertips. "HAPPY SWEET SIXTEEN," read the silver script above the flowers. And inside . . . Rose opened the card. A twenty-dollar bill and a photograph fluttered into her lap. "TO MY GRANDDAUGHTER," read the words in slanted script. "I WISH YOU LOVE AND EVERY HAPPINESS ON YOUR SPECIAL DAY." Followed by a signature. Followed by an address. And a telephone number. And a P.S. that read, "Rose, I would love to hear from you. Please call me any time!!!" It was the three exclamation points, Rose thought, that broke her heart the most. She looked at the photograph. It was a picture of a little girl—round-faced, brown-eyed, with bangs and two neat pigtails tied with red yarn ribbon and a serious look on her face, sitting on an older woman's lap. The woman was laughing. The little girl was not. Rose flipped the snapshot over. *Rose and Grandma, 1975,* it read, in the same blue ink, the same slanted script. Nineteen seventy-five. She would have been six.

Rose got to her feet. "I have to go now," she said.

"Rose," her father called, helplessly, toward her back. She ignored him, walking out of the house. Then she sat behind the wheel of her car, with the card still in her hands, and closed her eyes, remembering her mother's voice, her mother's pink-lipsticked smile, a tanned arm reaching out from behind a camera. *Smile, honey! Why such a sourpuss? Smile for me, Rosie Posy. Smile pretty, baby doll.*

FORTY-NINE

"Read more!" Maggie said.

"I can't," Lewis insisted, and gave her an extremely dignified look across Ella's dining room table. "It would be a breach of journalistic ethics."

"Oh, come on," Ella pleaded. "Just the first few sentences. Please?"

"It would be very, very wrong," he said, and shook his head sadly. "Ella, I'm surprised that you'd even want me to do such a thing."

"I'm a bad influence," Maggie said proudly. "At least tell us what Irving ordered."

Lewis threw his hands in the air in mock resignation. "Fine," he said. "But you're sworn to secrecy." He cleared his throat. " 'Irving and I do not care for French food,' " Mrs. Sobel's latest began. " 'The dishes are much too rich for us. We have also found that many French restaurants are noisy and dim, which is supposed to be romantic, but makes it hard to read your menu, let alone see your meal.' "

"Poor Mrs. Sobel," Ella murmured.

Lewis shook his head at her, then kept reading. " 'Most cooks do not know how an omelet should be made. An omelet should be fluffy and light, with the cheese just melted. And I am sorry to report that

Bistro Bleu is no exception. My omelet was overcooked and rubbery. The potatoes were not as hot as they should have been, and they were made with rosemary, which Irving does not care for.' "

"Again with Irving," said Ella.

"Irving's trouble?" asked Maggie.

"Irving's allergic. To everything," Lewis explained. "He's allergic to things I didn't know you could be allergic to. White flour, shellfish, all seeds, all nuts . . . half of that woman's reviews are devoted to how long it took her to find Irving something to eat, and then there's another quarter of the review reserved for the discussion of how whatever Irving ended up eating didn't agree with him . . ."

"This is Irving Sobel?" asked Mrs. Lefkowitz, shuffling toward the table. "Feh. He came to a party I had once and wouldn't eat a bite!"

Maggie rolled her eyes. Mrs. Lefkowitz, their dinner guest, was not in a good mood. She wore a pink sweatshirt, explaining that if she spilled her borscht, it would blend right in, and tan polyester pants. She didn't explain her pants, but Maggie figured that if she spilled anything at all on them, it would only constitute an improvement.

Mrs. Lefkowitz seated herself with a small groan, picked up a kosher dill pickle, and began expounding on the state of the nearby mall. "Hooligans!" she said, through a mouthful of pickle. Maggie relocated her textbooks from the Makeup for Theater class she'd enrolled in at the local community college and set dishes and silverware in their place.

"I think it's called Houlihan's," she said.

"No, no, hooligans," said Mrs. Lefkowitz. "Ruffians! Hoodlums! Teenagers! Everywhere! The mall is full of them, and all of the clothes are these teeny-tiny things with, with ruffled sleeves," she said. "Miniskirts! Shirts that you can see right through! Pants," she continued, glaring at Maggie, "that are made out of leather. Have you ever in your life heard of such a thing?"

"Actually—" Maggie began. Ella bit back a smile. She knew for a fact that Maggie owned a pair of leather pants, and a leather miniskirt, too.

"What's the occasion?" Ella asked instead. "What were you shopping for?"

Mrs. Lefkowitz waved a dismissive hand over the bowls of borscht. "My son. Remember him? The actuary? Mister Excitement? Well, he calls me up and says, 'Ma, I'm getting married.' I say, 'At your age? You need a wife like I need tap-dancing shoes.' He tells me that his mind's made up, and that she's a wonderful girl. I tell him that at fifty-three he's got no business going with girls, and he tells me I've got nothing to worry about, she's thirty-six, but a very mature thirty-six." She glared at Ella and Maggie as if they were responsible for causing her son to fall in love with a very mature thirty-six-year-old. "This I should live to see," she concluded, and helped herself to a piece of rye bread. "So now I need an outfit. Which of course I can't find."

"What are you looking for?" asked Maggie.

Mrs. Lefkowitz cocked a gray eyebrow. "The princess speaks!"

"I talk!" cried Maggie, affronted. "And it just so happens that I am an expert shopper."

"Well, then, what would you suggest for my son's third wedding?"

Maggie considered Mrs. Lefkowitz carefully—her cap of tousled iron-gray curls, her eyes, bright blue and inquisitive, the pink lipstick she applied even to the drooping corner of her lips. She wasn't fat, exactly, but she didn't have much of a shape, either. Her waist had thickened, her breasts had drooped.

"Hmm," Maggie said out loud, considering possibilities.

"Like a science project, she looks at me."

"Shh," said Ella, who'd seen Maggie look this way before, curled on her couch at night, poring over her poetry books in a pool of lamplight with a concentration that almost made it seem as if she were hypnotizing herself.

"What's your favorite thing?" Maggie suddenly asked.

"Hot-fudge sundaes," said Mrs. Lefkowitz promptly. "But I'm not allowed to have them anymore. Only with frozen yogurt," she said, wrinkling her face to demonstrate her feelings about frozen yogurt, "and that fat-free fudge topping, that they aren't even allowed to call fudge, because it's not. Fudge topping," she said again, and shook her head, clearly prepared to deliver a speech on the failings of fake fudge topping. But Maggie stopped her.

"Your favorite thing to wear."

"To wear?" Mrs. Lefkowitz looked down at herself as if she were surprised she was wearing anything at all. "Oh, I like what's comfortable, I guess."

"Your favorite thing ever," said Maggie, twisting her hair into a ponytail. Ella perched on the edge of a dining room chair, eager to see where this was going.

Mrs. Lefkowitz opened her mouth. Maggie raised her hand. "Think about it first," she said. "Think carefully. Think of all the outfits you ever wore, and tell me what you liked the very best."

Mrs. Lefkowitz closed her eyes. "My going-away suit," she said.

"What's that?"

"My going-away suit," she repeated, as if Maggie hadn't heard her.

"Like you'd wear when you were leaving your wedding and going to the airport for your honeymoon," Ella explained.

"Right, right," said Mrs. Lefkowitz, nodding. "It was a black-and-white-checked print, and the skirt was very fitted here," she said, smoothing her hands along her hips. "I had black pumps . . ." She closed her eyes, remembering.

"What was the jacket like?" Maggie prompted.

"Oh, short, I think," said Mrs. Lefkowitz, sounding almost dreamy. "With jet buttons down the front. It was so beautiful. I wonder what became of it?"

"What if . . ." said Maggie. "What if we went shopping together?"

Mrs. Lefkowitz made a face. "That mall again? I don't think I could stand it."

Maggie wasn't sure she'd be able to stand it, either, making her way through the stores at Mrs. Lefkowitz's snail's pace. "Or how about this?" she said. "You tell me your size . . ."

"Oh, now she wants to get personal!"

". . . and you give me your credit card . . ."

Ella could see Mrs. Lefkowitz getting ready to shake her head. She held her breath and hoped.

". . . and I'll find you an outfit. A few outfits, even. I'll give you a choice. We'll have a fashion show here, you'll try them on for us, and you'll pick the one you like the best, and I'll return the rest of them."

Now Mrs. Lefkowitz was looking at Maggie curiously. "Like a personal shopper?"

"Just like that," said Maggie, walking a slow circle around Mrs. Lefkowitz. "Do you have a budget?" she asked.

Mrs. Lefkowitz sighed. "Two hundred dollars, maybe?"

Maggie winced. "I'll try," she said.

FIFTY

Maggie spent two solid days searching for Mrs. Lefkowitz's wedding finery. Which was good, she thought. It kept her from sitting by the telephone, wondering whether Rose had gotten her letter yet, and whether Rose would call.

Mrs. Lefkowitz was a challenge—no doubt about it, Maggie thought. There was no way she could put her in the kind of fitted suit she'd described, but Maggie could, she thought, find something that would make Mrs. Lefkowitz feel like she was wearing that outfit again. A suit would work, and the skirt could even be on the short side—from what she'd seen of them, Mrs. Lefkowitz's legs weren't bad—but a short jacket was out of the question. Something long, maybe, hip-length, but with a trim to make it look dressy, something that suggested those jet-black buttons. Something she'd seen before. Macy's? Saks? She finally remembered that it had been at neither of those places, but in Rose's closet. Rose had a jacket like that.

Maggie swallowed hard and kept shopping, visiting department stores, consignment stores, thrift shops, flea markets, and the community college's costume department, after she'd promised the head of the department that she'd help with the makeup for an upcoming production of *Hedda Gabler*. In the end, she came up with three choices. The first was an outfit she'd found on sale at the Nordstrom's outlet—a knee-length skirt, fitted but not too tight, in pale pink linen, heavily embroidered in hot pink and red thread, along with a modest matching tank top and an embroidered cardigan that went on top of that. Mrs. Lefkowitz fingered the fabric doubtfully. "This doesn't look like my going-away suit," she said. "And a skirt with a sweater? I don't know. I was thinking a dress, maybe."

"It's not the look we're going for," said Maggie. "It's the sensation."

"Sensation?"

"The feeling you had wearing your going-away suit," she said. "You can't wear the suit again, right?"

Mrs. Lefkowitz nodded.

"So what we're going for is an outfit that gives you the same . . ." She struggled for words. ". . . the same sense of yourself that the suit did." She handed Mrs. Lefkowitz the outfit, still on hangers, plus a wide-brimmed pink hat she'd snatched from the college's costume department. "Just try," she said, and ushered Mrs. Lefkowitz back to her bedroom, where she'd set up a full-length mirror.

"I feel ridiculous!" Mrs. Lefkowitz called, as Ella and Lewis sat on the love seat, waiting for the fashion show to begin.

"Just let me see it," said Maggie.

"Do I really have to wear the hat?" came the reply.

"Come on out," called Ella.

Slowly, Mrs. Lefkowitz emerged from the bedroom. The skirt was too long. Maggie could see that right away. And the cardigan sleeves fell past Mrs. Lefkowitz's fingertips, and the tank top gaped.

"They're making clothes for giants these days," she complained, and shook one fabric-covered fist at Maggie. "Look at this!"

Maggie stood back, assessing the look. Then she walked to Mrs. Lefkowitz and rolled the waistband up so that the skirt lifted just past Mrs. Lefkowitz's knees. She folded the cardigan's sleeves, pulled and tucked the tank top into some semblance of a proper fit, and plunked the hat on top of Mrs. Lefkowitz's head. "There," she said, and turned her toward the mirror. "Take a look."

Mrs. Lefkowitz opened her mouth to object, to say that the outfit was horrible and that this hadn't been a good idea at all. Then she closed it. "Oh!" she said.

"You see?" asked Maggie.

Slowly, Mrs. Lefkowitz nodded. "The color," she began.

"Right, right!" said Maggie, who was more excited, more animated, more happy than Ella had ever seen her. "It doesn't fit you right, but the color, I thought, with your eyes, and I know you like pink."

"Not bad, not bad," said Mrs. Lefkowitz, and she didn't sound snappish, or crabby, or anything except enraptured with this vision of herself, with her blue eyes sparkling against the pale of the pink. What was she seeing? Maggie wondered. Maybe herself as a young woman, a newlywed, standing on the steps of the synagogue, holding her new husband's hand.

"So that's choice one," said Maggie, gently pulling Mrs. Lefkowitz away from the mirror.

"I'll take it!" she said.

"No, no," said Maggie, laughing, "you have to see what else I found."

"But I want this!" she said, clutching the hat to the top of her head. "I don't want to try anything else, I want this!" She looked at her bare feet. "What shoes do I need? Can you help me find shoes, too? And maybe a necklace." She brushed her hand over her collarbones. "My first husband gave me a strand of pearls once . . ."

"Next outfit," said Maggie, pushing Mrs. Lefkowitz back toward the bedroom. Outfit Two was a long sleeveless tube dress made of some slinky black synthetic, heavy enough to drape gracefully. She'd found it on sale at Marshalls, and paired it with a black-and-silver wrap with a black fringe on the ends.

"Ooh la la!" called Mrs. Lefkowitz, slipping the dress over her head and sauntering out of the bedroom, waggling the ends of the wrap in a vaguely suggestive fashion. "Racy! I feel like a flapper!"

"Hot stuff!" called Ella.

"It's nice," said Maggie, studying her carefully. The dress fell in a single column, suggesting the outlines of waist and hip rather than clinging too tightly, and it gave Mrs. Lefkowitz the appearance of a figure. She'd need heels, for sure, to pull it off, and Maggie wasn't sure that an eighty-seven-year-old woman in heels was a very good idea. Ballet slippers? she wondered.

"What's next?" asked Ella, clapping her hands.

Outfit Three was Maggie's personal favorite, probably because it had been the hardest one to find. She'd found the jacket on a back rack at a consignment store in a too-hip-for-its-own-good neighborhood in South Beach. "Hand sewn," the salesgirl had assured her—which, Maggie supposed, was meant to justify the one-hundred-and-sixty-dollar price tag. At first, it looked like a regular hip-length black jacket—nothing special. But the sleeves were decorated with swirls of black embroidery, and the pockets—embroidered, too—were set into the jacket on an interesting angle, which served to create the illusion of a waist when there wasn't much in the way of an actual waist there. Best of all, the jacket had a fabulous violet-colored lining, so Maggie had paired it with a long violet skirt and a black top.

"Here," she said, presenting the three pieces together on one hanger, so that Mrs. Lefkowitz could get the idea.

But Mrs. Lefkowitz barely spared it a glance, just snatching it out of Maggie's arms and hurrying back to the bedroom . . . and was it Ella's imagination, or was she humming to herself?

When she came out of the bedroom, she was practically skipping—or skipping as much as someone who's recently suffered a stroke can skip. "You did it!" she said, and kissed Maggie carefully on the cheek, and Ella beamed from the love seat. Maggie looked at her. The skirt wasn't great—it didn't hang right and it wasn't quite the same black as the jacket—and the shirt was just okay, nothing more—but the jacket was gorgeous. It made Mrs. Lefkowitz look taller, and curvier, and . . .

"I look wonderful," said Mrs. Lefkowitz, studying herself in the mirror, appearing not to notice the way the left corner of her mouth drooped, or the fact that her left hand was still curved around her body at an awkward angle. She considered her reflection for a moment, then grabbed the pink hat from Outfit One and plunked it on her head again.

"No, no," said Maggie, laughing.

"But it suits me!" said Mrs. Lefkowitz. "I want it. Can I have it?"

"It's from school," said Maggie.

"Oh, school," said Mrs. Lefkowitz, and made such a sad face that Ella started laughing.

"So which one?" asked Maggie. And Mrs. Lefkowitz, still in the hand-embroidered jacket, looked at her as if she were crazy.

"Well, all of them, of course," she said. "I'll wear the pink to the service, and then the long black dress to the reception, and this," she said, looking at herself, "I'm going to wear for my next appointment with Dr. Parese."

Ella burst out laughing. "What?" she demanded. "Why?"

"Because," said Mrs. Lefkowitz, "he's adorable!"

"Is he single?" asked Maggie.

"Oh, he's about twelve," said Mrs. Lefkowitz, waving her hand, then pausing mid-wave to admire the embroidery on her sleeve. "Thank you, Maggie. You did a wonderful job." She walked back to the bedroom to change. Maggie started returning the clothes to their hangers.

Ella studied her for a minute. "I've got an idea," she said. "I think you should do this for other people."

Maggie paused as she was repositioning the pink cardigan. "What do you mean?"

"Well, there's lots old ladies who have a hard time getting

around the malls, and an even worse time finding anything nice once they're there. But everyone has occasions. Weddings, graduations, anniversary parties . . ."

"Well, this was just a favor," Maggie said. "I'm kind of busy with school and the bagel shop and all . . ."

"I bet that people would pay," said Ella.

Maggie paused, mid-fold. "Really?"

"Of course," Ella said. "What, you want to work for free?"

"How much do you think I could charge for this?"

Ella put one finger on her upper lip and gazed at the ceiling. "A percentage of the cost, maybe?" she said.

Maggie frowned. "I'm not so great with percentages," she said.

"Or a flat fee," said Ella. "Which might be better anyhow, because if you charged a percentage of the cost of the outfit, the cheapskates here would think you were trying to get them to buy more expensive things. How long did it take you to get all of these things?"

Maggie bit her lip, looking thoughtful. "Ten hours, maybe?"

"So charge, say, fifteen dollars an hour."

"Really? That's a lot more than what I'm making at the bagel place . . ."

"This is a little harder than slicing and toasting, don't you think?" asked Ella.

"And believe me, the women here can pay," said Mrs. Lefkowitz, who was back in her pink sweatshirt, looking flushed and pleased. "For all the moaning they do about their fixed incomes, for a beautiful outfit like this, they'll pay."

And now Ella saw her granddaughter's eyes light up and saw that Maggie was beaming. "Could I do it?" she asked. "Do you think it would work? I'd have to advertise . . . and I'd need a car of my own . . ."

"Start small," said Ella. "Don't jump in with both feet. Maybe dip one foot in the water, see how you like it."

"I already know I like it!" said Maggie. "I love to shop, I love picking out people's outfits. . . . I just can't believe—Do you really think people would pay me to do this?"

Mrs. Lefkowitz smiled, opened her suitcase-sized purse, produced her checkbook, and, in her labored, shaky script, wrote Maggie Feller a check for the amount of one hundred and fifty dollars. "I think they would," she said.

FIFTY*ONE

In retrospect, thought Rose, the mimosas had been a mistake.

She tried saying as much to Amy, but the words "the mimosas were a mistake" came out as a champagne-sodden mumble. "Mimoshas were a mistake," she said. Amy, who'd evidently understood her perfectly, gave a vigorous nod, and called to the bartender.

"Two more mimosas," she said.

"Right away, ladies," said the bartender. Where had it all gone so wrong? Rose wondered. Probably when she'd gotten the invitation to the shower that Sydelle Feller had decided to host weeks prior to Maggie's letter, the revelation of the grandmother, the invitation printed on heavy, gilt-edged, cream-colored paper, in a calligraphy so ornate that it was practically illegible.

"Who's throwing this thing?" asked Amy. "Lord and Lady Douchebag?"

"I don't even want to go," said Rose. "I want to go to Florida and meet this grandmother already."

"Did you call?" Amy asked.

"Not yet," said Rose. "Still working on the whole what-to-say thing."

"Well, if the grandmother answers, you say, 'Hello,'" said Amy. "And if Maggie answers, tell her that if she ever sleeps with your boyfriend again, you're gonna kick her size-zero ass from here to Elizabeth, New Jersey. Just try not to get the speeches mixed up."

"First shower, then grandmother," Rose said. And on the appointed day, she had gathered her courage, shaved her legs, and gotten herself to the appointed restaurant at the appointed hour, where precisely one of her friends and three dozen of Sydelle's were waiting to toast the bride-to-be.

"Rose," said Sydelle grandly, rising to greet her. Any trace of the vulnerability Rose had glimpsed on her stepmother's face was gone, buried beneath the familiar layers of makeup, Sydelle's familiar disdain, and high fashion.

"Come say hello to my friends," Sydelle said, trotting Rose over to her cronies, all of them, it seemed, with identical highlighted bobs and freshly lifted eyelids. *They must share a surgeon and a hairdresser,* Rose thought, as Sydelle ran through the introductions. "And here's My Marcia," Sydelle announced, leading Rose over to her stepsister, who was sour-faced, stringy-haired, and wearing a gigantic gold-and-diamond cross. Marcia gave Rose a limp wave and went back to quizzing the waitress about whether there was processed sugar in the pancakes, while her four-year-old twins, Jason and Alexander, wrestled underneath the table.

"How are you?" Rose asked politely.

"I'm blessed," My Marcia said. Sydelle winced. Rose gulped her mimosa, accepted a refill, and hurried over to where Amy was sitting. "Save me," she whispered, as Sydelle chattered away ("I would have invited more of Rose's friends," she overheard her stepmother say, "but I guess she doesn't have any!")

Amy handed her another drink. "Smile," she whispered. Rose grinned. Sydelle clutched her wriggling grandsons to her negligible bosom, got to her feet, and proclaimed, "Those of us who know Rose are so thrilled that this day is here!" And, to Rose's horror, there were two waiters wheeling in a television set. "What's going on?" she whispered to Amy, who shrugged. Sydelle gave her a brilliant smile and pointed the remote control at the screen. And there was Rose in sixth grade, scowling at the camera, all greasy hair and glinting braces. Uncomfortable laughter rippled through the room. Rose closed her eyes.

"We had our doubts," Sydelle continued, smiling brightly. "We watched her go through high school and college with her hair in her eyes and her nose buried in a book." She hit the remote again and there was Rose on her first break from college, with her Freshman Fifteen rippling beneath a pair of too-tight jeans.

"Of course, Rose had romances . . ." She hit the remote again, and there was Rose at her high school prom, in an ill-advised pink lace sheath, and a long-forgotten junior with a gummy smile gripping her waist. "But for reasons we could never understand, nothing ever seemed to work out." Another click. There was Rose at someone's bar mitzvah, shoving a miniature éclair into her mouth. Rose with hamburger juice dripping down her arms. Rose in profile, in late 1980s shoulder pads, looking roughly the size of an NFL linebacker. Rose at Halloween, dressed as a Vulcan, fingers splayed in Mr. Spock's salute.

"Oh, God," Rose whispered. "My 'before' pictures."

"What?" Amy whispered back.

Rose felt hysterical laughter bubbling in her chest. "I think Sydelle's been spending years collecting 'before' pictures, so if I ever went on a diet and got really thin, she'd have plenty of compare-and-contrast photos."

"I can't believe she's doing this!" Amy said, as Sydelle flicked through a series of shots of Rose looking dumpy, Rose looking sulky, Rose with a particularly splendid zit on the tip of her nose.

"Mommy, what's wrong with that lady?" Jason or Alexander demanded, as Marcia shushed him.

"Kill me now," Rose begged her best friend.

"How 'bout I just knock you unconscious for a few hours?" Amy whispered back.

"So let's all raise our glasses and toast the miracle of love!" Sydelle concluded.

More uncomfortable laughter, followed by halfhearted applause. Rose gazed at the stack of gifts, desperately hoping that one of them contained the knife set Simon had registered for, so she could kill herself in the ladies' room.

"Rose?" Sydelle asked, her smile still in place. Rose got to her feet and positioned herself in front of the stack of gifts, where she spent the next hour trying to act excited about salad bowls and Mixmasters, china and wineglasses, a state-of-the-art food scale from Sydelle with a note reading, "We hope you find this useful," with the word *useful* underlined twice.

"Tupperware!" said Rose, in a tone suggesting that she'd waited her whole life for someone to give her fifteen pieces of lidded plastic. "That's wonderful!"

"So convenient!" said Sydelle, smiling and handing Rose another box.

"A salad spinner!" Rose cried, smiling so hard that her face hurt. *I am not going to survive this,* she thought.

"Salad spinner," Amy repeated, writing down the gift and its giver, and stuck the bow through a paper plate for the bow bonnet Rose had already decided she didn't want to wear.

"How lovely!" said Sydelle. Another sharp glance, another gift-wrapped box. Rose swallowed hard and kept unwrapping. After half an hour she'd amassed three cake pans, a cutting board, five place settings, two crystal vases, and had told six different women on six separate occasions that she and Simon weren't planning to have babies any time in the immediate future.

Finally, the last gift was unwrapped, the last bow was affixed to the plate, and the whole arrangement was tied on top of Rose's head.

Amy ducked into the bathroom, and came back to the table looking as if she'd seen a ghost in one of the stalls.

"What?" Rose asked, untangling the bow hat from her hair.

Amy grabbed Rose's sleeve and two fresh mimosas, and dragged her friend into a corner.

"That woman," said Amy, "is breast-feeding."

"Which woman?"

"Marcia!"

Rose looked at Marcia, who'd just returned from the bathroom with Jason and Alexander trailing behind her. "Are you kidding me? They're four."

"I know what I saw," said Amy.

"What, was she squeezing it onto their Frosted Flakes?"

"First of all, I don't think those boys have ever been near a Frosted Flake," said Amy. "Jesus wouldn't approve. And secondly, I know what breast-feeding looks like. Breast. Child. Mouth."

Rose slurped another mouthful of orange juice and champagne. "Well, at least she knows it's organic."

Which was the precise moment that Sydelle Feller swept over.

"Thank you for arranging this," Rose said. Sydelle had wrapped her arms around her, leaning in close.

"You might try being grateful for a change," she hissed.

Rose drew back. "What?" she said.

"I hope you get exactly the wedding you deserve," said Sydelle, turning on her heel and heading for the door. Rose reeled toward her chair, feeling utterly defeated, and the tiniest bit scared. "Oh, my God," she whispered. "She must have heard us talking about Marcia the milk bar."

"Oh, no," said Amy, "I am so sorry."

Rose covered her eyes with her hands. "Boy, that's sure not the kind of thing my *New Jewish Wedding* said people would say to me at my shower."

"Just ignore her," said Amy, picking up the food scale. "Hey," she said, "do you know my thumb weighs four ounces?"

They'd wound up loading a cab with Rose's gifts, piling them in her living room, and heading to a bar down the street, where they drowned their agony in fresh mimosas and speculated on how long Sydelle had been saving up all of those atrocious pictures of her stepdaughter, and whether she might have a similar slide show prepared if Maggie ever got married. Rose came home to an empty apartment. Simon had left a note saying he was out walking Petunia and shopping for dinner. She stood in the center of the kitchen and closed her eyes.

"I miss my mother," she whispered. And it was true, in a non-specific way. It wasn't that she missed her mother; it was that she missed a mother, any mother at all. With a mother around, that fiasco of a shower wouldn't have been nearly so bad. A mother would have enfolded Rose in her arms and sent Sydelle back to whatever sulfur-scented depths had spawned her. A mother would have tapped Rose once on her head with her magic wand, and Rose's drab dress would have been transformed into the perfect wedding gown. A mother would have known how to handle everything.

"I miss my mom," she said again. But saying it out loud, Rose realized that she missed Maggie more. Even if Maggie didn't have a magic wand or a wedding gown, she would have at least been able to make Rose laugh. Rose smiled a little, imagining Maggie making a mimosa-fueled toast, or asking My Marcia whether she could have a little breast milk for her coffee. Maggie would know how to handle this situation. And Maggie, God help her, was all she had.

"I've got to get out of here," she whispered. She pulled her suitcase out of the closet and filled it with stuff she thought she'd need for Florida—shorts and sandals, a bathing suit and a baseball cap, a copy of *Chastity's Voyage* that she'd borrowed from Simon's mother. Ten minutes on the Internet yielded a two-hundred-dollar ticket to Fort Lauderdale. Then she picked up the telephone and punched in the numbers from Maggie's letter—the numbers she hadn't even realized she'd committed to memory. When her sister answered the phone, she forgot the speech that Amy had dictated and simply said, "Maggie? It's me."

FIFTY-TWO

"Okay," said Maggie. "Places, everyone!"

Mrs. Lefkowitz stood to the left of the boarding gate. Lewis stood in the center. Ella was next to him. Maggie rolled back and forth in Mrs. Lefkowitz's motorized scooter, looking them over closely. "Signs!" she said. The three of them lifted their handmade posterboard signs into the air. Mrs. Lefkowitz's read, "Welcome," in pink. Lewis's sign said, "to Florida." Ella's sign, which Maggie had supervised herself, said, "Rose," and Maggie herself carried a poster with a collage of roses on it made of pictures she'd cut from Mrs. Lefkowitz's gardening magazines.

"Now arriving, flight five-twelve from Philadelphia," said the voice on the PA system. Maggie stomped on the brake so hard she almost fell off the scooter.

"You know what?" she said. "I think it would be better if you guys waited by baggage claim."

"What?" asked Ella.

"What'd she say?" asked Mrs. Lefkowitz.

Maggie twisted her sign in her hands and talked fast. "It's just that . . . before I left . . . Rose and I kind of had a fight. And maybe it would be better if I just talked to her first. Alone."

"Okay," said Ella, leading Lewis and Mrs. Lefkowitz off toward baggage claim. Maggie took a deep breath, squaring her shoulders and lifting her sign, scrutinizing the passengers making their way off the plane.

Old lady . . . old lady . . . Mom and toddler, inching down the walkway . . . Where was Rose? Maggie set her sign down, wiped her hands against her shorts. When she stood up, Rose was walking through the door, looking taller than Maggie remembered, and tan, with her hair loose and flowing over her shoulders, held off her face with two cloisonné barrettes. She wore a long-sleeved pink T-shirt and khaki shorts, and Maggie could see muscles moving in her sister's legs as she made her way across the lounge.

"Hey," Rose said. "Nice sign." She peered over her sister's head. "So where's the mysterious grandmother?"

Maggie felt a pang of hurt. Didn't Rose want to know how she was? Didn't she care? "Ella's in baggage claim. Let me take your backpack," she said. "Is that all you brought? You look really good. Have you been working out?"

"Riding a bike," Rose said. She walked down the hall, moving so fast that Maggie had to break into a half-trot to keep up.

"Hey, slow down!"

"I want to see the grandmother," Rose said without looking at her sister.

"She's not going anywhere," Maggie said. She looked down to check out Rose's footwear and saw something glinting on her sister's left hand—a platinum band with a square cut diamond. "Oh, my God. Is that an engagement ring?"

"It is," said Rose, still staring straight ahead.

Maggie felt her heart stop. So much had happened since she'd been gone, and she didn't know about any of it! "Is it . . ."

"Different guy," said Rose. They reached the baggage terminal. Ella and Lewis and Mrs. Lefkowitz stared at Maggie uncertainly. Lewis raised his sign.

"There she is!" Ella called, and she hurried toward her grand-daughters, with Lewis and Mrs. Lefkowitz trailing after her.

Rose stepped forward and nodded, studying Ella's face carefully. "Hi," she said.

"It's been so long. Too long," said Ella. She stepped forward and Rose awkwardly allowed herself to be hugged, standing stiffly in Ella's embrace. "Welcome, dear. I'm so glad you're here!"

Rose nodded. "Thanks. This is all kind of strange . . ."

Ella looked her granddaughter over carefully. Maggie, meanwhile, had resumed her spot on Mrs. Lefkowitz's scooter, and was driving it in small circles, looking like the world's smallest Shriner as she peppered her sister with questions and comments. "Who are you marrying?" she asked. "Where'd you get those barrettes? I like your hair!" She pulled right up to Rose's feet and looked down at her sister's sneakers. "Hey," she said, "aren't those mine?"

Rose looked down and smiled faintly. "You left them in the apartment," she said. "I didn't think you'd need them. And I wouldn't have known where to send them. And they fit."

"Come on," said Maggie, getting off the scooter and leading her sister out of the airport. "And tell me what's new. Who's the lucky guy?"

"His name is Simon Stein," said Rose. She stepped beside Ella, leaning her head in close, leaving Maggie and Lewis and Mrs. Lefkowitz following the two of them, trying to overhear scraps of their conversation. Rose looked so different! She didn't look pale; she didn't look prissy; she didn't look as if someone had stuffed a bug up her butt and she was in a hurry to find the nearest rest room in order to remove it. Her clothes were items that Maggie might have selected, and her stride was fast but relaxed. Rose didn't look thinner, but she did look firmer, as if her mass had been redistributed and rearranged. She seemed totally at ease in her own body, for perhaps the first time in her life, and Maggie wondered what had caused such a transformation. Simon Stein, perhaps? The name sounded familiar. Maggie wracked her brain and finally came up with a picture from their night at Dave and Buster's, a snapshot of a frizzy-haired guy in a suit and tie, trying to interest her sister in the firm's softball team.

"Hey, Rose!" she called, catching up. Rose and Ella's heads were close together, and they were talking softly. Maggie felt a fast stab of jealousy. She swallowed hard. "So this guy you're marrying. He's in your law firm, right?"

"My former law firm," said Rose.

"What? Did you change firms?"

"Oh, I changed more than that," said Rose, and then turned her back and walked away, with Ella at her side. Maggie watched them go, feeling sad and frustrated . . . and feeling like this was no more than what she deserved. After what she'd done to Rose, did she really think her sister would come running back, ready to forgive and forget? She sighed, hefted her sister's backpack, and started off down the hall.

FIFTY-THREE

Rose Feller felt the way she imagined an astronaut would feel after crash-landing on a strange new unexplored planet. Planet Grandma, she thought, and swiped at her forehead. It had to be more than ninety degrees out here. How could anyone stand it?

She sighed, readjusted the visor that Ella had lent her, and followed Maggie out the door. "Don't forget your sunblock!" Ella called.

"We won't!" Maggie yelled back, and reached into her pocket to show Rose the tube she was carrying. It was bizarre, Rose thought, as they started off down the baking sidewalk that ran along the perfectly manicured (if somewhat small) green lawns of Golden Acres. But in the months since she'd last seen her, her little sister had somehow transformed herself into a reasonable facsimile of a responsible young adult. And, more mystifying yet, she'd befriended old people. Rose didn't understand that at all. Her own experience with the sixty-five-and-over set was limited to the occasional *Golden Girls* rerun, and her newly found grandmother made her a little uncomfortable, the way she stared, and sniffled, and seemed perpetually on the verge of tears when she wasn't peppering Rose with a million questions about her life. What was her apartment like? How had she and Simon met? What were her favorite foods? Did she like cats, or dogs, or both, or neither? What movies had she enjoyed recently? What books had she read? It was like being on a blind date with no promise of romance, Rose thought. It was exciting, and exhausting, too.

A little old lady on an oversized tricycle pedaled up to them. "Maggie!" she said.

"Hi, Mrs. Norton," said her sister. "How's your hip?"

"Oh, fine, fine," the old woman said. Rose blinked in the sunshine and tried to make sense of what she was hearing and seeing, but the best explanation she could come up with involved her sister being brainwashed, or body-snatched. And how had she managed to survive out here without a steady stream of men who didn't have pacemakers and great-grandchildren? Who was flirting with her, who was buying her drinks and giving her money for her manicures and generally confirming Maggie's own opinion of her worth and beauty? Rose shook her head in disbelief, nodded at Mrs. Norton and her hip, and followed her sister toward the swimming pool. She'd planned on being furious with Maggie, but now she just felt confused, as if the girl she'd been ready to kill didn't even exist anymore.

"Okay, so explain this to me again?" she said.

"These are my pool friends," said Maggie. "Now, Dora's easy, because she's the only woman, and she talks basically nonstop."

"Dora," Rose repeated.

"She was one of my first clients," Maggie continued.

"Clients?" asked Rose. "What are you doing, massage?"

"No, no," said Maggie. "Personal shopping." She dug into her pocket and produced one of the business cards that Mrs. Lefkowitz had whipped up on her computer. "Maggie Feller, Personal Shopper, Your Favorite Things," it read. "That's my catch phrase," said Maggie. "With all of my clients, I ask them what their favorite item of clothing was, and then when I shop for them, I try to reproduce the feeling of whatever that was. Like, if your favorite thing was a blue linen sundress, I don't necessarily buy you a blue linen sundress, but I try to find something that makes you feel the way you felt when you wore it."

"Great," said Rose. And she had to admit that it did sound good. If there was one thing Maggie had always been good at, it was picking out clothes. "So who else are we going to see?"

"Okay, there's Jack, who I think has kind of a crush on Dora, because he insults her all the time. He's the one who used to be the accountant, so he's going to help me with Your Favorite Things. Then there's Herman," Maggie continued. "He doesn't say much, but he's very nice . . . and he's obsessed with tattoos."

"Does he have any?" asked Rose.

"I don't think so," said Maggie. "I haven't exactly made a study. But they know all about you."

Rose wondered exactly what that meant. What would Maggie say about her? "Like what?"

"You know, where you live, what you do. I would have told them you were engaged," she said, "but that was news to me, too. When's the wedding?"

"May," said Rose.

"And how's the planning going? Everything under control?"

Rose felt herself stiffen. "It's fine," she said shortly. Maggie looked hurt, but instead of throwing a tantrum, marching off in a huff, or pouting, she just gave a small shrug.

"Well, if you need any help," she said. "I'm a professional, you know."

"I'll take that under advisement," said Rose. And then they were at the pool, and Jack, who was tall, with a sunburn, was squinting at them, and Dora, who was short and and round and talking a mile a minute, was waving frantically, and Herman was carefully studying Rose's bare arms and legs, no doubt prospecting for body modification. Maggie waved and headed toward them. Rose shook her head in disbelief and spread a towel over one of the creaky metal lounge chairs. Relax, she told herself sternly, arranging her face into a smile and crossing the hot concrete to meet Maggie's new friends.

"Are you two going to be all right in here?" asked Ella. The pull-out couch, which had been sufficient for Maggie, suddenly seemed too small now that two young women would be sharing it.

"We'll be fine," said Rose, flicking a fresh sheet out over the bed. She was still feeling dazed and groggy (and slightly sunburnt) from her first day in Florida. She and Maggie had hung out at the pool, then gone out for an early dinner with Lewis, who was very nice, and Ella, who'd kept staring at Rose in a most disconcerting way. After dinner they'd watched an hour of television, and were now in the small back bedroom. Rose saw that Maggie had taken over, the same way she'd invaded Rose's apartment, transforming both bedroom and porch into a makeshift office-*cum*-boudoir. There was a card table covered with sketches and notebooks and guides to starting and running a small business. There was a dressmaker's dummy that Maggie had bought at a tag sale and had draped with swatches of different fabrics—a length of fringed ivory satin, a piece of plum-colored chiffon. And there were familiar piles of clothes and cosmetics joined by unfamiliar stacks of books. Rose picked one up. *Travels,* by W. S. Merwin. She remembered it from college, and flicked through the dog-eared pages, many of them decorated with Maggie's careless scrawl.

"You're reading poetry?" she asked.

Maggie nodded proudly. "I enjoy it," she said. She pulled a book out of the stack. "This is by Rilkee."

"Rilk*uh*," Rose corrected.

Maggie waved her hand. "Whatever." She cleared her throat. "A good night poem," she said, and began to recite:

> "I'd like to sing someone to sleep,
> By someone sit, and be still.
> I'd like to rock you and murmur a song
> Be with you on the fringes of sleep
> Be the one and only awake in the house
> Who would know that the night is cold.
> I'd like to listen both inside and out,
> Into you, and the world, and the woods.
> The clocks call out with their toiling bells,

And you can see to the bottom of time.
Down in the street a stranger goes by
And bothers a passing dog.
Behind come silence, I've laid my eyes
On you like an open hand,
And they hold you lightly and let you go,
When something moves in the dark."

She nodded, pleased with herself, as Rose stared at her, openmouthed.

"How did you . . . Where did you . . ." She blinked at her sister. *Body-snatched,* she thought again. Somehow, Maggie's greedy, obsessive, shoe-stealing, fame-seeking soul had been sucked out and replaced by Rilke.

"I particularly enjoy the line about the passing dog," Maggie said. "It reminds me of Honey Bun."

"It reminds me of Petunia," said Rose. "That little pug you left in my apartment."

"Oh, right right right," said Maggie. "How is she?"

"She's fine," Rose said shortly, remembering how Maggie had stuck her with the dog, and the mess, and the unerasable mental image of her fornicating with Jim Danvers. She brushed her teeth, washed her face, and got into bed, clinging to the edge of the pullout mattress, her back to her sister.

"Now don't kick me," Maggie warned. "In fact, try not to make any physical contact with me at all."

"Not a problem." Rose said. "Good night," she said.

"Good night," said Maggie.

Silence, except for the croaking of the frogs. Rose closed her eyes.

"So!" said Maggie cheerfully. "You're marrying Simon Stein!"

Rose groaned. She'd forgotten this about Maggie, how she'd say she was going to sleep, how she'd get into bed, turn out the lights, yawn, stretch, say good night, and give every impression of meaning it, and then, just when you were right about to drop off, start up a conversation.

"Didn't we cover this at dinner?"

Maggie ignored her. "I remember him from that party," she said. "He was cute! Short, but cute. Tell me what kind of wedding you're going to have."

"Small," said Rose, who'd decided that the shorter the answers, the better off she'd be. "Sydelle's helping."

"Oh, no. Disaster waiting to happen. Do you remember My Marcia's wedding?"

"Vaguely," said Rose. "I was only there for the ceremony." Sydelle, considerate as ever, had slated My Marcia's wedding for the weekend of Rose's last law-school finals. She'd stayed for the vows, then ducked back home to study.

"Oh. My. God," Maggie breathed. "It could've been a Fox special. *America's Worst Weddings*."

"I saw pictures. It looked beautiful." But Rose was starting to get a nagging feeling that there had been some story about My Marcia's nuptials, something her father and Sydelle hadn't wanted to talk about.

"Did you notice," asked Maggie, "that none of the pictures showed anybody's feet?"

Rose couldn't remember.

"Let me tell you why," said Maggie. "The wedding was on the lawn behind this fancy country club, remember?"

"Silver Glen."

"Silver Glen, Silver Lake, Silver Something," Maggie said impatiently. "And it was really pretty—gardens, lawns, all of that—except the automatic sprinklers malfunctioned, and the tent didn't have a floor and there was, like, six inches of muck on the ground. All of the tables started sinking, and it was freezing cold . . ."

"You're kidding," said Rose.

"I'm not!" Maggie said gleefully. "My Marcia was, like, crying her eyes out in the bathroom." Maggie raised her voice to a hysterical warble. "'My special day is ruined! Ruined!'"

"Oh, God," said Rose, who was starting to feel sick—and a certain degree of sympathy for My Marcia.

"Oh, there's more," said Maggie. "Sydelle forgot to get a parking variance, so everyone had to keep running out of the reception to move their cars. Then the sprinklers went off again, in the middle of their first dance, and everyone fled. And," she concluded, "they forgot to assign me a seat, so I had to sit with the band. We had boxed lunches instead of surf and turf."

Rose decided that Maggie's absence from the seating chart was probably not an accident, but decided not to say so.

"It was a horror show," Maggie concluded happily. "But there was an open bar. The one redeeming feature. I enjoyed many cocktails."

"I'm sure," said Rose.

"There was a drink parade with me as grand marshall," Maggie continued.

"Were you even twenty-one then?"

"Not so much," said Maggie. "So what else, what else?"

"Not much," said Rose slowly. It wasn't true, she knew, but why fill Maggie in on her disastrous shower, her fight with her father, running into Jim Danvers? It wasn't time yet. She still had to figure out what was responsible for her sister's miraculous transformation into a responsible, non-attention-seeking, job-holding, senior-citizen-appreciating citizen of Golden Acres.

"Tell me more about the wedding. Are you going to have bridesmaids?"

There was a short, tense silence. "Just Amy, I think," said Rose. "And you, too, I guess. If you want."

"Do you want me to be a bridesmaid?"

"I don't care that much," said Rose. "If you want to be in it, you can."

"Well, it's your wedding," said Maggie. "You should care."

"That's what everyone keeps telling me," said Rose.

"Well," Maggie said stiffly. "Good night, then."

"Good night," said Rose.

"Goodnight," said Maggie. Silence.

"Rose?" Maggie said. "Hey, Rose, could you get me a glass of water with one ice cube, please?"

"Get your own water," said Rose. But even as she was saying it, she swung her legs out of the bed, realizing that she'd forgotten this fact, too: she always got Maggie's water. She'd been bringing it to her since they were little. She'd supplied Maggie with her evening glass almost every night during Maggie's stint in her apartment. And, probably when they were in their eighties, after they'd out-lived husbands and left their jobs and moved to whatever the 2060s version of Golden Acres would be, she'd still be fetching her little sister glasses of water with one ice cube.

When Rose got back to the bed, there was something glimmering on her pillow. She looked at it carefully, thinking it could be a bug of some sort. But it wasn't a bug. It was a foil-wrapped square of chocolate. "Just like in the fine hotels," said Maggie.

"Go to sleep," said Rose.

"Fine, fine," said Maggie. But before she finally closed her eyes, she set the chocolate on the bedside table, so that it would be the first thing that her sister saw in the morning.

In her own bedroom, Ella released the breath she hadn't realized she was holding and sank onto her bed. Her brain was spinning with questions. What was the story with Sydelle? Who was My Marcia? Why wasn't Rose really talking to Maggie? Why did Maggie seem so desperate to please her older sister? Would Rose really have a wedding without including Maggie? Would Ella even be invited?

She bit her lip and closed her eyes. There was a story here. Ella was sure of it. There was a reason why Maggie had left Rose's apartment and gone to Princeton, a reason she hadn't talked to her only sister in ten months. Give it time, Lewis had told her. "I'll try," she whispered to herself, and blew two kisses toward her granddaughters' bedroom wall.

FIFTY❖FOUR

Rose shoved one gloved hand into a pot filled with boiled turkey legs, extracted one of them, and began pulling the meat off the bone.

"Thank you so much for coming to help," said Ella, who stood beside Rose, peeling carrots, in the synagogue recreation room where they served lunch to the homeless every Friday. "Are you sure you're okay with that?"

"Fine," said Rose. "It's better than the onions, right?"

"Oh, absolutely!" said Ella, wincing at her too-enthusiastic, too-loud tone. She bent back to the carrots, trying hard not to stare at her oldest granddaughter.

Rose had been in Florida for three days, and she was still mostly a mystery to Ella. She answered all of Ella's questions completely and politely, and asked plenty of her own, mostly all of them couched so well that Ella could tell that asking questions was part of what she did for a living. Or part of what she'd done, since Rose explained that she was taking a break from legal life.

"What do you mean, taking a break?" Maggie had asked.

"I meant what I said. Taking a break," Rose had said, without looking at her sister. Something bad had happened between the two of them, Ella knew. But she couldn't guess what it was, and Maggie had been tight-lipped on the subject while she trailed her sister around Golden Acres like a lost puppy dog.

Rose peeled off her gloves, put her hands on her hips, and stretched, rolling her neck. Even in a hairnet, her granddaughter was beautiful, Ella decided. Rose looked the way she'd imagined a biblical heroine to look—tall and strong and stern, somehow, with powerful shoulders and capable-looking hands.

"Are you okay?" she asked.

Rose sighed. "Well, I'm done with the turkey."

"Let's take a break," said Ella. They walked over to a card table in the corner, where Mrs. Lefkowitz sat, reading the latest issue of *Hello!* (because, as she'd said, the gossip from England was always much more interesting).

"The bride-to-be!" she hailed Rose. Rose smiled faintly and sat down in a folding chair.

"So let's hear about the wedding," said Mrs. Lefkowitz. "You got your dress?"

Rose flinched. "The wedding. Um. Well, Sydelle's helping."

"What's a Sydelle?"

"My stepmother," Rose said. "The Cruella De Vil of Cherry Hill." She looked at Ella. "What was my mom's wedding like?"

"It was small," said Ella. "They planned it themselves. They got married in the rabbi's study, on a Thursday afternoon. I wanted to help . . . to make her a wedding . . . but Caroline didn't want much, and your father didn't want anything that Caroline didn't want."

"Sounds familiar," Rose said. "My father's not . . ." Her voice trailed off. "He's not a very strong-willed person."

Except when he's cutting me out of your life, Ella thought. "He loved your mother," she said instead. "Anyone who saw them together knew that. He tried to take care of her, to make her happy."

"I want to talk about your wedding!" said Mrs. Lefkowitz, setting aside her account of Fergie's latest dalliance. "Tell me everything!"

Rose sighed. "Not much to tell, really. It's being planned by a monster, who completely ignores me when I tell her what Simon and I want, and keeps trying to cram her ideas down our throats."

"A lemon," said Mrs. Lefkowitz, and nodded.

"Huh?"

"Think about fruit," she continued. "When you squeeze an orange, what do you get?"

Rose smiled. "Trouble?"

"No, no, Mrs. Smart. You get orange juice. You don't get grapefruit juice, you don't get apple juice, you don't get milk. You get orange juice. Every time. People are like that. They can only give you what they have inside. So if this Sydelle character is giving you so much trouble, it's because she's nothing but trouble on the inside. She's just delivering what's in her heart into the universe." And Mrs. Lefkowitz sat back, looking pleased with herself.

"Where'd you learn that?" asked Ella.

"Dr. Phil," said Mrs. Lefkowitz.

Ella made a mental note to find out who Dr. Phil was.

"So," said Rose, "what kind of fruit is Maggie?"

"A sweet one," said Mrs. Lefkowitz.

Rose laughed. "If that's what you think, then you don't know my sister very well."

"She's not sweet?" asked Ella.

Rose got to her feet. "She takes things," she said. Finally, Ella thought, as Rose started pacing. Finally, we're going to get to the root of this, and find out what went wrong. "She takes everything," Rose continued, her voice cracking. "Haven't you noticed? My sister feels a certain sense of entitlement. Like, she's entitled to anything that's yours. Clothes, shoes, cash, cars . . . other things."

Other things, Ella thought.

"Don't tell me that in all the time she's been with you nothing's ever gone missing."

"I don't think so," Ella said.

"We don't have anything she'd want," said Mrs. Lefkowitz.

Rose shook her head. "Figures," she said, "that once she was done with me, she'd decide to walk the straight and narrow."

Other things, Ella thought again, and she took her best guess at what the heart of the trouble might be. "What did Maggie take?" she asked.

Rose's head whipped around. "Huh?"

Ella repeated the question. "I think she took something that meant a lot to you. What was it?"

"Nothing," Rose said. And now she didn't just sound angry, she sounded furious. At Maggie, Ella thought. And maybe at her, too. "Nothing that meant that much."

"Dear," said Ella, stretching out her hand. Rose ignored her. "I think Maggie's okay," Ella continued, blundering desperately forward. "She's saving her money, I know, and I think her business idea's a good one. She's found outfits for a bunch of people that I know of. Her friend Dora, my neighbor Mavis Gold . . ."

"Just be careful," Rose said. "If she hasn't taken anything of yours yet, it doesn't mean she isn't going to. She might look sweet, but she isn't. Not always." And Ella sat, openmouthed and frozen, as Rose walked out the door.

FIFTY⚡FIVE

Two days later, Maggie watched Rose as she slept on the lounge chair beside her.

"She's tired," Dora observed.

"Your insights are overwhelming," said Jack.

"She seems nice," said Herman, in one of his rare non-tattoo-related remarks.

"She is nice," said Ella.

Maggie sighed. "I think she's going home," she said. She'd heard Rose on the phone that morning, when she was coming out of the shower, talking quietly to someone who must've been Simon, apologizing quietly, asking him to check flights back to Philadelphia for her.

But Rose couldn't leave. Not like this. Not without Maggie convincing her that she really had changed, that she really was going to be better, and that she really was sorry.

She rolled onto her side, thinking. Rose needed peace and quiet, and Maggie had made sure that she got naps every day, quiet time at the pool, walks at night after dinner. She made sure that Ella had laid in a stock of her sister's favorite foods, including the cheese curls and ice cream that Rose was secretly fond of. She always let her sister have the remote control when they watched TV and didn't complain when Rose went pawing through her library books in search of the poems she'd remembered from college. None of it seemed to be working. Rose stuck close to Ella, asking her questions about their mother, looking at pictures, accompanying her on her rounds. The two of them were thick as thieves, a perfect circle of two. And Rose wasn't inclined to make room for Maggie. Maggie, it was clear, had not yet been forgiven. And Maggie had no idea how to *get* forgiven, except for telling Rose that she was sorry. Which she'd done over and over again, to no avail. There had to be something she could give Rose, some act she could perform to convince her sister that she was sorry and that she'd do better from now on.

Well, she thought, flipping onto her belly, at least Rose had another boyfriend. A husband-to-be. A wedding she was probably planning with all of the ruthless efficiency she'd once brought to bear on her career. Maggie imagined the guest list on a spread sheet. A computer-generated seating chart. A florist cultivating the perfect blooms for her bouquet. But what about wedding dress? Maggie sat up so fast she spilled her water, causing Dora to shriek and Jack to scold and Ella to pass her a towel.

"Hey, Rose!" she called. Rose woke up with a start and stared at her sleepily. "Do you have a wedding dress yet?"

Her sister closed her eyes again. "I'm looking," she said.

"Go back to sleep," said Maggie. It was perfect! If she could find Rose the right wedding dress . . . well, it wouldn't fix every-thing, but it would be a start. More than a start, it would be a sign—a sign that Maggie was sincere, and that she meant well.

Plus, the more she thought about it, finding the perfect dress for her sister would be symbolic. She remembered that from her class called the Manufacture of Myth, when the professor had talked about sacred quests, how the hero had to go into the world and bring something back—a sword, a chalice, a glass slipper, or enchanted beans. *Gawain and the Green Knight,* the professor had said. "Jack and the Beanstalk." *Lord of the Rings. And what were the objects a symbol for?* the professor had asked. *Knowledge.* Once the hero has acquired this knowledge, he can live happily in the world. Well, Maggie wasn't a hero, and she wasn't sure she quite understood all the stuff about self-knowledge and symbolism, but she was a fabulous shopper. She knew style, and, more, she knew her sister, and she could find Rose a dress.

She flipped open her appointment book. She was pretty busy, what with the Liebermans' fiftieth anniversary party to shop for, and Mrs. Gantz going on her cruise, but she could rearrange her schedule. Where would she start? The bridal department at Saks first, for inspiration. They wouldn't have anything in Rose's size, probably, but at least she could see what they were showing. Then, once she had some idea of what she was looking for, she'd hit her three favorite consignment shops. She'd seen wedding dresses at all of them, had flipped past them casually, hunting for other items, but she knew they were there, and . . .

"Hey," called Maggie, trying to sound casual. "Hey, Rose, how long do you think you'll be staying?"

"Until Monday," said Rose. She got up from the chair, walked slowly to the swimming pool, and dove in. That was four days. Could Maggie find a wedding dress—the right wedding dress—in four days? She wasn't sure. She'd have to start immediately.

"What was your favorite thing?" Maggie asked her sister. "Your favorite thing to wear."

Rose swam to the edge of the pool and hooked her arms over the ledge. "I liked my blue sweatshirt with the hood. Remember that?"

Maggie nodded, her heart sinking. She remembered the blue sweatshirt with the hood very well, because Rose had worn it practically nonstop throughout sixth grade. "I like it," she said stubbornly, when their father tried to get her to take it off so he could wash it.

"You wore that until it fell apart," said Maggie.

Rose nodded. "Old blue," she said affectionately, as if she were talking about a dog or a person instead of a sweatshirt. Maggie felt her heart sinking even further. How on earth was she supposed to figure out a wedding dress from a ratty blue sweatshirt with a zipper running up the front?

She'd have to start from scratch. And, if she only had four days, she'd have to get help. While Rose swam laps Maggie beckoned to Dora and Ella and Lewis. "I need you guys to help me with a project," she whispered.

Dora inched her chair closer, her eyes shining. "Well, that's wonderful news!" she said.

"Don't you even want to know what it is?" Maggie asked.

Dora looked at Lewis. Lewis looked at Ella. The three of them looked at Maggie, and solemnly shook their heads.

"We're bored," said Dora. "Give us something to do."

"Let us help," said Ella.

"Okay, then," said Maggie, flipping to a fresh page in her notebook and mentally mapping out her course of action, "here's how this is going to work."

FIFTY-SIX

"Are you ready?" asked Ella, fussing with her folder full of typed pages. "You might want to sit down."

"I'm old," said Lewis. "I always want to sit down." He pulled up a chair behind his desk in the *Golden Acres Gazette*'s office and stared at Ella expectantly. Ella cleared her throat and glanced at Maggie. Maggie gave her an encouraging smile, and Ella started to read the poem that she and Maggie had written together and called "The Senior Howl."

"I saw the best minds of my generation destroyed by
senior moments, dyspeptic, forgetful, polyester'd
dragging themselves toward the handicapped-parking spaces at
four, looking for an early-bird special."

"Oh, my," said Lewis, trying not to laugh. "I see you two have discovered Allen Ginsberg."

"We have," said Maggie proudly. "Now, I'm going to want a byline, of course."

"Co-byline," said Ella.

"Fine, fine, whatever," Maggie replied.

"How's the top-secret mission coming?" Lewis asked.

Maggie's face fell. "It's harder than I thought," she said. "But I think I'll be okay. You're still going to help, right?"

"Of course," said Lewis. Maggie nodded, hopped off the edge of the desk, and picked up her purse.

"Gotta go," she said. "Mrs. Gantz is waiting for her bathing suits. I'll see you back at the apartment at four."

Ella watched her go, smiling.

"So, my dear," said Lewis. "How goes the grandmothering?"

"Fine," said Ella. "Well, better, anyhow. Maggie's doing terrific. Business is really taking off. She's busy all the time now."

"And Rose?" asked Lewis.

"Well, I think her wedding's making her a little crazy. And I think that Maggie makes her crazy, too. They care about each other, so much. I know that, at least." Ella remembered the way, in the months before Rose's arrival, that Rose would pop up in odd moments of Maggie's conversation—never by name, Ella had noticed, but just as "my sister." As in, "My sister and I used to go to football games with my father." Or, "My sister and I used to share a bedroom, because Sydelle the Terrible made me move out of my bedroom and move in with Rose when she redecorated." Ella treasured every brief mention, every scrap of conversation, every glimpse she got of the two of them as little girls, especially in the early days of Maggie's time in Florida, when Maggie was saying hardly anything at all. Ella could almost see them sometimes, in the room with two twin beds, Rose lying on her belly on the floor, poring over—what? A Nancy Drew book, Ella decided. That seemed about right. And Maggie, a tiny little thing in—what? Red overalls, thought Ella. Maggie would be bouncing back and forth, back and forth, until her red legs and brown hair turned into a blur, shouting, "The quick! Brown! Fox! Jumped over! The lazy dog!"

"I wish," said Ella, then closed her mouth. What did she wish for? What did she want? "I wish I could make everything right between them. I wish I could give Maggie the life she wanted, and tell Rose how to handle her stepmother, and just . . ." She lifted her left hand, waved it as if it were holding a magic wand. "Fix things. Fix everything for them."

"Well, but that's not what grandparents do," said Lewis.

"They don't?" Ella asked morosely.

Lewis shook his head.

"What do grandparents do?" Ella asked plaintively, feeling sorrow for all the years when she was supposed to have learned the answer.

Lewis gazed thoughtfully at the ceiling. "I think you give them unconditional love, and support, and the occasional cash infusion. You give them a place to come, when they need somewhere to go, and you try not to tell them what to do, because they get plenty of that from their parents. And then you let them figure it out for themselves."

Ella closed her eyes. "I wonder if Rose hates me," she said so softly that Lewis almost didn't hear her. She hadn't told him, or Maggie, or anyone, but she'd been both joyful and terrified the first time she'd seen Rose; and how part of her was still waiting for Rose to ask her the questions she couldn't answer.

"How could anyone hate you?" Lewis asked kindly. "You're worrying too much. They're smart girls. They won't blame you for not being there when it wasn't your fault, and they can't expect you to fix everything for them. Nobody could do that."

"Does it make me wrong that I still want to try?" Ella asked.

Lewis smiled at her and took her hand. "No," he said, "it just makes me love you more."

FIFTY·SEVEN

The first problem with trying to find an off-the-rack wedding dress, Maggie learned the next morning, was that they only came in two sizes, neither one of which was the size she thought her sister wore. "Sample sizes," the bored clerk had explained, when Maggie asked to see something that wasn't an eight or a ten. "You'll try 'em on, find what you like, and we'll order it in your size."

"But what if you don't wear an eight or a ten?" she asked.

"We pin 'em if they're too big," said the clerk.

"But what if they're too small?" asked Maggie, fingering the gowns and knowing there was no way they'd fit her sister. The clerk had shrugged and scribbled a name and address on a piece of paper. "They've got larger sizes," she said.

And the next store—a branch of a gigantic bridal-gown chain—did indeed have larger sizes, hanging in its coyly named Diva section. "Do they come with their own entourage?" Ella had asked. Maggie wasn't sure about entourages. But she did know that the dresses were awful.

"I don't know about this," said Ella, showing Maggie the umpteenth empire-waisted A-line dress they'd seen. This one had bunchy silk flowers on the bosom.

"It's okay," said Maggie. "It's adequate, you know? But I want

to find something that's perfect, and I'm not sure this is the place."
She sighed, leaning against a glass case of discounted garters. "I'm
not even sure what the right thing is. I feel like I'll know it when I
see it, but I'm not sure I'm going to see it!"

"Well, what does Rose like?" asked Ella.

"She doesn't know what she likes," said Maggie. "Her favorite
piece of clothing was a blue hooded sweatshirt with a zipper up the
front." She sighed again. "I guess I'd better start talking to dress-
makers." She shook her head. "Maybe we'll get lucky." She gazed
around the store. "Not here, though. Where's Lewis?"

Lewis, as it turned out, was back in the dressing room, offering
helpful critiques to brides-to-be.

"I don't know," said a tiny redhead in a puffy meringue of a
dress, "do you think it's overwhelming me?"

Lewis looked at her carefully. "Put the third one on again, the
one with the low back," he said. "That's still my favorite."

A black girl with shells and beads laced through her braids
tapped his shoulder and twirled around.

"Definitely you," said Lewis, nodding his approval.

"Lewis!" called Maggie. "We're going now!"

A chorus of complaints came from a half-dozen dressing room
stalls. "No! Not yet! Just one more dress!"

Lewis smiled. "It seems like I've got a talent for this. Maggie,
maybe you should put me on retainer."

"Done," said Maggie. "But we've got two days until Rose
leaves, and no dress yet, so we've got to keep shopping. Let's go."

Later that night, Maggie and Ella drove back to Golden Acres through
the night air that was thick with moisture, and the whirring of cicadas,
and disappointment. The dress they'd driven to see had been a disaster—the polyester-satin blend too shiny, the sweetheart neckline too
plunging, the beads around the hem sewn so loosely that a few fell off
to rattle against the fake linoleum of the would-be seller's kitchen floor.
When Maggie said that it wasn't quite right, the woman had told

them they'd be doing her a favor if they just took it with them.

"Was it yours?" asked Maggie.

"It was supposed to be," she said.

So now they were driving back home with the dress swaying from its hook over the backseat like a ghost, and Maggie was feeling pissed-off and panicked.

"What am I going to do?" she asked. And she was surprised when Ella answered.

"You know what I think? I think that this really is a case where it's the thought that counts."

"How's she supposed to wear a thought down the aisle?" Maggie asked.

"Well, she can't, but just that you're doing this, and trying so hard, it shows how much you love her."

"Except she doesn't know that I'm doing this," Maggie said. "And I really want to find her something. It's important. It's really important."

"Well, you don't have to find a dress before Rose leaves. You've got five months. You could always find something you like and order it. Or you could sew her something."

"I can't sew," Maggie said morosely.

"No," said Ella. "But I can. That is, I could. It's been so long, but I used to make all sorts of things. Tablecloths, curtains, dresses for your mother when she was little . . ."

"But a wedding dress . . . well, wouldn't that be hard?"

"Very hard," Ella confirmed. "But we could do it together, once you've figured out what you want."

"I think I know what I want," said Maggie. In fact, after looking at more than a hundred different dresses, and pictures of perhaps five hundred more, she was starting to get a sense of what was going to look perfect on Rose. She just hadn't seen the actual dress outside of her imagination. A ballgown, she was thinking, because Rose had a nice enough shape, and enough of a waist to make it work. A ballgown with maybe a scooped neckline, low but not indecent, maybe with a row of beads or seed pearls along the edge, nothing too flashy, and certainly nothing too itchy. And three-quarter-length sleeves would be the most flattering length, certainly better than the short sleeves, which were somehow matronly, and the sleeveless dresses, which she knew Rose would never wear. And a full skirt, a fairy-tale kind of skirt, a skirt that would sort of remind Rose of Glinda the Good Witch in *The Wizard of Oz,* except not quite that costumey, and definitely a train, although not too much of a train. "And I think Rose would trust me." Which wasn't quite true, Maggie admitted to herself. She hoped Rose would trust her. She *hoped*.

She drove, and thought, picturing the dress in her mind. "When you're sewing," she asked, "do you have to find a pattern of exactly what you want to make?"

"Well, that's the way it's normally done."

"What if you want to sew something different than any patterns you can find?"

"Hmm," said Ella, tapping one fingertip against her lower lip. "Well, I guess what I'd try to do is find parts of patterns and put them all together. It would be tricky. Expensive, too, once you've added up all those yards of fabric."

"Like a few hundred dollars?" Maggie asked in a small voice.

"More than that, I think," said Ella. "But I've got some money."

"No," said Maggie. "No, I want to pay for it. I want it to be from me." She drove through the thick darkness, hearing the far-off rumble of thunder as the skies prepared to deliver Florida's nightly shower. Every old insecurity, every high-school taunt, every boss who'd fired her and landlord who'd evicted her and guy who'd called her stupid rose up in a wave within her. *You can't,* they said. You're dumb. You'll never figure it out.

Her hands tightened on the wheel. But I can! she thought. She remembered the afternoons she'd spent putting her flyers up all over Golden Acres, a drawing of a dress on a hanger and the words *YOUR FAVORITE THINGS,* and *MAGGIE FELLER, PERSONAL*

SHOPPER written on them, and how the phone had rung so constantly for the next two weeks that she'd finally installed her own line. She thought about going over her budget with Jack, how he'd explained it to her over and over again, never once losing his patience, telling her that to save for her own shop she should pretend that her money was a pie, and that she'd need to eat most of the pie to survive—and that was her money for rent and groceries and gas and such—but if she could put away a little piece, even a little tiny sliver every month, that eventually ("Not soon," he'd cautioned, "but eventually") she'd have enough for the big things she wanted. She'd look at the figures again, and carve out a slice for Rose's dress.

And she thought of the little empty store she'd seen, around the corner from the bagel shop, empty for three months, with a sweet green-and-white-striped awning and a storefront of fly-specked glass. She thought of how she'd walk by it on her break and imagine polishing the glass, imagine painting the walls creamy white and dividing the back room into cubicles by hanging lengths of white cotton and gauze. She'd put padded benches in each changing room so the customers could sit, and shelves for them to stick their purses, and she'd find old mirrors at tag sales, and every price would be a round number, tax included. It wouldn't be Hollywood, but it would be what she was good at. What she was best at. Her favorite thing. And she was succeeding at it, which meant there was no reason that she couldn't succeed at this, too. She wouldn't fall down on her face and need to be rescued. She'd be the one who did the rescuing instead.

"Can we try?" she finally asked. The dress in the backseat swayed gently, back and forth, like it was dancing.

"Yes," said Ella. "Yes, dear, of course we can."

"House of Stein, Simon speaking."

"Do they know you answer the phone like that?" asked Rose, rolling over on the bed. It was ten o'clock in the morning. Ella was off holding crack babies at the hospital, and Maggie was on one of her top-secret missions, which meant that Rose had all four rooms of the apartment to herself.

"I knew it was you. Caller ID," said Simon. "How are things? Are you relaxing?"

"Sort of," said Rose.

"Sun and fun, fruity drinks, the occasional cabana boy?"

Rose sighed. Simon was teasing, as usual, and he was funny, as usual, but he didn't sound quite like himself yet. The Jim thing, she thought. And the whole secret-grandmother thing, and Rose's sudden departure for Florida. She'd have to go home soon and start making things right. "The only cabana boys here are eighty years old, with pacemakers."

"Watch out for them," said Simon. "It's the elderly ones who always surprise you. Are you okay?"

"I'm fine. Ella's fine. And Maggie . . ." Rose furrowed her brow. Maggie had changed, and Rose wasn't sure she trusted it. She got out of bed, carrying the phone as she strolled toward Ella's living room. "Maggie's become a businesswoman," she said. "She's a personal shopper, which actually makes a lot of sense. She's got really great taste. She always knows what to wear, and what's going to look best on other people. And the people here, lots of them don't drive anymore, and even the ones who do sometimes have a hard time getting around the malls . . ."

"I have a hard time getting around malls," said Simon. "It's genetic. The last time my mother was at Franklin Mills, she called the police because she thought her car had been stolen, when in reality she'd just forgotten where she'd parked it."

"Oof," said Rose. "So is that why she put twenty stuffed animals in the backseat, and tied all of those ribbons to the antenna?"

"No," said Simon, "she just likes ribbons. And stuffed animals." There was a pause. "I was kind of angry at you when you left, you know."

"About Jim Danvers?" Rose swallowed hard, even though she'd been expecting this.

"Yeah," said Simon. "About that. I'm not upset that it happened. I just want to feel like you can tell me things. Like you can tell me anything. I'm going to be your husband. I want you to lean on me. I want you to say good-bye before you go somewhere." Across the line, Rose heard him swallow hard. "When I came home, and you weren't there . . ."

Rose closed her eyes. She remembered that feeling too well, of what it was like to walk into an empty house and find that the person you loved had disappeared without a word.

"I'm sorry," Rose said. "I'll try." She swallowed hard and walked in front of the bookshelf filled with the pictures of her, and Maggie, and her mother in her wedding dress, smiling a smile that said that she had her whole life in front of her and that it was going to be a life filled with happiness. "I'm sorry about leaving the way I did, and not telling you about Jim. You shouldn't have had to find out that way."

"Probably not," said Simon. "But I was too hard on you about it. I know how stressed out you've been, with all the wedding stuff."

"Well," said Rose, "I'm the one with time for it."

"Oh, along those lines," Simon said. "You got a call last night from a headhunter."

Rose's pulse quickened. When she'd worked at Lewis, Dommel, and Fenick, she'd get calls from headhunters a few times a week, people who'd come across her name and résumé in some legal directory and would call her trying to get her to jump to another firm, where she would undoubtedly wind up working even longer hours. But since she'd taken her leave, the phone had stopped ringing.

"Someone from the Women's Association for Women's Alternatives."

"Really?" Rose was trying to remember whether she'd heard of the group, and what they did. "How'd they get my name?"

"They need a staff attorney," said Simon, sidestepping the question, which gave Rose her answer—Simon had called. "They do advocacy work for low-income women. Custody, child support, visitation, stuff like that. Lots of time in court, I'd bet, and the pay's not great because it would be a part-time position at first, but I thought it might be interesting." He paused. "Of course, if you're not ready yet . . ."

"No! No," said Rose, trying not to shout. "It sounds . . . I mean, I'm very . . . Did they leave a number?"

"They did," said Simon, "but I told them you were on vacation, so no hurry. Go enjoy yourself! Put on your bathing suit, go give some old man a coronary."

"I've got to call Amy first. She's been leaving me messages every day since I've been here, and we keep missing each other."

"Ah," said Simon. "Amy X."

Rose grinned. "You know she only called herself that for three weeks in college."

"I thought she called herself Ashante in college."

"No, Ashante was high school," said Rose, remembering when

her best friend had renounced her "slave name" midway through Mr. Halleck's honors U.S. history class.

"Give her my best," said Simon. "Which will probably not be good enough for her."

"Amy likes you just fine."

"Amy doesn't think anyone's good enough for you," said Simon. "And she's right, but I'm not bad, generally speaking. And you know what?"

"What?"

Simon dropped his voice to a whisper. "I love you very much, my bride-to-be."

"Love you, too," said Rose. She hung up the phone, smiled as she imagined him at his cluttered desk, then dialed her best friend.

"Girl!" shouted Amy, "tell me everything! How's the grandmother? Do you like her?"

"I do," said Rose, surprising herself. "She's sharp, and nice, and . . . happy. I think she was really sad for a long time, and that she's really happy now that Maggie and I are here. The only thing is, she stares at me a lot."

"Why?"

"Oh, you know," said Rose, feeling uncomfortable. "Not seeing me and Maggie grow up. I told her she didn't miss much."

"*Au contraire,* my sister. She missed you winning all those science fairs. She missed you dressing like a Vulcan for three years' worth of Halloween parades. . . ."

Rose cringed.

"She missed us in leg warmers and ripped sweatshirts," said Amy. "Okay, granted, I wish I'd missed that, too."

"We were trendy!" said Rose.

"We were pathetic," Amy corrected her. "Let me talk to the g-mom! I've got stories!"

"Forget it," Rose said, laughing.

"So tell me this . . . is Maggie coming to the wedding?"

"I think so," said Rose.

"Is she going to replace me?" Amy demanded.

"Absolutely not," said Rose. "Your butt-bow is secure."

"Good deal," said Amy. "Go have a piña colada for me."

"And you go keep our drinking water clean," said Rose. She hung up the phone and considered her day. No dogs to be walked, no wedding crisis to resolve. She wandered into her grandmother's living room and picked up a photo album from the top of a stack on the coffee table. "Caroline and Rose" read the label pasted on the front. She opened the book and there she was, a day old, wrapped in a white blanket. Her eyes were squinched shut, and her mother faced the camera, smiling tentatively. God, thought Rose, she was so young! She flipped through the pages. She was a baby, she was a toddler, she was riding a bike with training wheels, her mother behind her, pushing a stroller in which baby Maggie rode in like Cleopatra on her barge. Rose smiled, turning the pages slowly, watching herself and her sister grow up.

FIFTY-NINE

Maggie sat back, gave her ponytail a businesslike tweak, and nodded. "Okay," she announced. "I think that's it." She beckoned Ella and Dora over to her table in the back of the fabric store. "This skirt," she said, showing them the pattern. "This top," she said, laying a second pattern carefully on top of the first. "And these sleeves," she said, displaying yet a third pattern, "only three-quarter-length, not full length."

"We'll make it from muslin first," said Ella. "We'll take our time. We'll be just fine." She gathered up the patterns. "Let's get started first thing in the morning, and we'll see what we shall see."

Maggie sat back and smiled proudly. "It's going to be great," she said.

That night, Maggie came home from her shift at Bagel Bay, and a last-minute stop-off to return three of Mrs. Gantz's rejected bathing suits, and found her sister's bags stacked neatly by the door. Her heart sank. She'd failed. Rose was leaving, and she didn't even know how hard Maggie had been trying to find her a dress. She didn't know how sorry Maggie was. Her sister was still barely talking to her, barely looking at her. It hadn't worked out at all.

Maggie walked toward the back bedroom, hearing Rose's and Ella's voices from the screened-in porch.

"You'd think the little dogs would be the easy ones," Rose was saying. "But really, they're the most stubborn of all. And they bark the loudest, too."

"Did you girls ever have a dog?"

"For a day," said Rose. "Once."

Maggie headed into the kitchen, thinking that she could make dinner for her sister, and at least that would be something, a small but meaningful gesture, an act that would show Rose she cared. She pulled swordfish steaks out of the refrigerator, sliced up purple onions and avocado and teardrop tomatoes for a salad, and set the basket of rolls right by her sister's plate. Rose smiled later when she saw them.

"Carbohydrates!" she said.

"Just for you," said Maggie, and passed her sister the butter.

Ella looked at them curiously. "My stepmonster," said Rose, with her mouth full. She swallowed. "Sydelle. Sydelle hated carbs."

"Except when she went on that sweet-potato diet," Maggie said.

"Right," said Rose, nodding at her sister. "Then she hated red meat. But no matter what diet she was doing, she'd never let me eat bread."

Maggie yanked the bread basket away, and flared her nostrils as wide as she could. "Rose, you'll ruin your appetite!" she said.

Rose shook her head. "Like that was going to happen," she said.

Maggie pulled up her chair and started on her salad. "Remember the traveling turkey?"

Rose closed her eyes and nodded. "How could I ever forget?"

"What is the traveling turkey?" asked Ella.

"Well . . ." said Rose.

"It was one of . . ." Maggie began.

The two of them smiled at each other. "You tell it," said Rose.

Maggie nodded. "Okay," she said. "We were both home for spring break, and Sydelle was on a diet."

"One of many," said Rose.

"Hey. Who's telling the story?" asked Maggie. "So we come home, and what's for dinner? Turkey."

"Turkey with the skin taken off," said Rose.

"Just turkey," said Maggie. "No potatoes. No stuffing. No gravy . . ."

"God forbid!" said Rose.

"Just turkey. We had poached eggs for breakfast, and then it's lunchtime, and out comes the turkey. The same turkey."

"It was," said Rose, "a very big turkey."

"We had it for dinner that night, too. And lunch the next day. And that night we were going to one of Sydelle's friend's houses for dinner, and we were so excited because we thought we'd finally get something that wasn't turkey, except when we got there we found out that Sydelle . . ."

". . . took the turkey with her!" Rose and Maggie concluded together.

"It turns out," said Rose, buttering a roll, "that her friend was on the same diet she was."

"We all had turkey," Maggie said.

"Traveling turkey," said Rose. And Ella sat back, feeling relief wash through her as her granddaughters started to laugh.

That night, for the last time, Maggie and Rose lay side by side on the flimsy pullout mattress, listening to the croaking of the frogs and the warm wind rustling the palm trees, and the occasional squeal of brakes as another resident of Golden Acres made his or her unsteady way home.

"I'm so full," Rose groaned. "Where'd you learn to cook like that?"

"From Ella," said Maggie. "I paid attention. It was good, wasn't it?"

"Delicious," said Rose, and yawned. "So what about you? Do you think you'll stay here?"

"Yes," said Maggie. "I mean, I liked Philadelphia okay. And I still think about California sometimes. But I really like it here. I've got my job, you know. I'm going to grow my business. And Ella needs me."

"For what?"

"Well, maybe she doesn't need me," Maggie conceded. "But I think she likes having me around. And I sort of like being here. I mean, not here here," she said, gesturing to indicate the room, the condominium, the Golden Acres Retirement Community in general, "but Florida. Everyone here is from somewhere else, did you ever notice that?"

"I guess."

"It's good, I think. If everyone went to high school someplace else, it's not like you're always running into people who remember what you were like in high school, or college, or whatever. So you can be different, if you want to."

"You can be different anywhere," said Rose. "Look at me."

Maggie leaned on her elbow and looked at her sister, the familiar face, the hair spilling over the pillow, and saw Rose not as a threat, or a scold, or someone who was always going to tell her that she was doing things the wrong way, but as an ally. A friend.

There was silence for a moment as the sisters lay side by side. In her bedroom, Ella cocked her head and held her breath, listening.

"I'm going to do it, you know," said Maggie. "Your Favorite Things. I'm going to open a store someday. I even know where."

"I'll come down for your grand opening," said Rose.

"And I want to tell you . . ."

"You're sorry," recited Rose. "You've changed."

"No! Well, yes, I mean. It's true."

"I know," said Rose. "I know you have."

"But that's not what I wanted to tell you. What I wanted to tell you is, don't buy a dress."

"What?"

"Don't buy a dress. That's going to be my wedding present to you."

"Oh, Maggie . . . I don't know."

"Trust me," said Maggie.

"You want me to get married in a dress I've never even seen?"

Rose gave a nervous laugh, while picturing the kind of dress Maggie would come up with—cut low, slit high, sleeveless, backless, and fringed.

"Trust me," said Maggie. "I know what you like. I'll show you pictures. I'll let you try it on first. I'll come home. We can do fittings."

"We'll see," said Rose.

"But you'll let me try?" asked Maggie.

Rose sighed. "Fine," she said. "Go for it. Knock yourself out."

Silence again.

"I love you, you know," said one of the girls, and Ella wasn't sure which one. Rose? Maggie?

"Oh, please," said the other sister. "Don't be so sappy."

Ella waited in her bedroom, holding her breath, waiting for more. But there was nothing. And, hours later, moving carefully, when she eased the door open and walked into the bedroom, both of the sisters were sleeping, both curled on their left sides with their left hands tucked under their cheeks. She bent down, hardly daring to breathe, and kissed them each on the forehead. *Luck,* she thought. *Love.* Your heart's every happiness. And, as quietly as she could, she laid two glasses of water, each with a single ice cube, on the bedside table and tiptoed out the door.

SIXTY

"Calm down," said Maggie for the eighteenth time, and leaned close to Rose, who flinched. "If you don't relax, there's no way I'm going to be able to do this."

"I can't relax," said Rose. She was wearing a thick white terry-cloth bathrobe. Her hair, thanks to the hourlong ministrations of Michael from Pileggi, was an elaborate updo of curls, bobby pins, and tiny white blossoms. Her foundation was on, her lips were lined. Amy, resplendent in a simple navy sheath that she'd ornamented with a bed-pillow-sized butt bow, was bustling around looking for the caterers, and the platter of sandwiches they'd promised, and Maggie was currently trying, unsuccessfully, to curl her sister's eyelashes.

"Hello!" Michael Feller, resplendent in a new tuxedo, with his thin hair artfully arranged over his bald spot, stuck his head in the door. "Everything okay in here?" He recoiled as Maggie maneuvered the eyelash curler into place. "What is that?" he asked, sounding scared.

"Eyelash curler," said Maggie. "Rose, I'm not going to hurt you. I promise. Now, just look right at me . . . Don't move your head . . . there! Got 'em!"

"Agh," said Rose, cringing as much as she could with her eyelashes trapped between the metal pincers of the curler. "Ow . . . hurts . . ."

"Don't hurt your sister!" Michael Feller said sternly.

"It . . . does . . . not . . . hurt," said Maggie, easing the curler along the length of Rose's lashes. "There! Perfect! Now I just have to do the other one!"

"God help me," said Rose, and looked at her feet. They looked very nice, she had to admit; she'd been dubious about the whole notion of a pedicure. "I'm not a pedicure kind of person," she'd said. But Maggie, who'd become extremely bossy in the months since Your Favorite Things had been written up in the *Fort Lauderdale Sun-Sentinel,* was not taking no for an answer.

"Nobody's even going to see my feet," Rose had protested, but Maggie had said that Simon was going to see her feet, wasn't he? And so Rose had given in.

Maggie maneuvered the curler toward Eyelash Number Two, curled it carefully, and stepped back to study the effect. "Did you see my date?" she demanded. "I mean, I know this is your special day and all, but . . ." And she paused, looking at her sister.

"Maggie!" Rose exclaimed. "I do believe you're blushing!"

"Am not," said Maggie. "It's just that I know it's a lot of pressure, inviting a guy to a wedding. . . ."

"Charles seems very comfortable," said Rose. In fact, Charles seemed just about perfect, the kind of guy she'd always hoped Maggie would find once she'd gotten over her thing for the semi-employed bass-players-slash-bartenders of the world. He was younger than she was, someone she'd met at Princeton, although Maggie had been evasive about the details. "And he's crazy about you."

"Do you think so?" Maggie asked.

"Definitely," Rose said, just as Amy arrived, brandishing a platter of sandwiches over her head and Maggie ducked through the door.

"I found the food!" she announced.

"Where?" asked Rose, waving at her father as he left.

"With Sydelle, where else?" Amy asked, carefully wrapping half of a turkey sandwich in a napkin and handing it to Rose. "She was scraping mayonnaise off the bread. And My Marcia was asking the rabbi whether she could do the Lord's Prayer."

"You're kidding, right?"

Amy nodded. Rose took a single bite and set the sandwich aside. "Can't eat. Nervous," she said, as Maggie swept back into the room, carrying a large, vaguely dress-shaped bundle wrapped in white plastic.

"Ready for your dress, Cinderella?" she asked.

Rose swallowed hard and nodded. Inside, she was dying. What if the dress wasn't right? She imagined herself walking down the aisle, thread trailing, half-sewn seams gaping open. *Oh, God,* she thought. How stupid had she been to let Maggie take this on?

"Close your eyes," Maggie said.

"No," said Rose.

"Please?"

Rose sighed and gently closed her eyes. Maggie reached over to the zippered plastic bag, gently tugged down the zipper, and eased Rose's dress off the hanger.

"Ta da!" said Maggie, and twirled the dress through the air.

At first all Rose saw was the skirt—layers and layers of tulle. Then, as Maggie held the dress up, she could see how beautiful it really was—the creamy satin bodice dotted with tiny seed pearls, the fitted sleeves, the neckline that she saw was just deep enough. True to her word, Maggie had sent pictures and had flown up to Philadelphia to do a fitting. But the finished product was more beautiful than Rose could ever have hoped for.

"How long did this take you and Ella?" Rose asked, stepping into the skirt.

"Never you mind," said Maggie, fastening the dozens of buttons she'd sewn by hand along the back.

"How much did it cost?" asked Rose.

"Never mind that, either. It's our gift to you," said Maggie, straightening the neckline, and turning her sister toward the mirror.

"Oh," gasped Rose, looking at herself. "Oh, Maggie!"

And then Amy was walking toward them, holding Rose's bouquet of pink roses and white lilies in her hand, and the rabbi was sticking his head around the door, smiling at Rose and telling her that it was time, and Ella hurried in after him, her corsage tilted to one side, a shoe box in her hands.

"You look beautiful," said Ella and Maggie at the exact same time, and Rose was staring at herself, knowing that the dress was the exact thing she was supposed to be wearing, knowing she'd never looked prettier, or happier, than she did at this moment, with her sister on her right side and her grandmother on her left.

"Here," said Ella, opening the shoe box. "These are for you."

"Oh, I've got shoes already. . . ." Rose peeked inside and saw the most perfect pair of shoes—ivory satin, with low heels, and embroidered in the same thread as her dress. "Oh, my God. They're so pretty. Where did you find them?" She stared at Ella and took a guess. "Were they my mom's?"

Maggie looked at Ella and held her breath.

"No," said Ella. "They were mine." She wiped her eyes with a handkerchief. "I know I should probably lend you earrings or a necklace or something, if you still need something borrowed, but . . ."

"They're perfect," said Rose, slipping the shoes on her feet. "And they fit!" she said.

Ella shook her head, and her eyes filled with tears. "I know," she whispered back.

"Don't start crying yet," said Lewis, poking his head through the door. "We haven't even gotten started." He grinned at Rose. "You look lovely. And I think they're ready when you are."

Rose hugged Ella, then reached out for her sister. "Thank you for my dress. It's unbelievable. The most beautiful thing I've ever seen!"

"You're welcome," said Ella.

"Oh, it was nothing," said Maggie.

"You guys ready?" asked Rose, and Maggie and Ella nodded. The caterer threw the doors open, and the guests looked at Rose and smiled. Camera bulbs flashed. Mrs. Lefkowitz sniffled. Michael Feller lifted Rose's veil. "You look so beautiful," he whispered in her ear. "I'm so proud of you."

"I love you," Rose said. She turned. At the end of the aisle, Simon was smiling at her, his warm blue eyes glowing, the yarmulke perched on top of his carefully cropped curls, his parents beaming beside him. Ella grabbed Maggie's hand and squeezed.

"You did it," she whispered, and Maggie nodded happily, and the two of them looked at Rose and caught her eye. *We love you,* Ella thought, and smiled, sending all of her good wishes through the air . . . and, in that instant, Rose looked at them through her veil and smiled back.

"And now," the rabbi intoned, "Maggie Feller, sister of the bride, will read a poem."

Maggie could feel the tension as she stepped forward and smoothed her dress (sage green, sleeveless, and without the slit in the skirt or the plunging neckline she knew her big sister was dreading) and stepped forward. She was certain, she thought, as she cleared her throat, that Sydelle and her father would be expecting her to bust out something that began, "There once was a girl from Nantucket." Well, they were in for a surprise.

"I'm so happy for my sister right now," said Maggie. "When we were growing up, Rose always took care of me. She always stuck up for me, and wanted what was best for me. And I'm so happy because I know that Simon will do the same things for her, and that we'll always be a part of each other's lives. We'll always love each other, because that's what sisters do. That's what sisters are." She gave Rose a smile. "So, Rose, this is for you."

Maggie took a deep breath and, even though she'd practiced the poem a dozen times on the plane, had long since committed it to memory, she felt a tremor of nerves work its way along her spine. Ella raised her chin in the exact expression that Rose and Maggie both wore at times, and Charles smiled at her proudly from his seat in the back. Maggie exhaled, and nodded at her grandmother. Then she fixed her eyes on Rose, wearing the beautiful dress she and Ella had made, and began:

> " 'i carry your heart with me(i carry it in
> my heart)i am never without it(anywhere
> i go you go,my dear;and whatever is done
> by only me is your doing,my darling)
>   i fear
> no fate(for you are my fate,my sweet)i want
> no world(for beautiful you are my world,my true)
> and it's you are whatever a moon has always meant
> and whatever a sun will always sing is you' "

Maggie's throat closed like a fist. In the front row, Lewis nodded at her, and Ella was smiling through her tears, and her father was pushing up his glasses and taking fast swipes at his eyes, and the assembled guests were staring at her expectantly. Under the chuppah Rose's eyes were wide and her lips trembling. And Maggie could imagine her mother, too, a ghost in the back row, the brightness of her red lipstick and gold earrings, watching over her daughters, knowing that in spite of everything both of them had grown up brave, and smart, and beautiful, that they'd be sisters to each other, and friends, too, and that Rose would always want what was best for Maggie, and Maggie would always want what was best for Rose. *Breathe,* Maggie thought, and began again:

> " 'here is the deepest secret nobody knows
> (here is the root of the root and the bud of the bud
> and the sky of the sky of a tree called life;which grows

higher than the soul can hope or mind can hide)
and this is the wonder that's keeping the stars apart'

" 'i carry your heart(i carry it in my heart)' "

She smiled at the crowd and smiled at her sister, and it was as if she could see the future—the house and the babies that Rose and Simon would have, the vacations where they'd visit her and Ella in Florida, where they'd swim together, Rose and Maggie and Ella and Rose's babies, in a wide blue pool under the sunshine, and where they'd curl up together at night on Ella's bed, side by side by side until they fell asleep.

"E.E. Cummings," she said, knowing that she'd done it, that everyone's eyes had been on her and she'd said every word perfectly; she, Maggie Feller, had gotten it just right.

ACKNOWLEDGMENTS

This book would not exist without the help and hard work from three incredible women. My agent, the divine and beneficent Joanna Pulcini, is a tireless advocate and a brilliant reader. Liza Nelligan's passion and commitment (along with her own tales from the Sister Zone) helped me more than I can say. Greer Kessel Hendricks not only took me under her wing and agreed to publish me, but also appointed herself the unofficial queen of my fan club and de facto personal publicist. No writer could hope for more careful readers and more vigorous champions, and I'm blessed and lucky to have them as my colleagues and my friends.

Teresa Cavanaugh and Linda Michaels helped Rose and Maggie see the world. Joanna's assistant, Anna deVries, and Greer's assistant, Suzanne O'Neill, dealt swiftly with my telephone calls. Laura Mullen at Atria is a miracle worker and incredibly cool to boot. My thanks to all of them.

Thanking all of the writers who've inspired me, encouraged me, and been incredibly generous would constitute a book in itself, so I'll settle for making mention of Susan Isaacs, Anna Maxted, Jennifer Cruise, John Searles, Suzanne Finnamore, and J. D. McClatchy.

Thanks to all of the members of my family who give me love,

support, and material. Special thanks to my sister, Molly Weiner, the quick brown fox, for her grace and good humor.

Thanks to my friends, who indulged me, encouraged me, laughed when they heard pieces of this book, tactfully refrained from mentioning the disastrous state of my home and my personal hygiene when I was knee-deep in revisions, and let me borrow pieces of their lives, especially Susan Abrams, Lisa Maslankowski, Ginny Durham, and Sharon Fenick.

I want the world to know that Wendell, King of All Dogs, is still my muse; and that my husband, Adam, is still my traveling companion, first reader, and an all-around fabulous guy.

Finally, most important, I'm more grateful than I can say to all the readers who came to my readings or wrote to tell me they liked *Good in Bed,* and to hurry up already with this one! I thank them for their kindness, and their generous support, and for taking the time to tell me that what I'd written hit home in their lives, and I look forward to telling them many more stories in the future. My Web site is www.jenniferweiner.com, and you're all invited to stop by and say hello!

Thanks for reading,
—Jen

In Her Shoes

Jennifer Weiner

A Readers Club Guide

ABOUT THIS GUIDE

The suggested questions are intended to help your reading group find new and interesting angles and topics for discussion for Jennifer Weiner's *In Her Shoes*. We hope that these ideas will enrich your conversation and increase your enjoyment of the book.

Many fine books from Washington Square Press feature Readers Club Guides. For a complete listing, or to read the Guides online, visit http://www.BookClubReader.com.

A Conversation with Jennifer Weiner

Q. Tell us a little about how *In Her Shoes* went from a bestselling book to a major motion picture. How involved were you in the process? What was the most nerve-racking part of the experience? What surprised you the most?

A. I'm still astonished by how easily *In Her Shoes* made it from book to film. In the spring of 2002, months before the book was even published, I gave the manuscript to my brother Jake, who works for a production company in Hollywood, with a note saying, "I hope you like this, but I'm not sure it's a movie." After all, the major parts are played by women—one of them's gorgeous, one of them is anything but model-like, and the grandmother's in her seventies! There are no big parts for men, no chase scenes, no time travel, and parts of the book are set in a retirement community in Florida—not exactly a locale screaming "Film me!"

But Jake read the book, liked it, and said, "I think there are producers in town who will really identify with this material." He was very smart about it—he circulated the book to a group of women in powerful places. Many of them had their own sister stories. In fact, the executives at Fox 2000, where the book landed, told me that they had meetings where all of the women at the table sat around asking the question, "Were you Maggie or Rose growing up?"

Once the book was optioned, I made what may well stand as one of the most mentally healthy decisions of my life. I said, "I'm keeping my hands off this." I figure, movies tell their stories in a different language than novels do. I don't know a thing about screenwriting, or how Hollywood works, but I do know novelists who've lost years of their lives trying to adapt their own work for the screen, only to have the project scrapped. I decided I'd be better served working on my book, taking care of my baby, and hoping for the best. At that point, "the best" was just having the movie actually made, because it's very, very common for things to get optioned and never get made—the executive who fell in love with the material left the company, the script never worked out right, the actress who was attached got pregnant or shipped off to rehab, whatever.

So I sat back and waited, and things quickly moved into the "yeah, right" stage. Jake would call me up and say, "Susannah Grant's doing the screenplay." And I'd say, "Yeah, right," because, come on—the woman who wrote *Erin Brockovich* and *Ever After*? Adapting my book? Pinch me already! Then it was, "Cameron Diaz is interested in starring." And I'd say, "Yeah, right." Then he'd call to tell me, "Curtis Hanson wants to direct!" And I'd say, "Yeah, right." I think I'm still in a state of pretty total disbelief—first, that the book got optioned; second, that it got turned into a movie; and finally, that it all happened with such an astonishing group of talented people, from the screenwriter and director to the stars!

As for the most nerve-racking part, I was concerned about the casting of Rose—specifically, Rose's size. I didn't want her slimmed down or dumbed down, and I didn't want her to be the typical Hollywood ugly duckling, someone who looks like Drew Barrymore in bad glasses, and as soon as she takes the glasses off . . . poof, she's Drew Barrymore!

I guess in an ideal world they would have cast an unknown plus-size actress who's been told all her career that she's too big for this and too big for that, but having an actress as amazing as Toni Collette agree to gain weight for the part was a pretty decent compromise. I've been a fan of Toni Collette's since *Muriel's Wedding*, and I was so thrilled when she got the part . . . and even more thrilled to hear the first word back from the set. My sister was an extra during one of the Rose-at-work scenes, and she called me at lunch. "Okay," she reported, "her butt looks enormous and they've got her in these horrible maroon palazzo pants, with this ridiculous hairdo. . . . She looks JUST LIKE YOU!" She was kidding. I think.

My biggest surprise is that this book is actually a movie. I think I'm going to be in that state of disbelief until I actually see the movie on the screen. The producers asked if I wanted to see a rough cut when I was in Los Angeles on my last book tour, and even though it was tempting, I declined. I want to see it on the big screen, with my Kleenex and my popcorn and my family!

Q. How did your experience in the film industry compare to your experience in the publishing industry? Were there any aspects of one that you would like to see in the other?

A. I've been so lucky in both the film and the publishing industries, but there are definitely different constraints. When you're writing a book, nobody cares how big your heroines are, or how old, or how unusual. With movies, it's all about "Well, who can we cast?" Or, more commonly, "What name actress can we cast to play this role?" Writing is very solitary and insular—it's just me, the story, and the laptop—whereas movies are enormous collaborative efforts requiring all kinds of fancy scheduling, teamwork, and coordination, and the efforts of thousands of people. I'll never forget driving to Briny Breezes in Florida—the mobile-home community whose clubhouse the producers were using in one of the scenes—and seeing block after block of trailers, cables, lights, sound trucks, catering tents, cameras, and dozens and dozens of people. "I can't believe this is all because of something you thought up," my Nanna said. I couldn't believe it, either!

The other thing I noticed about movies versus books is that movies can proceed at what feels like a snail's pace. Once the set's been built, the costumes have been chosen, the blocking's finished, the lights and sound equipment and cameras are all in place, the actors have to do a scene—maybe it's only a thirty-second scene—over, and over, and over, and over again, bringing the same energy and intensity to the thirty-first take that they brought to the first. Now that I've seen bits and pieces of how the movie actually got made, I think I've got the easiest job of anyone. I don't have to worry about the weather, I don't have to track down permits to get permission to close off a block in Philadelphia, or find a machine that can make it look like it's snowing in April, or worry about whether the leading lady's getting along with the director or the guy who's cast as her husband. All I have to do is sit in front of a laptop and come up with a story.

Q. Did the process of watching your book become a movie change the way you write?

A. Not really. I'm not a very visual writer to begin with—the physical descriptions of people and places are always things I really struggle with. I'm more likely to hear how a character sounds in my head than picture how she looks, so it's not like I'm sitting around thinking of a character who looks exactly like Ashley Judd or Angelina Jolie.

I haven't started writing my books with movies in mind, either. I think it's wonderful when someone in Hollywood sees potential in the finished product, but I think that novelists can get themselves in trouble when they begin tailoring their fiction for the big screen. The books tend to read more like screenplays.

Q. Will there be a Jennifer Weiner cameo in the film?

A. Oh, please. I got my whole damn family into this movie!

Yes, I make a cameo, but I would like to state for the record that I had no hair and makeup before the filming. REPEAT: NO HAIR AND MAKEUP! So when you actually see me walking behind Brooke Smith and Toni Collette in the Italian Market, please keep that in mind. I can—and have—looked much better! I blame the whole thing on my sister. When she was an extra, they did her hair and makeup. What I didn't know is that Molly was what's called a featured extra—i.e., one whose face and form you can actually see in the shot; whereas my friend Joanna and I were what is known as background—i.e., "Background! Go!" So no hair and makeup for us.

My favorite family cameo story, though, is my Nanna. My Nanna has eight grandchildren and I've never risen higher than where chronology put me, in the number-five slot. When I found out they'd be filming parts of *In Her Shoes* in Florida, I figured it was my chance . . . especially after Nanna ignored articles in *The Miami Herald* and *The Fort Lauderdale Sun-Sentinel* and got all excited about the article that appeared in the free newsletter she receives in her retirement community. "Jen," she told me, "they're making a movie out of one of your books!" I told her that I knew, and asked if she wanted to be an extra.

Nanna thought it over. "Well," she said, "I'm not much of an actress."

"That doesn't matter!" I said, meanwhile noticing that she'd already given herself a speaking role. "You just have to be in the background!"

She agreed to do it, and after a lot of begging ("Please! She's my Nanna! And I want to be the number-one grandchild for once in my life!") Nanna was cast. I flew down to Florida with my mom and my baby to watch my grandmother make her screen debut. It was an incredible thrill. We arrived on set at about six in the morning. Nanna was whisked off to hair and makeup. I felt my stock rising. Then she was escorted to wardrobe and given this lovely green dress, and I felt my stock rising even higher. Finally, they gave her a primo spot on the set, at a table a few feet away from Cameron Diaz and Shirley MacLaine, and I knew I'd finally made it! When they took a break from shooting I snuck onto the set. Nanna threw her arms around me and whispered, "I am so proud of you!" So for one bright and shining moment, I was number one! Of course, a few months later my cousin Rachel had a baby, so I'm currently back down to the number-five slot . . . but I can still hope for a rebound.

Q. To what extent is your work autobiographical? In *Good in Bed*, for example, Cannie's résumé is strikingly similar to your own. How much do you write yourself into a character? Also, how much do you base other characters on the people in your life?

A. I think that everything I write—whether it's set in the here-and-now in the United States or takes place in a mythical land that exists only in my imagination—is necessarily going to be influenced by my place in a particular moment in history. The pop-culture references, for example, or the characters' preoccupation with finding love (in Rose's case) or stardom (in Maggie's) by the time they turn thirty very much reflects the pressures exerted on women in the 1980s and 1990s, when I was growing up.

However, this story is a lot less autobiographical than *Good in Bed*. I'm not a lawyer or a dog groomer. My grandmother isn't much like Ella; my mom is one of the sanest people I know; my father vanished in a very different way than Michael Feller did; and my wedding . . . well, let's just say that I welcomed the opportunity to revisit a wedding in fiction and make it full of love, glitch-free and picture perfect, the way real-life weddings don't always turn out to be.

But, as always, there are elements of autobiography. Rose's very specific longing to be accepted by the right girls in junior high—the ones who have Diet Coke and cut-up carrots for lunch, and who always know the right thing to wear, and the right haircut—is something I remember well from my own days at Henry James Junior High. And Simon Stein, Master of the Menu, instigator of intramural softball, has certain things in common with my husband, Adam, although he'd deny it vigorously.

And with the characters who have nothing in common with me or my experiences—the senior citizens especially and someone like Lewis, who's both a different generation and a different gender—I try to imagine who they are, how they'd sound and behave by first trying to hear their voices in my head, and working backward. Once I know how someone sounds—or I have a gesture or a characteristic in my head—it's a little easier for me to step into their shoes and start to really figure out who they are and how they got that way.

Q. Do you have a favorite character in *In Her Shoes*? Do you relate to one sister more than the other?

A. I have a special place in my heart for all the characters in this book. Rose is the sister I most resemble, both physically and in terms of being responsible to the point of anal retentiveness. (Her cluelessness about fashion and makeup is all me, although I have to say that she's got embarrassingly bad taste in music. George Michael! Please!) Maggie is very, very different from me, but it was a very interesting exercise trying to slip into the skin, and the mind-set, of someone who's not like me at all, from the itsy-bitsy body and the constant flow of male attention to the spotty employment history.

Ella was the most interesting character for me to write because her life required me to imagine things I'd only seen or heard second-hand, or read about. My grandmother, Faye Frumin, lives in a place that's a lot like Golden Acres, so I was able to take some of the details of retirement-community living in Florida from my visits over the years. But thinking of what was going on inside Ella's head—how it would feel to lose a child, to feel a degree of responsibility for that child's death, and all of the guilt and longing she'd feel about these granddaughters she couldn't save—was a real challenge.

And in terms of favorite supporting characters, Mrs. Lefkowitz wins, hands down.

Q. **Which authors have influenced you the most, and how have they helped shape you as a writer? Are you more influenced by journalists than fiction writers?**

A. Besides newspapers and magazines I rarely read nonfiction in my free time. I much prefer novels. I figure there's enough reality in real life, and when I read I want to escape, and novels are what work for me.

There've been a lot of writers who've been influential, whose books I turn to again and again. Stephen King, for one. He's an amazing storyteller, with an unbelievable imagination. Susan Isaacs, for another. Every one of her lead characters is someone you'd want to sit down and dish with over coffee. It's interesting, but I just realized that both of them are writers I discovered in my adolescence. I remember devouring *Pet Sematary* in one fevered gulp when I was in seventh grade.

In addition to Sapphire's *Push,* I also reread Russell Banks's *Rule of the Bone* when thinking about Maggie's voice. Precious, the lead character in *Push,* is, like Maggie, at war with the world—she's someone who's been through incredible pain in her life, who's been judged as expendable and told that she's stupid, and yet she has this voice that's so sharp, so full of rage and sorrow and dead-on observations about the world.

And then there were the novelists and poets I discovered in college and keep coming back to, and it was fun to give them little cameos during Maggie's time at Princeton. The Elizabeth Bishop poem is a particular favorite of mine.

Q. In both of your novels, the idea of body image is a central theme. Do you think this concept is a constraint that we place on ourselves, a restraint that society places on women, or a combination of the two?

A. Um, all of the above? I think it starts out as being a societal mandate—a kind of signpost outside of life's roller coaster, reading "You Must Be Less Than This Fat Or Nobody Will Ever Love You"—and it's something that women internalize, and carry with them in different ways. One of the things I was trying to do with this book was to show both sides of the coin, and the different ways that buying the beauty myths can harm you. Rose, for example, who's a normal size and healthy, gets the message that her body is something to be ignored and concealed, swathed in sweatpants and unfashionable-length skirts, until she learns that however it appears, her body is, first and foremost, something to use—to get her around, to ride a bike, to walk a dog, to hold the people she loves. And then there's Maggie, who's got this ready-for-its-closeup body (which, as we see, requires a tremendous investment in terms of effort and time), but it doesn't bring her all the happiness that the plastic surgeons and diet merchants promise. It gets her scads of attention—good and bad—and it gets her judged, the same way Rose's body earns her judgments. I hope someday the idea of "you are how you look" will change, and I hope that in some small way my books will be part of that change. . . . But I worry that there's so much money to be made off of convincing women that they're inadequate, too big, too little, or otherwise completely unacceptable that change is going to be painfully slow.

Q. What do you consider to be the greatest challenge that you face as a fiction writer? Are the challenges different from those that you encountered as a journalist?

A. I think the greatest challenge I face as a fiction writer is character economy. I usually wind up with so many characters—all of them vying for space and attention, all of them wanting to do things—that a few of them wind up miserably on the cutting-room floor. In *Good in Bed,* for example, Cannie had another sibling, a second brother, who got lost in the revisions (my two real-life brothers spend lots of time fighting over which one actually made it into print, and which one got abandoned). In the early drafts of *In Her Shoes,* there was a lot more about Josh, the guy who menaces Maggie at Princeton, and what turned him into the creep he became. (It was actually a rotten father, who'd founded a *Survivor*-inspired weight-loss service: Dieters were dropped in the middle of deserted, bug-infested islands with only a handful of rice and some waterproof matches . . . and don't think for a minute that he's not coming back in a book someday!)

And the biggest difference between fiction and journalism is, far and away, the lack of immediacy. Working for newspapers, you can respond pretty much immediately to something that's happening in the world of politics or pop culture. As a novelist, if you're lucky, your book will be out within a year of whatever event you're outraged or amused by. It's been a challenge to strike a balance between writing about current events that aren't going to be interesting by the time the book comes out, and writing books that still feel contemporary and current and relevent.

Q. **Is there a message that you wish your readers would take away from your novels? Any themes or issues that you would like to get people thinking about?**

A. It's always funny trying to answer this question, because I don't think many novelists sit down in front of the blank page with any specific message in mind. They just want to tell a story, with characters their readers will care about, and keep them turning the pages—and in my case, give the characters as happy an ending as possible. The "message" part comes organically. It grows up around the plot and characters, usually without the writer having to do anything overt about it.

That being said, there are issues that seem to pop up in my fiction, and that I think are always interesting ones to think about. There's the question of interior versus exterior, and how much what you look like reflects, or determines, who you really are. And in this book I think there's the theme of the redemptive power of words, the way a good book can literally save your life. One of the parts I most enjoyed writing was turning Maggie into a reader, and showing the way her world, and her character, expanded as she read more and more.

Q. Do you have another project on the horizon?

A. My new novel, *Goodnight Nobody*, is about Kate Klein, a reluctant mother of three who finds herself stranded and friendless in an upscale Connecticut suburb inhabited by a tribe of supermommies. ("If one of those women is feeding her kids carrots," she complains, "the woman next to her is feeding her kids organic carrots that she grew herself in soil she personally composted.") Lonely and bored, with a husband who's never home, a mother who's rarely in the country, and a best friend who's never forgiven her for leaving Manhattan, Kate's life takes a dramatic turn when she shows up for a play date—only to find one of her fellow mommies lying on the kitchen floor with a German carbon-steel butcher knife sticking out of her back. When the police can't come up with a suspect, Kate decides to solve the mystery herself (of course, she can only fight crime between the hours of 8:30 and 11:45 when her kids are in nursery school). As she unravels the dead woman's double life, Kate ends up facing some surprising facts about her neighbors, her marriage and, ultimately, herself. It should be out in September, God and baby willing!

Questions and Topics for Discussion

1) Through the eyes of these two young women, we get a pretty modern view of the world. What then, do you make of the rather traditional ending: the fairy-tale marriage that seems to embody all the hopes of the future? Do you think the author is playing with this concept, or using it to offset her rather *un*-traditional story line?

2) The author utilizes a rather unusual technique when she tells the story through shifting points of view. How did this affect your reading of the story? Why might the author have chosen to do this? Do you think there are insights that could only have come out through multiple perspectives, or do you think the author wanted the ambiguity and clashing perspective that shifting points of view can elicit in a reader?

3) In many ways, this is really a story about growth, change, and transformation. Discuss the ways that virtually all of the characters alter their old, comfortable ways of being, acting, and thinking (or lack of thinking, in Maggie's case) throughout the course of this story. How easy does it seem for the characters to change? Would you consider intense pain or disillusionment (with a person or a job) to be the main catalyst for much of this change, or do you think something else sparks it?

4) Body image, for both sisters, obviously affects how they view the world around them. While Rose, at least in the beginning of the story, seems almost apologetic about her body, Maggie uses hers like a weapon, moving through the novel with a confidence that borders on aggressive. In what ways do you think their physical bodies, or perhaps the reactions that they receive from others regarding their physical bodies, helps create the people that they ultimately become?

5) Early in the novel, we get a rather painful and disturbing view of Rose's childhood during the scene on the dodgeball court. And while we would expect, or at least hope, that her sister might step in and try to protect Rose in such a humiliating moment, Maggie stands watching, obviously in pain, but frozen. In fact, Maggie goes so far as to blame her sister, asking herself, "Why did she have to wear those [underwear] today" and reassuring herself that "[Rose] brought this on herself." Were you shocked by Maggie's coldheartedness? Do you think that there were mitigating circumstances that help to explain this cruelty?

6) Forgiveness plays a central role in this story, as many of the characters struggle with their need for family and their inability to let bygones be bygones. To what degree do you think forgiveness paves the way for the story's resolution? Would you have forgiven Maggie? If you were Ella, would you have forgiven Michael Feller for having shut you out of Rose and Maggie's childhood? What seems more central to this story: the idea of self-forgiveness or forgiving others?

7) At times, it seems as if Maggie has created, in herself, the antithesis of her sister, and Rose heartily rejects and criticizes all things that seem to her Maggie-esque. Do you think the sisters' rejection of each other is a form of self-rejection? Do they actually share more traits than they would care to admit? Do they want to be like each other? Have they accepted their respective roles as screw-up and good girl so wholeheartedly that they unconsciously squelch any behavior that might help them to step outside of those lines?

8) Do you see this story as a common one in terms of sibling rivalry, or does this go above and beyond what you would consider "normal" sisterly animosity? If so, what do you think accounts for this? Obviously, the strain of losing a mother—one whose life was filled with struggle even before her death due to a debilitating mental illness—can lead to misplaced anger and bitterness, but why do

you think the girls turn on each other like they do? Were you surprised that their shared experiences didn't forge an absolute, unbreakable solidarity?

9) Although Rose seems to have a strong and loyal friend in Amy, we get the sense that Maggie really has no female friends; it seems that male relationships are the only ones that she chooses to foster. To what extent do you think Maggie's relationship with Rose affects her ability to make lasting, trusting bonds with other women in her life? Why is it that Rose seems more capable of these relationships?

10) At one point, Rose says to a waitress upon Maggie's departure, "She's not my friend, she's my sister." How might this shed some light on Rose's feelings of obligation and resentment toward Maggie? Do you think that, given better circumstances, Maggie and Rose could have been friends? Do you think family members can ever truly be friends?

11) What significance does the title have regarding the larger themes that this novel encompasses? Do you think it is ever possible for someone to ever truly put themselves in someone else's shoes? What do you think the author might say?

12) Where do you imagine Rose and Maggie in ten years? Has their relationship grown and gotten stronger? Do you see them finally as friends, or do you think they ultimately will fall back into the same patterns?

Turn the page for a look at the first chapter
of Jennifer Weiner's newest novel

GOODNIGHT NOBODY

Available September 2005 from Atria Books

ONE

"Hello?" I tapped on Kitty Cavanaugh's red front door, then lifted the brass knocker and gave it a few thumps for good measure. "Hello?"

"Mommy, can I ring the doorbell?" Sophie asked. She stood on her tiptoes and waved her fist in the air.

"No, it's my turn," said Sam, kicking his sneakered foot against one of the half-dozen perfectly spherical pumpkins beside Kitty's front door. Halloween was a week away, and we'd only gotten around to carving our single jack-o'-lantern the night before. It had come out crooked. Its right side had rotted and caved in overnight. Now it looked like we had a sadistic stroke victim parked on our porch. When I'd lit the candle, all three kids had cried.

"MY turn!" said Jack, shoving his younger-by-three-minutes brother.

"Don't push me!" cried Sam, shoving back.

"Sophie, then Sam, then Jack," I said. Two degrees in English literature, a career in New York City, and this was where I'd ended up, standing on a semi-stranger's doorstep in a Connecticut suburb with uncombed hair and a purse full of bribe lollipops, wrangling three kids under the age of five. How had this happened? I couldn't explain it. Especially not the part about getting pregnant with the boys when Sophie was just seven weeks old, courtesy of an act of intercourse I can barely remember and can't imagine I condoned.

Sophie reached up, pigtails quivering, and rang the bell. A dimple flashed in her left cheek as she gave her brothers a smug look that said *This is how it's done.* Nobody answered. I looked at my watch, wondering if I'd heard Kitty wrong. She'd called on Friday night, when the boys were in the bathtub and Sophie was sitting on the toilet, applying lipstick and waiting her turn. I was kneeling in front of the tub, my shirt half-soaked, a washcloth in my hand, scrubbing playground grime out from underneath their fingernails and enjoying one of my most persistent and vivid daydreams, the one that began with two men knocking on my front door. Who were they? Police officers? FBI agents? I'd never figured that out. The younger one wore a beige suit and a clipped inch of sandy moustache, and the older one had a black suit and thinning black hair combed over his bald spot. He was the one who did the talking.

"There's been a mistake," he would tell me, and he'd explain that, due to some glitch I'd never quite fleshed out (Bad dream? Alternate universe?) I'd wound up with someone else's children, living someone else's life. *Really?* I would ask, careful not to sound too eager, as a woman—these days, she was usually the lady from the Swiffer commercial who danced around to the Devo song, happily dusting—stepped between them, hands planted on her capable hips. *There you are, you little scamps!* she would say to the children. *I'm so sorry for the inconvenience,* she'd say to me. *No problem,* I'd graciously reply. And then she'd say . . .

"Telephone."

I looked up. My husband stood in the doorway, with his briefcase in one hand and the telephone in the other, staring at me with something that was either disdain or its close first cousin. My heart sank as I realized that getting slopped with the boys' bathwater was the closest I'd come to showering that day.

I reached for the phone with one soapy hand. "Can you watch them for a sec?"

"Let me just get out of this suit," he said, and vanished down the hall. *Translation: see you in an hour.* I stifled a sigh and tucked the telephone under my ear.

"Hello?"

"Kate, it's Kitty Cavanaugh," she'd said, in her low, cultured voice. "I was wondering whether you were free for lunch on Wednesday."

I'd been too shocked to stammer out "Sure" or "Yes." I'd wound up saying "Shes," even though lunch with Kitty Cavanaugh wasn't high on my to-do list.

Kitty Cavanaugh was the most beautiful, most perfect, most together of all of the beautiful, perfect, together mothers in my new hometown, the leader of a pack that had, so far, snubbed me. I remember the first time I saw her. After a morning of unpacking, I'd driven the kids to the park our realtor had pointed out. I hadn't washed my hair in three days and was looking more than a little disheveled, but the other mothers wouldn't mind, I thought, as I pulled into a parking space.

As we walked through the white picket playground gates, we saw four women seated on the green wooden bench by the seesaws: four women wearing the identical shade of dark-pink lipstick; four formidably groomed, exquisitely slender, terrifyingly capable-looking women. Each one had a monogrammed silk paisley diaper bag slung across her shoulder, like a Pink Lady jacket. Or an Uzi.

"Hi!" I said. My voice seemed to bounce off the pebbled rubber mats underneath the climbing structure and echo through the swing set. The women took in my outfit (loose, syrup-stained cargo pants, fingerpaint-smeared sneakers, one of my husband's washed-out long-sleeved gray T-shirts with one of my own violet short-sleeved shirts on top), and my kids (Jack looked okay, but Sam was clutching his favorite pacifier that he hadn't used in years, and Sophie had pulled on a tutu over her pajama bottoms).

The buff-looking blonde in the middle, whose camel-colored boot-cut pants were topped with a zippered fleece vest, raised her hand and gave us a semi-smile. Her name, I'd later learn, was Lexi Hagen-Holdt, and she looked exactly like what she was—a former all-state athlete in soccer and lacrosse who'd worked as a high school coach before marriage and had started training for a triathlon six weeks after she'd had baby Brierly.

The brunette next to her, whose shoulder-length light-brown hair was perfectly streaked and styled and whose eyebrows had been plucked into perfect arches, then dyed to match, gave us half a wave. This was Sukie Sutherland, wearing Seven jeans and high-heeled pointy-toed suede boots to a playground—the kind of outfit my friend Janie would have worn out clubbing, and I never would have attempted at all.

"Hi!" said the redhead at the far end of the bench. Unlike the other three, who wore clothing in shades ranging from beige to taupe, she sported a pumpkin-colored sweater with a long skirt in swirling shades of red and orange and gold. Her little gold earrings were clusters of bells that jingled and chimed, and she wore little purple slippers with curling toes. This was Carol Gwinnell, whose husband, I would shortly learn, was head of litigation at one of the five biggest law firms in New York City. Carol and Rob and their two sons lived in a Bettencourt and had a summer house on Nantucket, which I guess gave her the right to dress like she was going to a Stevie Nicks concert if she wanted to.

Finally, the fourth and most formidable deigned to approach us. She squatted down gracefully in front of my kids and asked each one of them their names. Her straight, thick hair fell to the center of her back, a glossy chocolate-brown held back with a black velvet band. She had lovely features: full lips, a straight, narrow nose, high cheekbones, and a neat little chin. Given her hair, and her golden complexion, I would have expected brown eyes, but her eyes were wide-set and a blue so dark it was almost purple. The color of pansies. "And I'm Kitty Cavanaugh," she said to my children.

"Kate Klein," I managed, while making a series of mental notes—where could I buy a perfectly cut suede jacket like she had, lined in mushroom-colored silk; where did these women get their hair styled, their teeth bleached, their eyebrows plucked; and where in the world were the other overwhelmed, undergroomed, slobby moms like me?

The ladies had murmured hellos, smiled at my children, and gone back to their conversation, which seemed to concern whether the organic milk sold at the local convenience store was really organic. It had taken three playground visits and a trip to Mr. Steven, the local hairdresser, before Kitty and I had had an actual conversation, about what kind of baked goods I should bring to the Red Wheel Barrow annual holiday bake sale.

"No nuts, no dairy," she'd told me. I'd nodded humbly and managed to keep from asking, "How about crack? Would crack be okay?"

Our second talk had been less successful. We'd been standing side by side at the swings on the playground. Kitty was wearing a linen sundress, simple yet elegant, a look (and a fabric) I hadn't attempted in years, and I was wearing my usual: grubby pants and a cotton cardigan, feeling overweight and underdressed and entirely inadequate. *It's this town,* I thought, tugging at my waistband with one hand and pushing Sophie with the other. Back in New York I'd get the occasional whistle from a construction worker, an appreciative glance from a guy on the street. Sixty miles out of the city, and I was Shamu in a sweater set.

I was daydreaming out loud about a vacation I'd probably never take, describing some resort I'd read about in a travel magazine in my gynecologist's waiting room. Private open-air bungalows . . . individual swimming pools . . . fresh-cut pineapple and papaya set out on the terrace every morning. . . .

"Can you bring kids?" Kitty had asked.

Startled, I'd said, "Why would you want to?"

"We take our daughters everywhere," she said primly, giving little Madeline a push. "I would never, ever leave them."

"Never ever?" I'd repeated—a little sarcastically, I'm afraid.

"Not even for a Friday night at the movies? Not even to go out to dinner? Or for a snack?"

She'd shaken her glorious hair, a tiny smile—a smug smile, I thought—playing around her lips. "I never leave them," she repeated.

I'd nodded, plastered a smile on my own face, eased Sophie out of the swing, mumbled "Have a nice weekend" (without realizing until much later that it was Tuesday), hustled all three kids into the van, stuck a DVD into the player, turned up the volume, and muttered the word "freak" all the way home.

Since then, Kitty and I had had a nod-and-wave acquaintance, smiling at each other across the soccer field or the dairy aisle of the grocery store. I didn't want it to go any further than that. But I'd said yes—or "shes"—anyhow. Oh, well. *Mindless assent,* I thought, and brushed my hair out of my eyes with one shampoo-slick hand. It was what had gotten me three babies and a house in Connecticut in the first place.

"I think we have a friend in common," Kitty had said.

I rinsed off my hands and wiped them on my thighs. "Oh? Who's that?" For one giddy moment I was completely sure that she was going to say Jesus, and that I'd be stuck listening to a twenty-minute soliloquy about her personal relationship with the Savior, and how I needed one myself.

But Kitty answered my question with another one of her own. "You were a journalist, right?"

"Well, that's putting it a little strongly," I said. "I worked at *New York Night,* and I covered celebrity addiction. Not exactly Woodward and Bernstein stuff. Why?"

Here it comes, I thought, bracing myself for the invitation to edit the nursery school newsletter, or do a quick polish on the Cavanaugh Christmas card ("Dear friends! Hope this season of comfort and joy finds you well. It's been a busy and blessed year for the Cavanaugh Clan . . .").

"There's something . . ." she began. Just then Sam dunked Jack under the water. "Mommy, he's *drownding* the baby," Sophie observed from the toilet seat, where she was holding a gilt-edged mirror and trying to twist her hair into a chignon. I bent down to pull Jack upright. He was spluttering, Sam was crying, and Kitty said we'd talk on Wednesday.

At least I was pretty sure she'd said Wednesday. Positive, almost. I took a deep breath and lifted the knocker again, noticing the way that every inch of the Cavanaugh house gleamed under the cloudless blue sky. The hedges were trimmed, the leaves were raked, and there were charming arrangements of bittersweet and miniature pumpkins in the window boxes that complimented the dried-red-pepper wreath on the door. *Gah*. I gave an especially forceful knock, and the door swung open.

"Hello?" I called into the dim, echoing entryway. No answer . . . but I could see lights from the kitchen gleaming at the end of the hall, and I could hear music playing, a Brandenburg Concerto, which was familiar to me from my own childhood and undoubtedly more edifying than the polka tunes my kids enjoyed.

"Kitty? Hello?" I called again. Nothing. The wind kicked up, blowing a drift of brown leaves rattling against the hardwood floor. I was starting to get the proverbial bad feeling about this as I wiggled my cell phone out of my pocket, called Information and asked for the Cavanaugh listing at 5 Folly Farm Way.

The operator connected me. Inside the house I could hear Kitty's phone ringing . . . and ringing . . . and ringing.

"Nobody's home," Sophie said impatiently, bouncing up and down in pink sneakers which did not quite match her orange overalls.

"Hang on," I said. "Hello?" I called into the house. Nothing.

"Mama?" Sophie reached for my hand. The boys looked at each other, their foreheads drawn into identical furrows, their plump curved mouths turning into matching frowns. The two of them were all curves and dimples and alabaster skin that flushed when they were overheated or upset. Their lashes cast spiky shadows on their cheeks, and their brown hair curled into ringlets so beautiful I'd cried at their first haircuts . . . and second . . . and third. If they'd had wings and gone around naked they'd have looked like cherubs. Poor Sophie, unlike her brothers, was tall and lanky and serious-looking, with olive skin and fine brown hair that tended toward snarls, not ringlets.

"Stay here. Right here. On the porch. On the pumpkins," I said, in a burst of inspiration. "I want tushies on pumpkins until I say it's okay. And don't close the door!"

Sophie must have caught something in my tone because she nodded. "I'll watch the babies."

"We're not babies!" said Jack.

"Stay here," I said again, and watched as each of my kids copped a squat on one of Kitty's perfect pumpkins. I held my breath and walked inside. The Cavanaughs had the same house we did, the Montclaire (six bedrooms, five full baths, hardwood floors throughout). The investors in our development were Italian, plenty of the residents were Jewish, and yet the homes all had names that made them sound like members of Parliament. Evidently nobody would buy a model called the Lowenthal or the Delguidice, but if it was the Carlisle or the Bettencourt, we'd be lining up with our checkbooks.

I tiptoed through the entryway, into the warmly lit kitchen, where the solemn notes of the cello and an antique clock's ticking filled the air. No dishes in the sink, no newspapers on the counter, no crumbs on the kitchen table, and no lady of the house that I could see, until I looked down.

"Oh, God!" I clapped my hand against my mouth and grabbed onto the countertop to keep myself from sliding to the floor. Kitty had gone for the same upgrades that Ben and I had picked. Her countertops were granite, her floors were pickled maple, and the French doors leading to the garden had leaded glass insets. There was a Sub-Zero refrigerator and a Viking range, and between them was Kitty Cavanaugh, facedown on the floor with an eight-inch carbon-steel Henckels butcher's knife protruding from between her shoulder blades.

I ran across the kitchen and knelt in a pool of tacky, cooled blood.

Kitty lay facedown, arms akimbo, white shirt and dark-brown hair both a sticky maroon. I felt dizzy as I leaned over her body, queasy as I grabbed her shoulders, then the handle of the knife. "Kitty!"

I'd watched enough cop dramas to know better than to move the body, but it was like I was floating outside myself, unable to stop my hands as they grabbed her shoulders and tried to pull her off the floor. The music swelled to its crescendo, strings and woodwinds sounding in the still, copper-smelling air as her torso came loose with a sickening ripping sound. I let her go. Her body thumped back onto the floor, and I clapped my hands over my mouth to keep from gagging, and stifled another scream.

"Mommy?"

I could hear Sophie's voice, which sounded like it was coming from another planet. My own voice was shaking as I called back, "Just a minute, guys!"

I got to my feet, wiping my hands convulsively against my pants, and whirled around once, then again. Then I slammed my hip against her breakfast bar and forced myself to hold still. Should I call the cops? Get my kids? What if whoever had done this to Kitty was still in the house?

Cops first, I decided. It took me what felt like forever to work my hand into my pocket, extract my cell phone, and dial 911. "Yes, hello, this is Kate Klein, and I'm visiting my friend Kitty Cavanaugh's house on Five Folly Farm Way and she's . . . um . . ." My voice broke. "She's dead. Somebody killed her."

"That address again, please?" asked the voice on the other end of the line. "Your name?" I gave it. Then I spelled it. When she asked me for my Social Security number and date of birth, I whispered, "Just send someone! Send the police . . . send an ambulance . . . send the Marines if they're around."

"Ma'am?"

My voice trailed off as I saw a square of creamy, heavy-stock stationery beside Kitty's telephone. I saw ten digits that froze the blood in my veins.

A Manhattan area code, the same number he'd had when I'd known him, the same number I'd dialed all those times for the nine months we were together and had struggled almost daily ever since to keep from dialing again.

I think we have a friend in common.

Without even thinking I hung up the phone, reached out with one shaking hand, and grabbed the note. I crumpled it and crammed it deep into my pocket. Then I shoved my bloody hands under Kitty's kitchen sink faucet, scrubbed them with her lemon-verbena-scented soap, dried them on her cheery fall-leaf-printed dish towel, and ran down the hall on wobbly legs.

"Mommy?" Sophie's round face was pale, and her big brown eyes were wide and solemn. Sam and Jack were both holding her hands, and Sam had his thumb stuck in his mouth. Sophie pointed at the blood on my pants. "Did you get hurt?"

"No," I told them. "No, honey, Mommy's fine." I fumbled a Wet One out of my purse and took a few hasty swipes at my pants. Then I gathered all three of them into my arms, feeling the fierce engines of their hearts beating hard against my skin as I carried them down to the edge of the driveway and we sat there, waiting for help.

Dear Reader,

Greetings from Philadelphia, and thank you so much for reading *In Her Shoes*. If you liked it, I hope you'll allow me a moment to shamelessly plug my other books.

Good in Bed, my first novel, is the story of Cannie Shapiro, a plus-sized reporter in Philadelphia whose life is going fine until she opens up a magazine one day to read the headline "Loving a Larger Woman," and sees that the byline belongs to her ex-boyfriend. It's about shame and self-esteem, dysfunctional families, dreams coming true, and finding your place in the world . . . about being the hero of your own fairy tale, even if that means you don't magically get skinny.

Little Earthquakes is the story of three young women in Philadelphia navigating one of life's most thrilling and perilous transitions: the journey of new motherhood. And it comes complete with lovable and exasperating husbands, the work/family dilemma, sex scenes, vivid accounts of sleep deprivation and new-mom neurosis, and the mother-in-law from hell.

Goodnight Nobody is the story of a young mother's move to a post-card-perfect Connecticut town and the secrets she uncovers there while she solves a crime between the hours of 8:30 and 11:45, the time her kids are in nursery school. It's also coming out this fall.

Finally, if you want to check out upcoming tour dates, the first chapters of all of my books, or read about my writing life and my own life as a mother (sample topic: Why Is My Kid the Only One on the Playground Eating Dirt?), you can check out my weblog, www.jenniferweiner.com.

Thanks for coming this far with me, and thanks so much for reading *In Her Shoes*!

Jennifer Weiner